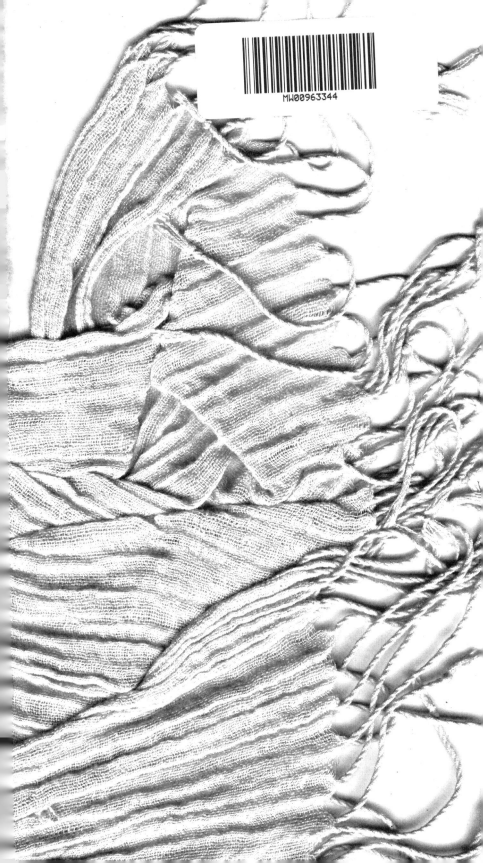

Arrhythmia

Arrhythmia

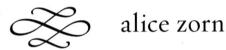 alice zorn

NeWest Press

Copyright © Alice Zorn 2011

Library and Archives Canada Cataloguing in Publication

Zorn, Alice
Arrhythmia / Alice Zorn.

ISBN 978-1-897126-80-6

I. Title.

PS8649.067A67 2011   C813'.6   C2010-906793-2

Editor: Suzette Mayr
Copy editor: Michael Hingston
Cover and interior design: Natalie Olsen, Kisscut Design
Author photo: Sadeesh Srinathan

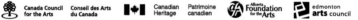

NeWest Press acknowledges the support of the Canada Council for the Arts, the Alberta Foundation for the Arts, and the Edmonton Arts Council for our publishing program. We acknowledge the financial support of the Government of Canada through the Canada Book Fund for our publishing activities.

201, 8540 – 109 Street
Edmonton, Alberta T6G 1E6
780.432.9427

NeWest Press   www.newestpress.com

No bison were harmed in the making of this book.

printed and bound in Canada   1 2 3 4 5 13 12 11 10

For Lorraine Zorn, 1960–1982

part *one*

Dear Harold, Thank you for asking me to see this pleasant 47-year-old lady with bleeding hemorrhoids. Plugged into the Dictaphone, Joelle types quickly. Frank is young for a staff doctor, only in his mid-thirties, but his writing style conveys a certain old-school flavour. Female patients are ladies he invariably describes as *interesting* or *pleasant* — the ladies, not their condition or disease. Joelle's fingers sometimes get mixed up.

Across from her desk hulk the metal filing cabinets with the patients' charts. Above them hang posters of a colonoscopy procedure. The colourful cartoons show a doctor guiding an endoscope up an intestinal track much like a miner with a lamp exploring a tunnel. Patients can more or less bear the cartoons. They avert their eyes from the magnified photos of real bowels, the glistening carmine and royal blue of live viscera. Frank believes in education, but honestly, Joelle sometimes thinks, his photos and posters must only tighten all those sphincters about to have an exam. A painting of a sailboat would make more sense.

She frowns as she types. Focuses on the words that herald varying degrees of doom. Polypectomy. Adenocarcinoma.

A few times this morning she felt the prickling of tears and had to blink wildly. Marc didn't say anything yesterday, nor this morning. Though he's always matter-of-fact before work.

Shower, coffee, and toast. Already dressed in nursing scrubs. Glancing through the paper he folds and takes with him. He can't have forgotten her birthday because they're going to his parents' on the weekend. Yesterday, when Diane phoned to ask if she wanted to go out to celebrate, the four of them, Joelle said that Marc had already made plans. She couldn't bring herself to tell Diane that he hadn't mentioned her birthday yet.

Joelle proofreads the letters she typed, signs them for Frank, and adds them to the manila folder in the top middle square of the imaginary tic-tac-toe of her desk. She snatches the phone on the first ring, but it's only Mr. Badanathan, who needs to change his appointment in December. His son invited him to Toronto for the holidays. How nice, she agrees, adding his name to the pencilled list at the back of her 1999 agenda. She doesn't have one for next year yet, though she's called Stores a few times. What's the holdup? Everyone keeps predicting Y2K disasters, each more crazy than the last. They're more excited by the fear of a worldwide crash, with bank balances wiped clean and jets plummeting from the sky, than getting on with day-to-day details — as in, please stock some appointment books because next year is coming, whether or not it also happens to be the new millennium.

Before the mail cart even edges into the doorway, Joelle hears the shivery chatter of dozens of bangles.

"No sun all week," the mail lady complains, her woeful eyes made more dramatic with kohl.

"But soon we'll have snow." Joelle loves the sharp, clean air of winter, the stone and brick cityscape of Montreal cloaked in white.

"Don't mention snow!" The woman flaps her hands — gold against gold objecting.

Joelle sorts the mail into piles. Labs and test results. Letters. The notice of a new head of Microbiology.

She knows Marc is tired. Overworked like every other nurse in the city. The stress gets to him. His legs twitch in his sleep.

At home he's impatient. When had they last even been to a movie? Gone shopping together? Had brunch? Made love? Sometimes she wonders what they share except for the same pot of coffee in the morning.

But *today* is her birthday, and even if Marc didn't think of it this morning, didn't he remember when he got to work and saw the date? What if he comes home tonight like it's any other night, cooks supper, and goes off to the den?

And now she yanks a tissue from the box, blots the corners of her eyes. She can't think like this or one of the other secretaries will ask what's wrong — and then she *will* start crying. She's lucky that Hermione, who keeps a calendar with everyone's birthday, is on sick leave. She would have organized a cake. Joelle doesn't want anyone wishing her a happy birthday if Marc hasn't.

The phone rings again — the private line. That has to be Marc.

"Joelle? It's Frank. Do me a favour, will you? Fill out a CT req for Soussan. Follow-up perforated bowel."

She writes the words on a memo pad. "The anastomosis," she hears him say on the other end as he hangs up, already talking to someone else.

What made him think of Mr. Soussan? She steps around her desk to the filing cabinets to get the chart for the MR number. Frank saw Mr. Soussan in the office yesterday — along with forty other patients. For all that he's a doctor, trained to process information in algorithmic steps, Frank's logic sometimes reminds her of a pinball machine. He strides down the hallway so swiftly that his lab coat billows. His body is skinny, with the square shoulders and ramrod posture of a sturdy man, his hair so densely curled and bunched on his crown that she knows who the residents mean when they say Broccoli Head — which is *not* nice, considering the many allowances he makes for their gaffes.

She deliberates taking the requisition to CT rather than

let it sit in the mail tray for hours. What if Marc calls while she's gone? She peeks at her watch, a gold Lannier he gave her a few years ago. She only wears it on dressy occasions. Today she wanted to be ready in case he called to suggest they meet after work. She has on her new black velveteen bell bottoms, a sea green blouse that matches her eyes, gold hoop earrings. Her boots with heels.

For over a month she's been glad that her birthday doesn't fall on a clinic day, so she won't be exhausted by the evening. Now she wishes the office was crowded with patients and that Frank was rushing from one examining room to the next, asking her to page GI or book a patient for surgery. Anything but to sit here feeling dull and forgotten.

∽

Ketia stands in the wide hospital corridor, rubbing disinfectant on her hands. Across her palms and around her knuckles, notching her fingers, circling her wrists. What next, the dressing in 38B or her pre-op IV? A young black man, his uniform drooped off his shoulders and hips, slouches from a patient's room. He's tied a red bandanna over the hairnet he's obliged to wear.

"Ça va?" she calls as she moves toward him. Ma's friend's son. She can't remember his name. "I don't see you up here much."

"Yeah…" The word dies between them. He's her age but she hardly knows him. Ma asked her to help find him a job. Ketia has only worked at the hospital for a few months herself, but she did what she could, and though she doesn't expect him to bow down and thank her, she doesn't like how he stands with his mouth — his whole body — sullen. What, did he think he'd get hired as a surgeon? He should have thought of that before he quit school.

"Were you delivering a tray?" she asks.

"…Don't like to do trays."

"But if they tell you to bring one up, you do it, don't you?" He traces the toe of his silver running shoe along the baseboard. "Supposed to be on the belt line."

A uniform that fit him would do more for his appearance than that silly bandanna. She has nothing to say to him but keeps talking, facing the nursing station where Marc sits, busy at some task. The focused angle of his head, his straight, brown hair.

∞

Black pen in hand, a pencil and a red pen before him, Marc transcribes doctors' orders from charts onto patient care plans and medication records. *Change dressing to N/S gauze. D/C Aldomet. Strict I-O.* When he finishes with a chart, he leaves it open, one atop the other, for the charge nurse, Raymonde, to co-sign.

He flips through the kardex for the care plan he wants and tightens his lips at the phone number scribbled on a torn edge of paper stapled to the front. There is an appropriate square on the care plan for contact info. In his boxy script he writes the phone number where it should go — where one would look for it in an emergency — balls up the torn scrap, flings it in the garbage.

Hidden behind his work, his aerie disguised by the ledge of the counter, he sneaks glances at Ketia in the hallway talking to some kid from the kitchen. Her satin brown skin. The moue of her well-cut mouth. Standing as if her spine were attached by a thread to the ceiling. All the nurses wear drawstring pants and tunic tops, but Ketia's are ironed and crisp.

The nursing station is a rectangle enclosed by an elbow-high wall that leaves the staff at all times visible and within hailing distance. In theory, the open concept inspires an atmosphere of trust and confidence. In real life, the air gets frantic with crisscrossed voices and demands. Who borrowed the bladder scan? There's blood in my mother's IV! Don't you want Lasix between the units? What's the number for Nuclear Medicine?

Just now, with the patients eating lunch, Marc offered to help Raymonde transcribe the orders that have been flagged since the morning. In the corner of the nursing station designated as the helm, Lou, the unit coordinator, empties the envelopes that threaten to avalanche from the mail basket. She waves down an orderly to go see why the patient in 40C complains that his bed is broken. She answers the phone and calls into the intercom for Carlene to pre-medicate her patient for the OR.

Marc opens another chart. Why is Ketia still talking to that do-nothing kid? The kid keeps shifting, all loose joints, like he wants to escape. So let him. Finally the kid pivots on his heel and ambles off down the hallway. Ketia calls after him in Creole.

Marc hears the words he doesn't understand and immediately resents them. If he could, he would erase every difference between him and Ketia. That she's only half his age. That she still lives at home. The way the other black nurses gesture, nudge, and draw her close within their circle. He minimizes the small detail that he's married, because it means nothing to him.

Ketia stops a family with a patient in a wheelchair, bending to check the tubing they've draped across the woman's knees. The family stand close, claiming their hold on their mother and wife despite the alien trappings of rubber and plastic. Ketia untangles the tubing from the urine bag and the intravenous line. "If these get pulled out," she says, "we'll have to put them back in again." The woman in the wheelchair winces. "Exactly." Ketia pats her arm. "We don't want that, do we?"

Darling Ketia, Marc thinks. Cocotte. Chérie. He's never liked endearments, which he always held were more appropriate for pets than people, but with Ketia he has discovered the tender links he can chain with no more than a whisper.

A group of residents and medical students move down the

hallway in a clot like a one-brain amoeba of lab coats. They crowd into the nursing station, and though there's room farther along, stop directly behind Marc. He hears them and he doesn't.

"I say we d/c Ampi and start Clox."

"How about we consult ID?"

"ID, ID..."

Marc swivels in his chair to reach for a blood requisition and snags a lab coat.

"Wha-at?" The resident, Shemi, lifts his hands in surrender. "You're practically standing on me." Marc would be more annoyed but Shemi is a good guy. He always answers his pages.

Shemi budges only a fraction of a step. "Do I page ID or what?" he asks his senior.

From her corner, Lou calls, "Marc, your patient in 36A has a potassium of 1.8."

Marc turns his head, notices that Ketia has disappeared, and whirls off his chair.

"Marc, your patient —"

"Tell Shemi." He jogs down the hallway, glancing into patients' rooms. He knows which are Ketia's as well as he knows his own assignment. Fernande swings open the door of the supply room where Ketia stoops, gathering rolls of gauze and a dressing kit. Marc darts in and stands next to her as if he, too, needs supplies to change a dressing.

"Who was that?" Not quite managing to still the tremor in his voice.

"Who, Fernande?" Ketia's head slowly rotates toward his mouth. His breath could be a magnet.

"That guy you were talking with. In the hallway."

"My mother knows his mother from church."

Marc's fingertips brush the hem of her tunic. "Your mother likes him."

"My...?" Ketia looks at him, surprised. Her movement shifts the fabric and his hand closes on air.

He tells himself he has to face facts. "Your mother would like to see you with him."

Her cheeks dimple. "Mais non!" As if he's too funny. "My mother wants us to meet someone with a good job. Him —" She lifts her chin in the direction of the door.

His fingers touch the edge of her tunic again. Neither move as he tugs on it gently.

The door bangs wide as the orderly Pietro shoves through with a heavy box he drops on the floor. "The way you guys go through this stuff." He tears open the box, slaps one plastic IV bag onto another in the bins that line the wall. "I spend half my day keeping this place stocked."

"That's why we love you," Ketia sings, her voice rich with the emotion of talking to Marc.

Marc hears it, whatever Pietro hears. He follows her graceful, high-shouldered walk down the hallway until she turns into a patient's room. He wishes he could call after her the way she called after that kid. A nobody with a lousy job in the kitchen, but who holds a secret bridge of language with Ketia.

Why, in all the years that he's worked with Haitians, has he never learned even a word or two of Creole? He thinks how Ketia would smile. A slow, sweet smile to curl around him.

∞

The butcher, the florist, the greengrocer, the patisserie. Marc strides into shops and out again with boxes and bags and a large paper cone, trailing the scent of vanilla, rosemary, chocolate, flowers. Whatever he would rather be doing, wherever he would rather be, he can't not celebrate Joelle's birthday. She holds to birthdays like a child avid for that one day a year that's hers alone. There was a time, too, when he had enjoyed her excitement. It didn't even take much. A new pair of earrings. A tiny parcel of Belgian chocolates. Supper at the upscale bistro on Bernard they like. Though he still recalls, all these years later, the tone of his mother's voice asking if that was what he wanted, a blonde doll who had to be told when to use her salad fork.

From a distance he sees the old grey stone Collège Montcalm, now converted to condos, where he and Joelle were able to buy because his father got their names on a list. Living there makes Marc feel proud — as if the stone arch over the entrance belongs to him personally. The marble tiles in the hallway. The sheen of light on the handsome, dark-grained moulding around the doors. The click of his key in the lock proclaims membership in an elite club.

In the kitchen he moves from the gas stove to the black granite counter to the sink. He washes the spinach. Peels cloves of garlic. Heats the cast-iron skillet to sear the lamb. Reaches for a whisk and a small glass beaker to mix a vinaigrette. He's arranged the flowers — lilies, snapdragons, and daisies — in the red Murano vase and set it on the table. In truth, he used to think he loved Joelle. At forty a man believes he knows what love is: a life together, marriage, the comfort of shared habits.

When he hears the door, he uncorks the bottle of Brouilly he set in the refrigerator half an hour ago to chill lightly. He pours a glass and carries it to the dining room, where Joelle stands with her hair mussed from her scarf, gaping at the flowers on the table. Yes, he makes his mouth smile, yes, he cooked. He doesn't let himself hear how grateful she sounds.

He's tired — exhausted — after a day at work, but roasting a gigot and lopping beans is still easier than an evening face to face in a restaurant with some officious waiter guessing that it was her birthday and sowing romantic hints around them. Like this, with him walking between the kitchen and the dining room, grating fresh Parmesan for the beans, carrying plates, topping up their wine, Joelle doesn't notice that he's only doing what he knows how to do.

Over supper she tells him about patients. An eighteen-year-old who swallowed nails and had to be rushed into surgery.

Madame Trintignant, who called for an appointment. Marc took care of Madame Trintignant when she had her bowel resected two, maybe three years ago. Joelle assumes he wants to hear about patients whose enemas he supervised once upon a time. What he hears is how they always talk about work or other people. Between himself and Joelle there's nothing.

When she's set her fork and knife across her empty plate and sits with an elbow on the table, humming a disconnected thread only partly in time and not at all in tune with the sax ballad that's playing, he suggests she go relax on the sofa while he clears up. He forces himself to restrain the coiled spring of his spine and push his chair back slowly. A little drunk, she trips to the sofa on the other side of the low dividing wall, drops into the corner facing the windows. Two rectangular pools of night sky. The building across from them is only three floors high. A full year it took him to get Joelle to understand they don't have to draw the curtains.

In the kitchen he rinses the dishes before slotting them in the dishwasher. Cutlery first, dinner plates, then salad plates. Vine beige Mikasa Tuscan. Tea towel and sponge in hand, he pushes through the swinging door into the dining room. He wipes and dries the salt and pepper mills, places them on the antique sideboard, grabs the placemats to toss in the laundry. Joelle sometimes folds and keeps them for another meal, though he's asked her not to. It cuts his appetite to see a dried fleck of food on the fabric.

First with the sponge, then the tea towel, he cleans and polishes the oval table. His arm circles like a piston drained of marrow and blood. Joelle lies stretched on the sofa, facing the windows, a bubble of blonde hair rucked up behind her head on the cushions.

Back in the kitchen, though he's already wiped the counters, he wipes them again. He brushes against a drawer handle, then presses closer, his breath already deeper, urging the current in his groin. Then he realizes what he's doing. I'm flipping, he thinks. I could fuck the refrigerator. A stainless steel block with a pull-out freezer drawer. At work they hear stories about people who show up in Emerg trailing all kinds of household gadgets. A refrigerator would be a first.

The coffee maker burbles. He opens the drawer for tea-spoons and dessert forks, which he adds to the fluted Spode cups and saucers on the tray. To one side lies a cream envelope with a gift certificate. Usually he buys Joelle a sweater or a blouse. Today, when he stood before the row of sleeves in burgundy and silver, he couldn't bring himself to touch them. Choosing clothes felt too intimate. Having to imagine what would suit her. The thought of her body. Her pale underbelly skin.

He lifts the platter of pastries from the refrigerator, each a gourmand's jewel of chocolate or fruit set in mousse, marzipan, crème Chantilly. Joelle likes to sample. He adds a serrated knife so she'll cut the pastries and not use her fingers to pull them apart.

The coffee, the tray, the pastries. Should he tell her now? Yes, he decides, now — before she runs her toes along his legs and hints that they move to the bedroom.

He swings through the door. Joelle has once again set her wineglass too close to the edge of the coffee table. It's a wonder they still have any crystal left. As he skirts the table, he moves the glass. There — notice? Of course she doesn't. She bends her legs to make room for him to sit by her, but he perches at the far corner of the sofa.

"Marc, that was *so* good! And after you worked all day. We could have gone out, you know."

"That's fine. I wanted to cook."

"You're right," she sighs. "This is better — more special. Just the two of us."

He rolls down his shirtsleeves and buttons his cuffs. Straightens his watch. The metal armband is slightly too large for his wrist, but the watch is his grandfather's. He prefers to keep it as it is, though Joelle has often asked why he doesn't get it fixed. "Listen. I had a needle stick today. We can't make love tonight."

She lifts her head from the cushion, alarmed. "Why didn't you tell me?"

"I just remembered." He gestures at the kitchen where he was busy. "I had to get tested for hepatitis and HIV."

"How long before you get the results?"

He makes himself meet her wide-set aqua eyes that so used to entrance him. Now he sees that they make her look like a sightless, deep-sea creature. "Don't worry," he says. "The patient is an elderly woman."

"Elderly woman," Joelle says sharply. "What about her husband? Maybe he's been going to a hooker for the last twenty years."

Marc frowns. She never had such crass ideas before she started working in a hospital. "I doubt it," he says, quick to defend his alibi. "He visits her every day. They've got kids who are already grown up — who've got kids of their own. In any case, you know it's only a precaution." He's surprised by how easily the lies come. How convincing he sounds.

She takes a deep breath. "I know. Frank's always cutting himself in the OR and he's always fine. Don't worry, you'll be okay."

Marc nods. Good. He waits a beat, then says, "The coffee's done. Are you ready for dessert?"

She rolls her head against the cushions, half-closing her eyes. "Chocolate," she moans. "I hope there's chocolate. You know it's as good as sex."

Her voice and her expression. Her neck open in abandon, her body lax. In that instant he could take back his story. Guess what? No needle stick. It was only a joke, ha-ha. He sees her against the cushions, black pants tugged down, the wiry soft hair, the slit of her cunt. She is his wife. There is no reason why... His hand on his thigh almost opens, almost lifts.

He lurches from the sofa, escapes to the kitchen. Pig! he thinks fiercely. You are a pig! You don't even *want* Joelle. Except that it excites him — it does! — to imagine Joelle in her ignorance spread beneath the pump of his lust for Ketia.

He grips the edge of the granite counter. The overhead light gleams on his cherished gas stove. The ceramic holder — high-fired Burgundy clay — where he keeps ladles and whisks. The double sink with its Swedish faucet and handles. His heart slows. The platter of desserts, yes. Joelle's birthday.

∞

Dessert was scrumptious. Well, of course. Every meal Marc prepares is.

Joelle hugs her arms as she watches his reflection in the window, carrying the tray with their empty cups and plates to the kitchen. She's always thought he moves like a dancer, sylphlike and slender. Over supper she noticed how tired he seemed. His mouth tense with fatigue. Offering her salad when she'd already taken some.

She feels sheepish remembering how hurt, even angry she was all day — and look, the whole while he was planning this intimate souper à deux. She's not being fair to him. Her and her stupid rat nibble of worry. Just because he doesn't say he loves her every day. People don't after twelve years. What matters is that he knows when it counts, like tonight.

She nestles her head deeper against the cushions, admiring the broad, high windows. She loves their view of the sky — the thick dark of a moonless night, the sun-shot blue of early morning, the pelting shafts of approaching rain. When she stands at the window she can see across the tops of the fine houses and brick triplexes of lower Outremont, toward the skyscrapers and lights of downtown Montreal. To one side lies the humped bulk of the mountain: a dinosaur of stone, earth, and trees resisting the encroaching push of the city.

From behind her she hears, "You're still up? I thought you were..."

"Go ahead." She knows he wants to brush his teeth. The sofa is too comfortable. She could sleep right here. Idly, feeling a bit tipsy, she raises a foot and glances down her leg. She likes these black bell bottoms, fitted along the thigh and flared at the bottom. Diane says she doesn't care if they're the new fad. She's not doing bell bottoms again. She did them the first time around, thank you! But Joelle thinks they suit her even better now than when she was a teenager.

You see, she scolds herself. Turning forty doesn't have to be a tragedy. Some things get better with age. Wine, bell bottoms, and many more years with Marc.

∞

Diane scoops water to her face. She can't sleep with a day's worth of city grime on her skin. If she did, just imagine. Before long she'd look like the buildings downtown. Etched with pollution, haggard with caked dust.

Not that the water from the tap is likely to win any purity awards. If not direct from, it's still the St. Lawrence, an artery of sewage, toxic oils, dumped cars, and drowned kittens. Even filtered, three guesses how many letters and numbers stay soldered to the chemical compound of Montreal H_2O? She shudders. Best not to think about washing in so many parts and varieties of crap per million. Better to take comfort in the ritual, gently sudsing and rinsing.

She pats the towel to her cheeks, under the jut of her chin, around her neck. With the years her sharp features have only grown more defined. So, she thinks, so? She's becoming more and more herself. She doesn't know why Joelle gripes so much about aging. Diane told her, Age doesn't *change* who you are. It's just a refrigerator. The older you get, the more the mould sets. Like me. I used to be a skinny girl with big boobs and hips.

Now I'm a heron waddling like a goose, Joelle objected. She didn't like Diane making fun of herself. Diane pointed at her head. Heron: note the nose and the neck. Then at her bottom. Goose: look at that bum! I'd be crazy to pretend I'm a *Vogue* model with slinky hips. Anyhow, I need the weight here, she said, patting her bum, to balance the full frontal effect. Talk of her bust cut all argument short. Diane had *bosoms,* as her grandma called them. At eleven years old she'd surpassed all the women in her family. She grew up believing that the word was plural. When she finally learned differently and said, It's just one, Grandma, bosom, her grandma laughed. *I* have a bosom. Your mom has a bosom. You, my dear, have bosoms.

Bosoms, indeed. The prow of her ship. Diane straightens her shoulders at her softly hazed reflection. The old mirror needs to be resilvered, but Diane doesn't mind. As long as she can comb her hair when she gets out of the shower in the morning and trace a line of Dusky Rose Plum across her lips. Nazim, too, seems to be able to shave more or less by feel. Who needs to analyze each minuscule wrinkle and blemish?

She would sooner keep the old mirror in its tongue and groove cabinet than whatever Jimmy, her Greek landlord, would replace it with any day. Last year he took advantage of a plumbing problem to install a fake marble-topped vanity with a scalloped sink. He keeps threatening to rip out her claw-foot tub. That old thing, he clicks his tongue. He wants to put a prefab shower unit in its place.

Diane steps into darkness. Nazim already turned off the lights in the kitchen and the living room at each end of the hallway that runs like a side tunnel down the length of the apartment. Only a dim arc of light from the bedroom doorway touches the catalogne rug in the hall.

Before Diane met Nazim she lived alone. She'd had two trial experiments with live-in boyfriends in her twenties. Nice guys, but hey. Bras shouldn't be stuffed into the washing machine with jeans. And *no,* she didn't want to pay for half a stereo.

If she bought a loaf of bread, why wasn't there even a heel left for her breakfast the next morning? With tennis racquets and monster-size running shoes jammed across the bottom of the closet, excuse me, but where was she supposed to keep *her* shoes?

She liked having a boyfriend. Lazing around Sunday morning, going for a walk on the mountain, both eating shish taouk so they both had revolting garlic breath. She didn't even mind watching hockey. But why did men always want to settle down? Move in together? Have a more committed relationship? To Diane it seemed so wide-eyed obvious that keeping separate apartments was *smarter* than having to wait to take a shower when you were already late for work. Inevitably the men decided she was more a friend than a girlfriend — and felt free to see her less and less as they met women who wanted to get married, have a baby, and cheer for les Canadiens.

A couple of years ago Diane met Nazim. She liked how he pressed his hand flat on his heart to show he was earnest. His earlobes like funny, little pincushions sewn to his ears. How solemnly he prepared mint tea, first sprinkling a pinch of black tea, then stuffing the pot with fresh mint he doused with sugar, so as not to bruise the leaves with boiling water. He held the pot high, pouring in a yo-yo stream — up and down — into tiny, filigree glasses.

So much decorum around mint tea, and yet he accepted the relaxed informality of their relationship. As far as she could tell, he had no get-serious-and-settle-down agenda. A year ago, when he said he was looking for a new apartment, she invited him to move in.

He's slid low in bed, his crime novel propped on his chest, pillow scrunched against the headboard.

"Doesn't your neck hurt like that?"

"My what?" In the light from the lamp his hair glistens as if washed in ink.

"Doesn't your neck hurt like that?" She drops her robe at the foot of the bed.

He doesn't move.

"You'll give yourself a crick."

She climbs into bed, edging her cold toes under his hairy calves. And then he shifts — his neck and his legs.

∞

Ketia sits in the dark in the kitchen, one leg crossed over the other. She wears pyjamas and slippers. The foot that dangles nods to the beat of the song in her mind. *Loving you...* She takes another small spoonful of caramel fudge ripple ice cream, cold and rich with that extra vein of candy sweetness. She bought a tub on the way home from work. She and Bastien, her eight-year-old brother, love ice cream. Winter or summer, they'd eat it every day if they could. But after supper she forgot about the ice cream in the freezer. Ma had served rice with oxtail simmered until the meat fell from the bone. Gabrielle wouldn't stop bragging about her math results and finally Ma exhaled loud and long. Salt doesn't boast that it's salted. An Island proverb. For a moment the only sound in the kitchen was the burbling of the refrigerator. Gabrielle was sometimes too smart for her own good. This evening she shrugged and asked Ketia if she'd had to read Molière at school. Dumb, eh?

Ketia only remembered the ice cream later when she was already in bed. She squirmed around to face the wall, dug her head in the pillow. She imagined herself tiptoeing down the hallway to the kitchen, easing open a drawer for a spoon. She could almost taste the frozen caramel. Slowly she edged a foot out from under the sheet, let it hang off the mattress, then slid from the bed.

Loving you... She's carried the chair to the window close to the electric heater beneath it. The lights in the kitchen in the apartment across from them are off, but one floor down two men play cards with their girlfriends. Ketia has an angled view onto one of the couples, the scatter of thrown cards, the small juice glasses of amber drink on the table. Rum, she guesses. Or maybe whiskey. The couple sits close, but not touching. He rests his hand on her chair. The back of her yellow sweater dips low, exposing the edges of her shoulder blades.

What's the name of that bone? The scapula. Ketia mouths the word.

The woman shifts in her chair and the lines of shadow flatten. The nakedness of her back is both flaunting and delicate. The man's hand lies so close. He could easily touch her. Trace his fingers down the groove of her spine.

Instead he lifts his hand to fling a card on the table, closes his deck, swings his free arm wide. Only after a moment does he return his hand to her chair.

Ketia presses her spine against the oval back of the chair. Maybe if Marc saw her somewhere in the city and she wore a top with a low back... Or what if he walked into the change room at work? Her mouth softens, playing out how it would happen, Marc opening the door when she's pulled off her tunic and standing in her bra. Of course, she would grab her shirt to cover herself, and he might reach to help, his fingers grazing her shoulder. The frisson of touch on skin. Not touching her, not *really*, only...

Ketia tucks her chin close. Marc is married and older, and even if he weren't, he's white. She knows how Ma thinks. What she would accept and what she wouldn't. What's right and what's wrong. But that's just it: because none of the scenes Ketia imagines can ever happen, there's no harm. As long as she keeps them a secret. Says nothing when Marc looks at her the way he does. Or stands nearby.

She hears steps in the hallway. Ma's tread would be heavier. The click of the bathroom light. It must be Gabrielle, who, if she noticed that Ketia's bed is empty, will come see what she's doing. Ketia wonders if she should turn on the light — in which case Gabrielle *will* come — or risk being found in the dark, spying on the neighbours. Careful not to make a sound, she picks up her chair and sets it at the table again.

When the bathroom door opens and the feet shuffle off down the hallway, Ketia tiptoes to the sink, where she rinses her bowl and spoon under a dribble of water. Even in the dark the dull burnish of the spoon catches light.

She hesitates and steps back to the window. The woman's dark back inside the soft yellow jaw of wool, the man's hand on her chair, so close. Ketia sees it then. The impatient flex of his fingers.

∞

Frank has been in the OR all day. He called Joelle between cases to ask her to pull Suzanne Dubuc's chart. A med student told him she was back in Emerg. Poor Suzanne. Joelle leaves the chart on the top-left corner of her desk. That square, closest to Frank's office, is his.

Joelle has been working for the last hour on billing. A maze of codes on the screen. The government makes the page harder to read all the time. She doesn't want to think that perhaps she needs glasses. One of the other secretaries, Venita, clacks past the doorway with her trenchcoat belted. Catherine Deneuve's fat cousin.

Joelle decides to leave, too. She closes the program, turns off the computer. Slides the memo pad next to the phone as if it could magically take its own messages. From the shelf behind her desk she lifts the foil-wrapped loaf Mrs. Peters brought for Frank and sets it on Suzanne Dubuc's chart. She doesn't know if Frank actually takes home the baked goods that patients give him. Marc won't let her. At first Joelle thought he was just being fussy. If a patient brought her Greek butter cookies or homemade brownies, she shared them with the other secretaries over coffee. She couldn't bring herself to tip them in the garbage — all that effort, all that goodness. But there's ever more talk at the hospital about bacteria that's resistant to antibiotics, spores that live on surfaces much longer than was previously thought. You could never be sure if people washed their hands or licked their fingers while they cooked.

Joelle drapes her scarf around her neck and slips into her jacket. In the hallway she hears typing. Who's still at work past four o'clock? Pei Yi. Joelle would wave but Pei Yi sits in profile, back straight, facing her screen. Her dedication excites no end of comment from the other secretaries. They say she wants to become executive assistant when Maryse retires. Who cares, Joelle thinks. They all claim they wouldn't do it for any amount of money. Working for Collier? No way. And yet they resent Pei Yi for trying. Joelle never ceases to be amazed by the viciousness among the secretaries. If whispers could slice, their pretty dresses would be hanging in tatters.

Of course, years ago, when Joelle studied film, she never expected that one day she'd be working as a secretary. In the eighties, a degree in the arts was qualification enough for a desk job with the government. She assumed her contract would be renewed every year — until one year, with budget cuts, it wasn't. The counsellor at the employment office told her that her decade with the government had left her with no skills to compete in the modern workforce. Could she use Word? Excel? Did she have experience dealing with clients?

Joelle mailed her carefully formatted CV to government offices and private companies across the city. No one responded. She began to wish she'd been more practical, like Marc, about her degree. Film studies, *why?* She didn't actually want to make movies. She simply loved film.

Marc got her this job. Frank had asked the nurses if they knew of anyone. He'd just lost his third secretary in a row — two to motherhood, one to higher education. Office temps answered the phone and booked appointments, but patients' charts and paperwork piled up like shoreline debris.

When Frank interviewed Joelle, he didn't even look at the

bold print headings on her CV. That she was Marc's wife was as good as the guarantee on a muffler. Not the most flattering comparison, but that was Frank. The only question he had was whether she planned to return to school or have children. On both counts, no. His lips crimped with the skepticism she'd come to expect — doesn't every woman want a baby? But he didn't ask again. As she would soon learn, Frank shied away from personal details. Examining as many rectums as he did a day, he already got his share of life's seamy underside.

Through the sliding doors at the Emerg exit a whirligig dance of snow blows along the sidewalk. The first snow of the season! The wind prods her along, air fists pummelling her back and legs. She breathes the cold deep into her lungs, almost laughs.

This evening she'll ask Marc if he wants to see a movie. It will be good for him to relax after the constant go-go-go of his day at work. She smiles, remembering the lamb and desserts he prepared for her birthday. *That's* what matters — not the way he zipped his jacket and left for work this morning with only a curt goodbye. She has to keep hold of the good times. The proof.

∞

Diane sits in her corner of the sofa, a quilted blue pillow behind her back, the weekend paper open on her knees. She's had the old sofa for so many years that the frame sags like a barge riding low and the nap of the corduroy is permanently flattened on the armrests and seat cushions.

Eight letters for a poisonous shrub, first letter o. OLEANDER, she prints with her fine-tip felt pen. A brilliant pink mouth, lush with death.

The crossword puzzles in the local papers barely flex her brain, but like an addict she has to do them. English and French. There are no blank spaces, no empty squares in her recycling box.

The phone rings. She reaches over the armrest. "Allô?" It's Joelle.

"So," Diane asks, "did Marc wine and dine you in style?" The question, though the one she knows Joelle expects, isn't as sincere as it sounds. Diane doubts that Marc would even know how to celebrate a birthday simply. After all these years, she still wishes Joelle were with a more *comfortable* man. Marc does nothing wrong. He's polite. He smiles — but not as if he's even in the same room.

"Such a surprise," Joelle says. "I wasn't even sure he remembered."

"But when I asked if you wanted to go out, you said you had plans."

"Well, I didn't think he forgot. But he didn't say anything, so I wasn't sure he remembered."

"You weren't sure if he remembered but you didn't think he forgot." Diane aims this pirouette of illogic at the plaster frieze of angels on the ceiling. They continue to play their silent harps.

As Joelle enthuses about her birthday meal — flowers on the table, gigot d'agneau, her favourite salad of spinach and figs — Diane's look drops to the hot-water radiator across the room. Paint coats the iron bars so thickly that their decorative moulding trails like lumpy varicose veins. A rag rug, striped brown, green, and blue, lies before the door with Nazim's pointed yellow babouches splayed at one end. The slippers are so old that the leather bulges where his big toe protrudes. Once, when he stopped by the boutique where she works, she showed him a pair of hand-stitched, suede moccasins. Nice, he said, but kept his hands in his jacket pockets. He didn't get the hint.

"So when are we going out?" Diane asks. "I want to celebrate with you, too."

"Oh!" Joelle sounds pleased. But then she whispers, "We have to go to Marc's parents for supper tonight."

"For your birthday?"

"Yes." No joy in that.

"The dreaded in-laws," Diane says, since it seems Joelle can't. "You're lucky Nazim's family is in Morocco."

"Right — lucky because we'll go there one day to visit. I *want* to go to Morocco."

"Well, sure. You'll go see his family if you get married."

Diane doesn't answer. Joelle knows how she feels about marriage: if a couple stays together, they do so regardless of a piece of paper or rings. And if they don't, the piece of paper and rings are only that much more hassle to untangle. Just because she and Nazim are living together doesn't mean she's changed her mind about marriage.

What Diane never understands is why Joelle, of all people, believes so fiercely in marriage. Diane remembers waking in the night as a child to the swish of red light on her bedroom wall. The police had been called to Joelle's house again. And those were only the times when the neighbours called the police. How often did Joelle wake to bawling and the crash of glass? Her mother — or her father — with a gashed lip or a bruised eye. And yet, all through high school, Joelle pored over bridal gowns in magazines. She choked in her excitement, crying on the telephone, when she called Diane to tell her Marc had proposed.

It's almost eleven when Diane hangs up. Nazim won't be home for a few hours yet. She should go for a walk, buy a bottle of wine, think about supper this evening — not lamb with spinach and figs, excuse me, but maybe something less routine than everyday pasta or a stir-fry.

She folds the newspaper and sets it on the corner of the coffee table with her felt pen on top, so Nazim knows she's still doing the crossword and won't touch it. Rule Number One when he moved in: crosswords are hallowed. Or if not rule number one, certainly among the top ten. She has to rock to heave herself out of the trough in the sofa. One of these days they'll have to buy new one. Or a crane.

∞

33

No one has told Bastien to go to bed yet. He hunkers in the corner of the sofa, wheeling the model car Pa gave him across the nubbly cloth, into the treacherous dip between the cushions, over the obstacle of piping. Beside him Ketia hears how he makes rumbling motor noises.

Ma stands at the ironing board, watching a TV movie about a missing teenage boy. Her long, high hips. Her flat feet shoved into threadbare slippers that gape along the instep. She keeps her new slippers for when company comes.

The ironing board pokes across the screen, but Ketia's not really watching the movie. Only when the neighbour appears. His slender frame, thin-lipped mouth, and quiet assurance remind her of Marc. She even feels a twitch of jealousy when he steps close to his wife and clasps her hand.

With the commercial Ma thunks the iron on the board again, nosing it down the leg of Gabrielle's jeans. The woman on TV swings her silken drapery of hair around her shoulders. Ketia will never have hair like that. She looks away from the TV at Bastien, still rolling his car across the sofa terrain. For Bastien, one of the highlights of Pa's visits home is bringing their old Volvo wagon out of their uncle's garage. For nine months of the year Bastien lives in a household of women.

Ketia stretches out her foot and nudges him. "Don't you wish you were a girl like us?"

He hesitates, not sure what she means, then shakes his head no.

"Wouldn't it be easier if you were a girl?"

"I like being a boy."

"Come here." She holds her arm out, waves him closer.

Still puzzled, but curious, he wiggles across. She squeezes a springy bunch of his hair, pulls it out straight. "Maybe," she considers with pursed lips.

"Maybe what?"

"Ma," Ketia says, "we could do cornrows on Bastien."

"No!" He wrenches away.

And now Ma notices that he's still up. "Timoun à cette heure-ci?" She tells him to brush his teeth and get to bed vite-vite. Bastien grumbles. It's Saturday. But he pockets his car and trudges off down the hallway.

Ma tugs one of Ketia's uniforms over the end of the ironing board, straightens the neckline, reaches to the coffee table at her knees for the can of starch, and sprays a fine mist. Another hair commercial. Long, smooth tresses to taunt the little knot of hair at the nape of Ketia's neck. She's worn it like that since she started studying to be a nurse. It's practical and easy. Extensions pull and itch and give her a headache. But what if Marc likes extensions? More and more she wonders if he likes that she's black. She loves his narrow nose, green eyes, and fine, straight hair. Though, of course, his looks wouldn't matter if he weren't who he was. She doesn't know why Marie-Ange at work, who used to have a white boyfriend, says she won't ever again. Hein, les filles? Stick with your own kind! Everyone agrees.

At the ironing board Ma inclines her head to the hallway, listening to hear if Bastien is in bed yet. "Go to him," she says.

Ketia drops her feet to the floor and pushes off the sofa. When she and Gabrielle were younger, Ma always came to smooth their blanket and say a prayer with them before they fell asleep.

∞

At night Joelle burrows downward, dragging a corner of her pillow along. Marc never follows. Even so, when she wakes that morning, she immediately knows she's alone. The sheets and duvet beside her feel slack. Empty.

She lies without moving, remembering her dream. Frank was examining glossy photos of bowel. Slick, red tunnels with mushroom-head polyps. Were they malignant? He fingered his lower lip, reluctant to say what he suspected, when suddenly she understood that the pictures were hers.

Joelle groans and turns on her back. No wonder she had bad dreams, eating at Marc's parents. Annie and Vincent are excellent cooks, but of the many meals they like to describe and relive — saumon en papillote, pork medallions with creamed fennel — they always serve beef when Marc and Joelle visit, and in their house beef is served rare. To Joelle it doesn't matter how choice or expensive the cut, it still looks like flesh. She can barely force herself to eat it.

Yesterday Vincent carried the platter high from the kitchen, around the butcher block counter to the table. "Birthday roast for the birthday girl!" he cried. On the walnut sideboard sat a gift wrapped in yellow and silver paper — obviously a book. Joelle would open it once they had sung and she blew out her candles. Chez Annie and Vincent holidays are celebrated exactly, step by step.

"Tenderloin," Vincent murmured as he nestled the platter onto its sisal mat. "Encrusted with herbs." As they sat admiring it — Vincent and Annie's version of saying grace — Joelle hoped hard that the crispy, toasted herbs meant that the meat was at least partly cooked. Then Vincent flourished the carving knife and peeled free the first slice. The meat oozed blood.

Joelle's usual tactic was to mince the severely underdone meat into the smallest possible pieces and smother each tidbit with vegetables. Asparagus tips in saffron butter, braised endive and caraway, corn flecked with chopped habaneros. Annie and Vincent prided themselves on a variety of side dishes to intrigue both the eye and the palate. Joelle tried hard to ignore that the vegetables on her plate were tinged red.

Throughout the meal Vincent and Annie volleyed animated banter on the high art of fine gourmandise. They triumphed that they'd found asparagus from California at this time of year. The corn came from their freezer, cut from the cob, parboiled and packaged by yours truly. They defied any talk of mad cow nonsense. Roasting beef too long ruined its succulence. Their butcher personally knew the farmers who stocked his refrigerators. An excellent man! Their saviour in a time of fools.

Joelle shivers, remembering the watery pool of blood on her plate. At least she and Marc won't have to go again until Christmas. She kicks the paisley duvet aside and reaches for her robe, a dark green kimono. In the hallway she hears the click of the mouse from the study. She finds Marc scrolling through photos of Venetian canals.

"What are you looking up?" She stands behind him.

"My dad asked me to check out some hotels." Next to his hand lies a sheet of foolscap with a handwritten list of names.

"They're really serious about going to Italy next summer?"

"Why not."

"At their age wouldn't it be easier to travel with a tour group?" Joelle brushes her fingers through his hair. So smooth and straight. Her eyes, like his, are fixed on the screen. A gondola in the foreground, a cream stucco façade. "Do you think we'll ever go?"

He doesn't answer.

"Italy, just you and me..." She slides her hand down his neck to his shoulder. "We could, you know. The money doesn't all have to go into RRSPs. We should travel while we're still young." She squeezes his shoulder. "Aren't you tempted?"

"Joelle." Clipped and precise. "I can't do this with you talking in my ear."

Her hand stops. Carefully she lifts it away. "You're just looking at pictures."

"I'm trying to do something for my parents — which is more than you do, making a face like they put poison on your plate."

"You know I don't like beef."

"And I don't cook it at home, do I?" He clicks with the mouse. "Even though I like it very much."

"But I told your mom I loved the cake. I asked for some to bring home."

"Once the damage was done. You don't think she noticed?" Joelle had no idea he was so upset. He'd said nothing in the car on the way home. He used to understand, even taking the meat from her plate, telling his father he'd given Joelle too much. "Never mind." Marc closes the window, disconnects from the server, waits for the computer to shut down. "I have to go. I've got things to do."

"What things?" she asks, her voice timid.

"If I don't get there soon, the gym will be too crowded. And I promised Justin I'd stop by." He swivels off his chair, pushes it straight against the desk.

"I thought that today..."

"Yes?" He hesitates in the doorway.

"I thought we might see a movie. The other night you were too tired."

"We did something yesterday. That was for your birthday, remember? I can't help it if you didn't enjoy yourself. Today I really need to get some of my own things done."

He's right, Joelle thinks. Of course he's right. The weekends go by so quickly.

"And in any case," he adds, "if there's a movie you want to see, you know you don't have to wait for me. Just go ahead and see it."

He's already gone. His steps in the bedroom. The slide of the closet door. The cabinet in the bathroom. He didn't suggest she come along to Justin's. Is he going to stay out all day or be home for supper? She doesn't dare ask. She stands staring at the blank computer screen.

∞

Marc walks fast along the sidewalk, crossing against the light, his gym bag hooked on his shoulder. He doesn't drive to the gym because it's only three blocks away — more bother to park the car than take it. When he's finished he'll come back and get the car to drive to Justin's. He won't go back upstairs.

He's as annoyed with himself as with Joelle. He shouldn't get angry. He doesn't want to get angry. But why does she wheedle? She knows he doesn't like it.

Wheedling — after the way she behaved at his parents. Making that wretched face, mouth pinched at her plate. Mincing with her fork through her food. Of course they noticed. He can even understand why his mother refuses to play along. At *their* table, one eats comme il faut.

The chrome wall of the gym reflects the brisk scissor of his walk. He looks like a man being chased. Hounded by Joelle's incessant whining. As if he needs her to dream up things for him to do on his only free day!

He's lost the bench press to a skinny kid who heaves and puffs, his shorts and T-shirt still creased from the package. Good luck. Marc goes directly to an upright bike, drops to the floor beside it to do leg stretches. On the bike he gets into rhythm, notching up the resistance, keeping steady. He's always exercised, but more than ever these days he wants to look fit — twenty years younger if he could.

He tucks his shoulder blades and arches his back. Not much good youth will do if you're a lazy do-nothing. Ketia isn't interested in young men. Them, too, they've no idea of the treasure concealed by her modest airs.

His legs pump hard. Sweat leaks down his arms. The force of striving against the machine stokes his anger anew. He remembers Joelle's pleading look. Eyes wide, lips parted. As if she's so innocent. Pretending that she doesn't know how she goads him. How he hates her clinging. The feel of her hand in his hair. Expecting him to plan his whole weekend around her. Like a child she is, so needy and dependent.

Sweat bathes his neck, his chest, his ribs, the backs of his knees. He rakes in breath, his lips tighten. Any reasonable man would get fed up. His irritation is entirely — and deservedly — her fault.

∞

Rancid popcorn warmth. People clumped in a chain that leads to the cinema doors, still closed. Joelle unbuttons her coat and unwinds her scarf.

"Can you believe it." A monotone voice behind her. "Chris said she'd sooner put in a deck than go on vacation next year."

"You should see this new supervisor they dumped on us at work. Brown shoes with black pants. A total geek. He doesn't talk, he uses a calculator to communicate."

Same postures, same attitudes. The repertory cinema crowd doesn't change. Only the hairstyles and clothes. Longer, shorter, messier, tighter. Everything's familiar, except herself. She's the stranger in a known place. The only one alone, too. She hunches her scarf and collar closer. Turns her head away from all the couples and roommates and friends.

The wall next to her is shellacked with posters of movies, side by side, top to bottom, edges overlapping. Bold print, faces, close-ups of mouths, a tortured tree against a skyline, a camel in the desert. She saw this movie and this one. That one she didn't because she doesn't like the French actress who plays the lead. And here, Bruno Ganz. His sad mouth and Hamlet expression. Once upon a time she saw every movie he made.

The man behind her in the line-up still complains loudly. "He even clocks us when we go to the john. Isn't that like, an invasion of privacy — some kind of harassment?"

The cinema doors open and the crowd from the previous show straggles out, slowly at first, then in a stream. Joelle watches people to see if they look restless or content. Well and truly catharsised, as her film professor used to call it. The satisfaction of conflict resolved — which wasn't the same as a happy ending. What *has* to happen, does.

But these people zip up jackets, ask if anyone's hungry and wants to go for a bite. They look neither pleased nor upset — nor even as if they feel they wasted their time. The movie equivalent of white noise.

The people in the line-up shuffle into the dim boudoir-lit

cinema. Rows of seats shoulder the gloom. Peachy footlights dust the pillars of the proscenium arch, the heavy folds of drapery. David Bowie plays on the sound system overhead. David Bowie… another time bubble.

Joelle drops into an aisle seat halfway down, elbows her arms free of her jacket, pulls it high around her shoulders, slouches in her seat. Her body finds the pose easily. Ready prey for the vortex of colour and sound.

When she studied film, she saw four or five movies a week. She kept the listings from the paper sticky-tacked to her fridge door. In those years Montreal teemed with repertory houses — old theatres with ballroom ceilings, the backrooms of cafés.

Today, when she looked in the paper, she discovered almost none of them are left. When did they all close?

When people like herself starting renting videos, trading the big screen for the comfort of their sofa. At home you could watch a movie by yourself and hardly notice you were alone.

Up until when she zipped her boots and locked the door, she didn't think she would go to a movie by herself. Maybe, too, if the bus hadn't braked at the curb just then, she might only have walked to the store and bought bananas. Crept home again.

The overhead lights dim. David Bowie fades and the curtains slide open. Only the red EXIT sign stays lit, but it's small and far away. The darkness all around presses close. Strikes her fear like a match. Her eyes brim with tears, hot and helpless, released by the sudden blare of colour and surround sound. She could be a child in the night, her pain gashed and raw.

∽

Marc fiddles with the catch on the back of an electronic thermometer as he walks into the nursing station. Lou, who has just come back from lunch, glares at the mess on her desk. Patients' charts, a whirl of requisitions, a blood tube basket sprouting an octopus of rubber tourniquets. "What is it with you guys?" she demands. "Why do you dump all this junk right here?" She shoves the blood basket farther along the counter. "I *don't* draw blood — or did that get added to my job description while I was gone? And this," she knocks a clipboard in Marc's direction, "isn't this yours?"

He looks up from the batteries he's changing. The clipboard holds a page of uneven printing he can read from where he stands. *get me one of those blue feeder bag's were did you go find a sink and make warm dry towel slipper's pillow your not being any help its been so long I figered you left ask for blue feeder bag*

He shrugs. "I didn't put it there." One of his patients has a trach and can't speak. Constrained to pen and paper, her demands bristle, bare and stripped-down. Her sister who spends most of the day with her stormed off, exasperated, half an hour ago.

The charge nurse, Raymonde, leans against the counter by the patient board where names and diagnoses are printed on magnetic labels. "Lou," she says, "we need to isolate a patient."

"Don't tell me," Lou groans.

Somebody is about to lose their coveted private room. Do people know that the H up top stands for hospital and not hotel? To listen to them, no. Marc escapes to the med room, where he scans the shelves for the yellow bottle of acetaminophen which, as usual, is not in its place. There, by the sink.

"Marc!" Raymonde calls. He steps to the doorway with a pleated paper cup in one hand, the yellow bottle in the other, his trach patient's clipboard under his arm.

"We have to move your man in 42." She's already pushed aside the label. With the smallest decision, her cheeks redden like cartoon spots — a handicap, he's often thought, for someone in charge.

"Why him? He's nice."

"They're all nice people. The absolute best in the world."

Marc shakes his head. "Pick someone else."

Raymonde slaps another label aside. "Him then. Lou, tell the nurse to let him know he's moving."

Lou peers at the assignment sheet and calls on the intercom. "Ketia, to the desk, please."

"Wait," Marc says. "Don't. It's okay. My patient can move. I'll go tell him."

Lou swivels around in her chair. "I thought you just said —" she begins. Raymonde is already talking to a resident about meds that were ordered incorrectly.

Marc can't explain and feels caught, standing with his hands full and a clipboard squeezed to his ribs.

"Oui?" Ketia arrives breathless.

"Forget it. Disaster averted. Superman here just saved you a lot of bother." Lou waves one hand in Marc's direction and with the other reaches for the phone that's ringing.

The nursing station bustles with hurry and rush, voices querulous and strident — Lou shouting after a porter, "Not that way! The patient's in 36B!"— but for Marc, for those few seconds that Ketia looks at him, face to face, the world comes to rest, tranquil and golden.

∾

Ketia washes dishes while Gabrielle stands beside her with a tea towel, hip cocked, teasing Bastien at the table. "I don't think so." Gabrielle draws out the words. "I really don't think so."

"Je te dis," he says. "I saw him do it!"

Beside him at the table Ma darns a sock, her pharmacy glasses low on her nose. She'd made rice and red beans to go with the leftover griot from a big family supper with their cousins on the weekend. The adults drank rum and talked about Haiti and the family who still lived there. The children ran up and down the hallway, playing hide and seek. Ketia helped the two-year-old who toddled after the older ones as well as she could. Look-look-look, who's that behind the bed?

Angélie squealed as she staggered forward to pounce, although in her excitement, she often fell. Ketia scooped her up before she noticed, blew in her ear, hugged her close.

"No way," Gabrielle singsongs. "I don't believe it."

"But it's true!" Bastien insists.

Ketia wipes the sponge around a plate, front and back, and turns on the tap to rinse it. At work today Marc helped her move her patient from the bed to a chair. They fussed with the piqués and pillows, fingers brushing, tucked a blanket across the patient's lap, asked if he was comfortable. Then, behind the chair, Marc grasped her hand. Fingers around her wrist, the flat of his thumb pressed into her palm. She didn't pull away and as he stroked his thumb across her palm, slow and deliberate, a groove opened — from her palm to the warmth between her legs.

Here, in the kitchen, under the cover of the suds, she copies the circle of his fingers around her wrist, the caress of his thumb.

"Maman!" Bastien cries.

Even Ketia hears the decided tock of the spool of thread replaced on the table.

Gabrielle nudges Ketia, grinning. "He's making it up, isn't he? What do you think?"

Ketia hands her a rinsed plate.

"You're not even listening," Gabrielle sniffs. And to Bastien, "Ketia isn't listening because she knows it's not true."

"Maman!" Bastien is desperate to trump Gabrielle's scorn.

"Suspend." Ma's Creole is more forceful than her French. "Suspend, mwen dit nou suspend."

Bastien whines, "But she's laughing at me."

They all hear the annoyed suck of lips on teeth. Gabrielle's mouth straightens. Bastien holds himself silent. Ketia tries not to gush water when she rinses a handful of forks.

"I've got homework." Bastien slides off his chair, scoots down the hallway.

For a while the kitchen is quiet except for the tap turned

on and off, the splash of Ketia's hands, the dishes Gabrielle sets in the open cupboard. Then, as Gabrielle waits for the pot Ketia scrubs, she hums a phrase. She hums it again, swishing her thighs in a slinky dance move.

Ma claps her scissors onto the table. The metal and plastic rattle before coming to rest. Into the silence that follows she says, "You, Gabrielle, you've got too much mirth for my liking these days. And you," she pauses. "Tu m'écoutes, Ketia? I don't like the look of you at all. Not at all."

Gabrielle shoves the last pot in the cupboard, catching the door before it slams, flaps out her damp towel she hangs on the oven door handle. "Homework," she throws over her shoulder.

Ketia wrings out the dishcloth, wipes around the tap, rinses the sink. She doesn't want to be alone with Ma but can't think of an excuse to escape. She suddenly feels eight years old, convinced Ma can read her thoughts.

Then Ma sighs and says that Bastien has to take hot dog buns to school tomorrow. Ketia offers to go out and buy some. Gabrielle would roll her eyes if she heard.

Let her. Let them all believe whatever they want. Ketia will play at any game that hides how she yearns for Marc's hands on her body.

❦

"You never said how supper at Marc's parents went."

Diane and Joelle sit in low armchairs. Art deco sconces cast softly flared ovals of light on the wall. At the next table a couple downs pints of beer without speaking. It's late, almost midnight, but Joelle wanted to stop for a drink.

Joelle frowns as if she can't recall the supper in question. Then she says, "Don't ask."

Diane has already noticed that Joelle hardly mentioned Marc all evening. She doesn't seem in any rush to get home, either.

The waitress sets their brandies before them and strides off with a big-booted step, skirt flouncing from side to side. Joelle touches her balloon glass as if it's coded with Braille. "Not bad."

Diane shakes her head, not understanding.

"They warmed the glasses. You're supposed to do that to make the..." Joelle scoops the air over the glass toward her. "Marc always says that."

They'd had supper at the Ecuadorian restaurant Joelle likes. Bright orange walls hung with gourds and tapestries, wooden tables and chairs painted yellow, green, blue, and red. Kindergarten colours, Marc calls them. And cafeteria fare — wedges of lemon served with the fish. Diane wonders what Monsieur would prefer. Wild mûres flambéed in ice wine? Once, when she and Nazim came for supper, Marc set a narrow porcelain dish with a single row of green olives on the table. Nazim came from a country that grew olives but he'd never before seen an olive boat.

Diane wets her lips with brandy and licks them. Joelle twists her glass around and around on the table, the gleam of her wedding ring a slice of light on her finger. At supper she chatted about everything and anything — in the forced way people have when they're determined to enjoy themselves.

"Birthday girl feels gloomy?"

Joelle's hand stops. "Birthday girl getting older."

"Right." Diane nods. "While the rest of us are getting younger."

Joelle tilts her head, acknowledging the point.

"Did your mother call?"

"Yes." The word ends in a hiss. "She asked if Marc took me out for supper. I said no — and before I could say that we had this wonderful evening at home, she started to tell me about the restaurant where Roly took her for her birthday. Then she talked for ten minutes about some extension Roly was building on the house — something with a sliding door. And that was my birthday call." Joelle sips her brandy. "I still can't imagine a grown man going through life with a name like Roly."

"Even better if he was fat." Diane only met him once, when he came to Joelle's wedding. A man with scrub pad hair and a long sausage torso.

"She wouldn't say if he got fat, would she?" Joelle has never been to Wisconsin where her mother now lives, apparently more happy with Roly than she was with Joelle's dad.

The waitress clomps by again. A troll in a saucy skirt.

"How's your mom these days?" Joelle asks.

"Oh… there's a big brouhaha about Robin wanting to host Christmas this year."

"But your mom loves to do it."

"I know that, you know that, I think even Robin knows. But she wants to have Christmas at their house this year because of Jérémie. I get the impression that once you have a baby, you don't care what anyone else wants." Diane snaps a thread that dangles from the cuff of her sweater. "What about you? Now that you're officially forty."

"What about me?"

"Do you ever think about having a baby?"

"You know Marc and I agreed on that before we got married."

"That was ten years ago —"

"Twelve."

"Whatever. Things change in twelve years. How you feel about life, priorities… And you know your clock's ticking. You don't have forever."

"I don't want to be a mom. I never have. And you know Marc. He doesn't change his mind."

Diane winds the thread around the tip of her finger, lets it uncoil on the table, winds it again. It might be good for Marc and Joelle to become parents — tear a few pages from Marc's little rulebook, supplant the ghosts of Joelle's childhood.

"Anyhow," Joelle says, "what about your clock? It's ticking, too. Don't you want to have a baby?"

Diane misses her lip with the glass. "Damn." She wipes at the drops on her sweater. "Does brandy stain?"

"You'd be a great mom."

"You have to be really settled to have kids. That's not something I —"

"You're settled with Nazim."

Diane remembers how Nazim moved in with hardly any belongings, though he'd been living in Montreal for nine years already. His silver Moroccan teapot. A few jars of spices — cumin, turmeric, cinnamon. His clothes. His babouches. They've never discussed children.

She drops the thread on the floor, shakes her head. "It's not the same. You know it isn't. Teething rings and pureed carrots — all the stuff Robin can go on about for hours."

"I know." Joelle lifts her glass in a toast. "We'll just have to grow old together. And get electric wheelchairs, since we won't have kids to push us around."

∞

That afternoon it begins to snow. Frank's in the OR and Joelle keeps finding reasons to step into his office — with a tidy stack of memos, the mail she's opened, a CT film he requested — to gaze out his window at the soft, grey sky where the snow seeds down, gentle yet steady. Slowly the dead, matted grass and pocked asphalt disappear under a fluffy, scintillating quilt. She hears the other secretaries complaining and ignores them. Marguerite who doesn't have snow tires yet. Venita who had her hair done yesterday and didn't bring an umbrella.

At a minute to four, Joelle buttons her coat and runs down the stairs. The falling snow melts in tiny dabs — fairy tongues — on her cheeks. She scuffs her boots through the powdery snow, marvelling at the new landscape. Edges blunted and hillocks reign. In place of every landmark stands a new semaphore, cold and bright with new meaning. The bristly twigs of a hedge furred white. Gloomy brick and stone buildings formally iced façades.

She stops at the dépanneur half a block from home for cream for their coffee in the morning. Checks the due date the way Marc always does. Yesterday, when she went out to supper with Diane, she'd left him in front of the T V. He was already in bed when she got home.

His black and tan boots sit in the rubber tray outside their door, toes aligned, the ends of the laces dropped in their mouths. Does that mean he's home for the evening? She unlocks the door and opens it cautiously. The light in the den at the end of the hallway is off. She can't smell cooking, either. She hears a noise and then he steps from the bedroom, eyes wide, lips parted — as if he's been caught, but at what? One hand clenches his gym bag.

"You're going to the gym," she says. Sparing herself having to hear it.

His mouth closes. "I didn't think you were coming home. Yesterday you went out..."

"With Diane, for my birthday."

"The other night, too."

"I went to a movie because you told me you couldn't." Not a reproach, just reminding him. She keeps her voice light as she goes to the living room window to look at the snow drifting down. "Have you already eaten?"

Silence behind her. Then he says, "I could make something. But after that I'm going to the gym."

Suddenly the fresh, clean mood she brought in from outdoors feels right. The purity of the city mantled anew. Smiling, she turns around. "That would be great." She doesn't mind the gym — she really doesn't, she's glad he stays fit — if they have supper together.

"Is there still lox?" He drops his gym bag on the floor by the wall.

"Not much."

"I don't want a heavy meal before —" The swinging door to the kitchen slaps shut behind him.

Joelle doesn't offer to help. Unlike his parents, Marc prefers to cook alone. In the bathroom she combs her fingers through her hair, then gathers and pulls it through a scrunchie into a loose chignon. With her hair off her neck — the way Marc likes it — she decides to change her studs for earrings that dangle. Long silver rods with tiny sapphires on the ends. Marc gave them to her a few years ago. To accentuate her eyes, he said.

The slide of a heavy pan on the stove. The appetizing odour of pancetta browning. The tap of the colander in the sink. At the hutch she takes folded placemats and napkins from the drawer, sets the salt and pepper mills on the table. She pushes through the swinging door to get cutlery from the kitchen. Marc already has shallow pasta bowls on the counter. He stands at the stove spooning green peppercorns from a jar into his sauce.

"Did you get your test results yet?" she asks.

"What test results?"

"From your needle stick."

He doesn't answer.

"Marc?" His silence makes her wonder if he's had bad news. She steps closer to peer around his shoulder at his face.

He startles at her jutting bouquet of forks and pasta spoons, nearly spilling brine from the jar into the sauce. "*What* are you doing?"

"Your test results," she repeats.

"I don't have them yet. It takes weeks to get the results."

"You're not worried, are you?"

"No, but I'm cooking. Don't crowd me at the stove."

He's right, she thinks, not letting herself hear the annoyance in his voice. She gets the bottle of Riesling, already open, still half full, from the refrigerator and sets two glasses next to their placemats. She doesn't know if he'll want wine before going to the gym, but she'd like some.

While she waits for Marc, she turns on the TV, standing in front of it with the remote in hand, ready to turn it off.

"Is that the news? Can you leave it on?" He's brought their bowls of pasta to the table.

She can't object. She has no one to blame but herself.

∞

Ketia sits in the nursing station checking the medication records for her patients.

Beside her Carlene talks about her boyfriend, who'd better be waiting at the end of her shift. At the door downstairs, and not with any of his friends along, either. Carlene flicks her finger in the air, taps long, silvery nails on the counter. Her tone is haughty — lui là — but Ketia has seen how she scampers down the hallway when Lou calls on the overheard for Carlene to come to the phone.

Marc will never be able to call her like that. Or wait for her openly after work. Carlene has no idea how lucky she is.

"I don't care if he has to wait." Carlene shakes back her straight, glossy hair — a shoulder-length wig sewn to a net skull cap. She'd shown Ketia earlier in the change room. "He'd better be down there, ma fille. If he makes me walk to the subway in this weather..." She ends in a soft hiss of disgust that needs no explanation.

A doctor barges into the nursing station. "Where's the CPS?" he asks the air, assuming in doctor-fashion that the answer will appear.

Ketia scans the counter for the hefty blue pharmacy manual, but he's already swept it from under an armload of folded towels heaped next to a phone. He drops onto the closest chair — Lou's — to leaf through the pages.

Lou turns away from the printer with a sheaf of lab results in hand. "May I," she says dryly, "invite you to avail yourself of one of the many other chairs in the nursing station? Whoever sits in this one has to deal with all the families who want to know why the doctor hasn't cured their mother/father/wife/husband yet."

He stands, still reading the tome that hangs open from one hand, the other out until it touches the back of a chair, and he sits again, perhaps not even aware that he's moved.

Enid clanks two blood culture bottles onto the counter ledge before Ketia and Carlene. "Lou, stamp me labels for 36b please? Two of them." Enid's body looks stuffed into her uniform, the elastic stretched in a line at her waist, the hems of her short sleeves tight around her arms. She fills in the requisition, muttering, "This took way too long. Patient has no veins." And to Marc, coming from the other direction, "Hand me those, will you?" She lifts her chin at the stamped labels Lou slid on the counter.

"Oh, for Christ's sake." Lou points down the hallway as she answers the phone. An elderly patient has untied his gown and draped it over his shoulder like a toga without a bottom, exposing his long, scrawny body.

Enid says to Marc, "Can you get him?"

Marc doesn't move.

Enid waves the man over. "How are you today, Ronnie?" Gently she pulls down the gown. "Let's tie this in the back, okay? A nice, tight, double knot."

He gives the nurses a mirthful grin. No wits but all his teeth.

"I don't know why you get so offended," Enid says to Lou. "You work in a hospital."

"I'm *clerical*. I'm not paid enough to look at men's parts hanging all over the place."

"They weren't hanging all over the place. They were hanging just the way they hang. Right, Marc?" Enid waddles off down the hallway without noticing that Marc hasn't answered.

Carlene murmurs, "What does he want?" She leans close — the genteel musk of her perfume — nudges Ketia, and stands. "Are you coming?"

"I'm not finished, I've got..."

Carlene doesn't wait.

In an undertone Marc asks, "When are you leaving for lunch?"

"Fernande's not back yet. I'm covering for her."

She dares herself to look at Marc as if he were any other colleague who's asked a question about work. His narrow chin. The peaks of his thin lips. His green eyes. Both forget to talk. Then the senior resident, in surgical scrubs and still wearing an OR cap, strides into the nursing station. "Where's the chart?"

"Here." Lou prods her pen against the chart open on the counter ledge before her.

"Vitals q one," he says as he scrawls. "Increase his IV to one-fifty. He's third-spacing. If we don't keep a close eye, he'll end up in ICU. Call Shemi. Tell him I want him up here. I've got to get back to the OR."

"Who?" Marc asks.

Lou says, "Aditi's guy in 42C."

Marc jogs down the hallway. Ketia pushes back her chair to follow when Lou says, "You don't have to run after him. There are already three nurses in there. Why don't you check Aditi's other patients?"

Ketia blushes and stammers, but Lou is already talking to Locating, trying to track down Shemi. Ketia glances at the assignment sheet and grabs a blood pressure machine.

∞

Halogen lamps in the ceiling spotlight displays of pottery, carved wood, a glass jewellery case. Diane sits near the cash with a crossword magazine on her knee. Her chair is an antique, the wooden seat buffed to a satiny sheen, the cane back curved to fit her exactly — and *not* for sale. People often ask.

The bells on the door jingle and Nazim steps in, hands

53

shoved deep in the pockets of his leather jacket. Surprised, she stands to kiss him. "I thought you were going to see Hatem today."

"I am." He grins.

"I'm not exactly on the way to Hatem's."

"I've got a secret map." He jiggles his fist in his pocket.

"Secret map! You came to see *me* when you could already be diddling a dead hard drive or a motherboard or…" That exhausts her knowledge of computer innards. If he could, Nazim would spend every day in Hatem's basement shop repairing old computers. His job selling internet service bores him.

"Are you going to stay there all day?" she asks.

He doesn't need to answer.

She pokes his chest. "You two, you're the champions of old clunker computers."

"People buy them — people who can't afford to go to a fancy store downtown."

"But you should relax, too. It's your day off."

"Don't worry," he says. "I'll be home before you."

"Supper on the table?"

He squints, as if trying to read the answer in the air. "… Pizza, I think."

The bells on the door jingle again. She tweaks one of his pincushion earlobes, trails her fingers down his neck, tucks his scarf higher. "Say hi to Hatem," she says as he turns away.

The client wears a stylish, black overcoat. Expensive. She strolls around the displays, scanning, touching nothing.

Diane whisks a feather duster here and there around the raku bowls. Their merchandise is top-quality and personally selected. The owner, Marie-Claude, visits artisans in their ateliers and studios around the province, driving up to the Laurentians, through Charlevoix, out to the Gaspé, and the Eastern Townships. Diane has taken trips, too. Stained glass, moccasins, pottery, earrings. The judicious tap of a mallet on a chisel. Skeins of handspun wool swimming in a kettle of onion-skin broth to dye them yellow. She likes explaining the techniques to the clients, giving them the story behind a heathery woven scarf, a carved ladle, a jug.

The woman in the tailored coat slaps her bunched leather gloves against her thigh, keeps circling back to the slipware plates.

Diane approaches and lifts one. "Let me tell you how the potter gets that design. She paints lines of coloured slip across the plate. Slip isn't glaze but clay mixed with water. While the lines are still wet, she drags a feather through them — that's how you get all these little peaks."

The woman traces a finger along a peaked line as if to gauge the truth of Diane's words — to feel the feather's brush through the slip.

"Looks like an EKG reading, don't you think?"

"Primitive," the woman says. "African."

Diane starts to shake her head. Rosenda, who makes the plates, is a petite Guatemalan with runner's calves, working on a manual potter's wheel in her Plateau studio.

The woman is still talking. "But why are they blue? My interior designer has expressly forbidden any shade of blue."

Pauvre Madame. At the mercy of her designer.

The woman squeezes her leather gloves. "You see my dilemma. Or do you think the artist could make me one of these using ochre instead of blue?"

After an exchange of cards and likely promises, the woman swirls out the door as if the world were waiting for the vision of her presence: that easy stride in high heels Diane never mastered. Diane likes to feel her feet on the ground when she walks. The complete sole from heel to toe. The complete soul, she thinks, taking up her magazine again.

At the beginning this job was only supposed to be a stopgap, but she's worked for Marie-Claude for fifteen years now. She remembers when the scrolled silver lettering on the door — Boutique À Votre Goût — was in two-tone blue and cream.

Marie-Claude often dashes in, her Jag double-parked out-side, waving a bag of biscotti. Or calling Diane to come help her carry boxes of pottery from the trunk. Artisans stop by if they're in town to say hello. Twice a week Stéphane, the florist next door, invites her for espresso. He has a small machine, demitasses, tiny spoons. Diane doesn't even mind the slow hours. She never feels alone among the carved and polished wood, the shaped bowls and plates, the supple weave of cloth. Objects made by hand breathe with the shape and life the artist gave them.

Ensconced in her chair again, she frowns at her crossword. She's filled in the easy words and works her way from the top down and to the right. Across: seven letters for disorder, first letter H. They could be more specific. Social, medical, or personal. H, h, h... She doesn't try to think of the word so much as she lets the cogs tumble. She leans back in her chair, considering the scarves that hang from the rack. She remembers Vicki at her loom. The shed of taut threads, Vicki's fingers opening to catch the shuttle she threw across as her other hand thumped the beater toward her and her feet pressed the treadles. One move following another in an orderly rhythm. A grid of threads becoming a roll of cloth.

HAYWIRE, she prints, wondering how that fine word came into being.

∞

Nazim hustles past the chic stores. A florist, a patisserie, a bistro, a hair and makeup consultant, another patisserie. The wind makes him hunch his shoulders and squirm his hands deeper in the pockets of his jacket. Diane likes to vaunt the beauty of the four seasons. What four seasons, he asks? Spring is gone before it arrives. Briefly he's warm — only in time for his bones to freeze again. Back home, even in January, he could walk outdoors in his slippers.

A bus groans into view and he lopes the last few steps to join the line-up. He finds a seat near the back. He'll get to Hatem's soon enough. Stopping to visit Diane isn't quite the worldwide detour she makes it sound. He often comes to the store. If she's busy with a customer, he'll saunter around the displays, look at what's new — pick up a clay bowl, feel the coarse, unglazed bottom. Finger a shawl woven from handspun wool. In the town where he grew up the narrow, stone streets smelled of the sea and freshly cut cedar, bread baked in wood-fired ovens. People lived by what they could fashion with their hands.

He can't recall why he happened to be walking through that highbrow neighbourhood the day he first saw Diane's store. He definitely wasn't shopping or meeting anyone for lunch. He stopped before the wooden bowls in a storefront window. Small and round, their lids topped with a pert button handle. Though the shape wasn't at all alike, they reminded him of the bowls his grandfather used to carve. He'd never seen wood like this, though — strangely veined, a tawny brown riddled with nervous black lines.

"Are you waiting for me?" A woman, holding a bottle of juice, dangled keys to unlock the door. She wore a soft, lapis blue sweater that would make a wooden stick look sexy —and she was no stick. He followed her inside.

"You're interested in the bowls?" She handed him one from a shelf.

He hesitated then lifted the lid and inhaled deeply. All he smelled was the oil used to polish the wood.

"I've never seen anyone do that!"

Was she laughing at him? He tried to explain. "My grandfather used to carve bowls with lids. The lids keep the scent of the wood inside. Cedar, thuya, lemon…"

"Thuya?"

"A Moroccan wood."

"You're Moroccan," she said, as if she were telling, not asking him. "We have an old man in Charlevoix — maybe like your grandfather in Morocco — who carves these for us. He uses spalted maple." She took the bowl from him to trace her finger along the zigzag veins in the wood. "The maple gets a fungus that makes the grain swell. He calls it bois fou. Crazy wood. That's why people buy it — for the look, not the smell. But I like your idea that the lid keeps the scent of the wood inside. It makes me think of..."

"Think of what?" Her wide mouth and regal nose. The confident rhythm of her voice. He imagined his hand on her hip. The roll of her stride against his palm. Though it happened years ago, when he was a boy, he still remembered Abdul's older brother walking with an Australian girl on the beach, his hand on her hip in a way no Moroccan would allow. The thin fabric of her skirt against the sun so Nazim and Abdul, hiding behind the rocks, could see the V at the top of her thighs.

"When we were kids," Diane said, "we watched cartoons about Arabs who lived in caves with heaps of treasure. They always had an oil lamp they rubbed and a genie came out in a cloud to grant their wishes."

"A djinn. They can help you if they want. But they don't do your bidding — and in fact, they can do harm. They live anywhere, not just in oil lamps." As he spoke, he curved both hands to demonstrate an oval shape coming to a V at his fingertips. "That's an oil lamp. The bowls my grandfather carved are more like this." He made deep brackets with his hands to show how the wood enclosed aromatic pockets of air.

In the weeks that followed, Nazim invented reasons to return to the store. To tell her about the lamps made of goat skin stretched over iron frames. The donkeys with woven reed baskets buckled to their sides. How a girl about to marry and leave her mother's kitchen searched along the beach for a stone the right size and shape for a pestle to grind spices. (Though, in fact, that was his mother's story. He had no idea if other brides did that, too.) Buttery cornes de gazelle stuffed with marzipan. Hot beignets tossed in a dish of white sugar. Diane shook back her wispy hair listening to him talk. You make me want to go to Morocco! she cried. I want to stand on the beach and eat a hot beignet.

One day he arrived at the store just as she was about to close. She told him to wait and they could have a beer at the pub around the corner. Oh, she said then, do you drink beer? Are you allowed? He'd lived long enough in Montreal, among people who believed the world spun on the axis of Santa Claus, to be touched that she asked. Though he did drink beer. I'm a catholic sort of Muslim, he said. I've been corrupted. Which made her laugh. Let's see how else we can corrupt you, she said.

His family would be horrified. But his family was far away.

∞

Joelle sits upright on the sofa with her legs tucked close, eyes on the fading light framed by the windows. Even if Marc went shopping after work, he should have been home by now. Or maybe he went to the gym. Lately he doesn't always tell her. She can't call him during the day to ask because he's taking care of patients. He told her a long time ago not to call him at work unless she absolutely had to. Before, though, he used to call her when he took his break. He's too busy now.

She doesn't know if she should keep waiting for him. He won't like it if he comes home and she's already cooked noodles and eggs, her standby meal when she's alone. She doesn't bother with fresh herbs or whatever little chopped and sautéed bits he would add.

The grey sky grows darker. The slow, steady leaching of the day. Her body on the sofa immobile.

She could look in the bedroom closet to see if his gym bag is gone. She could. She should.

But she still doesn't move. She keeps her face lifted to the sky through the windows.

Marc tries not to stare at the door. To sit still. The sounds around him camouflage the focus of his waiting. The shushing hiss of milk being steamed. The piano tinkle of jazz overhead. The aimless talk of students plugged into Walkmans, their belongings strewn across the tables and chairs where they're encamped with papers, jackets, knapsacks, and books.

The door yawns and Marc glances. A kid saunters toward a girl, slides his load of books on the table, and collapses in slow motion in a chair. Both mumble, hardly even bothering to look at each other.

Marc despises their lazy inattention. His back and shoulders are rigid. He tries to calm his pulse by breathing slowly. He knows Ketia will come. She has to. She can't not. The impetus of their kisses, touching, clinging to each other in hidden corners and behind closed doors, all leads here. Marc can no longer even help what he should and shouldn't do. He *has* to have Ketia alone in a room — for more than a moment, not knowing who might surprise them or knock on the door. He's booked a hotel nowhere near the hospital or where either of them lives. He went after work to sign in and pay. He wants the least amount of fuss when he walks in with Ketia. He's been in and out of the room a few times already. Opened the window to freshen the air. Closed it again and turned up the heat. Washed the grapes he set on a towel next to the bottle of Pinot Noir and the toothbrush glasses from the bathroom. The clerk who sat at the counter last time Marc stepped off the elevator didn't even turn his head. Surfing the net was more engrossing than clients. Let him surf.

Marc feels as pleased with himself for planning the arrangements as a Cro-Magnon hunter daring life and limb to kill a beast to throw before his woman. Of course, he didn't tell Ketia he was booking a room. He asked if she wanted to meet for a coffee. *How about we go for a coffee this evening?* He replays the line again and again in his mind. Why shouldn't they get together? They know each other from work. They're friends. Ketia didn't answer, but she listened when he told her. Café de Ville on Côte-des-Neiges. She stood with her back straight, eyes lowered, his words a current feeding into her blood. For weeks now they wait, alert for when everyone's busy and they can flee to the storeroom at the end of the hallway where the orderlies keep walkers. Lips and teeth nip collarbones, necks, ears, arms. He sucked a bruise at the neckline of her tunic — and whispered an apology — but against her dark skin it was hardly visible, and it excited him to see the bite of his mouth on her body when no one else did. He squeezed her breasts through her uniform, groped his fingers as far they would reach into her clothing. She touched only his face, his arms, his chest — but he loved her modesty. They only ever had moments before someone called on the intercom. "Ketia, your patient in 36B needs pain meds."

He hates the slyness and duplicity of hiding in a hotel room like thieves, but what choice do they have? He can't invite her home. Joelle might find out. And even if she didn't, he doesn't want Ketia to see the signs of another woman in his life. They need a place to meet. They run too many risks at work. They'll get caught yet. Two days ago, at the end of evening shift, when all the nurses sat in the nursing station, busy charting, he followed Ketia to check on a fresh post-op patient. She clicked on her flashlight. Both heard the patient snoring the deep sleep of morphine oblivion. The bed on the other side of the curtain, made up with fresh sheets and piqués, was elevated and empty, awaiting a patient. How much time did they have? She backed up against the mattress and he slid her tunic up her ribs, unhooked the front clasp of her bra. She gripped his hair as he mouthed her breasts. Crazy to do that in a patient's room. Someone could have walked in, wondering what that scuffling was. The orderly. Another nurse.

A hotel room is safer. He *needs* Ketia naked. So far he's only had glimpses of skin and flesh in opened clothing. He craves to see her body. Taste her flesh, nose along her thigh. Lick her every midnight nook. Ketia has roused an appetite he never even knew he had.

Oh come, Ketia, come! His hand around his empty mug opens. All those cars on Côte-des-Neiges slowing to find a place to park. One of them must be hers. This evening so precious, how can she delay?

He regrets the worn furniture and drab colours of the hotel room, but he can't afford the luxury he would heap around her if he could. Egyptian cotton sheets, richly woven drapes at the windows, the room velvety and dim in soft light. An evening alone together will be their luxury.

He wills her to walk through the door with that lovely, fluid step, her spine held queenly high.

∞

Ketia stands on the sidewalk in the dark, her chin ducked into the cowl of her yellow scarf.

She tells herself that she hasn't yet decided if she'll open the door. But she already called home and told Gabrielle she was working an overtime shift. She's spent the last two hours downtown pretending she was shopping. She fingered material, angled hangers toward her, and finally tried on a blouse for no other reason than to see herself in the mirror. Her new black bra with lace along the top of the cups. She takes care these days, never knowing what Marc might see. She glanced at the ceiling of the change room to check there was no camera then pulled down her jeans to look at her panties. The arrowhead patch of silky nylon pointing *here*. The firm cheeks of her bum in the mirror.

And so... tonight? Now that she's told them at home that she's working, Ma won't expect her until after midnight. If she goes home now, she'll have to say that she left work because she wasn't feeling well. Then she'll have to pretend to be sick. That would be a lie, too. Though less of a lie than the lie that she's working. Or meeting a man who's married. The whole while she drove from downtown to Côte-des-Neiges, she weighed the fine gradations of sin.

Except that she's only meeting him for a coffee. There's no reason why she can't meet a colleague for a coffee. Maybe there's something about work they have to discuss. Her lips tighten in a prim expression.

Still she stands in the dark on the sidewalk watching Marc through the glass. He lifts a hand to his temple to smooth his hair, rattles his wrist to resettle his watch but doesn't look at it. The sureness with which he knows she'll come compels her.

Hand back on the table, his fingers tap-crawl to his cup. She wants to be that cup. She steps forward and grasps the handle of the door.

part *two*

Joelle tries not to crunch her toast so as not to disturb Marc, who reads the paper on the sofa on the other side of the low dividing wall. He holds it open wide. Funny how his arms don't get tired. In build he hasn't aged since the day she met him. Only his hair, always fine, seems thinner. Against the light from the windows, she can see the top of his scalp through his hair. She wonders if he knows.

Alone in the morning she plays the radio. Music fills out the room. Marc usually only listens to the news. He doesn't mind the insidious creep of silence, doesn't hear how it hardens.

Joelle has finished her toast and debates easing off her chair to get more coffee. Should she offer to top up Marc's mug? He might think she's interrupting. She's surprised that he's still home at all. Lately he's out the door on his weekends off. Busy, busy.

"Are you ready to go?" he asks from behind his newspaper pages.

"To go...?"

"I'd like to get downtown early. We need a new coffee maker. The timer's shot on this one."

Joelle sets her plate and mug in the sink and darts to the bedroom. Yanks on socks, prods her feet into yesterday's jeans. They've always bought furniture and appliances together, Marc asking her opinion, if only for form's sake. She's grown

used to the ochre and brown leaf pattern of their sofa and armchair, though at first she found them dull. She'd have liked blue. But as Marc said, autumn colours wore well.

Hurry, hurry, she thinks. Before he changes his mind. She clips up her hair, which she'd meant to wash.

∞

The kitchen department is on the fourth floor. Marc stays two steps ahead of Joelle on the escalator. Whenever she climbs a step closer, he mounts another. Why does she crowd him?

"Look," she says as they glide past the second floor. "A shoe sale."

He faces straight ahead. He said a coffee maker. Wasn't she listening? He has no intention of waiting for her to try on shoes, wondering out loud how much the leather will stretch, if the heels are too high or too low.

He only suggested this trip to halt any suspicions she might have had about the other evening. Though of course she has none. Not even smart enough to question that he spends as little time as possible with her. So stupidly trusting. He can hardly believe he ever found that loving.

From behind she nudges his arm. "Didn't you say you wanted a new crêpe pan?"

He gets off the escalator on the fourth floor. Now that he is sure of Ketia, he'd thought he could afford an easy kindness to Joelle — a shopping trip, maybe a coffee and pastry. His mouth twitches. There's no way he can sit at a table with her.

He strides past the display of Italian glass bowls like the ones his parents have. Doesn't stop to look at the price. Doesn't stop at the wall of utensils, though he always does. Then he jerks his head around. Where *is* she? He has to backtrack, scanning heads across sets of dining ware, stockpots, madeleine tins, until he finds her holding a crêpe pan.

"Will you please not walk off when you're with me?"

Those dumb blue eyes. Hesitating then replacing the pan on the stack. "I was just here. You were going to look at the coffee makers. I would have..."

He retraces his path through the dishes in the direction of the small electrical appliances. Doesn't stop until he reaches the shelves with the coffee makers. She stands beside him, hands hanging, watching him lift the carafes, examine the display controls, read the specifications. Why did he even bring her along?

To make his point, he taps his finger on a white plastic machine. "I think we should get this one."

"Okay."

"It doesn't match our kitchen."

"But you just said..."

He raps a knuckle on a stainless steel carafe. "Why didn't you say this one?"

"I thought you liked that one."

"Don't you have an opinion?"

Joelle looks away, then says, "You always decide what you're going to buy."

"That's not true," he snaps. "I always ask what you think. Why else did I ask you to come? I could have done this more quickly by myself — and not had an argument in the middle of the store."

He hefts the box from the shelf and marches to the cash. The cashier is wrapping four water goblets in tissue paper. She tucks them in a box, closes and slides it in a bag, angling the handles of the bag toward the woman who is waiting. She smiles at the woman, smiles at the cash register, and softly — as if it were a secret — announces the price. The woman flips back the top of her purse to unzip the compartment where she keeps her wallet.

Marc coughs. Didn't the woman know she had to pay? He already has his wallet in hand. In his impatience he leans back and bumps into Joelle.

She whispers.

"Pardon me?"

"I wasn't arguing. I was letting you decide."

The cashier pulls the box with the coffee maker toward her. He doesn't return her stupid smile. He would sooner she were efficient. He holds out his credit card and speaking over his shoulder says, "I'll drive you home. I have some other things to do." Joelle fiddles with her purse strap, head lowered, probably waiting for him to tell her what. He knows she won't ask.

∞

The mismatched armchairs and sofa in the nurses' lounge are rejects from offices elsewhere in the hospital. Raymonde has spread her report sheets on the table where she leans forward on crossed arms, reading in run-on point form. "41A two days post-op anterior resection, hemoglobin 76, transfuse two units PRBC, Lasix between, CBC in a.m. 41B appi last night, hasn't voided but if she does she can be d/c'd, it's written. 42A three days post-op gastrectomy, still on PCA."

The six nurses coming onto evening shift sit in the armchairs that line the walls, clipboards on their laps, taking notes on their patients. Ketia doesn't look at Raymonde, because then she'll see Marc, who sits behind her. Like an alcoholic who can never idly pick up a bottle or a gambler who can't watch even a child tumbling toy dice, she can't look at Marc. Every nerve in her body, every neuron of her will are primed to guzzle, to grab, to plunge. She yearns for his hands — the whole length of his body. Without his touch, she feels only half awake. She automatons down the hallway with a bag of saline, the broken ghost of her longing on the IV room floor. She didn't know she could want a man so desperately. No one ever told her. Not that she imagines the women she knows — the nurses with their multiple-choice quizzes about *what men like,* her mother a bulwark of piety with her church-going friends — have ever been prey to this undertow. They wouldn't be able to talk and act normally, each movement leaden until electrified by a man.

When the head nurse told Ketia she had to work straight evenings this schedule, Marc asked to be scheduled for evenings, too. Here at work, even if they have to pretend to be only colleagues, they can orbit around each other. Sneak a word or a kiss.

Today, in the change room, Marc breathed in her ear, while Enid rushed to kick off her boots and stamp her feet into her running shoes. He wants Ketia to name another day when they can lock the door on the world and root every byway of their newfound map of each other. But she can't escape for a whole day from home. Ma needs Ketia to drive her to the West Indian store for goat, plantain, chayote, and burnt sugar. The floors have to be scrubbed, the furniture vacuumed and polished. On Sunday there's church, followed by a big family meal. If Ketia asks to go out, Ma will want to know why, with whom, and why Sunday. Ketia has a harder time wondering what to tell her mother than it seems Marc does to tell his wife. (Not that Ketia ever asks about his wife. He, too, shies away from the word.)

Raymonde drones on, "48A query bowel obstruction, arrived Air Ambulance from Florida, swabbed for MRSA and VRE. 48B hernia this morning, still in Recovery."

In the hotel room Marc whispered not to move. He slipped the buttons of her blouse through the holes. Pinched only the zipper on her jeans. Peeled them down her legs by the belt loops. Tugged her socks by the tips. Gentle with her bra. Hooked her panties with one finger, slid them down. Her skin tingled, craving the flat of his palm, his fingers, his face pressed into her neck, the solidity of his hips against hers, but he didn't touch her. He stood and gazed, still dressed himself. Then he dropped to the floor, his mouth hot on her ankle, lips trailing up the inside of her leg, unfurling ribbons of longing, a moan from deep within her throat.

Other couples date, see friends, go to restaurants, movies, dancing. What she and Marc share is different. More vital.

Beyond guidelines and conventions. It doesn't matter that he's married or the difference in age, she's decided — has had to decide, knowing how Ma would denounce her. Devègondé! Libetinaj! A man and a woman marry and live in the sight of God. They don't meet in hotel rooms to lunge at each other like rutting dogs. Ketia has heard Ma talk about goings-on. The disgusted suck of her lips on her teeth. Ma with her church rules at the ready, her Island talk of voodoo and the devil.

Raymonde slaps her hand on her report sheets. "That's it, all yours." She bounds off her chair and out the door. Ghislaine, the evening charge nurse, clicks her pen non-stop, which means she's impatient or in a good mood. The other nurses stand slowly, Aditi lifting her clipboard high and yawning, Fernande asking where Aditi bought her uniform. Except for noting a few numbers — intake, output, a low potassium result to be checked later — Ketia more or less missed report. She'll have to read through her patients' charts later. She manages not to look at Marc's face as he lets her precede him out the door.

In the hallway the orderly Abi beckons her. "52A, he's yours? He says his chest feels funny."

"Can you bring me the EKG machine?" Ketia drops her clipboard on the counter of the nursing station, wheels a blood pressure machine to the room.

"Mr. Apostolakis, you don't feel well?"

His blunt fingers tap his chest, mid-sternum. "A little," he admits.

BP 135 over 80, pulse irregular at 140. "I'm coming back," she tells him, sidestepping the EKG machine Abi pushes into the room.

At the nursing station she tells Ghislaine that her patient is complaining of chest pain with an irregular pulse of 140, BP normal.

"Do an EKG. I'll call..." Ghislaine squints at the patient board to see who the doctor is. "Urology." And as Ketia trots down the hallway, Ghislaine calls after her, "Does he have Nitro ordered?"

Ketia points at her clipboard on the counter. "I don't think so, but look."

Mr. Apostolakis has an almost hairless chest. Good. She doesn't have time to shave circles. She rips open a pack of electrodes she quickly connects to the leads.

"My heart is bad," he says.

"You might need a little medicine."

The paper with the EKG reading slides from the machine as the urology resident swipes through the curtains. "My friend!" he hails Mr. Apostolakis, as if their mothers picked flowers in the Greek hills together. He snatches the sheet of red graph paper with its zigzag tracing and bats through the curtains again.

The old man glances at the billowing cloth, then at Ketia. She taps his hand. "I'll go see."

In the nursing station the urology resident sits by the phone, flicking the unevenly jointed black strings that hang from a drawer handle — where med students practice their surgical knots.

Ghislaine tells Ketia, "Give your patient Nitro. We're waiting for Cardiology."

Mr. Apostolakis lies as if he's already in a coffin, mournful eyes closed, hands flat on his chest.

"Here," Ketia says. And after a minute, "Any better?"

He purses his fleshy mouth, lifts the fingers of one hand, drops them again.

She hurries back to the nursing station where the cardiology resident stands flipping through the pages of the chart, reading only here and there. The urology resident watches from a chair as if it's no longer his problem. Ghislaine rakes a hand through her flyaway hair, making it look wilder. With the other she clicks her pen repeatedly.

"He needs Digoxin," the cardiology resident says. Then scowls. "You didn't notice he was on Coumadin?"

"We had to hold it," the urology resident says. "For the procedure."

"Ever heard of Heparin?" The cardiology resident lets the chart slide off his hand so the urology resident has to tip forward to catch it.

Ketia stands appalled. Where was her head yesterday? She saw that Coumadin was held, but didn't once ask herself why Heparin wasn't ordered instead. She should have noticed. She should have asked.

"No need to call *us*," the cardiology resident sneers, "when you already have a well-documented history of chronic a-fib, but give him a few more hours without coverage and you can call Neurology — when he's thrown a clot."

Ketia grabs an IV basket and jogs to the room.

"Don't cry for me," Mr. Apostolakis says. "I'm an old man."

"I'm not crying. You'll be all right. I'm just going to start an IV." She traces a finger along his arm, looking for a vein. She'll use a 20-gauge needle, she won't hurt him, she'll —

She doesn't know what she'll do if he has a stroke because she had her head flipped around, daydreaming about Marc. Don't make this man pay, she pleads with a God she's forgotten in the past month. It's not his fault.

The urology resident sweeps through the curtain. "You haven't started the IV yet? He needs Heparin stat!" And to Mr. Apostolakis, "You'll be fine, don't worry. As soon as the nurse gets your IV going."

Ketia pops the cap off the end of the intravenous tubing and inserts it in the IV bag. She squeezes the chamber until fluid drips, unrolls the clamp, flushes air bubbles from the tubing. "Soon," she whispers. "As fast as I can."

∞

Early evening, walking home, Joelle kicks through the snow, peering into the sky dissolving into billions of ice crystal stars.

All day it's been snowing. The ground, parked cars, every flat and inclined surface are draped in radiant felt. Behind the sweep of their windshield wipers drivers stare grimly ahead. A woman shovels her walkway. A full-grown Lab snaps at the fresh snow, burrowing his muzzle into the frozen fluff, haunches high, tail wagging.

The dog's game reminds Joelle of digging in the snow when she was a child. Scalloped ridges of white skidded across the field behind their house, ending in a drift in their backyard. One winter the snow was so high she scooped out a hole large enough to crawl inside. She polished the walls smooth with her mittens, marvelling at how the snow glowed blue inside her cave. With every snowfall the walls grew thicker, the light more somber, her snow cave deeper. Inside it she felt protected from shouting and thuds and drunken screeching. For a child it's easy: a cave in a snowdrift.

Today, when she left work, she stopped in a cheap bistro where students bragged and told stories over pitchers of beer. She ordered avocado and Jarlsberg on baguette, and while she waited, opened the *Mirror* to the movie listings. Nothing interested her. She couldn't decide.

Marc has been scheduled to work a stretch of evenings. She's not sure why he agreed. The odd overtime shift, okay. He's helping out. But he has enough seniority that he shouldn't have to work steady evenings.

She takes a meandering route through the McGill ghetto toward St-Laurent. Grey stone façades with long windows. A glimpse of book-lined walls. Diamond sparkles of snow on gables over dormer windows. A patio table on a balcony so smoothly laden with snow that it's an enormous white cake on legs.

The tables in the cafés and restaurants on St-Laurent are almost empty. The few people on the sidewalks trudge with their heads lowered. Yet the snow falls so gently — a feathery hush. A man walking toward her seems as entranced as she is, face lifted to the sky. He nearly slips, one arm wheels, he rights his balance, and grins at Joelle.

She comes to the square where, in the summer, men play pétanque on the hard-packed ground. Now the empty benches are mounded with snow the exact shape and length of small coffins. Children's coffins, pristine and white, glowing faintly in the shadowed darkness.

She hadn't looked at her dad in his casket. Seventeen years old and unwilling to face death. Matante Huguette said to pretend he was only sleeping. As if anyone would sleep in a satin-lined box in a room full of people. When Joelle heard people murmuring how good he looked, she especially knew she didn't want to see. She would sooner remember him the way he was in the last months in the hospital, gaunt and jaundiced but still able to talk. She would have done without the funeral home entirely. The dimly lit room, the unctuous phrases. The funeral home director who assumed that Joelle and her mother were close in their shared loss. Joelle knew her mother was more relieved than grieving. Her dad was probably glad to be gone, too. Released from the pain that scraped through his abdomen until he could no longer lie or sit. Free, too, of his wife. Her tight barmaid's clothes in the closet. Plastic baskets of makeup, curlers, a hair iron, and brushes, crowding the vanity in the bathroom, though many nights she didn't even come home. When she did, she bellowed. Joelle's dad wasn't easy to rouse from his gin-heavy sleep, but if her mother succeeded in yanking him from his armchair to his feet, he roared.

A few years later, when Joelle saw her first Bergman film, it seemed more essentially true than anything she'd ever heard or read about relationships. The punishment couples inflict on each other. The compulsive damage of that bond.

She might have ended up like that had she stayed with Emile. His sneer flits through her mind. The way he always leaned against doorways with his hip cocked. She didn't know it then, but Emile did her a favour when he dumped the key on the kitchen table. Among the crumpled bags from the patisserie and the junk mail, she didn't see it. She worried, waiting on the couch facing the door for two days before calling his friends, and finally even his sister to ask if she knew where he was. He called her then. You idiot. The key's on the table. Stop harassing everyone, compris? She still curves her shoulders when she remembers. Feels ashamed.

Except then she met Marc, who was so different from Emile. Honest and meticulous, a caring man — a nurse. He never says mean things. Even when he's angry, which is rare, he only gets cold and withdrawn. It's not his fault that lately he's more stressed. Edgy. He's overworked, that's all.

That's *all,* she repeats to herself, as she kicks through the snow, looking up at the Morse code of flakes drifting across the nimbus heads of the street lamps.

∽

The bedroom is just large enough for two single beds pushed into the corners, a dresser, and a small desk. The flowered comforters match the pale peach walls. Ketia and Gabrielle went with Pa to the hardware store, chose the colour — peach passion — and painted the room themselves, including the baseboard and window frame.

Ketia sits at the small desk where she and Gabrielle used to do homework. Gabrielle has claimed it now with a weighty economics text, coloured plastic folders, pens, highlighters, lipstick, a nail file. Ketia had to clear herself a bay where she's set her Visa bill and a small stack of receipts she checks against the list of purchases. Twice she's had to start again. Didn't she already see this receipt? She must have returned it to the wrong pile. She frowns.

Gabrielle lies on her bed, propped against her frilly pillows, dancing her slender hand and freshly painted nails through the air. "You are one classy chick," she sings. "Oh yeah… définitivement."

Ketia blocks out her voice as well as she can. Gabrielle in all her vainglory and strut. She's told Ketia she's crazy to work as a nurse. Emptying bedpans, huh! Plugged into the old stereotype about black maids and servants. You bet that's what people think when they see her with her little tray of pills and her towels, all meek and efficient. Gabrielle scoffs. She intends to aim high — a degree in administration des affaires at the HEC, where students from around the world come to study.

Ketia grimaces. What did she buy at Royaume des Chapeaux? Not a hat. Then she remembers the scarf, canary-bright and soft against her skin. Prettier than the striped blue scarf — a perfectly good scarf — she already had. Except that she's supposed to be saving to start university next year.

Irritated, she jabs her pen at the lipstick and bottles of nail polish crowded among Gabrielle's things. "What's all this doing here? This is supposed to be a desk, not a makeup counter."

Gabrielle continues her game with her hands, undulating her fingers and wrists.

Ketia fingers the next receipt. Eighty-nine dollars for *jeans?* Oh. Yes. The temptress jeans that led to the first illicit touch. She'd finished work, changed out of her uniform, and was walking past the nursing station to the stairs, coat on her arm, when she heard Marc call. She turned on her heel and saw how he watched her. She knew the jeans squeezed every curve. A porter, who was pushing a bed down the hallway, motioned with his head for them to step against the wall. Hidden by the bed, Marc let the breath of space between them become the lightest possible graze of his fingers across her bum. She didn't move away, mesmerized by his daring. The tight denim moulded and held her: offered her up to Marc.

Then Gabrielle says, "Hey, you know what you need? A fuck buddy."

Ketia twists around in her chair. "What are you talking about? You don't even —"

"Oh chill, why don't you? Spare me the lecture."

"Maybe you could use a lecture, talking about sex like it's a game!"

"A game?" Gabrielle grins. "Why not, if you've got a capote in your pocket?" She lifts her hip off the bed and makes as if she's reaching for her back pocket.

"You don't carry condoms!"

Gabrielle pouts her lips in fleshy defiance. "Why not? I could. Just because you're a Miss Goody Two Shoes doesn't mean I have to be one. Me, I want to have some fun before I end up getting old and fat like Ma."

"Ma is not old and fat! And even if she were, you shouldn't say so. She's our mother."

Gabrielle groans and squirms her narrow hips around to face the wall. Ketia sees the resistant set of her shoulders and knows she should say more. Try to find out what Gabrielle has been doing.

But her thoughts stall before Gabrielle's word. A fuck buddy. She refuses to believe that's all Marc wants. His mouth on her belly, his hands gentle on her breasts, cupping her face — isn't that *love?* Except that he's never said it. Of all the desperate whispers that spill from his mouth, calling her his dear heart, his darling, cocotte, honey girl, the one word she craves to hear — that in her heart would mollify, if not excuse her wrongdoing — rings loudly in its absence.

Which leaves her where? Snared between what he doesn't say and that he's married. Married, which is not just a word but a fact. What does it mean to him that he has a wife? Does he love her? Ketia bites her lips to keep them from trembling. The nurses say that his wife is pretty.

Suddenly she hears the silence in the room. She turns her head. Gabrielle lies flat on her back again, watching her.

"You spent too much, didn't you?" Gabrielle gives a long

cat stretch against her pillows. "Bon. Vas-tu finir là? I've got homework to do — and you're sitting in front of it."

∞

Fine snow lace tempers the light that washes across the sofa, the rich ochre wool of the carpet, the sheen of the hardwood floor. Marc sits in his flannel robe, reading the opinion section of *La Presse*. The rest of the paper lies in a neat stack aligned with the edge of the coffee table. Stories about people hoarding jugs of water, gasoline, cans of food, and toilet paper in dread of Y2K. *Toilet paper.* He smirks.

Marc doesn't believe anything will happen. Even if it does, he'll escape to his parents' in the Laurentians, as he did two years ago during the ice storm that bombed the city, tearing power lines, cracking trees, leaving homes without power for days and the downtown core deserted. His parents have a fieldstone fireplace, four cords of wood, bins of flour and grains — their usual stock — excellent well water, even a gas-powered generator for their freezer if power fails.

Y2K paranoia. He snaps the pages, folds them, and sets the section on the rest of the paper on the table. He'd sooner think about Ketia. Her girlishly slim hips, her agile waist. When she lies on her back, her small breasts flatten except for the perk of her nipples. Marc's fingers close in a soft pinch, though he keeps his hands on the cushions as if they're manacled. He won't touch himself here on the sofa, though his cock thickens. The only place where he dares masturbate is in the shower. He doesn't see the drain where he kneels, but Ketia before him. He does it even when Joelle is home, asleep in bed on the other side of the wall. If she woke, all she'd hear would be the drumming of the water. He pumps rapidly then more slowly, relishing his lust, clenching his teeth when he comes. The water from the shower washes all proof away. Even so, he squirts disinfectant around the drain.

It's still too early, only eleven. He'll take a shower before he leaves for work. He took one last night when he got home. How many showers can a man take in a day? Ah, he smiles, fantasizing about Ketia, many.

He tries to focus on the books in the cabinet. A hefty surgical-medical dictionary. An anatomy text. Next to that, Joelle's book on Chaplin. And the handsome book on herbs with watercolour illustrations his parents gave Joelle for her birthday. Has she even once leafed through the pages?

Her sweater hangs on the back of a dining room chair. Her slippers lie one atop the other against the wall divider. Why can she never put her things away? Even when she's not home, her presence insinuates. Taunts him.

On the wall hangs the African mask he bought a few years ago because the dark-grained wood matches the colours of the carpet and the leaf-patterned sofa. The carved face isn't as stylized as masks usually are. The pouting cheeks and full lips seem almost lifelike despite the blind eyes.

And slowly now he stands and walks to the wall. His fingers barely graze the dark wood, not wanting to feel its hardness, only the line of the lips. Ketia's mouth that opens, the nip of her teeth, her tongue.

One hand fumbles through the folds of his robe as he hastens to the bathroom, locks the door, shrugs his robe to the floor, kicks free his pyjamas, yanks on the shower handle.

∽

Diane left work with a major Medusa headache. Stéphane, the florist from next door, gave her a pill that shrank the snakes' spread but not their writhe. Before she took the pill, they nearly burst her skull. After the pill, they bored inwards, strangling her brain.

Each step on the sidewalk jars the ache. She longs to lie down, blot herself against the cushions, die for a few hours.

Nazim won't be home until later. He's not working today, but he went to Hatem's — some story about someone's cousin finding a dozen old computers in the garbage.

She whimpers when she turns onto their street of low apartment buildings. Red brick, bay windows. Climbs the stairs, each step a bang in her head. No, not in her head. She winces. Some idiot is *hammering*. Don't people know how sound carries in these old buildings?

Louder on her landing. Christ. Stupid boys who live beside her. If her head wasn't a bruise about to fall off her neck, she'd throw her boots at their door.

She fumbles out her keys, unlocks her door. Stops. No way. In *her* kitchen? The landlord can't come in without calling first! He's got her number at work.

The tables and chairs are shoved against the wall. Nazim stands amid boards more or less joined in a bookshelf structure, hammering a nail in place. He hasn't heard her walk in. On the floor a handsaw, curled shavings, stub ends of wood, a box of nails. She said she wanted another bookshelf. She never thought he would build one.

She creeps back down the hallway to the sofa, where she pulls the blanket folded on the armrest over her. He must have bought wood and nails, borrowed tools from his friends. The sides and the bottom were together. He was hammering the top. Each bang reverberates pain. How much longer can it take?

The doorbell rings. Brief. Peremptory. Can't Nazim hear? He doesn't stop. It rings again. Twice, longer.

The woman from downstairs — spiked hair and flared skirt — stands with both hands on her hips. "Do you know what that sounds like in my apartment?"

"He's almost done," Diane says weakly.

"*Almost?* How about right now?"

Diane can't talk. Even her teeth hurt. How many times has this woman and her boyfriend woken her at three in the morning having Betty Boop and Tasmanian Devil sex? Her giggly squeals, his slathering growls.

The neighbour stomps downstairs. Diane hugs herself feebly. Flinches against the echoing booms of the hammer in the hallway. "You have to stop. The bitch from downstairs is complaining."

Nazim bends to take another nail from the box.

"I said stop. You have to. I can't take it, either. My head..."

Nazim lays the hammer on the top board, drops the nail in the box. The pain makes her smell everything. The sawdust. The bananas in the fruit bowl. Nazim's faint sweat as he walks past. From her end of the tunnel hallway she watches him grab his jacket from the closet. Open the door. Close it.

The crack of hammering still seems to sound against the walls. The kitchen looms larger — her grandma's cabinet on one side, the tables and chairs where Nazim piled them. The almost-finished bookshelf the centrepiece. Four shelves in a box frame. Exactly what she wanted.

Her head throbs. She can't figure out one plus one, much less what it means that Nazim was building her a bookshelf and she told him to stop.

In the living room she tucks herself into her blanket and pillow nest. The woman downstairs has turned her music up loud. A repetitive techno-mechanical sound. Motorized bedsprings.

Diane wakes to a dark apartment. The TV from next door through the wall. Nothing from downstairs. She clicks on the lamp. She's slept four hours. She rotates her head. Normal size, normal weight. No more snakes.

In the kitchen, leaning against the counter, she eats some yogurt from the container. Considers the bookshelf in the dim light from over the stove. It could have been finished by now, all the wood shavings swept away, the table and chairs in the middle of the room again.

She brushes her teeth, washes her face, goes to bed.

Nazim obviously didn't just walk around the block. He

escaped to a café where men congregate with small glasses of coffee or tea before them, the air rancid with black tobacco, faces animated by talk, jabbing the air with their fingers.

She trailed him once, the first year they lived together. She was coming home from work when he stepped from their building, head lowered, shoulders dogged. She decided to follow him. He only had to turn around and he would see her. He strode for blocks, heading north. She sometimes had to jog to keep up. On Jean-Talon she lost him in the crowd streaming from the market with bags of vegetables and fruit. Or did he slip in somewhere? She backtracked. A discount luggage store. A halal butcher. A starkly lit room where only men sat at the tables. A discreet sign in Arabic in the corner of the window. She retreated, then peeked through the open doorway. There, Nazim. At a table with two other men, his shoulder pressed against the tiled wall.

It makes sense to her that every now and then he needs to *be with his own.* Who wouldn't? She's always lived here and can't imagine not having that inalienable sense of belonging. What must it be like to leave home and move to another country where, even after living there for years, people still — always — treat you like a foreigner? If the colour of your skin doesn't mark you, your accent does. And all the while the home you remember — the home you left — changes. You no longer belong there, either. Your only true familiars are the other immigrants who order fish soup in Cantonese or sit, elbows on the table, over ouzo and cards above a barbershop in Montreal.

In the night, Diane wakes to the careful but loud click of the deadbolt. She looks at the lit numbers on the alarm clock. Almost one. The soft tap of his babouches to the bathroom, the toilet, the sink, then into the bedroom. The static of his sweater pulled over his head. The slide of his jeans down his hairy legs. The gentle thud of his belt lowered onto the chair. He eases himself under the quilt, careful to keep to his side of the bed.

She slides a hand across the space between them and touches his back. He twists around, pulling the sheet with him. He stinks of black tobacco. Acrid. He only smokes when he goes to a café with other Moroccans and Algerians. Neither says a word. They sleep facing each other.

∞

The patient, a fresh transfer from ICU, has three chest tubes, a naso-gastric tube, and O2. While Ketia, Abi, and the ICU orderly get the woman settled in bed, Ghislaine checks that the chest tubes are connected properly and fluctuating with no bubbles.

Ketia hugs the patient's chart, a thick mass of pages threatening to spill from the manila folder, to her chest as she walks to the nursing station. Doctors' orders, lab results, EKGs, RT records. The ICU flow charts, filled with numbers — all readings from machines — mean nothing to her. She sets aside the transfer orders, which she'll do in a minute. First she wants some sense of the history. Page by page she sorts through the notes for an entry in handwriting she can more or less decipher.

Carlene drops a plastic bag of boxes and bottles on the counter next to Ketia and swivels a chair around. Some patients bring the entire contents of their medicine cabinet rather than make a list. They don't trust themselves to copy the names. Carlene upends the bag and lifts a bottle. Her nails gleam lavender with long white French tips. "They shouldn't give you a heavy patient like that. You're still junior."

"Ghislaine said she'd help." Marc, too, but Ketia keeps that to herself. She's reading a note dated a week ago. *Thoracic aortic aneurysm. Large something something hemothorax. Pleural effusion. No something hemorrhage. Resp status 2 ° to atelectasis airway edema. Something something renal function.*

Carlene tuts under her breath. "Fish oil tablets! That's not medicine." She shows Ketia the bottle and for an instant their hands pose side by side. Next to Carlene's nails and silver rings, Ketia's hands are plain workaday tools, and briefly she wonders why she never does her nails. Gabrielle has enough bottles of polish on the desk at home. Nail polish, lipstick, eyeliner, mascara. Gabrielle likes to primp. Lately she's started wearing thongs and lacy boy shorts, though she has to wash them in the bathroom sink and hang them in the closet to dry so Ma doesn't find them. What a lot of trouble, Ketia said. And for what? Who even sees it? *I* do, Gabrielle said. They make me feel hot.

Ketia throws a sidelong look at Carlene and guesses that a layer of her sophistication stems from sexy lingerie.

Marc strides from the med room with a patient's med sheets he tosses in a swirl of pages in front of Carlene.

"Hey!" She flings up her hands and sits back. "What's your problem?"

"That's yours?"

"What about it?"

"Can I point out that on my watch"— Marc swings up his wrist as if to check — "it's only six o'clock?"

"Good for you, you know how to tell time."

"It seems that some of us don't. You've already signed off your eight o'clock meds."

"Because I got them ready!" Carlene glares at him.

"Ghislaine, could we maybe have a talk with Carlene here? She seems to have forgotten that we sign meds off *when* we give them, not at some indeterminate time when we happen to have a pen in hand. The nurse's initials on the med sheet are proof— legal proof, let me add — that the meds were given."

Ketia focuses on the ICU orders she's transcribing. Marc is right, of course. But she wishes he wouldn't use that tone.

"And what's the rationale?" Marc continues. "In the event that there's an emergency, which can always happen in a hospital, or if for some reason the nurse has to leave the floor,

we can at any time look at the med sheet"— he points at it —
"and verify whether or not meds were given. However, in this
case, we'd be mistaken if we looked at the med sheet, because
Carlene has not actually —"

"Okay! Okay!" Carlene flaps a hand as if at a bad smell. "Get
off your bloody high horse."

"My bloody high horse?"

"Stop it, both of you," Ghislaine snaps. "You're worse than
my kids. You know the procedure," she tells Carlene. "You sign
off your meds when you give them." She clicks her pen with
manic emphasis.

"Look at Ketia," Marc says. "She's a new nurse. She only has
a few months of experience, but she would never do something
like that." He stalks back to the med room.

Carlene shouts after him, "What business is it of yours to
look at my med sheets?" And more quietly, "Flexin' his chest
at me. Asshole."

Ketia keeps writing on the Patient Care Plan.

"Huh! Sounds like you're his favourite, aren't you lucky."
Carlene stands and pushes her chair aside.

∞

Joelle doesn't expect to see Marc's boots in the tray outside
their door. It's his day off, but when she called home this
morning to ask if he wanted to go out for supper, he said he'd
already made plans.

She opens the door onto the news on the radio. "...China
has now announced that it is ready for Y2K. To prove their
confidence, top airline personnel will be flying on December
31st and January 1st." She hangs her coat next to Marc's on the
coat tree. He doesn't seem to have heard her come in. He sits
on the sofa, paper held high like a sail, with only the feather-
fine cap of his hair visible.

"Hi," she says from the edge of the room.

He lowers the paper a fraction. The island becomes a forehead of moderate height, his eyes in shadow, his nose and mouth still submerged.

"I thought you were going out."

He lowers the paper to his lap and nods at the gym bag on the floor. "I'm leaving in a minute." He's wearing the brown and cream shirt she likes. His beige fisherman sweater lies across the armrest next to him. He seems not to know what else to say, then asks, "What will you eat?"

What's it to you? she thinks. Nearly says it, but then only shrugs. "Something."

Marc raises the paper again to keep reading. She walks across to the window, where she can see the flat roofs, gables, pyramid skylights, and mansard angles of lower Outremont. All summer the tops of the buildings were hidden by the dense foliage of trees. Autumn brought the stark edges into view again. She loves the view from here. The seasons in the city. The etched outline of lights. Signs over shops, cars in the street, apartment windows. As dusk thickens, everything that's not lit grows fuzzy. Disappears. At the same time Marc's reflection in the window grows more distinct. He hides behind his paper in the soft radiance cast by the lamp. His sweater across the armrest.

"Did you get your test results? You never told me."

The newspaper doesn't move. Then he says, "Yes." He lowers a corner of the page. "Everything's fine. It was just a precaution."

"I know."

"And finally," the radio announcer's voice rises a pitch, "did the Christmas truce of 1914 really take place? Legend has it that on Christmas Day in 1914, enemy met enemy between the trenches. British, German, French, and Belgian soldiers, who only hours before were trying to kill each other, climbed from their trenches to shake hands."

Christmas. Joelle grimaces. She hated the tense car trips to relatives with her parents. She only saw her cousins at Christmas and felt too shy to play their rowdy games. She knew to heap her plate from the table in the kitchen — pigs' feet in gravy, tourtières, coleslaw, an enormous pot of beans — and find a corner to sit by herself before the grown-ups got soused on gros gin and scotch, and her mother or her dad blamed a brother, a cousin, or a parent for some grudge that would take until next Christmas to forgive. When the arguing started, Joelle knew her parents were about to get flung from the house or they would stomp off, and she snuck off to the bedroom to grapple with the dead-weight mound of coats on the bed to find hers and get ready, terrified that her parents would drive off without her in the cold Christmas night, the black sky and the stars pierced by angry cursing, the uncle who whipped off his belt and hit their car, threatening to strap Joelle's mother because she insulted his wife. The car lurched. They drove fast. A couple of times slid into the ditch or a snow bank. Joelle, her hand gripped tight, as her mother strode to the closest house to call for a tow truck or a cab. That could take hours on Christmas Eve. Once the man who lived in the house where they knocked drove them home. Joelle asked about her dad. Her mother told her to lie down and be quiet. She sat in the front with the man. Joelle woke, wondering where she was. The back seat of a car that had stopped. Her mother's voice low and urgent. When Joelle woke again she was under her blankets in her bed.

Years later, once her dad died, Joelle spent Christmas with Diane and her family. And of course, since she's been with Marc, they spend the holidays with his parents, who host a festive meal of many courses, each of which Joelle must enjoy — with double emphasis on the *must* this year, since Marc was so annoyed with her after her birthday.

With the sky growing ever darker outside, the reflection in the window grows larger. Marc next to the lamp, the sofa, the bookshelves, the walls. Their home in the glass. Marc shakes his wrist to right the armband of his watch and checks the time.

Since he said that he was going, she wishes he would go. Leave her to her solitary evening. She's hungry and wants to eat.

As he shakes the paper to fold it, she turns from the window and watches him.

"Maybe," he says, "you should go out with Diane more often."

"I think she likes to spend her evenings with Nazim."

Marc nods. Hears no reproach. He pulls his sweater over his head.

"Your hair," she says, because he doesn't like it messy.

He goes to the mirror in the hallway and brushes his fingers through his hair. Straightens his collar inside the crew neckline of the sweater. "Okay, bye." He stoops for his gym bag. "I don't know when I'll be home."

She waits until she hears the door close before she heads to the kitchen. As she passes the hallway she smells the damp citrus scent of his shaving cream from the bathroom. Why did he shower and shave before going to the gym?

She runs water into a copper-bottomed pot she sets on the stove. Noodles and eggs was the meal her dad always made when her mother wasn't home. He sipped his glass of gin, with the bottle on the floor next to his overstuffed chair in front of the TV, until he fell asleep. Then she could watch whatever she wanted while he snored. Or she took a bath, stealing one of her mother's coloured perfume balls so the water smelled nice.

What she wonders now is how her dad felt. Rejected and lonely? Or glad not to have to rouse himself from his chair when his wife accused him of being a fucking loser who ruined her life. Joelle knows they were miserable together. Of course she knows. She had to live it, too. But before the misery — the drinking and the shouting — how did her dad grow to love his bottle of gin more than his wife? The comfort of his chair to a job where he would have felt productive? How did it start?

Not like this, she tells herself. Marc never raises his voice. And she doesn't flirt with other men the way her mother did. She and Marc don't fight. They're not alcoholics and not in debt. Everything about her marriage is different from her parents'. She made sure of that when she chose him.

∞

Ketia has smeared a wide swathe of Vaseline along her hairline to protect her face, ears, and neck. Her arms ache from the strain of holding them high to massage relaxant — a pretty word for a stinky product — into her roots. By the time she has finished rubbing cream into her scalp, her head looks electrified. A cartoon of a deranged scientist.

She's never tried to straighten her hair on her own without Gabrielle's help, and can only hope she didn't miss any, because if she did, the kinky strands will stick out like grasshopper legs. She probably should have waited until the weekend when Gabrielle was home. Except Gabrielle would ask too many questions. Hey, Ketia, who are you trying to impress? One of Ma's boys from church?

Ketia allows herself a smug, tiny smile. She's fooled them all — Ma and Gabrielle, even Carlene at work. No one suspects.

A towel draped over her shoulders, Ketia squats at the side of the tub, bent forward, holding the shower hose over her head to rinse out the cream. Water makes the smell stronger. Sulphuric. The insides of her nostrils cringe. But she's thorough, easing her fingers through her hair. Already she can tell that it's softer. She wants it to hang free. Sometimes she and Marc only have a single, stolen moment at work. He can never seem to kiss her without touching her neck, mussing her knot of hair, leaving her with a tuft of afro bobbing.

She squeezes her head lightly with the towel. Pulls off her T-shirt and panties, and steps in the shower. She shampoos her hair carefully, rinses that out, and gently works in conditioner — which doesn't get rinsed. Gabrielle taught her that. Anything to add gloss and flatten.

Yesterday she couldn't keep her hands out of Marc's hair. She wound it around her fingers, tugged on it, bunched it in her fists. Their second hotel date — their anniversary, he called it. He brought champagne, chocolate, and peaches. She leaned against the tiny bathroom sink and watched him shower through the gap in the curtain. The water streamed down his back and buttocks as he soaped himself. What a marvel, a man in the shower. His wet flesh looked leaner, his muscles more defined. Hands practical yet tender as he cupped his testicles. Rivulets of water smoothed the hair on his thighs. And how roughly he towelled himself dry and raked his fingers through his hair. Naked, his body exuded more power than when he was clothed.

Ketia uses the hair dryer on low heat, holding strands flat with her brush. She hasn't got time for Gabrielle's big rollers. Gabrielle believes in rollers, not an iron. Every woman Ketia knows has theories on hair care. Except for holidays, Ketia rarely bothers with the rituals and fuss. But if Marc likes her hair straight, she'll do it for him all the time. She doesn't think how long this is taking and how sore her arms are. She smiles at herself in the mirror, turning her head from side to side. Her hair looks prettier, more like a lady's. She props a coquettish hand on her hip, resting her fingertips on the jut of the bone. She likes that edge — the crest of the ilium — that cradles her flat tummy.

But now she's late for work and flings wide the bathroom door, rushing to the bedroom to dress. Her camisole and green scrubs. Heavy knee socks against the cold outdoors. She drops a pair of ankle socks to wear at work in her knapsack. Quickly she scampers down the hallway past the kitchen.

"Ketia," she hears.

She was so excited about her hair she forgot Ma was home. She makes her face blank. "Oui, Ma."

Ma sits at the table, her hands flat on her thighs. The counter is scrubbed and free of dishes. Her braids, pinned around her head, gleam in the sunlight that slants through the window behind her. Her hair is still rich and black. As far as Ketia knows, she's never straightened it.

Ketia avoids looking at the set of Ma's features. The expression on her face. "Oui, Ma," she repeats.

"Where are you going?" And before Ketia can answer, she adds, "Tonight?"

The word slaps panic into Ketia. "To work," she manages.

"That was what we thought yesterday."

How does Ma know? What happened? "Did you… call at work? Did something happen?"

"Where were you?"

Ketia has an excuse ready. "We were overstaffed yesterday and they asked if someone would work on another floor where they had three sick calls. I should have let you know but I didn't think of it. We were so busy."

"When Bastien called, they told him it was your day off."

"Bastien didn't understand. Why did he call? What happened?"

Ma doesn't speak.

"Next time that I'm asked to work on another floor I'll make sure that whoever is at the desk knows where I am. It's not like in the daytime when Lou's at the desk. She keeps track of everything. But Cassie doesn't…" Ketia trails off. Ma's not listening.

"I'm late. I have to go."

Ma speaks below her breath.

"Pardon me?"

"Bastien didn't make a mistake."

Blinking rapidly, Ketia scurries down the hallway and fumbles her coat from the closet. Maybe she lied yesterday, but today she's going to work. Ma can ask Bastien to call. She's going to work.

Joelle holds the phone to her ear, waiting for a blood result. Patients sit in the chairs across from the filing cabinets, around the wall, up to her desk. She took the blood to the lab herself, tripping down the stairs, heels clacking. She had to get back to the office pronto. Frank's clinic was running more than an hour late.

Back in the office, with the phone ringing and a new patient arriving every few minutes, she forgot about the blood until Frank stood before her, motioning with his head at Mr. Belmontadillo. "Nothing yet? We should have the result by now." He took the next manila folder from the stack on her desk and called for Madame Fleury.

Joelle phoned the lab, who put her on hold. The tech returns. The blood wasn't left at the right window, so it's being processed with the hundreds of tubes of routine bloodwork.

"I didn't know there was a window for stat blood." Joelle tries to keep her voice low. She doesn't want to alarm Mr..B, who is sitting close enough to hear. "Didn't you see it was stat? I marked it in red pen."

"Can't help that now, dear. It's in the machine. It'll be done when it's done. Next time leave it at the right —"

"But this is important!" Still an urgent whisper.

"This is a hospital, dear. Everything's important."

Joelle hangs up, as annoyed with herself as the lordly lab tech. She hasn't yet looked at the man who's walked in. Any closer to her desk and he'd be on it. The edges of his sheepskin jacket brush the manila folders. Black jeans and a worn leather belt. He taps a blue-edged paper — a referral — against her pencil sharpener.

She glances up at him. Then stops. Good God. *Emile.* For a heartbeat time freezes. She still lives with Emile in their apartment with the yellowed walls in NDG. Nothing has changed. She never escaped. Dread seeps through her, holds her immobile.

Then she sees that he's older, his skin more rugged, his eyes pouched. The lines that used to bracket his mouth when he frowned are now etched in place.

He chuckles deep in his throat. "Salut, Beauté."

Beauty and the Beast. One of his nicer tags for their relationship. He liked playing the beast, too, rough in his habits and person. He didn't seem to know — or care — that in the story the Beast was loving and kind.

His eyebrows arch as if puzzled by her silence, though she can see he enjoys the surprise. "You don't look happy to see me."

"What are you doing here?" The question sounds feeble. She's aware of the patients sitting close by, pretending not to watch.

Emile flaps the referral in the air. "I'd just as soon avoid the whole quack profession, but it looks like I need one of these fancy check-ups. Kodak up the bum, whatever you call it."

She reaches for the referral but he lifts it away. "Never thought I'd see you in a place like this." He waves the referral at the filing cabinets and, above them, the large poster of a colon polyp magnified to the size of an adult fist. "I thought you were going to... what? Make movies? Do those write-ups in the paper?"

Joelle used to tell him he should try to better himself. Didn't he want to do more with his life than sell tickets at the train station? He could take courses, maybe get a degree. She doesn't answer now. She deserves his taunt. But she wishes the patients couldn't hear. Hear, too, how he includes them in his scorn.

He dangles the referral just beyond her reach. She refuses to grab for it. She taps the eraser end of her pencil on the ledger-size appointment book open before her. "Do you need to be seen quickly?"

"Since I've got some pull here, why not? Let's get the butt check over with."

She flips pages a month ahead, two months ahead, waves with her hand across the dense list of pencilled names on every clinic day. "We're booked solid."

"Squeeze me in," he drawls.

She keeps her eyes on her appointment book. Not that that's any better the way he stands with his crotch right across from her face.

And suddenly she flushes, remembering the time he walked into the kitchen behind her where she sat at the table copying recipes onto cards. At first she felt only how he prodded at her hair and her neck. She didn't understand until she heard the rapid skin-on-skin pump of his hand. The words between his teeth. Think you're a princess, eh? Lotsa girls'd be happy. She cowered into herself, eyes squeezed shut, hands spread across her new recipe cards. She hated that willful, whacking sound. Still she stayed in her chair. Didn't move. Couldn't. Wished he'd just finish. She never thought he'd come in her hair, spraying her like a tomcat. She's never told anyone, not even Diane.

The phone rings. Joelle grabs it thankfully. Ginette Blais, who'd called earlier to ask whether she should stop a medication. "I haven't talked to the doctor yet. I told you I would call you when I knew." And though there's nothing more to add, Joelle lets Ginette explain again. "Yes," she says, "yes." What she'll do is ask Frank to refer Emile to someone else. She'll tell Frank she doesn't want him in the office. Frank won't even ask why.

Emile shifts his stance and drops the referral on her blotter. Automatically she reaches for it and reads the scrawl across the top. *46 yr male, right-sided abd mass, constipation +++, family history.*

All she saw before was that he looked older. Now she notices that he's paler, the creases around his mouth deeper.

He misses her quick once-over. He's staring at the shelves behind her. "That him?" he asks.

"That's him," she confirms. Framed photos of Frank and his two girls. Patients love to see the family side of the doctor, a dad with his kids.

She holds the referral curved toward her, hiding the poisonous words. Though Emile must have read them. Doesn't he know what they mean? What did his doctor tell him?

The phone rings. The lab with the stat result Frank wanted. Mr. B's hemoglobin has dropped to 68.

She answers the other line.

"Joelle, it's Sandeep. Where's Frank? He's not answering his beeper."

"He's with a patient."

"Tell him to page me tout de suite when he comes out."

As she hangs up, Emile sniffs. "I can't picture you a mom."

Joelle looks up, surprised. "I don't have children."

He points at the shelves behind her.

"That's the doctor. And his daughters."

Madame Solteis, sitting closest to the desk, chimes in, "Lovely! Aren't they lovely?"

"Ah," Emile's voice gets as light as his gruffness allows. "I thought that was hubby and the brood." He half-laughs, shakes his head.

"My husband and I don't have children," Joelle says, glad to let him know that she's married. "It's a decision some couples make."

"A decision, yeah." Emile smirks. "Except that for you the big decision would have been to have kids, right?" He winks. "I never had any, either — or none that showed up calling me Dad. Just as well, eh?" He gestures at the referral. "With cancer."

Joelle immediately says what she would tell any patient. "This doesn't mean you have cancer. That's why your doctor sent you here — to find out what's wrong."

"You think I don't know? The same thing that got my two uncles and probably would have got the third except his heart got him first. Don't know how my old man made it to seventy." Emile shrugs. "So what's going on here? Are you giving me an appointment or aren't you?"

"I need to ask the doctor…"

Emile exhales loudly. The people in the waiting room — all having gone through the routine of referrals and tests, surgery and follow-ups — resettle purses on their laps, shift legs. Doesn't this man know to be nice to Joelle?

She looks past Emile at the door to the examining room where she can hear Frank's voice. The door opens and Madame Fleury, her face grim, appears first, followed by Frank, trying not to look as if he's rushing her. He sets her chart on the desk, takes the next patient's and the note she hands him. The hemoglobin result.

"Mr. B." Frank turns around. "We're going to have to bring you in for a transfusion and some tests. I'm sorry, it doesn't look as if we have much choice." And in Joelle's direction, "You'll call Admitting?"

"Sandeep wants you to page him right away and —" She holds out Emile's referral. "How soon do you need to see him?"

Frank scans it without expression. "This week. No, I'm…"

"Next week," Joelle says.

Frank reads the name on the chart he's holding. "Monsieur Seemon?" he asks in French. And in English, "Mr. Simon?"

"Don't forget Sandeep," she calls after him.

Joelle turns pages in the appointment book slowly, taps her pencil on the desk, wondering where to put Emile.

"Why not this week?" he asks.

Joelle doesn't answer. Frank is already doing him an enormous favour. Emile should have seen a doctor long ago. With his family history especially. He deserves to be told to waltz his abdominal mass right back out the door and get in line. She takes an appointment card, writes out a day and a time next week, hands it to him.

"Nine's no good."

Joelle could change the time, since whichever slot she gives him is already booked, but she shakes her head. "That's your appointment."

Emile looks at the card again. Shrugs. Then grins. "Great seeing you, Beauté."

The phone rings. A secretary from another office wants to know if she can borrow some requisitions for Nuclear Medicine. Joelle's look follows Emile out the door. His dark hair curls with silver. She'd forgotten how from the back he looked thinner, more stooped. All that up-front bravado and then he turned around and you saw he had a flat bum.

She had hoped never to see him again. Out in the street or in the city, she would have backed into a doorway, covered her face. But this is different. He's probably — almost certainly — got cancer.

She reaches for the phone and dials Admitting for Mr. B.

∞

Diane's crossword magazine lies askew on the seat of her cane back chair. She stands refolding the scarves a client left in a heap. The woman had flapped open each scarf on the rack, exclaiming at the vibrant colours. Unfortunately, she said then, wool gave her hives. Right, Diane thinks. So don't bloody touch it in the first place! Her hands move mechanically, bringing edges together, smoothing folds, overlapping colours from greens to blues to purples, all the while that her muscles feel geared to slam and rip.

When the phone trills, she takes her time draping the last scarf on the rack before answering. "Bonjour." Deadpan. "Boutique à Votre Goût."

"Diane, it's Joelle. Are you busy?"

"Cleaning up after middle-aged brats who seem to think I've nothing better to do."

"Busy, eh? Me, too. Frank's leaving tomorrow for a conference so he rescheduled everyone from Friday for today — between all the patients that were already booked. I can't wait to get home and soak in the tub."

A woman who has just walked into the store upends piece after piece of pottery to look at the prices. Diane rolls her eyes. Why doesn't she go into a department store with the prices clearly marked on the shelves, since that seems to be her major concern?

"You'll never guess who showed up today. Completely out of the blue. Emile."

At first the name doesn't register. Then Diane stands straighter. "What do you mean, Emile? What was he doing there?"

"His doctor referred him."

"I hope you told him you're booked solid for the next fifty years and sent him right out of the building to another hospital!" Diane remembers Joelle's hair hanging lank and stringy. The absent way she tucked it behind her ear again and again. Her jeans sagging loose below her belt. How much weight did she lose when Emile dumped her?

Joelle's voice drops to a dramatic hush. "Diane, he's got an abdominal mass so *big* his family doctor could feel it."

"Maybe he swallowed his wallet."

"He's really sick, Diane."

"That's *not* your concern. Not after the way he treated you — and the way he walked out." Diane had brought Joelle to live with her, both sleeping in Diane's bed in their underwear, watching movies together, eating yogurt and salads with berries and mangos. Diane doesn't feel a speck of sympathy for the egotistical prick who left Joelle in such a mess.

"I know how he —"

"Sounds to me like you forgot."

"Diane, you can't turn your back on someone who's sick."

"Oh, please! You're a secretary, not a doctor. You can't do anything for him if he's sick. And even sick, he can still hurt you. Guys like that don't change."

"He's older and weaker. You can tell he's sick just by looking at him."

"So let whoever's folding his socks now worry about that." Diane sighs loudly, exasperated. "I was hoping he'd self-combusted. Too much of an asshole jerk for his own skin. Or that he slimed back into whatever hole he crawled out of. And if that was too much to hope for, then I hoped that you would have enough sense to ignore him if you ever had the bad luck to bump into him again!"

The woman juggling the pottery whips her head around and stalks to the door, making the bells rattle hard when she slams it. That's right, Diane thinks. This is *not* good news.

Stiffly, Joelle says, "You never liked him."

"Oh, come on, Joelle! He wasn't very likeable — especially not the side of him that I got to know."

"You don't have to make it sound like he hit me. We just weren't..."

Diane waits for whatever innocuous word Joelle will use, but Joelle can't think of one.

Two teenage girls in funereal black coats jostle through the door, giggling and whispering. They've come in a few times in the past week to look at the jewellery.

Diane says, "Even if he didn't hit you, which would have left bruises, so you could have gone to the police, he was mean to you. You know he was." The evening they drank far too much wine and Emile stood over Joelle, waggling his hips and grinding his thumb on her head.

"I work in a hospital," Joelle says primly. "I see all kinds of things. And when you're looking at sickness and the possibility of a person dying, you can't hang onto grudges."

"*Grudges?*"

"Anyhow, I'm with Marc now. Emile can't hurt me."

"So let me understand. You've decided to let bygones be bygones."

"Yes."

"Because he's sick."

"Yes."

The girls at the jewellery cabinet have turned to look for Diane. She waves a hand to signal that she's coming. "Joelle," she says, "let me tell you something. Emile was always a sick man. Always." And before Joelle can protest, "I have to go. I've got clients."

Despite their artful, black rattails of hair and gloomy garb, the girls chatter with excitement, gleeful. One says, "My brother gave me money for my birthday." The other, "These earrings are so cool." She taps her indigo fingernails on the glass.

"Which ones?" Diane's hand hovers over the polished agates set in silver. The girls exclaim and nudge, ooh and ah, dangling the earrings Diane hands them against each other's cheeks and necks.

"How long have you been friends?" Diane asks.

"Since grade four," both answer, breaking into a laugh at their timing.

Diane nods wryly. Good luck, she thinks.

∽

It hasn't snowed for a week and the old snow is drying up into pockets of dirty white at the base of buildings, in the shadows and crevices, behind garbage bins. Joelle walks along, only half aware of the buildings and traffic. Her thoughts swarm with the surprise of seeing Emile again. For years she's avoided NDG where they used to live, the streets lined with brownstone walkups, maples and oaks, Cinema V on Sherbrooke, and near it the restaurant where Emile knew the crazy chef… what was his name? An excellent cook, but the last person who should have worked in an open kitchen. The diners saw how he crashed pans into the sink, slammed ladles, cursed his kitchen prep.

Today she discovered that Emile doesn't even live in NDG anymore. He had an apartment downtown on de Maisonneuve. She certainly never expected that he would one day resurface on her territory, and in a situation where *he* needs *her* help. She'd watched Frank's expression when he scanned the referral, saw how he didn't even look at Emile.

It *has* to be significant that she and Emile have met again in such circumstances. Diane is too suspicious. Emile won't be the same in a johnny shirt and bare legs.

Joelle holds the door to the grocery store for an elderly man, encumbered by his shopping bag and floppy galoshes. She doesn't need a basket. She chooses a tomato, a ripe avocado she hopes isn't bruised, a package of soup mix.

Walking down their street, she glances up at the windows. Dark. Of course. Marc is at work.

Lately, when she gets home in the evening, she feels her old uneasiness about dark rooms. Even with a switch right by the doorway, having to creep her hand inside makes her skin prickle. When she lived alone, she used to leave the lights on when she went out. Now, with Marc working evenings, he leaves before she comes home. She can't ask him to keep a light on. She can't explain.

She steps off the elevator. Focuses on the tidy click of her boot heels on the marble. The hallway is well lit with small brass chandeliers. She reminds herself that she's forty years old and married. The bogeymen of childhood long gone. She unlocks the door and swings it wide for the protective spill of light from behind her, darts a hand along the wall for the switch, which is... right there. From the living room to the kitchen, the bathroom, the bedroom, the study, she turns on the lights. She feels better once she knows for a fact that the rooms are empty. She still leaves all the lights on.

She munches whole-grain crackers from the box, standing at the stove, stirring her instant soup while it heats, remembering when she hadn't even met Emile yet, though they lived in the same building. It was shaped in a square-edged U with her window looking onto the bevelled glass front door with its heavy oak frame and three broad stone steps. The faded richness of a once-better neighbourhood. Mrs. Holley, who'd lived there for sixty years, told Joelle there used to be a potted plant in the entrance. Imagine, Mrs. Holley said, what would happen to a plant there now. Candy wrappers and cigarette butts, that's what!

Joelle often leaned by her window, watching the tenants come and go. The woman from down the hall who played piano and had a boyfriend with a blue Volkswagen beetle. Mrs. Holley in her hat and gloves. The two cousins from Trinidad. The man with the black curls. His easy amble up the steps. The hang of his jacket. Joelle imagined his voice was deep. He always lingered when he met the cousins on the steps. He helped the woman from the second floor manoeuvre her stroller through the door.

Then one day Joelle was struggling with the flyers wedged in her mailbox and the door behind her opened. Salut Beauté! And he sounded exactly as she'd dreamed.

∞

Fluorescent lights, shoppers with their coats hanging open, their faces bled of air. Ketia has driven to Carrefour Laval to buy a purse. Ma has a nice one in dark red leather with a gold buckle, which she uses on Sunday when she wears her beige coat with the cherry sprig brooch on the lapel. But her everyday purse slumps from her arm. Even the strap looks stretched. Gabrielle said why not get her a new one for Christmas. Ketia can buy it, and Gabrielle and Bastien will sign the card, too.

Yet Ketia strays past the stores that sell purses, scanning the crowd. Two or three times she holds her breath because she thinks she sees Marc. Should she flee, feign blindness, or smile? She's not sure she can bear to be introduced to his wife. Then she realizes the man only has hair like Marc's. Or he walks briskly, his head at that decided angle.

Her steps slow when she reaches the food court. She's hungry, tempted by the smells of frying meat, garlic, and onions—if not the greasy plates of food being served. She wants rice and red beans. Tassot. Plantain with chopped pickled pepper. The kind of food Ma cooks.

Or ice cream. Yes.

The young man who serves her sprinkles cocoa on the scoop of caramel in the dish. "Keep you brown." He winks. He's brown, too, long-waisted and lean, the electric-white glint of a rhinestone in his ear.

She looks at the next stand, where a Chinese woman with a food-stained apron double-tied around her waist ladles sauce onto noodles.

"Just somethin' to say," the young man drawls. He butts the counter with his hip as he takes his time making change.

She holds her hand out for the coins and takes her ice cream. No tip. At the tables people sit gobbling pizza and stir-fries with self-absorbed speed, their shoulders and arms hunched as if guarding their kill.

She perches on a seat at the edge of the crowd, torn between savouring and not wanting the ice cream to melt in the dish. She takes wee spoonfuls that she lets melt on her tongue. That lovely dairy-smooth creaminess.

The sizzle of frying comforts her. The scrape and knock of a spatula on a griddle. A gabble of languages she can't understand. Voices and fast-food noise.

And there... a thread of sound from long ago. A wispy singsong that rises and dips to the shake of a rattle. Curious, she twists around in her seat.

A woman who must be Ma's age sits with her legs well apart, knees straining her skirt, singing to a toddler in a stroller. His hands stretch to grasp the green plastic ring she shakes in time to her tune. "Les souliers neufs et le beau veston!" Her voice drops to a more natural speaking register. "Mais oui, mon coeur, Mommy is buying shoes for 'tit François. She'll be back soon, won't she?" And beginning again, "Les souliers neufs et le beau veston!"

Ma sang the same tune to Bastien. He couldn't even walk yet. He was still a baby — Ketia remembers the milk-warm smell — but when Ma sang, Ketia saw him as a little man with shiny new shoes and a handsome jacket. The words breathed a spell of promise.

∞

Marc sits at the computer, trending a patient's amylase results. Enid marches into the nursing station, grabs a chart from the rack, slams it on the counter. "That's it! This time I'm writing an incident report." Frustration makes her doughy shape brisk, even agile. "I'm sick of picking up after T-P. He doesn't do dressings, his IVs are infiltrated, he lets his patients lie in bed all day. Can someone please tell me just *what* he does except twinkle his buns up and down the hallway, flirting with the orderlies?"

Past Enid, at the other end of the nursing station, Ketia bends to a cupboard. She stoops gracefully, her neck a dark stem rising from the neckline of her pale green tunic. Marc approves of her new bobbed hairstyle — as he approves everything Ketia does — though he still prefers the schoolmarm knot at the nape of her neck. The tease of her restrained appearance.

"I've told Pascale and you know what she says? *You have to give the new nurses a chance.* A chance to what? Kill a few patients? She has to do more than hire them to make her stats look good. She has to follow through, make sure they're doing the job.

"Today T-P tells me he didn't give a patient her Dyazide because the doctor ordered 12.5 mg and it only comes in 25." Her finger jabs at the page as she reads. "Dyazide 1/2 tab — *comma* — 12.5 mg. How much more clear can you get? You break a 25 mg tablet in two! You don't need a friggin' Ph.D. I tell him and he goes 'Duh?' I mean, is he a nurse or what? Every time I get his patients, it's the same story. Stuff not done because he couldn't figure it out — or he just didn't do it." She pauses. "And *you*, what's up with you? You're not even listening!"

"You're complaining about T-P."

"I'm complaining about this floor going downhill fast!" Anger spots her face in patches of red and white. She wheels off her chair and yanks open the drawer where incident reports are kept. "I mean, what? Are we that desperate for nurses that we have to work with inept twits? We'll see what Pascale has to say when she starts getting incident reports on all the mistakes around here. Let her explain that to her boss!"

Ketia has her back turned to them in the med room. For sure she can hear. Anyone getting off the elevator can hear.

"Not all the new nurses —" Marc begins.

"T-P takes the cake."

"Some of the new nurses —"

"Oh, for God's sake," she cuts him off. "I'm talking about T-P! Have you heard a word I said? Obviously we need new nurses. I'm not an idiot."

Marc takes his clipboard to the med room, where he reaches for a container of sterile water and a bottle of Timentin. Ketia rips clear plastic packets of pills she drops into tiny paper cups. He adores how she stands, shoulders high, face bent to her task. He opens a drawer for a 12 cc syringe. Tear, snap, tear. Attaches a needle to the syringe, uncaps it, and pierces the gel cap on the container of water. "Enid's upset," he says, "because T-P didn't give a patient her Dyazide today. You know she doesn't mean you."

"…I know."

He injects the syringe of water into the small, glass bottle of powdered Timentin. "You're an excellent nurse. We're lucky to have you."

Ketia's already erect posture straightens even more. He wishes he could trace his fingers — his mouth! — down the arrow of her spine. Rapidly he rolls the bottle back and forth between his palms to dissolve the powder.

Ketia suddenly turns her head, staring at his hands.

"What?" he says, surprised, not hearing the repeated click of his wedding ring against the glass. "I'm reconstituting Timentin."

Aditi walks in, swinging the turquoise lanyard with the narcotic cupboard key. Marc moves by rote, drawing up the antibiotic, reaching for an IV additive label he dates and initials. Maybe Aditi only needs a pill. But no, she fiddles out a box of morphine vials. He must have imagined Ketia's strange look. She stands now as always, shoulders straight, checking the contents of her pill cups against the medication records.

Aditi starts complaining about a resident. "He wants to give me a verbal order and when I ask for his number, he tells me to look it up! No way, man. I paged his senior. We don't have to put up with attitude like that."

"Which resident?" Ketia asks.

Marc lingers, but Aditi and Ketia keep talking. He leaves the med room to give his Timentin.

∞

Ketia zips up her boots. She's already dressed. She and Carlene are alone in the change room. Carlene draws her sweater over her head, holding the neckline wide, not to disturb her elegant French twist. "He says his brother can get him a job in New York. I don't know if I want to live in New York, but just that he asks is like saying he wants to get married, don't you think?"

The knock on the door makes Carlene clutch her jeans against the triangle of lace over her crotch. "Don't come in!" she yells.

"I need my jacket," Marc says through the door.

Carlene wiggles her feet into her jeans and tugs up the waist, but instead of letting Marc in, she takes his big parka off its hook and thrusts it through the door.

"Is Ketia there? I have to —"

"No." Carlene closes the door again. And more loudly through it, "She already left."

Ketia frowns at her for lying but doesn't give her away. In her mind she still hears the click of Marc's ring. A tiny hammer of ridicule — married, married, married, married.

Carlene sucks her teeth in disapproval. "You watch out for him."

Ketia bends to check why her boot zipper pinches. Marc will be unhappy, but this evening she feels unhappy, too — yearning for a man she can only meet in corners, in the dark, behind a locked door. The gold ring on his finger binds him forever to his wife.

Carlene peers into her purse, shaking it from side to side. Finally brandishes her lip gloss and bangs open the bathroom door. "Wait for me," she orders.

Ketia cherishes every detail of the evenings in the hotel. The luxury of being naked together like man and wife on their honeymoon. But Marc hasn't suggested the hotel again since the last time. Instead, a week ago, he said he didn't bring his car to work, and would she give him a ride home? Before she even pulled out of the parking lot, he slid his hand up her thigh to her crotch. Rubbed with his fingers through the cloth until she felt too dizzy to drive. Told her to turn and where to park at the back of an apartment building. There, with her coat still on, her boots kicked off and her drawstring pants tugged down, she climbed on his lap. They've done this every night since, and in the moment, while it's happening, she grapples and thrusts as much as he does. But afterwards, when she drops him off at the head of his street and watches him stroll off, sure of himself, cock-proud, she can't believe what she's done — parked next to the rusty hulk of a dumpster, facing the slashed darkness and light of a fire escape, her knee jammed against hard plastic.

The bathroom door opens. Carlene prances out, pursing her shimmering lips at Ketia. "I'll check if he's gone."

Ketia wonders if he would actually check the parking lot for her car. This late, past midnight, with only the night nurses and orderlies working, the last stragglers from evening shift going home, he'd be able to spot it. But would he guess that Carlene lied?

They wait for the elevator. On the way down it stops at the second floor for an ICU nurse, going home, too. Carlene tells Ketia that maybe she'll write the New York state exams for nursing. As they approach the sliding glass doors, she nudges Ketia to look at her boyfriend waiting in his car, a clean-cut profile in the dark — an ad for cologne, Carlene the beauty who joins him. Ketia follows the ICU nurse across the parking lot, her boots crunching on the gravel strewn across the hard-packed snow.

And now she regrets not answering Marc. Even scrabbling like animals in the front seat of her car, they would have been together. All she's done now is send him home to his wife. Marc always wants to have sex, and when he can't with her, his wife is right there, isn't she? In his bed. Where he lives.

Alone in her car, Ketia's breath catches. She balls her fists against the steering wheel, helpless.

∞

The scuffed snow hides patches of ice and frozen lumps. Diane slides and tromps along, wielding the baguette in her hand like a balancing wand. Nazim worries about slipping. Their single-file conversation threads in and out.

"It's because," he says, "the older computers don't say 1999, only 99. No one knows if at midnight on New Year's, when they switch to 00, they'll understand 1900 or 2000."

"So what," Diane says over her shoulder. "In the morning you'll get up and have a cup of coffee regardless."

"Coffee, sure, but you might not have any money left in the bank. And if you run a small business, you might have lost all your files. I've been telling people to back up everything."

"But you just *said* you're afraid of everything backing up."

"Back up as in store," he explains. He can sometimes hardly credit how little Diane knows about computers. "On floppies."

Diane skids to a stop, shouting, "Badar!" at a man stepping out of a camera shop.

Nazim's friend Badar, still holding the door, turns to see who hailed him.

Diane no longer kisses him Montreal-style on both cheeks since Nazim told her it made Badar uncomfortable. Women weren't supposed to touch men who weren't their husbands or family.

Badar's wife, Noor, follows him from the store, a petite woman so bundled in winter clothing that her hijab is hidden by her scarf and the hood of her coat. She hangs back when she sees Diane.

"How are you?" Diane asks. "Where are the children?"

"With my sister," Badar says. He smiles because he is polite.

"Your sister is visiting?"

"She lives with us now."

Diane pokes her head past Badar to ask Noor, "Are you all right with that? I don't know that I'd like my sister-in-law living with us. Not even my own sister — in fact, definitely not my sister!"

Badar says, "Yes, she is a great help. Noor is going to school now to become a nurse."

"My friend works in a hospital — not as a nurse but a secretary. She likes it."

"Very nice," Badar agrees. "We must go now. The children, you know."

Nazim nods at them as they leave, his restraint as much acknowledgment of their discomfort with his relationship as he can offer. He appreciates that they're at least civil to Diane. In Morocco, in his village, people would hiss at her because they aren't married.

Diane steps across the frozen ruts, swinging her baguette. She has no idea she's offended Badar and his wife by suggesting they wouldn't welcome his sister. Diane's ideas and values — her body language and talk — are so alien. Of course, that very difference attracts him. He never wanted a wife like Noor. Diane doesn't hamper him with expectations, obligations, subtext. Life feels easy with her. He appreciates her frankness. Only when they meet his Muslim friends does he feel the conflict. Fortunately, these encounters are rare. His friends don't invite him and Diane to their homes. Diane doesn't realize how they're snubbed, since she so rarely invites people herself. And when he meets his friends at a café or in passing, they don't mention Diane.

∞

Joelle follows the Radiology clerk down aisles packed to the ceiling with large cardboard folders, thousands upon thousands squeezed side by side. The clerk says that soon everything will be on computer. "Tap, tap, tap." He mimes in the air with his fingers. "Bingo!" He snaps his thumb. "There's the film on the screen!"

Joelle wonders why he sounds so delighted. Doesn't he realize he'll be out of a job?

She pushes a cart. She only needs three files but each holds several large square films: cross-sections of abdomen blotted with disease. She waits for the clerk to sign them out and wheels the cart to the elevator.

Frank will need the films on Monday when he's back from his conference and in the OR, scalpel in hand, before she even starts work. She props them on his chair where he can't miss them — also the only available space. Papers, books, and medical journals spread across his desk, the shelves of the bookcase, the second swivel chair, the computer table, even the window ledge between the photos of his wife and daughters.

Back at her desk, her mail basket empty, typing and filing done, she decides that's it then. She's taking the rest of the day and tomorrow off. Before she went to Radiology, she left a message on her phone that the office is closed until Monday — but, of course, the light already blinks. By Monday the message box will be full. Monday? By tomorrow. She leans across her desk, punches the button. Mr. Mack *again.* Then a patient who was released from the hospital a week ago and needs an insurance form filled out.

As she listens, she fills out a requisition for staples and paper clips. Her pen stops at the sound of a gruff voice. "Listen, Jo, I can't make it next week. I figure anything I've got isn't going to change from one week to the next. I'll be there same time, same place following week... Hey, it's funny, eh? That you're working there." Emile hangs up without leaving a number. Or, for that matter, having identified himself.

Joelle replays the message, listening intently. The cadence of his voice. The easy presumption. No, she thinks, he's wrong. Between one week and the next will mean a delay on tests, on a date for surgery — on *survival,* doesn't he realize? She flips through the pages of her appointment book to Thursday where she's pencilled his name and number.

The phone rings only once. "What now?" Followed by a loud sigh.

"It's Joelle. You have to come to your appointment next week. You have to."

"...Joelle. Shit. I thought it was — doesn't matter. I'll hang up, you call again and leave a message. I don't have a pen on me. Give me another day."

"No, you're coming on Thursday."

"Can't."

"Oh yes, you can! You're going to change whatever else you've got scheduled. This is more important. You waited too long already. You're going to end up in Emerg completely obstructed, and believe me, that will be even worse."

Emile says nothing. Then laughs. "Obstructed? Is that like constipated up to my ears?"

"Stop joking. This is serious."

"Must be to get such a rise out of you. Wish I'd known. I'd have played sick long ago."

"This is my job. I'm telling you what the doctor would want me to tell you."

"Okay, okay." She can tell from the sound of his voice that he's grinning. "Hide behind your doctor and your desk."

"You're coming on Thursday then?"

"For you, babe. Just for you. Hey, I might even get *more* sick, seeing how it tickles your buttons."

"Good."

"Oh yeah," he murmurs, "Joelle's pretty buttons…"

She stands with the phone pressed to her ear, listening to him breathe. Then hears a click. Slowly she hangs up. Touches a finger to Emile's name in the appointment book.

∞

The swelling warmth between her legs wakes Joelle, though she keeps her eyes closed, longing to return to the dream. The lascivious tongue that licked. The muscled probe of its tip. Sleep, she wills, sleep, her body ripe to combust on that roguish tongue.

Beside her in bed a weight shifts. *Marc.*

Soft hot wet with desire creeping her hand across the space the fabric of his pyjamas snaking her fingers under the waistband her longing squirming her body ducking her head under the sheet freeing his flagstaff cock from his pyjamas obeying the growling command of dirty words from her dream her mouth her body grovelling to have him her own fingers sliding between her legs and him his hands grasping her head his fingers in her hair his moans when — "*No!*" he cries. Twists his hips and wrenches himself away, stumbling, flees the bed.

She crouches, half-exposed by the duvet he hurled back, hair hanging around her face, head bowed, not believing herself what she's done. She loathes the smell of down there, the fat bullying worm with its spew. She's always been so grateful Marc never made her put it in her mouth. What must he think now? The disgust of his cry.

Oh shame! She clutches her kimono and scurries to the powder room in the hallway, locks the door, and spits in the sink. Rinses her mouth. Spits again. Then gently on tiptoe leans against the door, cheek pressed, shoulders cowed, listening to the blast of the shower from the bathroom. Her lips move, begging that he leave. Please go. Please. Her eyes closed tight. Just go. Please go.

∞

Marc sudses himself thoroughly. Nails of water, hot as he can bear, pound his abdomen, scald his stupid penis. Joelle tricked him by playing the kind of wake-up game he fantasizes with Ketia. He'd surfaced from sleep with a grateful sob for the hot, greedy mouth, clutched her head with his hands, flexed his fingers through her sleek, straight hair. His fingers knew for a good long minute, his will choked between loyalty to Ketia and the driving immediacy of lust.

He scrubs the towel down his body, bats his penis aside angrily, winces. Scowling, he roots through the laundry basket for a T-shirt, underwear, and yesterday's cords. But he won't wear old socks.

Listening at the door he hears the whine of water from the faucet in the powder room. Darts to the bedroom to grab socks from the dresser. Ignores the tumult of sheets and duvet on the bed. Hurries down the hallway, scoops his parka and gloves, slams the door behind him. Hear that? I'm gone.

Outside the door he tugs on his socks, quickly laces his boots, folds the newspaper from the mat under his arm. He can have a café au lait and a croissant at the patisserie down the street. Then he'll go shopping, do something, it doesn't matter what. If he doesn't have a spare uniform in his locker at work, he'll get scrubs from the OR.

Why was Joelle even home on a Friday morning? He has no idea. This he vows, though: she will never trick him like that again, because from now on he's not sleeping in the same bed.

∞

Joelle hears the door slam but still waits before coming out. She had so looked forward to sleeping in late, spoiling herself with a manicure, dropping by to see Diane, maybe going to a matinee.

Now she wishes she'd set her alarm and gone to the office as usual. Even the furniture in the living room looks cold and blaming. The sofa and chair angled like a tribunal, the white light from the windows insistent and precise. The furniture is on Marc's side. Of course, he chose it. There isn't a chair or a corner that feels like it's hers.

In the bedroom she hesitates before the flung disarray of sheets. Then she lunges, yanking them off the mattress. Throws aside the duvet, still warm from their bodies, bundles the sheets, and stalks to the laundry room off the kitchen, where she stuffs them in the washer.

In the bathroom Marc's towel hangs on the rack as always. But she can't smell his citrus shaving cream. He never goes out without shaving.

How will she ever apologize for her disgusting and perverted behaviour? She no longer wants a manicure or to visit Diane, who will immediately see that she's upset. She eats her toast in the kitchen, standing up. Showers and dresses. On the street she runs for the bus that's coming, slips on a patch of ice, and nearly falls. The driver waits.

"Sorry," she apologizes.

"A bus is no reason to crack your hip."

At work she hangs her coat behind the door, changes from her boots into brown shoes, and sits at her desk, waiting for the familiarity of the chairs against the walls to reassert themselves. The rack of test requisitions. The colonoscopy posters. The magnified photos of a mushroom head polyp. The thin snare looped around its stalk. The cauterized stump after the polyp's removal.

Venita clacks past the doorway and stops. "You girls, you're crazy. Your docs are gone and you come in to work. Pei Yi, too. But you know her." Venita wags her head. "She isn't taking it easy. She's decided to reorganize the charts in the Colorectal Suite. Still trying to impress Collier. I tell you, she wants that admin assistant job."

Joelle has nothing to do once she's slipped the rubber band off the bundle of interhospital envelopes and opened them. Pathology results, notices, and memos Frank has to read before she files or chucks them. She startles when the phone rings. Looks at it. Doesn't move. Abruptly she pushes back her chair.

Pei Yi's manner is calm, her glance indirect. Among the secretaries she rarely speaks unless spoken to. And even then she might not answer. Joelle wonders if she's shy. Except that she wears such vivid colours — today a blouse that's sunflower yellow. She's pushed a trolley to the wall-length metal drawers and lifted out armfuls of folders. Everyone in the department will benefit, every secretary, nurse, and doctor trying to backtrack the results of previous tests, but everyone is either too busy, too important, or too cynical to help.

Quietly Pei Yi explains that she's sorting the folders into alphabetical piles, inserting dividers with coloured tabs to differentiate patients who've had surgery from those who return for routine checkups. She sets the piles on tables as they grow too high. "It's easy," she says. "It just needs to be done."

Joelle takes up folders, scans for an OR record, finds the right pile. Sometimes, when she reaches, her arm crosses Pei Yi's. When they softly bump shoulders, Joelle says, "Sorry."

"Next time I chop off your hand."

Joelle snatches her hand back then sees the faint hint of a smile.

Next time their arms brush, Pei Yi says, "Chop."

Slowly Joelle relaxes into a rhythm. Now and then she glances at Pei Yi. The smooth line of her mouth. The flat cushions of her eyelids. Joelle wonders how Pei Yi and her husband have sex. Of course she can't ask. What kind of a question.

Even she and Diane only talk about sex in a general, what-people-do kind of way. Or funny details — like Diane's first boyfriend in college, who thought she could supply breast milk at will. But they never say how they feel about sex or what they like. Joelle doesn't want to imagine Diane on her back, legs spread, as Nazim humps. Nor does she want to feel so naked before Diane. She's never told anyone about the things Emile did. Forcing her to her knees. Pushing his own finger in his bum because she wouldn't. How he made her straddle his face while he tongued her until she cried out. She'd always thought that years of proper sex with Marc had buried her memories of Emile and his filth. Only sometimes she wakes from a dream in the flare of a fire-bright orgasm. This morning she woke too early. Her shoulders cringe as she remembers Marc's expression. His lips tight with disgust, pyjamas clutched to cover himself.

"You girls still at this?"

Collier towers before them with his undertaker's joyless face, the hang of his impeccable suit. Since Pei Yi doesn't answer, Joelle doesn't, either.

Nor does he seem to expect a response. "Great work, girls. Need to see a little more initiative like this around here."

Joelle imagines that Pei Yi must be pleased, especially if she's hoping to come to Collier's attention, but Pei Yi juts her lips at Collier's back.

"Do you think we'll finish all the drawers today?" Joelle asks.

"We'll do what we do. At least we got started. It's better than nothing." She sounds as placid as ever, but Joelle hears the judgment levelled against the rest of the secretarial pool.

Then Pei Yi says, "I can do some more between Christmas and New Year's when it's not so busy."

"Frank's on call this year right after Christmas. I'll be doing the chicken with no head dance. But if I have time, I'll help."

Venita looks in on them. "Aren't you two breaking for lunch?"

Again Joelle waits for Pei Yi to answer. She doesn't. Venita shakes her head and heads off down the hallway, her stodgy weight deepening the beat of her heels.

Pei Yi closes the last chart before her and drops it on one of the newly organized stacks. "Good idea," she says. "Are you almost done?"

"In a moment. Go ahead." Joelle reaches for another divider with a coloured tab. If she joins the secretaries in the lounge, they'll ask why she came in when she said she was taking the day off. What can she tell them that they'll believe? Her mind stretches soundless, desperate for a reason. Her stomach grumbles. She'll go to the cafeteria and hope no one she knows sees her. Or no, she'll go to the coffee shop, buy a sandwich, and escape to the next pavilion, where she'll find a lounge to sit alone.

∞

Along the street stand buildings, three to four stories high, in weathered red brick with wrought-iron balconies. Nazim walks with his hands deep in the pockets of his leather jacket, a scarf wrapped tight, his toque pulled low. He hopes Diane's apartment is at least halfway warm. The hot-water radiators hiss and sputter deep within their depths, but for all their noise barely counter the draft that scurries along the floor down the hallway.

He corrects himself. *Their* apartment. Diane doesn't like him calling it her place. What can he say? She was living there for years already before they met. The furniture is hers, too. The corduroy sofa, the bedstead she stripped and varnished, the pots and pans, towels, cushions, throw rugs, and clocks. He unlocks the front door, then jiggles the key — a hitched tooth of steel — into its slot in the panel of metal mailboxes. A paper clip would open the box as easily, but people here have a mania for locking things.

Four families lived in the whitewashed building where he grew up, and no one ever locked their doors. No one would enter a home unless they were invited. The heavy slab door onto the street had stood open for so long it couldn't even be moved from the dip in the stone flags where it had settled. Beetles, termites, and worms had tunnelled colonies of clustered pinpoint holes in the wood. The iron bar and bolt on the back were rusted stiff. Nazim and his friends used to heave their weight against the bolt, trying to slide it. He felt so much older, only a year or two later, when he saw his brothers and their friends engaged in the same futile test of strength.

Nazim pulls a folded pizza flyer from the mailbox and only then sees the blue airmail envelope behind it. His fingers hesitate. His father can't write, his brothers only reluctantly, and Ghada, his sister, is too busy to send casual news. Mail from home always brings back the shock of the letter Ghada sent four years ago to announce their mother's death. When he'd seen his mother a few months earlier, on his one and only visit home, he'd found her skin sallow, her face leaner. She sat in the kitchen, watching Ghada mince onion and grate carrots. Roll dough paper-thin to make pastilla. Nazim thought their mother had aged. No one told him she was ill.

How had his family reached the decision not to tell him? Even once he returned to Montreal, Ghada didn't write and no one called, though he'd given them the country code and the number, instructions on how to call collect. He found the letter on the kitchen table where Jamal, his roommate, had propped it against a can of tomatoes. *Inna lillahi wa inna ilayhi rajiun. To*

Allah we belong and to Him we return. He has taken our dear mother after a long struggle. For three weeks she could no longer —

For three weeks? Nazim fumbled through the yellow pages, grabbed the phone, and booked the next available flight to Casablanca. He called work and told an answering machine that his mother had passed away. Pacing at Dorval, cooped in his seat on the plane, staring out the window during the long stopover at JFK where workers on the tarmac argued, he felt how truly far he was from family. Especially since it seemed he was no longer family, not even told when his mother lay dying.

He caught an air-conditioned bus from the airport into Casa, transferred onto a wheezing bus that heaved to a stop at every banana stall down the coast. When he finally arrived, limbs stiff, mouth dry from a night without sleep, he barely saw the backdrop of dirty white walls and windblown garbage as he strode down one corridor street to another, every shortcut through the maze tracked into the muscles of his legs since boyhood. He broke into a run when he saw the canted slab door, loped up the stairs and across the courtyard, not even knowing whom he'd find when he burst into the room, crying, "From now on if our father breaks his toe you will call me! If the young ones get a fever! If you can't afford medicine! If our father needs money for the truck! If —"

Nazim's sister-in-law cowered on the wall bench. Next to her his father gaped. Then Ghada stepped away from the wall. "We have had a death in this household. Would you please comport yourself appropriately."

Nazim bowed his head. "Please forgive me. Please excuse my behaviour."

Later Ghada told him that it was their mother's express wish that they not bring him across the ocean to look upon her wasted corpse. "Mâma didn't expect to see you again after your last visit. She said goodbye then."

"But *I* didn't!"

Four years later, Nazim takes slow steps up the stairs, trying to gauge the thickness of the envelope. Ghada has no time for long letters. She keeps house for their father, who makes deliveries up and down the coast, occasionally taking in passengers, calling himself un entrepreneur — one of his few French words — since the day he sold his donkey and cart, and acquired the small truck with the coughing motor and split upholstery patched with glued carpeting. Ghada also prepares the midday meal for Rachid's children because Leila works the noon shift in a hotel dining room to save for their schooling.

Nazim slips into his babouches and heads down the long hallway to the kitchen. He drops the envelope on the table, picks up a twist tie Diane must have dropped on the counter, and adds it to the jar in the drawer. He fills the kettle, reaches for the metal tin of tea he opens with a spoon, then realizes he's still wearing his jacket. Diane always teases that it's sewn to his shoulders. He shrugs it off, moves to drape it across a chair, then carries it down the hallway to the closet.

What has Ghada written? About their father? About...?

First he'll make himself a glass of hot sweet tea. Back in the kitchen he goes directly to the table and tears open the envelope. A single page covered with Ghada's dense script. With his hip he pushes the chair away from the table and sits. He doesn't hear the dull click when the kettle shuts itself off.

"Akhi Aazizi Zazou!" His eyes skim ahead, see no troubling words in the first lines. He returns to the top.

My dear Zazou!

We are all well, praise be to Allah. Father is age-less. He still carries Hashim on his shoulders. Hashim looks so much like you! Everyone has told him so often that he says it himself now. "I look like my uncle in Canada." Ahmed and Rachid are in good health, as are your sisters-in-law.

So, Nazim, what do you think? I am coming to see you! It's a project I've dreamed of since you left. When Mâma got sick, she decided we would put aside a portion of the money you send. She wanted to be sure that one day someone from the family could go see that your life is in order so far away from us all. Father, too, has begun to worry that you still haven't found a wife. He will take his meals with Ahmed and Selima while I am gone. Ahmed thinks we should choose a wife for you here and that I should bring her with me. What do you think? Don't worry, I'm teasing! I recall very well how particular you always were about girls. You were never interested in the same ones the other boys liked. You always had your own ideas, didn't you? But it's time now — high time, mon cher! — that you decide on a wife. I've already secured a list of good Moroccan families with eligible daughters in Montreal.

Zazou, I'm so excited! And curious! You left and made yourself a new home in Canada. You must have, since you did not return to us. I refuse to believe that you're lost and in exile the way the newspapers here write about people who emigrate. But it bothers me that I can't imagine you in your new home. I *need* to come see where you are! I want to see how a dishwasher works. Do you have your own car? Are there truly so many grand tall buildings?

I am coming, Zazou! January 2nd, arriving in Montreal at 10:10. You and I, we can celebrate Eid together.

Je t'embrasse fort!
Ghada

Nazim raises his eyes to the dark turquoise walls of the kitchen, the knotted jute basket where a philodendron nests, the walnut buffet where Diane keeps heavy crockery. Ghada, he thinks, his lungs filling as if with the fresh sea air from home. Ghada in Montreal!

Then the pot Diane left on the stove comes into focus. Diane's cabinet, her crockery, her knickknacks, her apron hanging on a hook, the calendar where she notes appointments. Ghada can't come here. In his family's eyes it would be like bringing her to a whorehouse.

From down the hallway he hears the door. He turns the page face-down on the table, though Diane can't read Arabic.

"Nazim?" She's already in the kitchen, swinging a bag of groceries onto the counter. She moves so quickly — easy with the forthright fullness of her figure — that he can smell the cold air from outside still on her coat. She sees the teapot with its lid off, the tin of tea beside it. "I think you forgot your tea," she says. Then she notices the page of thin airmail paper. "You didn't get bad news, did you?"

"No." He folds the page. "My father's doing well... and apparently my nephew looks like me."

"Good. Now I know where to get a replacement when you're ready for the glue factory." She leaves the room to hang up her coat. Nazim slides the letter into the envelope.

Swift steps and she's back, taking a new crossword magazine, a couple of red peppers, mushrooms, and chicken from the bag. "Look what I found." She waggles a tied bunch of greenery. "Arugula. Listen, do you mind throwing it together? I have to call Robin. Jérémie was running a fever yesterday and she was frantic. Even if he's better today, I'm in for thirty to forty minutes of high-level mom anxiety. I bought everything. Chicken, veg..."

"I'll cook," he says, pressing his hand to his heart.

She points at his hand and tuts. "You're so dramatic sometimes. It's just a meal, not a solemn, lifelong promise."

She sweeps from the room. He sits, hands inert now, on either side of the pale blue envelope where Ghada has printed Diane's address.

∞

It's long past midnight when Ketia drives down their street of apartment buildings. Most of the windows are dark, but here and there balconies blaze with Christmas lights. Red, green, blue, and yellow. The fiery gems offset the crisp darkness and cold around the buildings.

Their own Christmas will be subdued this year because Pa won't be home until the end of January. Not in Ma's hearing but to Ketia, Gabrielle grumbles that they have to spend Christmas half in mourning. No way, she says, will she ever settle for that! Not for herself, not for her children. She's getting her degree in economics, a job in a bank, a sporty Nissan, a husband who works nine to five. They'll have two children and he'll be home every evening, every weekend. Ketia, too, couldn't bear it if Marc were gone for nine months of the year. She's begun to wonder why Ma doesn't mind. Or Pa for that matter. He doesn't have to work for a cruise line in Alaska. Pa's friend, Monsieur Petit-Jean, got a job on a boat in the St. Lawrence.

Ketia turns in behind the Lessive Plus laundromat where Pa arranged with the owner that she could park so she doesn't have to find parking on the street late at night. She jogs down the alley, which she doesn't like either, but it's close to the side entrance and stairwell of their building. Even when she doesn't drive, Ketia almost always uses the side door to the building.

She unlocks their apartment door onto breathing silence. It's dark except for the pool of light from the lamp on the hallway table, its cream silk shade hung with fringe. The soft light dusts the outline of sleeves packed tight in the closet. She stands with her coat in hand, suddenly too tired to wrestle for a hanger, feeling the fatigue of the evening drain down her neck, her shoulders, her spine.

125

Two sick calls today, so everyone had an extra patient. IVs, dressings, trach care, patients calling for bedpans, needing pain medication or something for nausea. And always Marc trying to sneak a kiss or a squeeze.

Yesterday on their supper break he had a surprise. He'd found an examining room down a hallway, in another department. She was sure when they returned to the floor someone would notice the languor of her walk, his smug mouth. But Enid's fresh post-op had clambered out of bed on his own and fallen with his epidural, and everyone was running, paging Anaesthesia and Surgery.

Ketia tiptoes down the hallway to her room, sees the faint line of light under the door, eases it open.

Gabrielle lies on her bed, huddled under her comforter. "I'm dying," she groans.

Ketia immediately knows what's wrong. Gabrielle's period is always preceded by a few hours of gut-twisting cramps. "Did you take anything?"

"Hasn't started to work yet." Sly, rebellious Gabrielle becomes a baby in her pain.

"I'll rub your back."

"Can't lie on my stomach," Gabrielle mumbles into her pillow.

"Here." Ketia rotates Gabrielle's skinny hips toward her and sits with one leg curled under her, pressing soft, spiraling circles into the small of Gabrielle's back. "This always helps a little. Concentrate on my fingers. They're taking the pain away."

"You wish…"

"No, *you* wish," Ketia says.

A ruffle of frills edges the pillow behind Gabrielle's head. Sleepily she asks, "You didn't get yours yet?"

"Not yet." They always have their periods within a day or two of each other.

"Lucky," Gabrielle murmurs. "You're lucky."

The most Ketia ever feels is sluggish in her abdomen.

Bottom-heavy. She sucks in her stomach now, feels nothing. She hasn't had a period since she started the pill a month ago. Marc asked her to. She went to the Gyne Clinic in the hospital. The doctor didn't even ask any questions. Before that, Marc used condoms, ripping the packets open with his teeth, rolling them one-handed. There was only that time in the lounge when he locked the door to kiss her — except that, alone behind a locked door, once they started they couldn't stop. Pant leg hanging off her foot, leaning on the back of the sofa.

Only that once, Ketia thinks. And she's on the pill now. His wife never got pregnant.

That's another puzzle Ketia doesn't understand. Why don't Marc and his wife have children? Everyone she knows who's married has children. Even the men with a fam sou koté have children with their wives. Sometimes with their outside women, too. Marc never even mentions children. Maybe he and his wife couldn't.

Ma had six babies. Three lie in graves in Haiti, three souls to whom they pray for intercession on their behalf. Jean-Wilhelm, Alexandre, and Marie-Victoire. Baptized and pure, they sit next to God in heaven. Ketia sends them a fervent prayer now. Watch over me. Help me.

She wills her fingers, pressing circles into Gabrielle's back, to draw the magnetism of blood flow into her body. Even on the pill she's supposed to bleed.

∞

Marc clicks and drags the mouse. Jack on a Queen, red eight on a black nine. He's dressed and shaven. His gym bag stands ready against the wall. He glances at his watch. Not yet noon.

On his day off he used to clean or cook. Go to the gym. Shop. Meet his parents for sushi if they came to the city. Now a day off weighs uselessly. A day when he doesn't know where Ketia is or what she's doing.

This morning he woke early when he heard Joelle in the shower. Even now that she's gone, he would sooner stay in the study where he doesn't have to see her sweater or a glass she's used, the remote half-slid under a cushion. Joelle leaves a trail behind her like she's lost in a Hansel and Gretel story.

He has no idea what she was trying to prove the other morning. He's recast the scene as wild-eyed craziness, himself a victim. He moved his clothes to the study and now sleeps on the sofa bed.

Again he glances at his watch. At the periphery of his vision sits the phone on the desk. He has told Ketia she can call during the day. He didn't say his wife was at work. He knows Ketia understood. She still never calls.

He grips the mouse. The hard curve of plastic in his palm. When they're together, Ketia is exactly as he wants her to be. When he's alone, he realizes how little he knows about her — not enough to know what she's doing. He scowls, imagining a young man her mother invites to join them for supper, seating him next to Ketia, using their best dishes to impress him. Marc has felt how, the few times Ketia mentions her family, she doesn't expect he will ever meet them. She made him promise never to call her at home. She says her mother will immediately guess who he is even if he says he's a nurse calling from work.

Another glance at his watch. He pushes back his chair and walks to the laundry room. Scoops his uniforms piece by piece from the dryer, matching the colours, folding them in pairs of bottoms and tops. Carries the warm pile down the hallway, almost pivots into the bedroom, but catches himself and strides to the study. Not quickly enough, though. He saw the drag of the sheet hanging below the edge of the duvet. His lips tighten. Joelle.

He'll go to the gym. An extra fifteen minutes on the bike, the elliptical machine, the bench press. But how to spend the rest of the day? As he waits for the computer to shut down, he reaches to his back pocket for his wallet to see if he needs to stop at the bank. A card falls to the floor. He stoops to pick it up, slowly straightens again. Cream pasteboard with embossed green print. Hotel Modesto, where he brought Ketia. He could get the number from the phone book anytime, but the card is a talisman — both memory and promise of meetings to come.

∞

Ketia stands at the counter waiting for her toast to pop. The only sound in the kitchen is the toaster's red-hot clicking. She breathes in the smell, tells herself that hunger is a good sign. The jut of her hipbone presses against the handle of the cutlery drawer and she leans back to brush her fingers across her tummy. Flat as ever. No nausea. Her breasts not tender.

Except that all the signs she so carefully notes are duds as long as she doesn't bleed.

She drops her toast on a plate, peels the lid off the tub of margarine, and scrapes her knife across the bread. She spreads only the thinnest layer, right out to the crust — unlike Gabrielle, who smears her toast hastily and adds great blobs of jam. Gabrielle is a glutton. Reckless and careless. Something like this could happen to Gabrielle. Not to her. Something like this...

She hears how her mind dupes her. Not *if* or *when* or *maybe,* but as if it already knew.

She shudders then straightens her shoulders. *No.*

She carries her plate to the table and sits in Bastien's chair, facing the window. The angle of light between the buildings picks out the scars in the ochre brick wall opposite. Behind Ketia the apartment broods. Bastien and Gabrielle are at school, Ma at work. But even if they aren't home, Ketia senses how they fill the space. Bastien telling a meandering tale where he figures as the good boy/saviour/hero of the playground. Gabrielle in the bedroom, propped against her frilly pillows, chemistry homework open on her knees to show she's too busy to help prepare supper. Ma at the kitchen counter making a sweet potato pudding, her shoulders sagged with fatigue.

Ketia stops chewing her toast. Worse even than being pregnant — which she can't even imagine, it so terrifies her — would be the horror of Ma finding out.

∞

Yesterday, a Saturday, Joelle set her alarm early, showered and dressed, and slipped from the condo so that Marc wouldn't have to see her when he got up. She accepts the closed study door at the end of the hallway as punishment she deserves. Of course he doesn't want to sleep in the same bed if she behaves like a pervert. She used to take refuge on the sofa when Emile got too rough. She always eventually forgave him. For weeks afterward he was so sweet, too, clearing the table after supper, taking her out for fancy drinks, one time buying her a pretty turquoise and silver bracelet. Somehow she has to make that happen with Marc.

On Sunday she wakes to the drum of the shower through the bedroom wall. She slept late and Marc's already up. How will she get out now? She presses her face in the pillow, hunkers deeper under the duvet. The bedding is completely skewed by her burrow to the bottom of the mattress.

The water shuts off. Why is Marc even up, since he worked last evening and has to work again tonight? Or is he, too, trying to flee? Doesn't he know that she got up early yesterday and left? All morning she wandered through the shops in the Eaton Centre and Place Ville Marie, taking shoes off the shelf and putting them back, watching a demonstration on hot hair curlers, drinking a mochaccino, refusing hand cream samples, too fitful to get undressed and try on clothes — but satisfied that Marc would appreciate that she left him alone. It's *so* not fair if he didn't even realize.

All she can do now is hide in bed until he leaves. Neck tense, she listens, tracking his movements. The can of shaving cream set on the shelf. The bathroom door. The study door. After a few moments his steps pass the bedroom.

But that's not right, either, if he thinks she's just asleep. He should *know* she's obediently staying in the bedroom. She lifts her head from the pillow, looks around. A noise, she thinks. She'll drop her brush on the hardwood floor.

She's kicked away the duvet and swung her legs from the bed to get her brush from the dresser when she hears the front door close. Did he leave?

She sits for the longest time, not sure what to do. Her nightgown twisted across her legs. At the ends of her legs her feet. Long and slim with ten toes. Bizarre outgrowths. She wills them to move and they don't. She tries again. They jerk. Though that feels strange, too, the brush of the bedside rug against her bare soles.

∞

Ketia used to be able to sleep through Gabrielle's alarm, but these past few days she's awake every morning before it even sounds. Today again. She lies still, turned toward the wall. Her stomach like water. Anxiety shimmers along her nerves. She keeps her eyes closed, her shoulders tight, as if the danger came from outside and she could resist it. She won't let herself think that it's alive and growing in the crux of her belly.

When the alarm rings, Gabrielle lurches from her bed, grumbling. She closes the bedroom door softly but in the bath-room her voice rises because Bastien left a gob of toothpaste in the sink. "Do you have to be such a pig?" she shouts down the hallway. And then the dull tone of Ma's voice telling her to be quiet, her sister is still sleeping.

Gabrielle stomps into the bedroom, annoyance heavy in the balls of her feet. The snap of her bra strap, the crackling of static as she changes sweaters, choosing one then another, the stubborn tug of form-fitting jeans up her hips.

Distantly, as if it had happened to someone else, Ketia remembers how she used to dress to look sexy for Marc. Stupid, she thinks now, *stupid*. She knuckles a fist against her stomach.

Gabrielle is always the last to leave home in the morning, but even once Ketia hears the click of the lock, she doesn't move. She waits for the stillness in the apartment to settle. She wills her breath to slow, tucks her legs as she does when she sleeps, curls her hands under her chin. But even tucked and curled, her muscles are tense. Her jaw stiff.

She finally slides up on her elbow. Gabrielle's sweaters pool in floppy crowns on her bed, her blankets and bedspread thrown back as if she'd exploded from sleep. She's supposed to keep her bed and clothes tidy, but she argues that she can't disturb Ketia who's sleeping. And Ketia, rather than look at her mess all day, makes Gabrielle's bed. Her reward is the approval she gets for being the more dutiful daughter. She's seen how Ma purses her mouth and frowns at Gabrielle, heard how Ma's friends whisper, hoping that their safe and steady boys don't fall for Gabrielle. Ketia, now, Ketia is the daughter-in-law they would choose.

Ketia squeezes her eyes shut, sits clenched, knowing how everyone, *everyone,* will feel betrayed — and how that betrayal will infect the whole family. Ma will never forgive her. Ever.

When Ketia opens her eyes again, she still won't look at her knapsack hooked on the back of the chair where her clothes lie folded. All night it radiated blame. In her mind she hears Ma's voice. What's this, Ketia? Réponds tout de suite!

Yesterday Ketia stopped at a pharmacy. At work she's overheard other nurses ask someone to draw blood for a pregnancy test. It's the quickest way to know — but then everyone knows.

She sways as she stands and drops back on the bed again — not from nausea, she tells herself, but lack of sleep. She stands more slowly, unzips her knapsack, and eases out the small plastic bag. She has to remember to keep the package to throw away somewhere else, not at home.

In the bathroom she locks the door behind her. The instructions in the box are almost too easy. She'll have to wait five minutes, though. She should have brought her watch. Even with no one home, she won't take the chance to leave the bathroom with a dipstick angled in a vial of urine on the back of the toilet. She leans her head against the cool wall tiles. She feels feverish, her skull heavy. Though her feet are cold, even in slippers. Early morning sunlight plays in the folds of the shower curtain where green fish blow bubbles. Bastien must have been with Ma when she bought it. Gabrielle would have chosen a pink or a silver design. On her own, Ma would have picked white. Everything else in the bathroom is white. Tiles, tub, the sink, the toilet with its spotless white mat and toilet seat cover.

No change in the dipstick yet. Ketia takes up the paper with the instructions and starts to read the fine print. She's not interested in hCG or the variables of her last ovulation. Then she squints, reads again. The test is ninety-seven percent accurate if it tests positive, but only ninety percent accurate for a negative result. If it's positive, she's probably pregnant, but if it's negative that doesn't mean she isn't.

Why wasn't this on the outside of the box? She would have bought a more expensive kit with more accurate results. How will she go through all this again, sneaking another box home, standing here waiting for a stick to tell her if she's saved or doomed. In frustration she throws the paper in the wastebasket beside the vanity. Then she stoops and shoves the paper back in the box.

She rests her head on the tiles behind her, takes deep, calm breaths. Ignores her face in the mirror. Instead she looks at the convex of opaque glass that shields the light bulb. With one hand she traces the clean bracket of her hipbone. She can't begin to imagine losing it under a great ballooning belly.

But: until the dipstick changes colour, nothing has happened yet.

part *three*

Nazim showers and shaves while the coffee brews. In the pantry he frees a few dates from their cellophane package and picks a couple of clementines from the small wooden crate on the floor. According to the tiny black label that dots each fruit, they come from Morocco, which is why Diane buys them. He knows she means well. She's never had a clementine fresh from the tree.

The date he pops in his mouth is mealy with age, its sugar long turned to starch. At home their mother gave them dates to break their Ramadan fast. After a day of not eating, the scent alone — heady and sweet — made you dizzy. You bit and the date's skin broke into tender shards of glaze that dissolved on the tongue.

He hasn't fasted for Ramadan since before he met Diane — since he shared an apartment with Cuong and Orion, who cooked large, messy meals with ginger and garlic he didn't even try to resist. Though, of course, if he spends a day at the computer shop with Hatem during Ramadan, he prays and fasts with him. He can do it. He respects the purity and the ritual — acquiesces to the indolence that grows with each passing hour — but on his own he feels no such compunction. Maybe with Ghada expecting to celebrate Eid ul-Fitr, the fasting beforehand will make more sense. But how will he explain to Diane that he's decided to fast this year?

Nazim rubs his forehead. Usually he reads a page or two from yesterday's paper over breakfast. Or the Maghrebian community news. This morning he remembers lines from Ghada's letter. *Mâma wanted to be sure that one day someone from the family could go see that your life is in order so far away from us all.*

From his family's point of view, his life is not in order. Even if he can manage to hide the scandal of living with Diane, Ghada will wonder that he doesn't have the things she believes everyone in Canada owns — a dishwasher and a car. He never told her he did, but he never told her he didn't. He never expected that anyone from his family would one day come to test the myth.

You left and made yourself a new home in Canada. You must have, since you did not return to us. But how will she construe his life in Montreal once she sees it? Especially in January, with the snow and the wind. People living huddled away from the cold and each other. She won't believe that he doesn't know his neighbours except by sight and to nod hello. She'll find that barbaric.

And what would she make of these dates that have travelled around the world, packed in cellophane and boxes? No wonder they're dry and squeezed flat. Ghada could decide against a whole country, its industry, skyscrapers, highways, and hospitals, because life's very sweetener — dates and oranges — had to be imported. Back home they had an expression: the tar of my country is sweeter than the honey of yours. He can just hear Ghada: *is* there any sweetness here?

The clementines, too. Neither sweet nor juicy. The half-leathery rind mocks his memory of trees with bright balls of fruit peeking from between glossy leaves. When he was little, his mother told him that oranges drank the light from the sun. That was how they became orange. As a boy he believed he could taste the sun in the sweet flesh. Even the oil from the peel smelled of it.

Nazim lifts his fingers to his nose. They smell sour. Citrus peel in wintertime in Montreal. Clementines bought at a supermarket.

Ghada must still buy food the way their mother did: from vendors behind tables heaped with carrots, squash, garlic, fennel bulbs, and fresh mint. Basins of green, black, and red olives studded with pickled lemons. Round loaves of bread stacked upon each other like yeasty dinner plates. The jostle of bodies, the dull thunk of weights on a metal pan scale, the animal squawks, the stink of fish and dung. Nazim and his friends running through the market, dodging tables, making the vendors shout and threaten to pelt them with stones if they kept acting like dogs.

Ghada was the one who had to learn how to barter and stretch the weekly dirhams into meals to feed a family. A knuckle of mutton, a sack of brown lentils, a small paper cone of white sugar. She liked to lecture him on the seriousness of managing a household — until he began to wonder if he and his brothers didn't have it easier, being boys. He had to study and do his lessons, but Ghada went to school as well. His homework done, he escaped to play soccer on the beach. Hers done, she had to help their mother in the kitchen.

When Nazim was older, he sometimes strolled with Ghada to the market. Veal, please, she cried. I want it for cooking, not to sole my shoes. And this, tell me, is it cumin or sand from the Sahara? It looks about as old. The merchants appealed to Nazim. His sister was too difficult. How were they supposed to feed their poor families? Yet they winked at Ghada and sometimes added an extra bone to make soup.

Nazim throws the torn peel from his clementines in the garbage. He wants Ghada to come, even knowing how she'll criticize the weather, the dry dates and clementines, that he has to wash his own dishes the same as back home. But she can't stay here. And she can't meet Diane. And he doesn't have a clue yet how he'll organize that — or how he'll tell Diane.

∞

Marc waits in the small room where the orderlies store walkers and extra linen in long net sacks. The bare overhead light presses the close walls flat, making the stray nicks in their surface gouge deeper in relief. There's nowhere to sit. He's been waiting for a couple of moments already. He blows air through his teeth, the controlled escape of breath a hold on his nerves.

Ketia used to come as immediately as she could when he whispered supply room, IV room, change room, lounge. He knows she heard him just now, even if she was walking in the other direction with an armload of fresh piqués and sheets. She doesn't need to rush to change a bed. A bed can wait. Or she can ask the orderly to do it.

When rapid steps approach the door, he drops his hands from his hips, but whoever it is scurries past. Of course. Ketia walks softly. He never hears her coming. The door will simply open et voilà.

He stares at the doorknob, willing it to turn. His hands hang at his sides, bone and skin shells of themselves: starved for Ketia. His fingers twitch. He takes another long breath he holds and expels slowly. One, two, three, four, five, six.

He shifts a step, swallows a groan of impatience. Come, Ketia, come! It's all he can do not to kick the sagging net sacks of laundry. Torsos of linen slouched against each other. Pale washed-out sheets, yellow isolation gowns.

The intercom speaker in the wall scratches and Ghislaine calls, "Marc, I need to see you. Marc."

You need to see me, why? Anyone else would say, but Ghislaine has to do a mini psycho-social to pass on the simplest of messages. She'll call again in a minute.

He turns away from the door and faces the aluminum walkers jumbled against each other, an awkward brace of metal legs.

"Marc, come to the desk."

He feels the winking pucker of a tic at his mouth.

"Marc, I need to see you."

This had better be good. He swings the door wide, heads

to the nursing station. Slows, though, when he turns the corner. Ketia stands at the far end of the hallway neatly looping the tubing of a blood pressure cuff into its basket. He's positive she heard him.

Ghislaine glances up from the assignment sheet and shoves her glasses into her bushy hair. "You all right? You look like you just swallowed poison." She waits for him to answer, and when he doesn't, taps her pen on an open chart. "Antibiotics on your patient in 56A have been d/c'd."

"They're not due until ten. Why did you call me now?"

"So I don't have to remember until ten. I've got enough going on around here. How about you get a grip?" And turning away, she mutters, "Male menopause."

He shakes his arm, settling his watch on his wrist, grabs the chart to transcribe the order. Speak for yourself, he thinks. He isn't the one with old-witch hair and wobbly thighs. In fact, he's got a woman half his age hot for him.

∽

Emile's appointment today. It's Joelle's first thought when she wakes. The first morning, too, that she doesn't lie curled into herself, ashamed of the empty bed and the closed study door at the end of the hall. She has to look calm today. Emile could always tell when something was wrong.

She stands before her closet. Last night she decided on a dark blue pencil skirt, but now she's not sure. She slides it on and looks in the mirror. Marc prefers skirts, but Emile told her once that she had thick ankles. She unzips the skirt and steps into black pants with flared legs. Shoes with heels. Her pale green sweater that accentuates her eyes.

The morning begins busy, backed up before they even start. Frank got tied up with one of his post-op patients on the floor, and by the time he got to the office three patients were waiting. Within the half-hour more arrive.

Emile says nothing — doesn't even look at her — as he hands her his hospital card. Still wearing his jacket, he sits legs apart, hips forward, between Madame Grazia and Léon.

Joelle flips through next week's appointments for Mr. Al-Sayad's phone number. Frank wants him to come in for a blood test first. Phone to her ear, listening to it ring, she taps the eraser end of her pencil on the list of patients. Maybe it's better that Emile ignores her. She doesn't want him acting familiar in front of the other patients.

She leaves a message on the answering machine and answers the other line, repressing a sigh at the opening line of the spiel. Drug reps sound like Bible preachers hawking the end of the world. Are you up on the latest? Save yourselves while ye may. Stool softeners and bowel preps.

"I'll tell him," Joelle says. "Oui." And more firmly, "D'accord. Oui."

Madame Grazia sits with her legs crossed and angled toward Emile, her small foot, elegantly booted in kidskin, tapping the air. He takes no notice and finally she speaks across him to Joelle. "He's late today, the doctor." She makes her voice dulcet and pleasing. She can equally well do imperious and shrill.

Across from Grazia, Mrs. Klein and her daughter bridle and fluff like sparrows in a wind. To each other, loudly enough that everyone can hear, they say that you always have to wait. "He's such a popular doctor!"

Frank strides out of the examining room with Carla Maclean behind him. "Six months," he tells Joelle, who leafs ahead in her appointment book. Carla always needs a morning appointment because that's the only time her mother can babysit. Frank takes Léon's chart and beckons him to follow. Joelle writes down the date and time for Carla. There are too many people in the office to talk, or Joelle would ask about her daughter.

Pei Yi walks in. Since they worked on the colorectal files together, Pei Yi says hi when she passes Joelle's office. "Do you have a permanent marker?" she asks. "Someone took mine."

Joelle opens her drawer for the pen she hides behind a box of staples.

Mrs. Bedrossian arrives with her daughter, who announces defiantly that it's not their fault if they're late, they couldn't find parking. Joelle doesn't bother saying — can't she see patients sitting elbow to elbow? — that they're running late. The daughter looks around as if expecting someone to offer to move so she can sit with her mother. Grazia has coyly put her elbow on Emile's armrest as if they're together. Mrs. Klein's daughter sits with *her* mother. Mrs. Bedrossian, out of breath from her long trek from the car and through the hospital, sinks heavily in the closest chair. Her daughter gathers the folds of her long coat around herself and takes the seat on the other side of Emile.

A GI secretary calls with a referral for a patient her doc wants Frank to see ASAP. Joelle takes the details. When she hangs up, she hears Grazia talking to Emile. "Have you been here before? The doctor is…" Grazia's voice drops. "Not much you can do." She murmurs, fanning her prettily manicured hand in the air to the rumble of Emile's reply.

Frank is already out again. "You can call Admitting," he tells Joelle, dropping Léon's chart like a winning card on her appointment book. "Closure colostomy."

Joelle nods. Thumbs up for Léon, getting rid of his colostomy.

"À votre service, chère Madame." Frank inclines a courtly head before Grazia, who tucks her sequined clasp purse under her arm and slowly uncrosses her legs.

Joelle clears her throat. Frank doesn't have time to waste on such antics. She glances at Emile, expecting that he's watching the sway of Grazia's exit — everyone else is — but he's staring at her. A hard, almost accusing look.

"You might have to go for tests," she stammers. Those were the words she had prepared. "A CT scan. A colonoscopy…"

"You know I hate doctors."

She blushes at the intimacy of his tone. The heat of the

words. Mrs. Klein and her daughter carefully look away. Joelle turns to the computer and opens the billing page, making herself look too busy to talk.

The phone rings. "That's right," she confirms. "It's not a mistake, we're here the twenty-ninth. Yes... you have a good Christmas, too."

She hangs up and reaches for the mouse again.

"So tell me," she hears. Emile doesn't need her to look at him to know that she's listening. "Who's the guy convinced you to tie the knot?"

Joelle wasn't expecting the question. His mouth a straight line, his eyes brown stones.

"Who," he repeats. A low flat sound.

She forgets that Marc has been sleeping in the study since last week. That they didn't even talk on the weekend. Marc *married* her — which is more than Emile ever did!

Mrs. Klein stirs and fidgets in her chair. Marc took care of her when she had her operation. When she overhears patients say they need surgery, she tells them that if they're lucky they'll have Joelle's husband as a nurse. He never lets you wait for pain medication or a bedpan.

And quickly, forestalling her, Joelle says, "He's a nurse. He works here."

"A nurse." Emile smirks. "Thought you would aim higher. Why not marry a doctor."

Joelle answers the phone. Frank wants to know when Grazia's cardiac echo is booked. Joelle tells him to look on the inside cover of the chart to see if there's a date pencilled next to the outstanding test. "Oh... okay," she hears as he hangs up.

Joelle clicks with her mouse across the screen, pretending to work. She doesn't want to hear what Emile will say next. Something hurtful, she knows.

Let him, she thinks then. She slides open her bottom drawer and reaches for her purse. Normally she stays at her desk — fidèle au poste — during a clinic. But Grazia always takes a long time and the charts for the next few patients are ready. The answering machine comes on after four rings. Emile is the one who has to sit there and wait. Not her.

∞

Marc walks past the cafeteria, still on the ground floor, when he meets the orderly Pietro. "Hey —" Pietro spreads his arms wide. "What are you doing here in the morning? Thought you switched to evenings." Marc nods, keeps moving.

Then, outside the Nursing Admin office, his head nurse, Pascale. "Marc, why are you in the hospital at this hour — and on your day off?"

He smiles. Could he have some privacy, please? Maybe he forgot something he needs in his locker. Maybe he has a doctor's appointment. Since when is everyone so curious? Other nurses show up at the hospital on their day off and no one harasses them with what, when, and why.

Last night at home, over a glass of Merlot, irritated because all evening someone got in the way whenever he tried to approach Ketia — Carlene hovering like a paid chaperone, Ghislaine with some stupid nonsense about one of his patients — he decided it was ridiculous that he couldn't call Ketia at home. Ridiculous, too, that they couldn't get together on their days off. What was it with her family that they expected her to stay home all the time? A young woman! An adult with a responsible job. Well, he resolved, he was going to call. He hefted the phone book from the bottom shelf of the cabinet in the study. Didn't expect the long list of Dauphins. Didn't know her father's first name. Nor her address. Slapped shut the useless book. Poured himself more wine.

Right. He can get her phone number at work. The only problem will be sneaking the book with the staff numbers from Lou's desk. Lou makes everything her business. Fortunately, he knows that, no matter how busy it is, Lou leaves for her break

145

at exactly ten. No one even wants her at the desk if she hasn't had her mid-morning dose of caffeine.

Ten fifteen. He's timed it perfectly. He skirts the counter, hand already out for the top side drawer. The tattered black notebook edges out from under the vacation request sheets and assorted takeout flyers. He can't believe that he even has to look for Ketia's number. He should have it engraved on his heart.

He repeats it under his breath several times. An incantation. An open sesame. He won't write it down.

And in fact, now that he has it, why wait to call? If her mother answers, she'll hear all the background noises — the buzzing of the intercom, Fernande complaining, feeding pumps beeping. He won't be lying when he says he's a nurse calling from the hospital.

He punches in the number and waits, facing the desktop Christmas tree on the counter ledge. It bristles with a surfeit of dollar-store trinkets, tiny balls, ribbons, and miniature candy canes. Down the corridor, along the wall, hang loops of red and green streamers. A piece of tape has come unstuck. One loop drags as far as the handrail. A patient might get snagged on it. A health and safety obstacle. Doesn't anyone notice?

"Allô?" he hears in the receiver. The voice sounds too young to be Ketia's redoubtable mother. He still takes care to sound brisk and polite, asking to speak to Ketia, please.

"C'est moi-même."

Marc nearly laughs with relief. He didn't recognize Ketia in this formal mode. She sounds more Haitian, her French softly percussive. "It's me," he says. "Don't worry, I'm at work. I came here to call you. Can't you hear all the noise?"

Ketia doesn't answer. She must have someone close by. "Listen," he says, "can we meet today? I don't know what happened yesterday. We didn't even *talk*." Of course, he means touch, but he's being careful on his end, too.

Silence.

"I'll say where and you say yes or no. That's all you have to do."

Nothing.

"How about that café, the one beside the hotel? I'll wait for you there."

A fumbling, smothered noise, then a click. He stands with the phone still pressed to his ear. What happened? Did someone take the phone from her? Is her mother that strict?

From behind him he hears, "Let me guess. You'd sooner use one of our germ-infested phones than your own at home."

He carefully replaces the receiver and turns. "I had to get something."

Lou is looking at the phone book that lies open before him. There are six other Ds. She can't know who he was calling — or even that he was the one who used the book. There are patients' charts, a volume of Nursing Policy and Procedure, an x-ray film, an armload of towels, all within reach. Was he using those?

Before she can offer her precious opinion yet again, he takes up his gloves and leaves, pushing through the door to the stairwell. He will go to the café and wait for Ketia. She can lie to her mother. She did before. She has to come. She has to.

∞

Ketia wishes the sheets and blankets would press her flat. Make her disappear. Normally on her day off, she vacuums. Does some ironing for Ma.

Today she lies in bed, though Ma has long left for work, and Gabrielle and Bastien for school. School… Ketia longs for the innocence of school. Nothing more serious than a mid-term exam. How stupid she was back then, agonizing about exams and marks.

How stupid she is now. Everything ruined and it's all her fault. No one she can tell and no idea what to do next. Her mind shies away. Skitters in panic. She's sick with dread and self-loathing, terrified of the moment when Ma will find out.

Ketia turns in bed, twisted in a knot of bones that rejects the fruit that will soon bulge at her centre. Better to be dead, she thinks. Imagines her closed coffin. Ma's face sombre with grief. Grief hurts but it festers less than shame. How Ketia wishes...

She can wish all she wants. Conjure any number of unlikely what-ifs. No amount of regret, however sincere and repentant, will undo the baby.

When the phone rings, she stumbles from bed, expecting that Ma wants to tell her about some chore. She doesn't recognize his voice until he says who he is. She hears less what he says than his tone of yearning: a siren's call that makes her limbs and mouth soften. She wants not to listen, but her hand keeps holding the phone to her ear. The bewitching hum of her own flesh. His cunning. The lick of the devil's tongue up her spine. She grinds her teeth, finally splays her hand wide, and lets the phone drop. And quickly, as if it could scorch her, she snatches and fumbles it onto the receiver. She flees to her bed, in panic that the ringing will start again and this time she won't escape. What does he want? *Why?* He's already destroyed her, branded her with his lust, and still he woos her. She hides in her shroud of blankets and sheets. Help me, oh, Mother Mary, help me!

Her only solace are these few weeks before her crime grows visible. She's unable to imagine beyond the shame, contempt, and disgust that will flay her once Ma and her friends, the neighbours, the nurses at work, everyone knows.

She dozes and wakes, wondering why she still lies in bed in the middle of the day. Remembering gouges her anew with horror.

Just before Bastien and Ma are due to arrive home, she creeps from her bed and pulls the tangle of blankets and sheets straight. In the shower she notes symptoms. Her aureolae are darker, her breasts tender. Yet water and soap stream as ever down her flat tummy. If she could, she would exchange her body for the worst disfigurement. Illness. Cancer. Anything but this. She fastens her hair in a knot without looking in the mirror.

All through supper she feels Ma watching her. Suspicious. But the worst Ma will ever imagine is that Ketia has started dating a boy she hasn't brought home yet to introduce — a boy who doesn't have the manners to come forward.

Ketia fumbles her fork and spills rice on the table. Gets up for a rag to wipe it. If Gabrielle were home, they would have chatter and gossip. Bastien's little boy tales of school don't need more than a nod. Ketia tries to sound interested. A ball hidden? Where?

When she was younger, she used to think Ma could guess what was in her head. She sees now that Ma thinks so, too. So why *didn't* Ma guess when she should have? *Why,* Ketia almost cries out, didn't you stop me?

Ketia shoves the last forkful of tassot and rice in her mouth, pushes back her chair, and starts scraping the pots, rinsing them, filling the sink with soapy water. When Bastien grumbles about his math homework, she tells him to get his exercise book and she'll help. Anything but sit in the living room with Ma.

Bastien leans his elbow on the table, pencil idle in his hand, waiting for Ketia to tell him what to do. "You have to do it yourself," she says. "It's your homework. What don't you understand? Look." She points at the two circles on the page. "This is a whole one and this one is divided in three parts. Each part is…?"

His bottom lip hangs loose with incomprehension.

"Let's draw a new one." She flips the page and draws a circle, divides it in three like a pie. She can't believe he doesn't understand fractions. She and Gabrielle excelled at math.

"What don't you see?" she asks.

Silence.

"Here. The number one." She prints it. "It's divided by three, so we put a line here with a three underneath." She waits for him to nod. "And you see this number — this *fraction?* It's exactly like this circle divided in three." She waits again. "Now we'll make another circle we divide in four. Now you write the number for that."

She watches his lips moving as he counts the parts to himself. He glances at her, grips his pencil as if it were a rope about to slip away, and prints the number four.

"Very good! Now turn it into a fraction."

He makes a careful line under the four and slashes a one below it.

"No, that's..." She's not sure how to explain.

They both hear the trudge of Ma's steps. "Do you understand what she's telling you?"

Bastien's head sinks farther between his shoulders. Ketia pretends to be reading the homework instructions. Brother and sister breathe more easily when Ma continues down the hallway to the bathroom.

"We'll try another one," Ketia says as she draws a square she divides through the middle. She wonders if Bastien will remember how she helped him with his homework once he hears the things people will soon start to say about her. When the other kids ask him about his bastard nephew. What will it be like for him to have a sister everyone calls a slut? I'm sorry, she thinks at him. So sorry.

Ma took him to the barber just a few days ago. His close-cropped curls. Half-and-half babies always keep their kink. Not tight and wiry, but still far from straight. No telling about his skin, though. She's lighter than Gabrielle and Bastien, who are dark like Ma. But still not light enough to account for how light he will be.

She thinks of the baby as a boy because a man made her pregnant. A man tricked her. A man who was older and married and should have known better. She thinks *a man,* not Marc. She has always been a good girl. This could not — *should not* — have happened to her.

∞

Joelle nods sympathetically as Madame Repentigny talks in chopped, vague sentences. "What will I do if... my son in Abitibi. My daughter." She worries that the CT scan she had that afternoon confirms a recurrence of cancer. Both stand outside the crowded bus shelter in front of the hospital, their shoulders hunched away from the birdshot pellets of snow in the wind. Joelle reminds her the scan might show nothing.

Madame Repentigny's expression changes. "Mon mari," she says as a car pulls up to the curb. She knocks her boots free of snow before bending to duck through the door. Her husband grips the wheel at two and ten o'clock like a perfect driving student. Joelle wonders if he knows what kind of test his wife had and why.

From behind her she hears, "Isn't your job over?" That gravelly voice. She has to force herself to turn around calmly. Emile stands so close she can smell the pungency of a fresh-lit cigarette. But he isn't smoking. He's pulled the collar of his sheepskin jacket up around his neck. Of course he wouldn't do anything as sensible as wear a hat. He doesn't look cold so much as annoyed by the snow.

Stiffly Joelle says, "I feel badly for her."

"And?" The suggestion of a smile or a smirk on his lips. "Do you feel badly for me? I'm sick, too."

"I don't like to see anyone..." She falters and looks away, lets the wind whip hair from under her cloche hat across her cheeks. She read what Frank wrote in Emile's chart.

"Not anyone. Me. Do you feel badly for me?" And in a lower register, "Come on, Jewels, I want to hear you say it."

The old nickname, his deep almost-growl, the request — he

151

always made her say things — triggers too much. She quivers at how deftly he cracked her husk and reached in. It frightens her that he *knows* exactly how to get there. Marc never has. She always thought that meant her relationship with Marc was more normal. Except that even in their most private moments Marc doesn't look at her as deeply as Emile does now, standing in the blowing snow on the sidewalk with people to either side.

A woman struggles to pass with a stroller through the ankle-deep snow and people shuffle aside. Joelle blinks. Gropes for a stock phrase from the office. "You're lucky your surgery is so soon."

"You mean I'm lucky to have it so bad that they have to rush me in?" A bitter laugh. "That's not the kind of luck I need. Your doc there had better be good."

"He is. But you know," Joelle feels safer now, talking about Frank, "there's only so much any doctor can do at a certain point. You should have seen someone sooner. You had symptoms and a family history."

He shrugs. Then his mouth quirks again. "Any truth to what they say about doctors?"

She doesn't know what he means.

"In examining rooms... doctors, nurses, secretaries. Quick deke into the closet." He winks. "You said hubby was a nurse. I'll bet he knows."

Joelle looks away. "You've been watching too much TV."

"Right, right." She hears the grin in his voice. "Hubby's a good boy."

A bus tops the rise two blocks away. Two blocks in rush-hour traffic and with the snow could take minutes yet. At least she knows Emile won't follow her. He abhors public transit.

"Oh-oh." A low whistle.

Why doesn't he leave? She keeps her lips closed. Pressed shut. Protest only ever made him continue.

"What's going on with hubby makes you clam up like that?"

The bus creeps forward, however slowly. The wipers sweep arcs from side to side. The windshield is dark with crowded bodies. Only when the heavy wheels finally churn through the snow to the curb does she turn her head to look. He's gone.

Joelle pushes through the bodies bulked out with coats and knapsacks, grabs onto a pole already claimed by an octopus of mittens and gloves. She steels her face against the thump of techno-rap from someone's headphones, fixes her eyes on the snowman pin on a woman's lapel. She wishes now she'd objected. Told Emile he was wrong. Every marriage has its ups and downs. It's not the first time Marc has slept in the study. (Although never more than for a single night.) Even if he can't forgive her — not now, not yet — eventually they'll get back in sync again. Quiet weekend mornings. Marc going to the gym. Cooking... grilled ribs with wine-braised lentils.

Last night she thought of getting him a new computer or a leather coat for Christmas. She doesn't mind spending her personal savings on Marc. But she doesn't know how to pick a computer and Marc would sooner choose a coat for himself. What about a gift for his parents? That would touch him — show how much she loved him. Except... she has no idea what. The presents they give her, though chic and expensive, always range far wide of her tastes and habits. That strange book on herbs for her birthday. Lovely watercolour illustrations, but surely they know that Marc is the cook in their household. Last Christmas she unwrapped a jewellery box, which augured well until she saw the polished knuckle of jade set in a massive band of silver. The clunky ring weights her hand like a wrecking ball. She only wore it once. She's not at all sure she can choose the right gift for Marc's parents, but she counts on Diane to help. She imagines their surprise. The surprise on Marc's face, too.

She steps off the bus into the wind again, tugging her hat lower, hurrying past the patisserie, a hair and make-up consultant, a bistro. The florist has orchids on stems long as wands in the window. That's what she needs — abracadabra! Zap Marc from the sofa in the study back into their bed again.

Diane's storefront is bordered with white fairy lights. Fir boughs make wispy hills for carved toys on wheels and hand-painted soldiers. A couple stands just inside the door deciding on the perfect garlic pot. Diane counsels a woman fingering the woven shawls. When she sees Joelle she hula-hoops her hand in the air. Busy, busy.

Joelle nods. Not to worry. Slowly she walks around the displays. Stops to smooth her hand across a woven linen runner. Plain, yet elegant in its simple austerity. The indigo bowl in the middle attracts her, too. What about a serving dish? Wouldn't that be perfect for an eminently cook-'n'-dine duo? Diane has two large soup tureens, one with a rustic, coarse-textured glaze, the other with a lustrous, white sheen.

She bustles past, leaning in to whisper. "Joelle, I can't even stop to say hello."

"That's all right. I haven't decided yet."

"You came to shop? What are you looking for?"

"Christmas present. For Marc's parents."

Diane turns around and sights down her nose, as if she couldn't possibly have heard correctly. "For…?"

Joelle could almost laugh. What, is Diane the only one allowed to have bold ideas?

She pauses here and there as she strolls around the store. She considers a fish platter, a ceramic oval with a handle shaped like a tail. She lifts a handsome raku jug. But none of these are grand enough for the effect she wants. Again and again she looks at the polished white soup tureen. The translucent glaze reflects warm light.

Wasn't that what Marc said the last time they went shopping? She should have her own opinion. Well, then, she nods to herself. This is it.

∞

Marc lifts his cream-striped mug from the cupboard, unscrews the lid of the carafe, and pours himself coffee. His movements are slow, his look abstracted. He tightens the lid then stops, hands loose fists on the counter. Ketia never came to the café, though he waited all afternoon and evening. And yesterday at work, what happened? He's sure she saw him coming down the hallway when she about-faced and dashed to the blood cart as if Fernande, who stood puzzling over blood tubes, had called her. All evening, whenever Marc walked into the nursing station or the med room, Ketia scurried away or latched onto someone else. He finally surprised her when she was gathering piqués and towels from the linen closet. Both hidden from view by the wide wings of the doors he pulled her close, and she clung to him, gripped his shoulders. "Ketia," he whispered, "Ketia, what's going on?" She grimaced and shoved him away — he was so shocked that he let go — and ran down the hallway. *Ran.*

He lifts his coffee, sees that he hasn't yet added cream, and crosses to the refrigerator.

And suddenly he understands. The refrigerator handle, the carton of cream, the cupboard doors, the brushed steel thermos carafe. Whatever he touches, Joelle has touched, too. Even if he avoids her, sleeps in another room, and barely even talks to her, he still lives here. Ketia doesn't know that for him Joelle is no more than a dead appendage, wasted and dry. Though, yes, entwined around his life.

He pushes through the swinging door and there, look, the paper Joelle took from the mat and left on the dining room table. She can't even leave his paper alone. She has to touch everything. He looks around and can tell exactly where she's been. A chair left askew. The salt and pepper mills off-centre on the hutch. A cardboard box on the floor — buying things she doesn't even have the courtesy to put away. And on the coffee table, a red and white Santa candle, his head half-melted, wax drooled down his arms onto... Marc creeps on soft feet to verify what he can hardly believe. Doesn't she remember how much that sushi plate cost? Was she trying to prove how stupid she was? Years ago they'd agreed not to clutter their home with Yuletide kitsch. They —

Marc scowls. He doesn't want to think *they* anymore. Apparently Joelle can't be bothered to think *they* either. He snatches the plate to toss the fat man in the garbage when the answer comes to him as simply as that. Why is he still living here among these things in this life he no longer wants? He doesn't need *this*. All that matters now is Ketia — to be alone with her, the two of them.

Galvanized, he strides to the hallway, turns again, and paces to the dining room. Stops at the kitchen door. Goes to the living room. The dining room. The hallway.

He will furnish a new home where he can welcome Ketia. *Her* home too, if she accepts. He thinks *if*, though of course she will. She won't have to hide anymore from her mother, who will see how he loves her. His parents, too, will be thoroughly entranced by Ketia's grace and poise.

Still he paces. In the last months he's lived for whenever he can see Ketia again. Now he sees the future opening, a long, clear path before him. He ignores the oak dining table, the antique hutch, the treed and snowy hump of the mountain out the window, the much-prized view. He no longer wants anything tainted by his life with Joelle.

Yes, he nods. Yes. Except for the cooking implements, the copper-bottomed pots, the knives, the fine dishes and cutlery — which Joelle doesn't appreciate in any case — he will leave her everything. Whatever else she will think of him, she won't be able to say that he isn't generous.

∞

"You can't even see the Jacques Cartier Bridge!"

"The bridge? You can't see the mountain."

"Well, duh, that would make sense. It's farther away."

Pamela and Yasmine sit on the other side of Nazim's desk. He has no idea what they mean about not being able to see the bridge. The call centre is on the eighteenth floor with windows all around. From their corner, the spanned trusses of the Jacques Cartier Bridge lie directly in view.

"Excuse me? I *live* near the bridge. It's sort of important to me to know that it's there."

"You're worried the bridge disappeared because you can't see it?"

Nazim can hear them even while he wends his way through the spiel of offering a client internet service. The man says he's satisfied with the free service he already has, but Nazim's job is to convince him that he would be far more satisfied paying $39.95 a month.

"Do you bank online?" Nazim asks.

"Yes."

"Ah." Nazim lets the pause hang, then swoops. "Unless you have a firewall, you're not protected. With ours..." Nazim will tailor the information depending on how the man reacts. The sales reps have some leeway to make the offer — the kill — more attractive to the client. Nazim doesn't mind that the work is routine and bores him, but the product the company sells is a hoax. Basically there *is* no product, only a perceived need the company hopes to convert into profit.

The man on the phone is too polite to say no. He finally agrees to consider the offer. If not the ideal answer, it will do for Nazim who can now forward his name to the list for callbacks — a point in Nazim's favour. The man has just opened himself for a call from an agent who specializes in hard sells.

Nazim has a few seconds before the next call. Pamela and Yasmine are still unplugged and talking. He wonders how they do it. If he unplugs, his supervisor, Sami, appears to ask why he's gone off queue. The others think Nazim gets preferential treatment because Sami talks to him in Arabic. They don't know that Sami uses Arabic as a putdown. He believes his

Lebanese Arabic is more pure than Nazim's. He actually has less schooling than Nazim and speaks more dialect than he realizes. More than once Nazim has wanted to stuff his headset into Sami's supercilious mouth. But it was hard enough just to get this lousy job.

And technically it *is* a desk job. Waalid, who went to school with him, runs his father's fig and date shop in the market back home. In Morocco, without connections, an education alone wasn't enough to advance. For that, you had to pack your bags and leave home and family behind. How was Nazim to know that his Moroccan education wouldn't count here, either? He never told his family that the only work he could find when he arrived in Montreal was as a hotel clerk. He sent them as much money as he could, which wasn't easy in the first years. Finally he was able to write that he worked for a large telecommunications firm.

Of course, he never thought that anyone from his family would visit Montreal. He's read Ghada's letter so often he's memorized it. He keeps the page, still in its envelope, in his locker at work. He's decided he'll have to move into a small furnished apartment and pretend it's his home. The ones he's looked at so far are shabby with balding wood floors, windows that face a brick wall, suspect stains in the sink. He doesn't want to but he doesn't have much choice. He can't afford better on his own.

At least Ghada will be impressed by the tower where he works. He'll have to tell her — which is true — that she's not allowed on the eighteenth floor for security reasons.

She'll still want to meet his colleagues. Who? Yasmine, with her turquoise bed head? Pamela, with the studs in her nose, eyebrows, and tongue — and apparently her nipples and labia, a word she pronounces like a delectable fruit. He *cannot* introduce Ghada to a woman likely to describe the studs in her labia.

Sometimes he sits in the lunchroom with Ismael and Carlos to watch soccer on TV. If they happen to leave the call centre at the same time, they walk to the subway together and sit in a loose group on the train. But he's never met them outside of work for a coffee or a beer.

Ghada can't meet his friends, Hatem and Badar, either, because what if their wives invite him and Ghada for a meal — as they surely will? Can he rely on them not to mention Diane?

The details he will have to fabricate around Ghada's visit feel so precarious. A flimsy structure a careless knock will collapse.

And what about her intention to find him a wife? Nazim winces.

"Mais oui," he tells the woman who called to ask about virus protection. "Permettez-moi de vous l'expliquer."

Finished with the client, Nazim decides to unplug for a moment and risk Sami's ire. He stands to stretch his legs and stares. The bridge — the whole city of Montreal — has vanished. The tower where they work floats in a white stratosphere. Except for the towers close by, the city below is obscured by blowing snow. They could be in a fishbowl afloat in the sky.

"Crazy, eh?" Yasmine wags her turquoise head at the window. He's about to agree when he notices that she's plugged in and talking to a customer. She winks at him and grins.

∞

Marc jogs up the stairs. An orderly passes him on the way down. "You runnin' to get to work?" The enclosed walls amplify his full-lipped smack of derision.

Running, yes! If Marc could, he would fly to see Ketia. He'll tell her in a rush. He'll tell her slowly. The important word is *together*. From now on. You and me. All afternoon he pored over apartment listings. There aren't many just now, before Christmas. He has to think of money, too. He has realized it would be crazy to give up the condo, so he'll have to keep up with his share of the mortgage until they sell. Joelle can't afford to buy him out; nor can he her — unless his parents help. They might. He hates the idea of leaving his black granite counters. The dovetail efficiency of his kitchen cabinets.

He spots Ketia in the nursing station, turned away from the hallway, her hair tucked in a bun at the nape of her neck. How does no one else see how enchanting she is? The comeliness of her walk, visible even in loose-fitting scrubs. She goes to the med room without looking around.

He shucks his parka and boots in the change room and hurries back to the nursing station, but Ketia has left the med room. He grabs a worksheet and goes to the bulletin board next to Lou's desk to take note of his assignment for the evening. Nurses from day shift sit with their elbows on the counters, charts stacked before them, writing as if in a competition. Lou radiates an annoyed end-of-shift aura, though her hands move busily, sorting a thick sheaf of lab results to be filed.

"Do you..." Marc stops. He has to keep his voice steady. "Do you know where Ketia is?"

Lou doesn't look up from her lab results. "You've got 48A. We did all the pre-op bloods but the resident just came and she wants a CEA."

"Did you call the lab to see if they'd add it?"

"You know what? I'm finished. I'm beyond finished. I had fifteen minutes for lunch today. It's your patient. How about *you* call the lab?"

Lou always has a bite to her manner, but they used to get along. What's up her nose now? Up her whatever.

He skirts the counter and heads down the hallway. He expects to find Ketia in the lounge, but Ghislaine and Yadira are the only ones there. He steps back into the hallway. Ketia is here somewhere, close by.

There! Erect as a princess disguised in nursing scrubs, walking toward him, reading the care plans on her clipboard. Come to me, he thinks, as his hands and arms spread.

She lifts her head and freezes. He smiles at her reaction.

Hands still out, he advances. "Ketia!"

Her look careens wildly. She makes a sound deep in her throat and springs away, running. He would call after her, except that he refuses to do it like this, shouting down the hallway at work. He wants his hands on her arms, her face lifted to his as she listens. *That's* how he's imagined it. *That's* how it will happen.

Only then does he notice everyone in the nursing station. Abi, Carlene, Marie-Ange, Raymonde, Lou at the helm, a couple of the doctors. Faces surprised, a whole staring audience. He sweeps them a tight smile. Fuck you, he thinks. She loves me and I love her. We're beyond being hassled by your stupid opinions. Gossip all you want. You'll see.

He returns to the lounge and takes a seat. Every time the door opens, he expects Ketia, but it's always another of the nurses from evening shift. No one sits next to him, which is perfect. Ketia will. But Ketia doesn't come, and when Raymonde charges in, her report sheets dense with notes, she immediately starts reading. "36A, patient of Collier's, went for c-scope today, *wasn't clean,* rescheduled for tomorrow. Whoever's got him tonight, make sure he's prepped. Christ, we got an earful today. 36B five days post-op anterior resection..."

Marc watches the door. He realizes he startled Ketia. Frightened her. He's been so caught up with his own longing that he hasn't thought what it's been like for her — not just hiding how they feel about each other at work, but at home from her mother, too. She's so young still. He should have understood. But now he can take her out on dates. Seduce her all over again. Meet her family like any other man come courting. Bring desserts from the patisserie on Laurier when they invite him for supper.

Raymonde drones on. "44A has a bolus of NS running. Pain controlled with PCA. 44B has a bed at conval tomorrow. We need exit meds." Ghislaine scribbles notes on her evening report sheets, glasses slid low on her nose.

Marc wonders if something happened with one of Ketia's patients — if she needs help. But Raymonde doesn't mention any crisis, and when he comes out of report, the EKG machine is still in place. Lou is gone, too, taking her cloud of gloom with her.

Briskly, he walks past all the rooms but doesn't find Ketia. In the med room he starts to prepare his evening meds. Every now and then he glances into the nursing station. Finally, he sees Ketia with Ghislaine, her chair pulled close, getting report on her patients.

"Marc," Cassie calls on the intercom.

Marc lingers, passing Ketia, but she keeps her face lowered, writing on her worksheet, listening to Ghislaine.

Cassie points at a junior resident who says he wants to insert an NG tube on one of Marc's patients.

"They're in the supply room," Marc says. Since when does he play fetch for the doctors?

Then Ghislaine calls over, "I asked Cassie to get you. Go with him, will you? To the bedside?" She shakes her unkempt hair slightly. We don't trust this guy. Make sure he knows what he's doing.

When Marc finishes with the resident, who was clumsy but at least open to coaching, he scouts for Ketia again. She turns the corner, coming toward him, and he quickens his step, but she veers aside to talk with Abi, who's cleaning the bladder scan with disinfectant. Marc leans against the wall, hands behind him on the guard rail. He'll wait for her to finish. He'll just wait.

But she keeps talking to Abi. What can she possibly have to tell him that takes so long? Abi, too, has put aside his towel and bottle and stands bent toward her. Marc resents their easiness with each other — something he and Ketia don't have. There was always too much secrecy, creeping behind closed doors, hoping no one suspected. When they had time together, they didn't waste it in talk.

But now they can talk! They don't have to hide!

When he steps away from the wall, Abi moves, too, effectively blocking Ketia from view. Carlene, who minces from a patient's room, sees Marc and dashes to Ketia's side. They speak in low voices. Fine, Marc thinks, they're having a private confab. They don't have to act like he's a boor who's about to intrude. He's got work to do, too.

He goes to the supply room for a bottle of NS, sterile gauze, gloves, and a roll of Kling. He has to change the dressing on a fresh AV fistula — a minor surgical procedure to provide access for dialysis. The patient is an older Russian woman who speaks neither English nor French. He'll have to wait for the family before he does the post-op teaching: how she should no longer use her arm, how to check for the distinctive vibration of blood that indicates the fistula is patent.

He removes the initial dressing and lays his gloved fingers on the shunt. Blood hums under her thin flesh. "Good," he says, "very good." She responds with a tentative smile. He wonders if her family has told her that she'll be getting dialysis three times a week for the rest of her life, or if she believes that her malfunctioning kidneys have been cured by a simple incision in her arm. People are so naïve about their bodies.

He breaks the seal on the bottle of NS and cleans the site with gauze. "Lift your arm so I can..." He lifts his arm showing her. "Yes, hold it like that."

He winds Kling around the fresh gauze and fastens it with tape. With one hand he folds the paper packaging of the dressing kit around the dirty gauze, and with the other reaches for the bottle of saline.

Ketia can't still be talking with Carlene and Abi. He'll find her, whatever she's doing. He needs to tell her that they're free. He's leaving his wife.

∽

"You want me to tell him to get lost?" Carlene asks.
"No!" Ketia shakes her head.
Ketia, Carlene, and Marie-Ange sit at the table in the

lounge, eating supper from plastic containers. Ketia only picks at her kalalou and pork. She's hungry but doesn't want to eat —as if starving herself will stop what's happening.

"But he's bothering you," Marie-Ange says. "Did you see?" she asks Carlene. A stupid question. Everyone saw.

Carlene squishes elbow noodles onto her fork. "How about asking Pascale to work days on the next schedule? Stop doing evenings."

Ketia has thought of that, but the next schedule doesn't start for a week. How can she dodge Marc for a week? And what if he asks to work days as well?

"Comme ça," Marie-Ange agrees. "Don't work when he does. He only sees you here, right? He's not calling you at home, is he?"

"No." A punch of denial, small but definite. Not even a lie because she hung up on him.

Carlene and Marie-Ange look disappointed. They would have liked an all-out battle with Marc.

Marie-Ange points with her fork at Ketia's food. "You're not eating."

"I'm not hungry." She covers the food that's left with the lid. She'll throw it away so as not to tempt herself.

"I remember this one guy I knew," Marie-Ange starts.

"I'll bet." Carlene winks at Ketia, who knows they're trying to cheer her up with other bad luck stories. They have no idea how bad hers is.

"Well, *this* guy —"

The door to the lounge opens. Ketia doesn't face the doorway, but she sees how Carlene glares. The hostile pucker of her mouth.

"Does anyone have the key to the tub room?"

Marc's voice touches Ketia's ears and neck. The key to the tub room used to be their code for a quick rendezvous in the back stairwell.

Marie-Ange and Carlene pat their pockets.

"We don't," Marie-Ange says. "You can go."

"Ketia?" Marc's voice wavers.

"She doesn't have it, okay?"

A moment passes before the door finally closes.

"Man, he's got it bad," Carlene says.

Marie-Ange clucks disapproval. "You keep away from him," she warns Ketia. She and Carlene watch her with concern. They all heard the urgency in Marc's voice.

"Yeah," Carlene says. "Maybe you shouldn't wait 'til the next schedule. See if you can get someone to switch shifts with you now."

"A whole week of shifts?" Marie-Ange makes a face.

"I'm just *saying*."

They discuss her options — as if she has any. She knows she doesn't. Everyone will condemn her once they know. Especially him, who did this to her. She grew up hearing the stories Ma told about married men. They always stayed with their wives. Tales of warning. Bad tales. A man was a devil in pursuit until he planted his seed and made a devil child. A bastard. To Ketia those seemed like back-in-the-Islands stories. Things that happened to second and third cousins who lived in the hills, didn't go to school, and didn't know better. But the devil was here, too. He had a narrow nose and green eyes, kept his hair neat, his hands clean, his manners at work and with others polite. Only in secret did he whisper how he would slide his long fingers into her hidden slickness.

"I know!" Carlene slaps the table. "Jovi's got a problem with her babysitter. She was trying to switch from days to evenings. Why don't you call Jovi?"

When Ketia doesn't move, Carlene runs her hand along Ketia's arm. "Hey, sweetie, are you sure you're all right?" She keeps her fingers on Ketia's wrist, a loose link of flesh and bone. "Listen to me. Call Jovi. She wants to switch shifts."

"Jovi," Ketia says. She can hear how they're trying to help her.

"I'll get her number," Marie-Ange offers, lifting the phone

to the table and dialing. "Cassie, I need Jovi's number. I'm here in the lounge. That's right, I'm too lazy to move my fat butt and get it myself. You bet mine's bigger than yours! Okay, thanks."

She pushes the piece of paper towel, where she wrote the number, across to Ketia.

"Thanks," Ketia whispers. She wishes she could tell them the truth. She'll have to tell someone soon. There are all kinds of nursing tasks she should no longer do. Take blood. Start IVs. She could get into trouble with both management and the union. If she could tell just one nurse who could cover for her. Carlene would do it. But if she switches to days, she'll no longer be working with Carlene.

Phone to her ear, she waits. A child answers. Ketia asks to speak with Jovi.

The child cries, "Maman, c'est pour toi!"

Ketia controls her face, but her throat tightens, hearing the cadence of the words.

∞

Marc checks that Ketia's coat and yellow scarf still hang in the change room. All evening he was so busy he was hardly able to think of her. One of his patients returned from X-ray and had to be prepped and rushed to the OR tout de suite. Then ID opened a big abdominal dressing with packing that Marc had to do all over again. Whenever he saw Ketia, she had someone with her. The other nurses even dragged her off for supper. Why does she let them bully her?

Well, ha! He has a new plan. He grabs his parka and from the door to the stairwell calls to the orderly about a stretcher in the hallway, making sure that Carlene sees him leaving. She'll never guess that he's waiting downstairs, hidden behind the tower of public telephones. Carlene can't *think* that far ahead. He still doesn't understand how someone as smart as Ketia can tolerate Carlene, with her affected airs and preening. The very opposite of Ketia's alluring modesty.

He keeps his head angled low as if he were talking on the phone. Carlene only ever walks with Ketia as far as the exit, where her boyfriend waits. Marc will let them go, then follow Ketia across the parking lot to her car. He won't even call out her name until she's almost there. He doesn't want to frighten her, only to make sure no one else can hear. Just the two of them — the way they like to be. The way they'll be from now on.

He thought of waiting for her by her car, but if she's delayed, he could wait in the cold for a long time. There's also a security guard who patrols the lot at midnight. That's not a conversation Marc wants to have.

Oh come, Ketia, come! His news won't feel real until she knows.

From the end of the hallway he hears the chatter of women, and still keeping his head low, peeks around the edge of the steel tower that houses the phones. Two nurses from another floor, an orderly, and Ketia — with Marie-Ange. Marie-Ange, who brags she has the biggest ass in the hospital. Probably does, too. Her thighs churn as she walks. Marc quickly ducks his head again. Once they pass, he doesn't leave the phones but cranes his head to see if Marie-Ange has someone waiting for her. But no, the whole group trudges to the parking lot.

He finally lopes to the door and pretends to look down the street, though all the time he spies on Ketia. Even in her puffy down coat, at a distance, lit by the harsh white lights that angle across the frozen parking lot, he can distinguish the grace of her walk. The other nurses fan out to their cars. All except for Marie-Ange, who sticks with Ketia. Step for step. Ketia unlocks the passenger door and Marie-Ange gets in.

His hands open. Fingers rigid with what they can't hold.

∞

Joelle swings her grocery bag listlessly. A baguette, a grilled chicken breast, a small bag of apples. The apples weigh the arc of the bag's pendulum. The click of her heels on the marble echo the dull beat in her head. A disorganized day at work. Another long evening alone. Although maybe Marc wrote her a note about the box she left on the floor. He wouldn't open it uninvited but he might have wondered what she bought. Years ago, when he worked evenings, she used to arrive home to notes on the table. That he'd already washed lettuce and made a tarragon vinaigrette. Heat the Veal Marengo at 325°.

She hesitates when she sees Marc's boots in the tray beside the mat. Isn't he supposed to be working? Is she allowed to enter? After a week of pretending she doesn't live here, she feels too defeated to slink away again. She opens the door softly, alert for a clue. She smells garlic being sautéed. And something smoked... chipotle chilies or oysters. An impromptu burst of flavour. A rumour of sizzling from the kitchen.

Her shoulders and neck immediately relax. The sounds and smells of Marc cooking mean all is well again. Though she still moves stealthily, setting her bag against the wall on the floor, slipping the large buttons of her coat free, hooking it on the stand. With suspense akin to reverence she listens to the thud of the wooden paddle against the wok, the rush of water in the sink, the clink of plates set on the counter. The swinging door thwacks open and she hears him at the hutch, opening a drawer.

She tiptoes to the low dividing wall between the dining and living room. Marc's back is to her, but there are two placemats on the table. *Two.* She wants to hug him — so slender and boyish, his sweater rucked up on one hip — as he puts the salt and pepper mills in their exact spot in the middle of the table.

"I can do that," she says.

He starts at her voice, half-turns his head. "It's done."

"Do you want me to —"

"Everything's ready. I'll finish up now that you're here."

She knows how he likes to mastermind a meal from beginning to end and takes no offence at the shortness of his tone. She hears only that he's himself again. She's forgiven.

In the bathroom she traces blue along the edge of her eyelids and touches mascara to her lashes. She uses pale pink blush — almost natural. Lightly sweeps the brush along her cheekbones. Marc doesn't like a lot of make-up. She checks the fall of her blouse and feels behind her to make sure the zipper of her skirt is centred. Her hair hangs limp, so she gathers and twists it in a roll she fastens with a large barrette. Again she flattens her hand down her blouse and touches the zipper of her skirt.

In the kitchen Marc scrapes aside the vegetables in the wok and upends the bowl of shrimp he shelled and deveined himself to ensure they were properly cleaned. He has thought through his argument several times already. If Joelle objects, it will only be because she fears change. She has always been one to cower and clamp onto routine. She cannot possibly deny — it's so obvious! — that their marriage has failed. When was the last time they even did anything together? They're no longer a couple in any real sense of the word. He's setting *her* free, as well as himself. Maybe not today or tomorrow or even next week, but eventually she will thank him. He won't mention Ketia. That much he owes Joelle: not to make her feel she has been supplanted.

The shrimp glisten pink, a handful of plump commas in the bottom of the wok. The rice fluffs nicely — but still al dente. He sprinkles the lime zest he minced with lemongrass across the shrimp, then tosses the vegetables and shrimp together. Joelle likes shrimp. This might not be their absolutely last supper, but in the event that it is, he hopes she appreciates that he prepared a meal solely with her in mind.

Joelle fetches the box with the soup tureen from the living room and sets it on the chair next to hers at the table. Marc will ask what it is. He'll see that the gift for his parents proves how much she loves him. She's so ashamed about what happened — and so sorry. She was half-asleep. In the grip of a nightmare. Of course Marc fled in disgust. She remembers how molested Emile always made her feel. She wishes she could let Marc know she *understands*. But she also doesn't want to mention the incident. Better to forget it ever happened.

As she waits for Marc, listening to the heft of a pot slid onto the stove, she wonders if her little mise-en-scène with the box on the chair seems too coy. Why wait for Marc to ask what's in the box? She folds back the bubble wrapping and eases the tureen free of its nest. The opalescent sheen, like the glimmering skin inside an onion, matches the flattened onion bulb shape. Colour and form complement each other with pretty artistry.

Marc backs through the swinging door with two plates he sets on the table, carefully avoiding any contact with Joelle's shoulder.

"Shrimp!" She points as if he doesn't know what he cooked. "Snow peas, red pepper, oyster mushrooms, and... smoked oysters! I *knew* I smelled something smoked when I came home."

Her voice bubbles. Too overeager. Marc had hoped for a quiet meal. A reasonable tone. He had meant to wait until they finished eating to tell her. Suddenly he's not sure he can eat at all.

"Lemon?" she asks when she tastes her shrimp.

"Lemongrass. And lime zest." He stares at the shiny white pot on the table. "What is that?"

"A soup tureen. For your parents." She cocks her head like a little girl, smiling. "For Christmas."

The object is hideous, can't she see? He wouldn't want it in his home, much less give it to anyone — and certainly not his parents.

He angles the knife and fork he still hasn't used on the lip of his plate. He tries to keep his voice mild. "Why did you get my parents a gift?"

"You know how your mother likes to serve soup — and they've only got one soup tureen."

"The one they have is Royal Worcester dated 1885. When

you have antiques like that on your table, you don't need a dozen." Her ignorance exasperates him even more than her childish rationale.

"I know it's an antique," Joelle says quickly. Marc's mother always upends it to show her the stamp. Joelle doesn't care about the stamp. She doesn't like the fussy blue flowers that cover it, the worn gilt handles. "That doesn't mean they can't have another."

She wouldn't be so sure of herself if she hadn't bought the tureen in Diane's store. Although perhaps — Marc would know this better — the style isn't to his parents' taste. If they like the Royal Worcester, which she doesn't, then they might not like this tureen, which she does. More tentatively she adds, "Your parents have some modern dishes, too."

"They don't use contemporary lines when they serve soup. I'm surprised you never noticed."

"Well, now they can serve soup all the time if they want." Joelle persists, if ever more lamely.

Marc takes a long, slow breath. How have they gotten side-tracked into this ridiculous discussion about an ugly dish? "You don't recall that years ago we agreed that I would select gifts for my parents?"

"I thought I'd help." She leans her knife and fork on the edge of her plate as he has. For a moment she rests her hands on either side of her placemat. Then, as if to make herself less visible, she slides them under the table to her lap.

"You'll have to give it to someone else." He motions at the shiny white dish. Ugly objects are so complacent and obvious. Beauty glides without fanfare. "Why not," he suggests, "to Diane and Nazim?"

She's blinking. Is she going to start crying? He looks away into the living room — at the African mask on the wall. The dull burnish of light on the dark wood. The full, sombre mouth. Tell her, the mask says. Tell her now.

The distaste in Marc's voice helps Joelle see that the

shimmery glaze she thought so pretty looks cheap next to their own matte green plates and stainless steel cutlery. She remembers Diane suggested she get Marc's opinion, since the gift was for his parents.

Okay, she thinks now, biting her lips in reprimand against herself. She made a mistake. Another mistake. At least this one she can undo. "I'll return it," she whispers. And more loudly, "I'll return it. I just thought I would help you with the Christmas shopping."

Softly he says, "Who knows where I'll even be at Christmas?"

More than the words, his expression makes her nervous. "Are you supposed to work? Didn't you ask for Christmas off?"

When he doesn't answer, she turns her head to see where he's looking. The living room seems the same as always. Then she hears, "I'm moving out."

Did he say that or did she imagine it? His mouth is stretched in a grim smile.

"I'm moving out," he repeats.

Moving what? Moving where? What were they talking about? Oh — "I'll take it back!" Her voice catches, ragged with urgency. "You won't see it again!"

What is she babbling about? Marc doesn't understand. But he doesn't have to. He feels himself brimming with his own sense of purpose. Fists knuckled, wrists pressed against the edge of the table, he lets loose the words that will choke him if he holds back another instant. "We haven't been happy for a long time. We're living a sham here, side by side, sharing the same address, but really what else? We're not home together, we don't eat together, we don't —" He scans the room, the furnishings, the two long windows, all witness to the lie of their marriage.

"Why have we settled for this? We're both still young. We have years ahead of us yet. The rest of our lives!" His fingers stretch open as if to reach, though his wrists stay anchored against the edge of the table. "We have to take that chance — to meet someone we love who loves us, too. Not to live here entombed with each other as if we were already half-dead. There's no sense to this day in, day out routine we're living. That's not *living!* We're just paying off a mortgage. We're just—"

She watches him as if she could stop herself from hearing by holding her breath. Her face gapes a void where his words somersault without meaning or sound. And suddenly he understands that even if she cannot deny what he says, she would still hang onto their marriage. She will always choose the comfort of delusion over the hard, cold truth.

He groans in disbelief, scrapes back his chair, pushing himself away from the table. He's already swung out his arm to push through the kitchen door — escaping the plea of her face — when he whips around. "You always said you didn't want to end up like your parents, remember? Making each other miserable but staying together anyhow. Like dogs, you said they were, too stupid to know better. You always said they should have separated."

Joelle lets the words stream past. She's ready to prostrate herself, apologize for all she's ever done — for *everything* — if only he would stop denouncing their marriage. She doesn't know why he keeps saying we, we, and we as if he means her, too. Doesn't he, can't he —

Then he says the words she has dreaded since she was old enough to think them. End up like your parents. Too stupid. You. The words nick deep into her lifelong fear that she was fated to be miserable, too. Her mother so bitter, her dad unable to keep even the lousiest job. How hard she tried not to be like her mother, who criticized and argued. Didn't she always agree with whatever Marc wanted? Sweet and accepting, smiling and good. Marc, too, she counted on him not to be like her drunk and ineffectual dad.

She turns her face away from Marc, her protest strangled in the only stand of self-preservation she has ever known: not to be like her parents.

"I'm moving out," she hears. "We'll work out the details

later. But I'll be gone by the end of the month. I'm booked to work through the holidays. I've already told my parents that we aren't coming for the réveillon on Christmas Eve." He pauses. "You should be happy. You never liked going to my parents'."

Through the brimming water of her tears the soup tureen spreads wider. Its glimmer wobbles. She keeps her eyes open wide so the tears don't fall. She doesn't want him to see her crying. She makes no sound or gesture he could interpret as a plea. Finally he turns and lets the kitchen door swing shut behind him.

Swiftly she makes her escape to the bedroom, head lowered, tears streaming. She sits on her side of the bed, facing the wall, hands forgotten on her lap. Still as she is, she can hear Marc clearing the table. The tidy clatter of cutlery set on the plates. Like cooking, it's the sound of Marc being home. She listens with every pore of her being. She will be able to sob all she wants when the only other sound is the emptiness around her.

She grows yet more still when she hears nothing more from the dining room or the kitchen. She listens more intently. Nothing. Not the rustle of a newspaper nor the TV.

How long does she sit with her feet side by side, her hands numb, the salt dried on her cheeks? Finally she stands. Shuffles stiff and cold from the bedroom.

No light shines under the study door. The living room and kitchen are empty. The table is wiped, the salt and pepper mills returned to their places on the hutch. Only the soup tureen sits on the table, the box with the bubble wrap still on the chair next to hers.

∞

Minus thirty, maybe colder, breasting the freezing rake of the wind. Marc strides with the flaps of his sheepskin hat snapped across his mouth, the collar of his parka zipped to the highest notch. In his hurry to leave, he forgot his scarf.

He doesn't feel the cold. He's too triumphant that he finally made the break. He takes nothing back. He believes what he said. He's convinced Joelle will be happier with someone else. In fact, he *wishes* it. He doesn't want her on his conscience. Everything he said was true. Even about her parents. He knows that was cruel, but he had no choice. He can't help it if she didn't want to acknowledge the truth until he flipped it to its underside. Showed her the maggots.

He squints into the wind, his eyelashes frozen. He feels so excited, he could walk all night. Pound the Main all the way to the port, why not?

If he could only — *only* — call Ketia and tell her! He whispers, I'm free now. We can marry!

No, he thinks. He should *ask,* not tell her. He shakes his head in delighted pique with himself. No fool like a fool in love. Don't screw up now. Get down on your knees and beg for her hand.

Ice crystals — the frozen condensation of his breath inside the stiffening collar of his parka — scrape against his cheeks. He nearly starts laughing. He's going to lose his nose! Marching down the street in such exultation that he won't notice until it cracks off like a snowman's carrot!

He comes to an almost clownish stop and peers into the street-level windows of a bistro. The tables float like blond lily pads in semi-darkness. Most are empty. He trips down the stone steps and swings through the door, stooping to grab one of the weeklies from the rack.

He unzips his parka but keeps it on when he sits. His face and neck are thoroughly chilled. He can't feel his toes at all. A woman's voice, accompanied by bass strings, croons so deeply that he only now hears it.

The waitress sidles past, the band of suede around her hips either a skirt or a broad belt. On impulse he orders a double whiskey on ice. He never drinks whiskey. But here he sits, like a character in an American movie, alone in a bar at night, thinking about a woman he wishes could be with him. He's only missing a cigarette, easy in the crook of his fingers.

He opens the paper to the back pages. He needs to find a place as soon as possible, even if it's only temporary. He's not sure he can last until the end of the month with Joelle. What if she attacks him again? Or starts pleading.

Without a sound the waitress sets a heavy-bottomed glass on the coaster. He swirls the whiskey, making the ice cubes chuckle — still in that American movie — before lifting the glass to his mouth. Liquor fumes prickle his nostrils. Smooth heat flickers warmth down his throat to his stomach, en route to his blood. It's that fast. Like the sureness of his longing for Ketia.

Soon, he thinks. Soon. He tilts the pages to catch the light from the bar. The listing for an apartment that jumps out at him seems to do just that. A four and a half, clean, the second floor of a house in Outremont. He likes that it's advertised as clean. His parents will approve of the upscale address. He glances to either side. The waitress stands chatting with the sole client at the bar. Marc spreads his parka like a cape to shield him as he tears a neat corner, folds the piece of newsprint, and slips it in an inside pocket.

∞

Diane slumps low against the armrest, phone to her ear, listening to Joelle. In the other corner of the sofa Nazim reads the paper. An arctic wind batters the building. Both wear thick sweaters against the cold that seeps through the window and the poorly insulated walls.

"Is he there now?" Diane asks.

Joelle's voice sounds thick, bruised with crying. "He went out. I don't know where."

"You should come over here. Take a cab."

"...No."

"You think he might come back?"

"I don't know."

"And you're sure you weren't just having an argument. He really meant it?"

"You know Marc. He doesn't say so until he's decided."

Diane lets out a long breath. "What about discussing it with you?"

"He hated the soup tureen! He thought it was ugly."

"That's a question of taste, Joelle, not right and wrong. *You* liked it, remember?" Diane can't see what the soup tureen matters, but it irritates her that Joelle continues to defer to Marc even as he's waving sayonara.

"I don't like it anymore. I just... I don't know, I think I inherited this."

"What do you mean?"

"The way my parents were. I always thought they should have split up."

"They probably should have. But that's got nothing to do with you and Marc."

"I guess," Joelle says, but not as if she believes it.

When Diane finally hangs up, she drops her head back on the armrest. "I know I never liked Marc, but I thought he was going to *stay* with her. He's such a stick in the mud. Why did he —" She groans at the plaster angels doing their frozen dance on the ceiling. "What if she collapses the way she did when Emile left?"

Nazim lets the newspaper pages slide together in his lap. "Maybe she won't. She's older now."

"Years don't matter. Some things Joelle never learns. She says she still loves him." Diane sniffs. "If you ask me, she's well rid of him. Bon débarras."

"She's your friend, Diane."

"That doesn't mean I can't say when she's being stupid. She didn't even realize something was up. And you know Marc. For sure he had everything planned to the last detail. If she really cared about him, she wouldn't have been so clueless. She would have had some inkling. When people care about each other, they're in tune — like us."

She punches the cushion under her arm. "It doesn't even make sense that he's leaving — the way he had the furniture set up, everything matching, the accessories — even the pens by the phone, did you ever notice? The same colours as the living room. Where did he go shopping to find brown pens? He had everything *just so*. Like he planned to live there forever."

"Sometimes they're not," Nazim says.

"What, the pens don't always match?"

Nazim lifts the newspaper pages from his lap to the coffee table. "Sometimes people care about each other but they're not in tune."

"What are you talking about?"

"My sister's coming."

"Coming *here*?" Diane struggles to right herself on the sagging sofa. "But that's fantastic! I'll finally meet someone from your family. And you — you must be so excited! Your sister, that's the one you always talk about, right?" She stops. Why does he look so sad, brow furrowed, mouth glum? "What's wrong? Why aren't you happy?"

"She can't come here."

"What do you mean?"

"We aren't married."

Diane holds herself still, waiting, not believing what she's heard. Why in two years has he never mentioned that it matters that they aren't married? Or should she have guessed how old-fashioned his family was from his stories about oil lamps and donkeys?

Slowly she shakes her head. "You know I don't believe in marriage."

"We don't have to get married. But she can't meet you."

"Is this about me not being Muslim?"

"Even if you were Muslim, we aren't married. That's the problem. I can't just live with you."

"What you do mean, you can't? You are!" She kicks a cushion to the floor. "This is totally absurd! Why did you never tell me? Does your family even know I exist?"

He sighs but still she doesn't expect it when he says, "No."

"*No?* Just like that? You're telling me I've been kept a secret all this time?"

"I didn't think you'd ever meet them."

"I *told* you I wanted to go to Morocco one day."

"We can. Just not to my family. Or my village."

"And when did you intend to divulge that small detail? On the plane going over? And if we never went, I guess you *never* would have told me?" She props herself higher against the armrest, tucks her feet closer, her body a package she folds away from him as well as she can on the drooping sofa. "You live with me — you tell me you love me — but you're treating me like some stupid, naïve Westerner!"

His lips flatten in a grimace. "Well, stop acting like one."

She stares, not expecting that derisive tone.

"You know I'm Moroccan and that my family is Muslim." He makes a full stop as if waiting for her to catch up. "I left home nine years ago. I live here now — with you. And yes, I love you." He sounds more angry than loving. "But I haven't forgotten my family and what they believe." Full stop again. "If they knew we weren't married and living together, I would be dead to them."

"Oh!" Diane nods, derisive in turn. "So you think this is better. You pretend *I* don't exist. Between you and me, you decided *I* should be the dead one."

"You have more experience of the world than they do. I assumed you would understand."

"No." Diane jabs a finger at the space between them. "You never assumed I would understand because you never told me."

"I'm telling you now."

"Telling me now," she says under her breath. And louder, "How about telling your sister not to come? Tell her it's not convenient. Save her the bother of having to plan your funeral."

"She's been putting the money aside for years. This will be the biggest adventure she's ever had." His jaw determined. His mouth stubborn.

Diane has never heard him like this. "And what am I supposed to do, stuff myself into a magician's hat? Bye-bye, Diane?"

He rubs a hand along the top of his thigh, says nothing.

Diane exhales forcefully. She *knows* she's right. He should have told his family about her. Whatever they believe, it's a fact that she and Nazim live together — and love each other. Though she's suddenly less sure of that.

"When is this fiasco even supposed to happen?"

"In January."

"January? She's coming for polar bear weather?"

"She didn't ask me when to come. She decided on her own."

"Well, that part must be true. You hate winter."

"It's all true," he says stiffly.

"So if she can't come here, where do you propose she'll stay?"

"Abdullah said I can live at his place. She can stay with me there."

Diane thrusts her head forward, ever more incredulous. "You're planning to move out?"

"Just while she's here."

"I thought you told me he only has a room — over a falafel shop."

"He has two."

"Oh, *two*. Well, that's practically a palace."

"In Morocco two rooms for a single man would be luxury."

"But you're not in Morocco, you're here. Isn't your sister going to expect more — like why did you come to Canada if you can't do better than Morocco?"

He pinches the crease of denim on his leg, tries to smooth it flat, though it won't with his leg bent.

She doesn't like the idea of him moving to Abdullah's with his sister. She knocks another cushion to the floor, revealing ever more of the sofa's worn upholstery and jutting frame. "I don't know, Nazim. This isn't what I expected. I thought we were..." She scowls, remembering how moments ago she said they were *in tune.*

She waits to hear if he'll say more. That he's sorry. That he regrets not having told his family about her. That he wishes his family weren't so narrow-minded.

When he still says nothing, she unfolds her legs. "I think this whole thing is crazy. I wish you'd told me before." She slides off the sofa. "I'm taking a bath."

∞

Phone to her ear, Ketia winds the cord around her finger. Lou must be on the other line or away from her desk. Ketia bends her finger, encased in coils, remembering the childhood game of pretending it was a jointed caterpillar.

"Seven Surgery."

"It's Ketia."

"You'll have to speak up, Madame."

"It's Ketia."

"Ketia, are you all right?"

Her lips feel numb. "I'm calling in sick for this evening."

"You should talk to Pascale."

Ketia didn't know she had to speak with the head nurse. She's never called in sick before. "I think I've got the flu," she says weakly.

"Talk to her," Lou urges.

Ketia hears a click and the phone begins ringing again.

"Pascale Cloutier."

"It's Ketia." Her voice trembles. "I can't come in this evening. I think I've got the flu."

"Don't worry about this evening. Ghislaine already spoke

to me. Lou and Carlene, too. I hope this hasn't been going on since you started here."

Ketia stands very still, says nothing.

"You should have come to me immediately. I'm so sorry this happened, but I've never had a complaint about Marc before. I'm particularly bothered because he oriented several new nurses who transferred off the floor. Maybe there were other incidents that weren't brought to my attention. I need you to help me now — to make a formal complaint."

"...I can't," Ketia whispers.

"The hospital will protect you. You don't need to worry."

"I don't... I never said anything."

"Silence is no solution, Ketia. You have to think of other young nurses. I can't have someone like Marc harassing them. It helps that there were witnesses, but I still need you to make a complaint. Think about it, Ketia."

Her mouth stays closed.

"You rest this evening and I hope you'll call me tomorrow."

Ketia replaces the phone slowly and perches on the sofa. She was so impressed that first night that Marc had made all the arrangements for the hotel room. He knew exactly how to skirt past the desk clerk without drawing attention. The bottle of wine and the glasses next to the bed. The sureness of his hands on her body. The grapes he slid from his mouth to hers.

Even while it was happening, and she knew it shouldn't, she always thought it was for her alone. She has no defense against Pascale's words. *Other incidents.* His wife, okay. Ketia knew about his wife. But were there other women, too?

Other young nurses. The words reverberate as if her bones were hollow. Her solitude colder.

∞

A galley kitchen with veneer cupboards and beige Arborite. Marc's hands hang, thinking of his custom-designed kitchen with black granite counters.

The landlady nudges his arm. "C'est très propre, regardez!" She is short, her fluffy, mousy hair barely at his shoulder. She has talked non-stop since hearing that he's a nurse. She tells him that they usually only rent to women, but she expects that a nurse will be quiet and neat. Marc is older, too. More settled. Again she nudges his arm. The problem with young people is that they don't always pay the rent on time.

The apartment is small but bright. A pretty triptych window in the bedroom faces the yard behind the house. The living room is more the size of a sitting room. But the rooms are all separate, and, except for the kitchen, have doors. Marc doesn't like the open studio concept. He's not an animal who sleeps in one corner and eats in another.

But how will he reconcile himself to such a cramped kitchen? He steps forward, touching a finger to the iron grid of rounds that tops the small stove.

"Mais oui," the landlady says. "Gas is so much nicer for cooking."

All the other places Marc visited had electric stoves, one or two spattered with caked filth. This stove is as spotless as the rest of the apartment. He'll still clean before he moves in.

"Is the gas included in the rent?"

"All the utilities," she assures him.

He likes the Outremont address, which carries that aura of grey stone houses, fine cars, and wealth. "Is this the furniture?" He gestures at the small sectional sofa. Not his favourite style, but he supposes he can live with it for however long it will take to make arrangements with Joelle.

"Do you have your own?"

"Not at the moment."

She peers up at him with curious rodent eyes.

"Why are there clothes in the closet?"

"Chantale." She beams as if everyone knows Chantale. "She went home to Shawinigan for two weeks. She'll be back after

Christmas and then she'll finish moving out. She's being transferred to Ottawa." The landlady prods his arm to underline how impressed he should be.

He twitches it away. "Why didn't she move out all at once?"

"A few days, Monsieur. Only a few days. She was so good to us, Chantale."

A few days will drag out like a sentence living with Joelle. He wants to begin his new life with Ketia. Yesterday he got boxes from the SAQ and packed his old nursing textbooks and clothes. He has to be careful with items Joelle might argue belong to her, too. The kitchen is complicated because everything was his, but he obviously can't leave her with empty cupboards. Nor does he wish to discuss which dishes and pots she wants.

The landlady trails behind him as he does another slow circuit. Now and then she murmurs a word or two, pointing out the crown moulding, the Lazy Susan in the bathroom cupboard. "And here, look, Monsieur, how large the closet is."

He ends in the bedroom with its triptych window. The rent is at the upper limit of his budget, but he won't have to pay for utilities. Presumably Ketia will be able to help out, too. They won't be going out much. They will be too happy with the luxury of life together. He will cook for her better than in any restaurant.

The grandfather tree in the backyard must shade the bedroom and keep it cool in the summer. Now, in the winter, it thrusts aged arms at the sky. Ketia once told him how she loved big old trees. He imagines her nestled in an armchair, gazing out upon the tree. The rustle of its greenery. A glass of wine at hand. Just the two of them.

∞

Joelle has no memory of the day at work. She got out of bed when the alarm beeped. She showered. She opened the closet and pulled on the first blouse her hand touched, then the tweed slacks she normally wore with it.

Here she is again in front of the bathroom mirror. Maybe she never left.

She skims her reflection from the outline of her hair to her blouse to her arms. She can't seem to see herself all at once. She unbuttons her blouse, turns to drop it in the hamper, remembers that it needs to be dry-cleaned. Stands with it loosely bunched in her fist. The wicker hamper isn't even half full partway through the week. Only her things. Marc moved all his belongings from the bedroom to the study — apparently his laundry, too. He doesn't even want their dirty socks to touch.

She drops her blouse in the hamper. Reaches to unhook her earrings but she isn't wearing any. She stands with her hands on the edge of the sink, waiting for the water to run warm, the drift of her gaze stopped by her bra in the mirror. Beige with lace netting. Underwire cups. Who cares? She doesn't believe what Marc said about meeting someone else. Why would someone else want her if Marc doesn't?

The splash of the water recalls her. She reaches for the oatmeal soap and bends forward, but her hair falls around her face. She rinses her hands, dries them, and reaches for the soap again. No. She turns the water off and opens the drawer for an elasticized band, sees her barrettes and clips, can't remember what she wanted, closes the drawer. She unzips her slacks, peels off her pantyhose.

The kimono feels too watery and silky on her bare arms and backs. She fumbles for the ends of the belt, but the fabric is slippery, her movements disjointed, swiping uselessly at her hips. In the mirror she sees Marc's towel on the rack behind her. She wonders if it's damp. If he showered before going to work or the gym. Wherever he is now. Her hand opens but she still faces the mirror. She can't bring herself to turn around and actually touch the towel.

She's ready for bed, though she's only just come home. She

hasn't eaten but she's not hungry. She'll watch TV and have a glass of wine. Wine: the best at-home anaesthetic.

But she's still in the bathroom. Herself and the mirror. Herself and no one. The doorknob casts a jug-headed shadow on the floor. A portent. A bludgeon. A fleeting memory of a closed white door with shouting on the other side. Cowering in her bed when a body thumped against the door. Her mother or her dad. Both matched in anger if not size.

She forces herself to step past the shadow of the knob into the hallway. Leaves the light on. The door to the study is closed. No trespassing. She wishes she could open it and at least turn on the light. She can't if Marc closed it.

She forbids herself to cry. Cry for whom? Not you. Who are you.

All the lights blaze — in the living room, over the dining table, in the kitchen. She turns the TV on loud. Sitcoms, detectives, a Eurotrash movie. The program doesn't matter as long as it's not the news. Let the end of the millennium tear the face off the world as people know it. She'll still be alone.

The wineglass makes an echoing tock on the granite counter. A tiny but distinct sound of reproach. The kitchen has always been a hostile place — Marc's domain. She concentrates on the blare of theme music from the TV. There's barely a glass of wine left from yesterday. She didn't put another white in the fridge. Marc has a few expensive bottles of red stored in the laundry room for special occasions.

Such as when? When he invites a new woman for supper? Joelle stoops to the rack and grabs the neck of a bottle. *Château Margaux, Haut-Médoc, 1990*. In 1990 they'd been married for three years. She thought Marc was her saviour. He'd freed her from her parents. From men like Emile.

She pours her glass of white wine down the sink, rinses it, and takes the bloody *Château Margaux* through to the dining room where they keep the corkscrew in the hutch. The kitchen door swings shut behind her.

Ketia called in sick yesterday. Marc tried to call her at home, but each time someone else answered. He hung up on the deep voice — her mother's, he guessed. The boy, too, because before Marc even said a word, he heard him. "Allô?... Maman, c'est lui encore, le monsieur qui raccroche." How did the boy know he was a man? How often had he called?

This morning he flipped through the phone book to match her phone number against the long list of Dauphins to find her address. All he wants is to make sure she's all right. A flu, okay, but he's starting to worry about stories he's heard about arranged marriages and how the women have no choice. Why did Ketia make him promise not to call her at home? He imagines her walking down the street, leaning on a younger man's arm. A match her mother found.

Because she still lives at home, he assumes that she lives in a house. He doesn't know anyone who didn't grow up in a house, and doesn't expect the row of 1950s apartment blocks, built in postwar haste for burgeoning, low-income families. He's never been in this part of the city. He's surprised but then gratified by the shabbiness from which he will rescue her. He parks close enough to have a clear view of the front door. A cheap metal frame that's not even locked. Maybe she'll look from a window and recognize his car. Which window, though? A group of black girls crowd out the door, elbowing each other, screeching, laughing. Ketia would never behave like that. Still, he tries to spy her yellow scarf.

An hour passes. The minutes on his car clock advance. A small visual blip — a line, a corner. Almost no change at all. Yet it's all time lost. He curls his hands around the bottom of the steering wheel, grips it. He keeps the engine running to warm the car, then notices that people slow as they walk past. Dart a suspicious once-over. Not everyone is black, but no one is as white as he is. He takes the maintenance manual from the glove compartment and pretends to read it, so they think he's having car trouble. When his stomach won't stop growling, he finally drives away.

Patience, he tells himself. In a couple of hours he'll see her at work. He'll get her alone — in the back stairwell, in the storeroom — and tell her about the new place. Or perhaps he'll just tell her he's leaving his wife — and *hint* that he's looking for a new place. Then, in a few days, once he's moved and has a cassoulet baking, the air fragrant with duck and thyme, garlic and bay leaves, a bottle of Cabernet breathing on the table, he'll lead her up the stairs. Voilà — our new life!

∞

Frank stands reading a CT report. Behind him he hears Joelle on the phone. "We're booked up until March." The words don't seem to fit in her mouth. "March," she repeats.

Yesterday she stood before the filing cabinet with a chart in hand, not moving. When the phone rang, she didn't take it. Frank asked if she felt all right. She looked at him with her slightly protruding eyes that used to make him wonder if she was hyperthyroid. She said she was just... but she didn't say what she was. Today the collar of her blouse doesn't lie right. And her lipstick is smeared.

A couple of times lately, when he's been up on the floor to see patients, Lou has made comments about Marc. That he's behaving like a randy old lech. That *she* wouldn't be happy if she was his wife. Frank never responded because how and why should his secretary's husband concern him? But after that scene in the hallway, Frank sees what Lou means. How awful for Joelle. The poor girl deserves better. She so admires him, too. He's heard how she tells patients, who are booked for surgery, that they might get her husband as a nurse.

Joelle sighs as she puts down the phone, a great, sad sound, and in spite of himself — because he'd really sooner not get involved — he says, "Joelle?"

She seems to wonder how and when he got there, though she handed him the CT report.

"Can I...?" Can he what? He's not even sure. "Why don't you come into my office."

Obedient, she stands. Doesn't react when she bumps into the corner of her desk. He leads the way, stepping aside for her to precede him through the door. The office is large and messy with ceiling-high bookshelves stacked with texts and journals, his desk strewn with reports and Joelle's memo-pad reminders. On the computer an image of a double helix bounces from side to bottom to top, trying to escape the screen.

"Sit." He motions at a leather chair, only then seeing that it's heaped with journals. He shovels his hands under the jumbled pile and lowers it to the floor. There are other piles, sprouted like dishevelled paper mushrooms, against the base of the bookshelves. She drops more than sits, the toes of her high heels pointing inwards like a child's.

He swivels his desk chair toward her. Doesn't know where to start, though, or even what to say. She's always so poised and neatly dressed. Haven't the other secretaries noticed? What about her family and friends? She doesn't seem like herself at all. Hands drooped in her lap, stranded in the chair across from him.

In the silence, glancing at her and away again, he's reached for the bundle of file cards he keeps in the breast pocket of his lab coat. Each represents an inpatient he's currently treating or been asked to consult: the patient's addressograph stamp, diagnosis, planned intervention, pathology results. He slips off the elastic, starts to read the top card, realizes what he's doing. Puts the elastic back and returns the bundle to his pocket.

"Joelle... what's going on?"

Slowly she asks, "Did I make a mistake?" She doesn't even sound surprised. A week ago she would have been mortified.

"No, I mean... I mean with you."

She doesn't move or make a sound, and at first he doesn't notice the tears leaking from the corners of her eyes.

"I don't have any —" He looks around, though he knows he has no tissue in his office.

Softly she says, "Marc's leaving me."

So she knows. "Yes," he nods, "I'm sorry."

Her mouth opens. "You already knew?"

"Well, I could tell you were having a hard time. I didn't know…" He touches the knot on his tie. "I didn't know he was leaving you. I didn't know that."

"Then… what do you know?"

He sits back in his chair, elbows firm on the armrests. "You know, I don't pay attention to gossip."

"Gossip," she echoes.

"I actually only saw them together once."

Her eyes close, but tears still seep out.

Embarrassed, he turns his head to his desk. *Journal of Colorectal Disease*. The tray of letters Joelle left for him to read. The framed photo of his wife and daughters. Marie wears the yellow dress she bought in Florence. Hanna imps with a grin and Zoë tilts her head as she laughs. He can't imagine losing Marie — and doesn't believe he ever will. She's there every evening, no matter how late he finally pulls in the drive. Sometimes she's still cleaning the kitchen or doing the laundry and if he wants to talk to her, he has to eat from his plate leaning against the laundry room doorway while she folds heaps of little T-shirts, skirts, and panties, his boxers and socks. If the girls aren't in bed yet, he plays a game of chess with Hanna, trying to teach her strategy. Or he talks to Zoë about a butterfly she saw — she calls them flutterbyes — as she fits multi-coloured blocks into a cube. The girls, yes. Joelle and Marc don't have that bond. Of course, that makes a difference.

He peeks at Joelle again. Her eyes swollen, cheeks sticky. "Maybe you should take a few days off."

"No," she croaks. "I've got work."

He stands to help because she's struggling with the chair. "Do you want me to —"

But she bats away his outstretched hand, stumbles to the hallway, slams and locks the bathroom door.

∞

Joelle ignored the discreet knock a few moments ago. The clack of heels receding. Now someone knocks more loudly. "Il y a quelqu'un?" Venita's puffed-up voice. As if the staff toilet were a boardroom where she needs to hold a meeting.

Joelle squats on her heels with her back against the wall. There's a restroom for patients just a few doors away. Venita doesn't have to pee in her panties unless she wants to. The idea of Venita squirming her plump bottom and thighs to hold her bladder makes Joelle snicker. The crack opening in her face feels stiff — like something she used to know how to do.

She's comfortable here on the floor, level with the toilet, her back flat against the tiles that are smooth, hard, and cool. Good squatting heels, too. Just the right height.

She can't remember how she got here. Frank was talking... yes. He said he only saw them once. Men never realize that *once* isn't the word that hurts. Once simply happens to be the time you see them. Once always accordions out into more. The time she came home and Emile had Francesca propped, ass-wide, in their bed. Even when Emile shouted at Joelle's crying and swore that it was *just that once,* and even though she stuffed the sheets and pillows down the garbage chute, how could she know Emile didn't do it again? If not with Francesca, then someone else. She didn't catch him again, but she didn't have to. Men never stopped. Marc, too. She glances at the toilet. Remembers now that she threw up. Her mouth tastes sour.

There are more voices in the hallway. Knocks and calls. Joelle can see shadows moving under the line of the door. A bobbing crowd. Every secretary on the floor suddenly needs to pee. Why don't they goddamn *go* to the other restroom and leave her alone?

Then the lock clicks and the door opens. A security man with a ring of keys talking to someone in the hallway until he turns his head and sees her. "Oh boy. T'as une problème icitte."

Arms pull and help her. Muscular hands, shiny fingernails, the pudginess of a midriff clasping her close, a harness of bodies holding her up. They walk her to a room that looks familiar. Those filing cabinets with the black alphabet letters. The vivid posters on the walls. Slimy tunnels of innards.

Someone says to call her husband. What floor does he work on, Surgery Six or Seven?

"No!" she cries, pulling against their arms, her hair that's come undone swinging around her face. "Not him, no! Don't call him — *no!*"

∞

Gritty bits of snow whirl from the sky around the boles of the trees. Only a few stalwart dog owners have come out to walk on the mountain. Diane has wrapped her shawl high around her cheeks and mouth, tramping up the path to the top.

Nazim went directly to Abdullah's after work to help him paint his place. Diane didn't offer to go over. She's not even sure she'd be welcome.

Yesterday they argued because she said she didn't believe he'd only just found out about his sister's visit. There were too many plans in place already. Abdullah with his two falafel-stinky rooms. Hatem's wife sending Nazim home with her old winter coat for his sister.

Diane kicks through the snow. Bad enough that he never told his family about her. Bad enough that he never told *her* that he'd never told them — because that would have been some solace, being party to the dreaded secret that he's living in sin. Now she realizes she must be the last person to hear about his sister's visit, too. Hatem, Abdullah, everyone else seems to know!

Hands tucked in her pockets, she leans against the stone balustrade that encircles the lookout. The grey buildings of the city below are shrouded in blowing snow. The bridges that cross the St. Lawrence, connecting the island of Montreal to the rest of the world, head off into the obscurity of an early dusk.

Diane wiggles her chin free of her shawl, lifts it to the wind, shakes her head. She doesn't agree with this farce. Nazim lives here now. And if his family doesn't understand that his life has changed, well, they should.

∞

Joelle waits on the mat holding the key. Inside it will be dark. The air so empty it drones. If she had anywhere else to go, she would.

She unlocks the door and pushes it wide so she can see the hallway. Sneaks her hand inside along the wall to flick on the light. Walks from room to room turning on all the lights. Except the closed study door.

She knows now it means more than the end of their marriage. Maybe Marc brought *her* here. And did he... would he...

He would have shunned the bedroom. Marc always had clear and exact margins of privacy.

But what about the other rooms they still share? She eyes the sink in the bathroom for signs that the other woman washed her hands — with Joelle's soap. After sex with Marc. Her lips pull back with disgust. She shivers. Though, of course, the bathroom is spotless. Marc would clean up, wouldn't he? Align the edges of the towels, straighten the chairs at the table, brush the sofa, plump the cushions. All of Marc's tidy habits suddenly strike her as sinister. Not being neat, but hiding evidence. The creep.

Since Marc told her he was leaving, she no longer eats at home. She stops at a new Italian bistro on Querbes, the kind of place she once would have told Marc they should try. *Chorizo and red pepper penne. Mushroom tetrazzini.* She has no appetite but eats because the waiter will only clear away her plate once she's finished. She eats slowly, mechanically, delaying the moment when she has to go home.

Frank wrote her a prescription for Diazepam. Tiny white pills. Frank said if she felt really bad, she could take two. She does. They make her feel slowed down, gelled in her body, but the effect helps anchor her thoughts. Keeps them from straying and twisting with anxiety. She doesn't want to think about the blasted future. Nor the broken past.

If she remembers, she rents a movie. She no longer looks for directors or actors. She will take anything — Korean, Canadian, Italian, Swedish — if it's about a relationship breaking up. Even a generic Hollywood movie holds some detail she should have noticed about Marc.

A glass of wine, too, helps dull the evening alone on the sofa she and Marc spent a month's worth of weekends to find. Furniture store after furniture store before he was satisfied that he'd finally chosen the perfect sofa. Much good a perfect sofa did them. The asshole.

On the other side of the divider stand the table and chairs. An orderly rectangle. The salt and pepper mills side by side on the hutch. Whenever she cleared the table and put them away, Marc always moved them again. She could never get it right.

Why, she wonders now, did she even try? Emile was right. She should have aimed higher. Not settled for such a prig who measured out his smiles. All his silly rules about setting the pens next to the phone top side up. Draping scarves on the coat stand so the ends hung evenly. Every inane, little detail, and still he was leaving her.

The first year they lived here she bought a pottery dish to

decorate the wall divider. Marc said it was only a question of time before she knocked it to the floor. She hadn't, but he continued to predict that she would until a few weeks later she finally removed it.

And put it where? She tries to remember. Marc probably made her give it away.

∞

Marc runs lightly, rapidly down the stairs, one hand holding the head of his stethoscope flat against his chest so it won't bounce. Ketia called in sick again today — so he *still* hasn't told her. All these changes in his life and she still doesn't know!

He has to tell someone. The one person he knows he can find is Joelle. It will be easier to tell her here, at work, that he's found a place than at home where she'll be more likely to start crying. And in fact, now that he's walking down the hallway to her office, he realizes this is the best way. Perhaps, too, she deserves to hear before Ketia.

She stands by the fax machine on the counter beside her desk. Anyone else would begin another task and let the tray collect the paper, but Joelle waits for the paper to spit out. His lips tighten with disdain. She's as step-by-step plodding in her work as at home.

Pages in hand, she turns and sees him. Her cheeks suffuse slowly. She gropes for her chair.

"I wanted to tell you." He sits two chairs away, both feet flat on the floor, ready to leave as soon as he's spoken. "I've found a place."

Her pale, moonish eyes. So unlike Ketia's grave, listening expression that the two women might not even be the same kind of creature.

"I've found an apartment, so I'll be moving out next week. It's not available until then."

She looks at the pages in her hand. She makes no sign that

she's understood. He shifts in the chair, his impatience with Joelle never far from the surface.

"It's in Outremont," he says, as if that fact will impress her. "Small but very nice." He feels like he's talking in an empty room and raises his voice. "I appreciate your understanding. As I said, I think this will be better for the both of us even if it feels like an upheaval now."

"Is she moving in with you?"

Marc is confused. Who she? Who what? Then he knows. But who could have told Joelle? He and Ketia were always so careful.

"Is she?" Louder and clearer, a mean slice of syllables.

"She?" he repeats, hearing how weak it sounds. But he's always controlled the emotional muscle of their relationship, and he only falters for an instant. "That I met someone else only confirms what I said. We haven't been happy together for a long time. You'll meet someone else, too — someone who will make you happier than you were with me."

The grip of her fingers crease the pages she still holds. "You didn't answer. I asked if you're moving out of our place to move in with her."

Marc can't say yes until he's spoken with Ketia. He doesn't want to jinx himself. Since when has he become superstitious? But he also doesn't want to deny it. Nor can he bring himself to admit that he doesn't know. He brushes the leg pocket of his khaki scrubs where he keeps a pen holder with pens and nursing scissors. "I'm not going to discuss this with you. She's not your business."

"Really?" Joelle's voice rises. "Well, you listen. She *made* herself my business when she started fucking my husband."

His eyes widen in shock. "It wasn't like that!"

Joelle sneers. He's never seen her make such a face. "All right then, you fucked *her*. It doesn't really matter who fucked who at this stage, does it?"

"Joelle!"

"That's right, I forgot. You don't fuck, do you? You *make love*."

He jumps to his feet. She's crazy — she attacked him once in bed already! An irrational wacko who might stab him in his sleep in revenge. He whirls around and at the door nearly collides with Frank.

Frank doesn't answer his hello but looks past him. "Joelle, are you all right?"

Marc escapes down the hallway. When he hears the fast tap of his shoes on the tiles he slows. He's not running. He's perfectly within his rights. Divorce is rampant, for God's sake. It's not a crime.

He's furious with Joelle for having twisted the situation around so that he looks like a villain — here, where he works! He gives his arm an angry shake, settling his watchband on his wrist. Shakes it again. Joelle had no right to tell Frank. No right at all.

∞

The winter sunlight on the kitchen window is so thin the glass flattens it. Ketia sits at the table with a cup of strong black tea. Ma has just left for the West Indian store to buy plantain, gombos, piman bouk, cabri. Ketia usually drives her but she said she still felt ill.

She called in sick again yesterday to avoid Marc. Pascale's *other incidents* wither the last longing her body still felt for him. She's terrified of seeing him. Doesn't want him close. Though she wishes she could have gone to work, where she's so busy she can't think. At home she huddles in bed, her only distraction the afternoon soaps. The stylized agony of the characters, each hair in place, their make-up smooth. The sequence of commercials with their facile necessities. Laundry stains vanquished. Despondent husbands brought to life with a slice of pizza.

She feels guilty that she sent Ma to travel across town by

bus, having to wait with her bags on the sidewalk in the cold. But she's too afraid to be alone in the car with Ma. Afraid of Ma's friends, too. They might guess what Ma, in her complacence that Ketia is a good girl, doesn't. She's afraid even of the sounds and smells of the store. The memory of herself when she was young, waiting in the shadows among the crates of mangoes for Ma to pull herself away from the never-ending conspiracy of stories in Bajan, Creole, and Guyanese. The odd voice twanged with Cockney or rounded with school-taught French vowels. In the cellar-like gloom roots jabbed hairy arms from open boxes along the concrete floor. Bottles and jars of coconut oil and burnt sugar lined the dimly lit shelves. The butcher flirted insolently from behind his mounds of fat-yellow poultry, a goat's head, hanks of beef. The women teased him back. Vociferous laughter undercut with innuendo.

Soon Ma will be the butt of all the gossip in the store — Ma who was so proud of Ketia when she became a nurse. Too proud, maybe. Ma never said much, not one to push herself forward, but her friends knew she thought Ketia was better than their daughters. Of course, they'll gloat telling the tale of Ketia's shame. Suck their teeth with righteous censure.

The other night, past midnight, when Ketia was driving home along the highway, she thought how easily she could solve everything if she drove full speed into a pole. She gripped the wheel hard when she realized she'd started counting the poles as they flashed past — as if her mind had already set a goal.

From the hallway she hears the lazy swish of slippers. Gabrielle could have gone to the store with Ma. But Ma never asks her, because Gabrielle will sulk and embarrass her.

Gabrielle pours a glass of milk and plops herself, one leg folded under, across from Ketia. Her fleece robe hangs open on blue stretchy pyjamas. "Let me guess. You're sitting there wondering what to get me for Christmas, aren't you, dear favourite sister? Well, don't break your head. I'll give you some clues."

Ketia has hardly thought about Christmas, except to be

glad that Pa won't be home. She's not sure if she'll be showing yet when he comes at the end of January. Suddenly her tongue feels thick and dry. She sips her tea.

"I could use a new sweater. You know that tight style?" Gabrielle runs her hands down her torso. "Hey, what's up with you? You don't drink tea black."

Ketia is punishing herself with bitter tea. It's no longer even warm.

Gabrielle leans back in her chair, away from Ketia. "Are you still sick? Don't give it to me. I've got a New Year's party I am *not* missing."

Ketia closes her eyes against the memory of her stupid self, who dreamed of spending New Year's Eve in bed with Marc.

"It's actually a very private party. Just me and Laurent. His parents won't be home and he's —"

Ketia lunges forward to grab at her sister's hand. "You can't!"

Gabrielle snatches it away in time. "You can't tell me what to do. I'm nineteen, you know."

"But you'll get into trouble," Ketia hisses.

"No, I won't, I'm not *dumb*. And anyhow, Laurent's parents know and they don't mind. Not everyone's uptight like Ma — like we're living in some tiny village where people cluck about a girl's reputation. Wake up, honey. We're in Montreal, 1999. Eve of the millennium."

"No," Ketia breathes. "You don't know what will happen."

Gabrielle peers at her, still keeping her distance. "What's wrong with you?"

Ketia bites her teeth hard. Not saying. Not telling anyone. Except that she has to warn Gabrielle — before it's too late for Gabrielle like it's already too late for her. Beware devil men with their words that snake down your body. Beware how your body will open —

Ketia staggers off her chair as her stomach convulses. She hasn't eaten and vomits only tea and bile into the sink. She stands, head bowed, leaning on her elbows, then turns on the tap, rinses her mouth, and reaches under the sink for cleanser.

Gabrielle says, "Let me." She makes a moue of distaste but eases the cleanser from Ketia's hand. "Go to bed. You're sick, I told you."

Ketia creeps down the hallway. If only the bed would swallow her.

She curls on her side, the comforter tucked high around her neck. Gabrielle comes and sits on the bed by Ketia's knees. "Maybe you should see a doctor."

"I'm not sick," Ketia mumbles.

"Listen, I know I'm not a nurse, but *I* think you are. I just cleaned it up."

The desire to confess — to rid herself and to warn Gabrielle — surges and threatens to break. Ketia presses her mouth into the pillow. She can't, she thinks. She can't, she can't.

"You're not having your period, are you? Oh *man,* I hope I don't have mine at New Year's. I've got plans for some quality nooky."

Ketia frees her mouth enough to ask, "How far do you go with your boyfriend?"

Gabrielle sniffs. "None of your business." Archly she adds, "Obviously more than hold hands."

Ketia turns her head. "But do you... do you go all the way?"

"Hey. Just because Ma's not home doesn't mean you have to stand in."

"Ma would never ask that. She doesn't think we'd ever..."

Gabrielle leans closer. She heard Ketia say we.

"Because..." Ketia twists her neck free of the comforter and the sheets.

"Because...?"

"Because you might think you won't, but then... it only takes one time," Ketia whispers. "One time that he doesn't have a condom and... and... and you want to and you can't even stop. Not for anything." Tears slide from her eyes to her temples.

Gabrielle sits very still. "Ketia, what's going on?"

"I'm pregnant." The word escapes — a last susurration — the taut balloon of her pride already deflated.

Gabrielle's body tilts away and her hands slap her cheeks with a gesture that belongs to a much older woman. "Oh *God*. What will Ma do?"

The knot of Ketia's limbs relax. It's such a relief that someone else finally knows — and understands the worst of it. What will Ma do.

"Who was it? Who?"

Ketia's lips close. Everyone will eventually know about the baby, but she will never again say Marc's name out loud.

"You know who it is, don't you? Or was it a one-night stand?"

She's hurt by the question. "Not a one-night stand."

"But if it wasn't a one-night stand and you —"

Ketia moves her head on the pillow.

"You don't want him to know." Gabrielle waits. "He's out of the picture?" She wants to be sure she understands. "Like... he never happened?"

"Yes."

"Okay." Gabrielle nods. "Okay. So what are we going to do?"

Nothing has been solved — nor can be solved — but in that instant Ketia knows that for the rest of her life she will be grateful to Gabrielle for saying *we*.

∽

Diane knuckles her hands on her hips. A box sits open on the kitchen table.

The glass candleholders, they can go. She wraps them in newspaper and tucks them in the box. A clay figurine with pendulous breasts. The painted papier-mâché bowl from Ecuador.

She still needs her apron to cook. For that matter, Nazim uses it, too. Though he probably wouldn't have an orange flowered apron with a bib. They'll have to get a new one, something manly. PAPA FAIT LE BBQ. Or do men who live alone wear aprons at all?

The philodendron with its curling branches doesn't look like a man's plant, but she can hardly bundle it away.

And what about all the platters and dishes? She purses her mouth. The kitchen is too complicated.

She carries the almost-empty box to the living room. She can't pack her books because what will she put in their place? The books will have to belong to the woman from whom Nazim rents the apartment. Diane wraps the raku jug but leaves the shallow bowl where he keeps tiny anise candies. She won't pack the crossword magazines on the coffee table until the last minute. She leaves the clock. Men look at the time. Or at least they should.

Now that she's started to pack, she's determined. Nazim will object, but she's not giving him a choice. She doesn't like the whole business with his family and his sister, but she especially doesn't like him moving out. So keep him here. His sister won't know that she's staying in a home where the rightful *mistress* is missing, but Nazim will. His friends will, too. Let them remember that while they're drinking their filigreed glasses of mint tea.

The key turns in the lock as she's wrapping the framed portrait of her grandma in newsprint.

Nazim worms his feet into his babouches. "What are you packing?"

"Me."

He shakes his head as if he didn't hear right. He pulls off his toque and she winces. He got a haircut on the way home.

"A bit short," she says. His pincushion earlobes stick out even more.

From the hallway he calls, "I'm making tea. Do you want some?"

"Yes." Diane considers the sofa piled with embroidered and patchwork cushions — a woman's idea of comfort. But without the cushions for padding it's impossible to sit on it.

Nazim returns with two mugs and drops into his corner of the sofa. "Getting rid of some stuff?"

"Temporarily." She takes up her mug, still standing by the bookcase.

"Why?"

"Joelle called. Marc's moving out. When he does, I'll move in with her for a while."

Nazim doesn't stop blowing across his hot tea, though he furrows his brow, not understanding.

"That will solve two problems."

"Two?"

"I can keep Joelle company. And I disappear from your life. You can bring your sister here."

"Oh." An explosive sound like *no*. "I don't think that will —"

"Why not? You never had a problem living here. Why do you think your sister will?"

"I don't want you leaving your home because of my sister."

Diane swings her hand through the air. "Leave my home? Pretend I don't exist? It's all the same once you get used to it. Anyhow, you're not listening. I'm worried about Joelle."

Nazim sets his mug hard on the coffee table.

"Come on," she says. "It's a lot nicer here than Abdullah's."

"But all your stuff. Even if you pack everything, the furniture is all wrong. The way it's set up. She'll know I don't live here by myself."

"You can tell her you rent the place furnished. From some woman who's gone on a trip. Yeah... why am I packing any of this? I'll leave it all. I'll just take my clothes."

"No, Diane, it's not right. I don't want you to —"

"To keep Joelle company when her asshole husband dumped her? Don't be so selfish." She steps around the coffee table and drops onto the sofa. They're both in the trough now. "You'll see, it will work. It might even be fun. We can meet on the sly. If I'm going to be branded as the whore of Babylon, I might as well get the perks."

"The whore of…?"

"It's from the Bible. The *other* religion."

Nazim shakes his head, but she's not giving him a choice.

∞

Ketia sits in bed with the afghan tented over her knees and her nursing binder open. She told Ma she had to study for a procedure, for which she is already certified, but Ma doesn't know that. It's only a small lie, a tiny buzz of words — nothing compared to the grotesque falsehood her whole life has become.

Today she worked days and left early before Marc came — but working days means that she's home in the evening. She sat on the sofa, facing the TV, hands gripped in her lap, with Ma in the armchair beside her. Then Bastien tumbled onto the sofa, restless with his angular shoulders and little-boy questions. Ketia mumbled an excuse about studying and fled to her room.

The wind blows hard. Even with the electric heater turned up, the bedroom is cool. Ketia wears a fleece over a sweater over a turtleneck. When her bedroom door opens, she frowns in concentration at the page in her binder.

"Hey." Gabrielle tosses her knapsack on her bed. "How are you?"

Ketia shrugs, helpless before the question.

Gabrielle grabs a bulky, red sweater off the shelf in the closet and pulls it over her arms, careful to spread the neckline wide not to disturb her hair. Ketia envies her slender waist. Even though the mirror shows nothing yet, Ketia has already begun to feel misshapen. Off-balance.

Gabrielle lets the thick wool drop down her torso to her thighs. She makes a face, plucking here and there at the thick, sloppy knit.

"I put some feelers out," she says. "Made a few calls." She sits at the bottom of Ketia's bed, one leg tucked under, the other dangling off the edge. "A couple of people wanted to refer me to a clinic in a hospital, so I'm wondering, since you work in one...?" She peers sidelong at Ketia. "Did you ask anyone where you work? Or is that a problem because you work there?"

"Ask?" Ketia doesn't follow.

"A doctor."

Ketia huddles against her pillow. "I'll have to go to one eventually, but no, I haven't—"

"Not eventually," Gabrielle interrupts. "It has to be soon."

"I'm not even showing yet."

"Ketia." Gabrielle looks at her hard. "You know you can't keep it."

"You mean give it up? I *can't* do that! Ma is going to kill me when she finds out, but she'll kill me even more if I give up my baby."

Gabrielle shakes her head. "Why do you say *my* baby?"

"Who else's do you think it is? The father—" Ketia stops. Was Gabrielle trying to trick her?

"I got that part. The father's gone. Disparu. Jamais vu. Believe me, if you don't want to have anything to do with the prick, I don't, either. He doesn't exist — except for the mess he left behind." Gabrielle jiggles her shoulders with contempt. "I'm talking about *you*. You're saying *my* baby. Does that mean you want it?"

"No," Ketia whispers. This child will be her cross that will scar the rest of her days.

"So... isn't that what we're talking about here? An abortion?"

Ketia's throat constricts so suddenly she begins coughing. Eyes watering, she chokes out, "No!"

Gabrielle makes an annoyed mouth, sits straighter. "You're a nurse, aren't you? You don't have to act like the word is Sodom and Gomorrah."

"It is!"

"Oh, come on! Cut the righteous act. You're the one who

got pregnant — and by some guy who can't even foot the bill. I mean, what? Did he leave the country? Is he married? Were you drunk out of your gourd when it happened? I'm not stupid, you know. I can figure things out."

"But I can't —" Ketia squeezes her eyes shut.

"What? I'm trying to help." Gabrielle gets off the bed and begins to pace back and forth, arms crossed, at the foot of their beds. "What are your options here? You have the baby, you're a single mom, good luck for the rest of your sorry life. And like you said, Ma kills you. Or you could say, Sorry, fetus, I made a mistake. This time I flush you — and I promise it won't ever happen again." Gabrielle opens her hands and shrugs, an MC constrained by unfortunate but necessary truths.

"It's not even a fetus yet."

"Whatever." Gabrielle rolls her eyes. "Isn't that even better? You're just getting rid of some egg that got in the way at the wrong time."

When Ketia was a nursing student, she'd done a rotation on a gynecology floor. She and another student had agreed that they could never have an abortion. An abortion was murder.

"And don't you dare tell me that you can't have an abortion for religious reasons. Because if your religion didn't keep you a virgin, I don't see why you should let it turn you into a single mom. Or," Gabrielle props her hands on her hips, "are you worried about the baby's soul?"

Ketia hasn't once thought about its soul. The dictates of the church don't frighten her as much as her gut belief in God and the devil. The baby is the outcome of the devil prompting her to sin. How strange to think that a devil's child has a soul and belongs to God.

"Are you *listening*?" Gabrielle raises her voice and Ketia flaps a hand to shush her.

Gabrielle plops onto the bed again, next to Ketia's legs. "Okay. Forget everything you're thinking. Look at it this way." She pauses to make sure Ketia is paying attention. "If you had an abortion, Ma wouldn't ever have to know." She lets that all-important fact fill the air between them. "And you work in a hospital. It shouldn't be that hard for you."

∞

Lou reaches for the phone. The lab wants to give her an abnormal result. "The patient's not here," she says as soon as she hears the name. "She's in Recovery. *No*. Don't give me the result. Call Recovery." She mutters when she hangs up. "Are they calling? Who knows?" She dials Recovery.

As she waits for someone to answer, her abstracted look returns to Ketia. Everyone but Marc has figured out that she's trying to avoid him. Yesterday Aditi covered for her so she could leave early before shift change. Ketia moves inside a protective net of glances and bodies.

Over the years, from her vantage point at the helm, Lou has seen a few relationships wax and wane, strategic alliances between doctors get nasty, department heads disappear and be replaced. Marc and Ketia would be just another story — except that Lou thought Marc was one of the good guys. She was disappointed, then disgusted, to watch him act like a poster boy for testosterone, ruffling his newfound macho glory. See Dick. See Jane. See Dick want Jane. Dick, indeed.

Lou waves an X-ray requisition at a surgical resident coming down the hallway. "One of your admissions needs a pre-op chest." The resident plucks a pen from his lab coat pocket. He leaves the requisition and his pen on the counter. Lou snags the req and tosses it in the mail basket. She's already sorted the filing. It's not too busy these few days before Christmas. They even have empty beds. No one wants to come into the hospital unless they absolutely have to. There are no scheduled surgeries, only emergencies.

Ketia still sits at the computer, checking the morning lab results on her patients. Now and then she notes a number on her worksheet. She rubs her other hand slowly back and forth, cradling her lower abdomen.

Lou reaches for the intercom that's buzzing. A bedpan. She calls for Pietro. The phone rings. "Seven Surgery. Just a sec." Lou swivels around in her chair. "Do we have a bottle of Fleet Phospho-Soda to lend?"

"Who's asking?" Raymonde says. She looks more calm since she started wearing foundation to mask her red cheeks.

"Six."

"Sick Surgery," Alex says as he ambles into the nursing station holding aloft a large box of donuts a patient's family has given him.

Raymonde comes from the med room with a bottle of Fleet Phospho-Soda.

"We've got one," Lou says into the phone.

Alex lowers the box to show Ketia. "Look, sweetie. Cream donuts."

Ketia shakes her head. "No thanks."

"Don't tell me you're on a diet. You're hardly adult size as it is."

"I just don't want one."

"I've never seen you refuse a cream donut. What, are you pregnant?"

Ketia's hand jerks, knocking a chart to the floor. She springs to her feet. Her nostrils flare.

Everyone looks at Alex. He protests, "She doesn't want a donut. That's all. I asked if she was pregnant —"

Again Ketia flinches. And now Lou gapes. Raymonde, too. And as Ketia still stands petrified, Raymonde cups her shoulder. "Are you, Ketia? You have to tell us if you are. You know that." She slides her hand across Ketia's back and leads her in the direction of Pascale's office, murmuring gently.

A porter from CT hands Lou a chart. "Wow." He whistles through his teeth. "Someone's gonna get in trouble. You look like you could land a punch."

"A punch? I'd like to electrocute his balls, skin them, and hang them off his ears."

∞

Joelle steps around the open drawers of the filing cabinets where she shelves the patients' charts from yesterday's clinic. From B to U to K. She doesn't move as quickly, thanks to the calming purr of the little, white pills. Now and then she glances at the Christmas cards that parade along the top of the filing cabinets. Glittering bells and fireside armchairs. A cartoon of a family climbing out of a horse-drawn sleigh in front of a village church. Two days to Christmas and the cards keep arriving, many from patients with a message for her. *Wishing you a happy year, Joelle! Que cette fête de Noël soit remplie de magie! All the best, Joelle! You're the heart in that hospital! Merry, Merry Christmas!*

She's glad to be at work, where the patients need her. An office temp wouldn't know that Jean Bilodeau has to have an appointment in the morning so he can get to the nursing home to feed his mother lunch. And who would go to Radiology to fetch the CT scans Frank needs to operate?

Yesterday Pei Yi brought her no-bake, chocolate coconut cookies she'd made with her daughter. None of the other secretaries even knew Pei Yi had a daughter. Joelle felt honoured that Pei Yi told her. The cookies, too. She and Diane used to make cookies like this when they were teenagers. She asked Pei Yi for the recipe. Maybe she would surprise Diane.

The mail lady with the dozens of bangles on her arms gave her a sweet-scented sachet she said to keep under her pillow at night. Two of the secretaries, Marguerite and Iona, have told her about their divorces. Iona's was complicated by child custody. Her ex tried to kidnap their son and she had to get a restraining order. Joelle and Marc have only copper-bottomed pots. He can keep them.

Joelle crouches to slide a chart in a bottom drawer, stands and reaches for the next when she hears, "Why don't you put them in alphabetical order first? Wouldn't it be easier than going back and forth all the time?"

The intimate rasp of Emile's voice. The smug, amused question. How long has he been watching? So what? Let him. "They're too heavy to shuffle. Doing it like this is easier." She slots Kramer in place.

He leans against the door frame, the pockets of his jacket stretched into pouches, his boots clouded and scored with salt. He always bought himself good clothes —he was vain that way — but never took care of them.

"The doctor's not here," she says.

"Who cares about the doctor? I came to see you. You didn't look so hot the last time I saw you."

She can't remember what happened the last time she saw him. Or even when that was. Out in the snow waiting for the bus? She slides open the D drawer for Delisle. Hefts the next chart. Mogador.

"You didn't make up, did you?"

"What are you talking about?"

"Last time I saw you. You were fighting with hubby."

Did she tell him? Does it matter? She should have started taking those pills years ago.

"Yeah..." he drawls. "You were pretty upset."

She shrugs. "He's leaving." She almost smiles at how easily she says it. No tears, no big ado, no melodrama.

Emile shifts against the door frame. The rub of soft leather on wood. "You've got to be joking."

"Who would joke about that?"

"Well, that's really shitty."

"What's shitty?"

"That he's leaving you."

"Shittier than when you left me?" She's stopped moving and faces him. He looks more natural slouched against the door frame than when he stands straight. Too bad he can't carry a door frame around with him all the time.

He tilts his head. Considers her. "Getting over him pretty fast, aren't you? Seems to me when I left, you took it harder."

Joelle turns away to hide the colour she feels rising. "I know more now. I'm not as naïve about men." She manages to keep her voice steady.

Emile makes a sound deep in his throat. A chuckle? "Don't tell me. He's already got a piece of snatch on the side."

Still turned away, she leans against the desk. Even with the white pills, his words punch.

She doesn't hear him move, but suddenly his voice is right behind her, tender and low. "You didn't deserve this, Jo."

She straightens. Her back rigid. "Leave me alone! Don't touch me!" Imagines his hands on her waist. Her hips. Their grasp. She'll collapse against him if he does.

Moments pass. Nothing happens. She feels only air behind her and whirls around. He's gone.

∞

Christmas Eve, midnight mass. Ketia sits between Ma and Bastien in the pew. Bastien keeps twisting from side to side, gawking at the splendour of the church at night. Braided fir branches, studded with coloured lights, loop from the massive chandelier to the pillars. Candles in red glass cups wink in the dimness, reflecting glimmers of red on polished stone and wood. The vaulted dome of the ceiling seems to rise even higher in its unlit reaches, the voices of the choir to resound more clearly, the organ to rumble more deeply. The congregation, dressed in Christmas finery, mingles in the aisles before filing into pews. Again and again Ketia hears Joyeux Noël! Or when Haitians of her mother's generation greet each other, Jwaye Nwel!

The priest is a French-Canadian from Manitoba who worked in the Caribbean. He often interjects a word or two of

Creole in his sermons — enough to touch hearts, not enough to lose those who don't understand. He calls himself un homme du peuple, drives a scooter, sings rather than chants the liturgy. He is known for his practical sermons about living within one's means and understanding value. Did Jesus get the latest chariot so he and his apostles could travel in style? No, they made do with their sandals and donkeys.

Twice in the last month Ketia came to church to confess, but she couldn't bring herself to approach the confessional. She's terrified of the questions Père Christophe will ask. Why, Ketia? And with a married man? What were you thinking?

She joins in singing "O peuple fidèle," a hymn she's always loved, but it gives her no solace this evening. She moves by rote, sitting, standing, responding.

"Que l'amour de Dieu soit avec vous."

"Et avec Votre esprit."

Between the heads of the couple before her she can see the crèche with its figures of Mary and Joseph kneeling before a manger, but the story doesn't touch her today. Even if Mary was penniless, in a stable among shepherds and animals, she knew she bore the son of God. Not a bastard.

"Prions," the priest enjoins the congregation.

Ketia bows her head but cannot find the words nor the feeling. Pray for what? To whom? When she gives birth she will bring shame upon herself and her family. Ma will never again stand so proudly at midnight mass.

Gabrielle has removed her coat to show off a white Lycra tube, apparently a dress, that Ma let pass when Gabrielle argued that the sequined spray around the neckline made it formal wear. Out of habit Ketia tuts before she remembers.

At work the head nurse made Ketia promise to observe the necessary precautions for pregnancy. You have to think, Pascale said, of the risks you're taking for your child. Ketia whispered, I don't want anyone to know. Pascale traced her thumb along the edge of her desk. I assume you mean Marc.

She waited for Ketia to speak, and when she didn't, sighed. You're going to have to tell at least some of your co-workers, because they'll have to start your IVs and take blood on your patients. And the nurse in charge has to know so she won't assign you fresh post-ops. But you know, Ketia, it won't stay a secret for long. When Ketia still didn't answer, Pascale said, Are you sure you want this baby? Have you considered other options? Ketia looked at her quickly — to catch the blame and disapproval. But Pascale's face stayed smooth. A health care professional. Another woman. Her boss.

Père Christophe has come out from behind the altar to the steps. He raises his arms, his red and gold vestments swaying, and calls out for the children in the congregation to come forward. "Venez tous les enfants! Come hear a story that's two thousand years old!"

One by one the children edge past their family's knees, some hanging back, some tucking their thumbs in their fists for courage. Bastien slides off his seat and stands on tiptoe to see, but doesn't scoot past Gabrielle until Ma says, "Va, il t'appelle."

The priest has gathered his robes about him and sits on the steps with the children. Come, he beckons them closer. Come. And so he begins his Christmas sermon, sitting before the altar, speaking to the children about the birth of Jesus in a stable, while the microphone directs his voice onto the pews from above.

Ketia leans forward, hands on her knees. Flinches when Gabrielle touches her arm.

Ça va? Gabrielle mouths.

Ketia nods automatically, though she feels the whole of her known world receding, her insides hollow except for this hard stone she bears.

∞

Although it's Christmas, Marc arrives at work early. Alex and Enid are already charting, an open bag of chocolate truffles between them. A resident sits at a computer checking email. At the end of the hallway the orderly stacks piqués and towels on a trolley. The floor seems calm. Marc has worked holidays with more medical emergencies than seem statistically possible; others where the staff could lounge around the nursing station corked on champagne and shortbread and no one would notice.

In the change room Marc drops his parka on a hook and rifles through the puffy black coats until he finds Ketia's yellow scarf. She's here!

On Thursday she called in sick again, though he came an hour early to see her. When he asked Lou what was wrong with Ketia, she barked, You've got bloody nerve even asking!

Crazy, Marc thought. They were all crazy, including the head nurse who'd changed Ketia's schedule to days — which she *couldn't* once it was posted. Ketia should go to the union and make a grievance.

Yesterday he told his parents that he was leaving Joelle. He had already forewarned them that she wouldn't be coming for the réveillon. As he half-expected, his mother was relieved. You'll find someone else, she assured him. Only with restraint did he manage not to tell her that he already had. Then his father surprised him. You were never fair to Joelle, he told his wife. She always meant well. Marc and his mother didn't answer. Mark knew she would adore Ketia. His father, too.

In the time it takes Marc to untie his boots, sling his stethoscope around his neck, and grab his clipboard from his locker, the scene in the nursing station has transformed completely. Alex is gone and from down the hallway he hears Ghislaine calling the orderly to bring the crash cart and the defibrillator.

"Who's going sour?" Marc asks Enid, who has fetched a cup of ice and labels blood requisitions.

"44A. Hudson."

Marc unclips the assignment sheet to see who will have 44A on evenings. Yadira. He'll end up helping her — more likely take over. His shoulders sag. And who had Hudson today? Ketia. Marc sets his clipboard on the counter and jogs down the hallway.

The junior resident, Ketia, Alex, and Ghislaine crowd around the bed. Ketia leans across the patient, who is pale and visibly diaphoretic — ashen and perspiring — his oxygen mask pressed into his cheeks. The sheet and gown are pulled away, exposing the man's abdomen. The resident needs to draw blood gases from the femoral artery in the groin. He tells Ketia to remove the mask, which she lifts by its elastic strap to the man's forehead.

His eyes flutter open and Ketia says, "It's okay, Mr. Hudson. I'll put the mask back as soon as we do a blood test. We're trying to help you here."

Ghislaine sees Marc. "Take report for me, okay?"

Marc doesn't move.

The senior resident strides in. "Bloods done yet?"

Ketia says, "SMA, trops, calcium, magnesium, cbc."

"EKG?"

"There on the machine," Ghislaine says.

He scowls at the tracing on the graph paper, curses, and stalks from the room.

In the silence, as the junior resident pokes a needle into the tender groin flesh, angling for the artery, Ghislaine asks, "Who took the bloods?"

Alex says, "I did."

"Because I don't want to catch you taking blood again," Ghislaine tells Ketia. "You're not allowed to, compris?" She slides her glasses from her hair to her nose and back up into her bushy hair again. Then she notices that Marc is still in the room. "Didn't I ask you to go take report so these girls can get home? It's Christmas."

Marc hasn't seen Ketia for days. Her sombre expression as she checks that the IV drips correctly. Her well-shaped mouth. Fingers lightly resting on the patient's arm. Marc wishes he could be the patient, supine, barely conscious, soothed by the touch of Ketia's hand.

The resident caps the syringe of bright arterial blood while Alex applies pressure on the site. Ghislaine jabs a finger for the resident to hand the blood to Marc. "Get that on ice, Marc — and go take report!"

Ketia starts when she hears his name, but keeps her face down. Her hand, reaching forward to readjust the patient's mask, trembles.

Marc cries, "Wait for me, Ketia! I have things to tell you, I have —"

Ghislaine bounds around the bed, standing so close that he smells chocolate on her breath. "*What* is the matter with you? Are you fucking stupid standing there with blood gases in your hand? Can't you see the patient's crashing? And leave Ketia alone, for God's sake!"

The blood gases, right. He trots from the room. Enid sees him coming and shakes aside the ice cubes in the cup to make room for the syringe. "Blood gases at the desk," she calls into the intercom. Before she's even shut it off, the orderly has whisked the cup off the counter.

Marc reaches for Ghislaine's report sheets on the blotter and scoops a pencil from the can on the desk. To Enid he says, "What's up with Ghislaine telling Ketia she can't draw blood?"

Enid points a hand in the direction of the room when RT comes running. "44A," she yells. And to Marc, "For the same reason any nurse who's pregnant can't draw blood. Possibility of a needle stick. Infecting the fetus with who knows what. Geez, Marc, even if you're a guy, you're a nurse. You should know that." She answers the phone, grabs a pre-printed pad for panic blood results, jots some numbers. As she hangs up, she swivels off the chair to take the results to the room.

A muscle in his cheek twitches. Can it be true? Ketia pregnant?

The phone rings. Raymonde says, "I thought Ghislaine was coming to take report. It's Christmas. I've got family waiting. I want to get home."

"There's a patient crashing. I'll take report."

"Well, then, get in here, will you?"

The tic in his cheek puckers so hard that his eye winks. He needs time to absorb what this means. Ketia pregnant. A baby.

He opens the door to the lounge where the nurses sit waiting, clipboards on their laps. He sits where Ghislaine usually sits at the table. Raymonde begins to race through the patients. Last unit of plasma running, stat INR, 50 cc urine output.

"Marc," she snaps and points at his sheet. "I'm on 38A, not 36C."

Marc circles what he wrote in the wrong space and arrows it ahead.

"Pay attention, will you? I don't want Ghislaine calling me at home."

The other nurses in the lounge glance at each other. But Marc doesn't hear her tone. At that moment, Marc the nurse is a pull-the-string doll. His pencil moves from years of having sat through report and knowing the procedure.

Report over, Raymonde bolts from the lounge. Marc, too. But the orderly, who replaces Abi for the evening, stops him in the hallway. The patient in 40B has just pulled out his IV. The elderly woman who trails behind the orderly raises quivering hands to beg Marc to come. "He is bleeding," she laments. "My husband for fifty-six years. He is bleeding."

Marc drops the report sheets on the counter, grabs some gauze and tape, and heads to the room. He finds the patient not only bleeding, but also wormed so low in bed, with his shoulders twisted against the railing, he hardly looks human. Marc steps back to the doorway to call the orderly. "What's your name?"

"Ricky."

"Come on, Ricky, let's lift this guy."

Easier said than done. The man is a bony torso with limbs attached. His sheets and piqué are soiled with urine. The orderly helps Marc roll the man aside to spread fresh linen.

The words fetus, pregnant, and baby are all Marc can think. He doesn't care about the baby, but pregnant Ketia is tied to him, no matter what her mother says. He is the father of her child. Pregnant she *belongs* with him. No one — not even Joelle — can object to that.

When Marc finally finishes and rushes to 44A, he finds a crowd at the bedside. Nurses, RT, the surgical resident, the ICU staff doctor. But Ketia has disappeared. She's not in the nursing station, either. He lopes to the change room, but her coat with the lemon scarf is gone.

∽

Joelle stands at the counter waiting for her toast. She's already opened the tub of low-fat sour cream and a jar of blueberry preserves. Her blue mug and plate stand ready. Both are from Diane's boutique: the solace of friendship in what now feels like an alien home. Marc can keep his fancy dishes. His goddamn heirlooms.

Then she hears the study door. Marc must have got up to go to the bathroom. He worked yesterday evening. Christmas. She spent the day with Diane's family. Turkey with celery stuffing, squash, corn, and mashed potatoes, mincemeat tarts and shortbread cookies. She preferred Diane's sister, Robin, and her mom having an honest argument about how to make giblet gravy to the duet of Marc's parents' perfectly concocted gourmet events.

Though she's just gotten up, she's already dressed in jeans and a sweater. She doesn't want Marc to see her in her kimono. If she had anywhere else to live, she'd be gone. Wasn't he supposed to leave this week? But every morning the coffee is ground and the machine set to drip at the usual hour.

She returns the sour cream and preserves to the fridge, but hesitates to leave the kitchen. She didn't hear the study door close again. Can't he smell her toast? She opens a cupboard door and slams it. I'm home, can't you hear? Go back and hide in your study.

Plate in one hand, mug in the other, she eases through the swinging door. She doesn't see Marc standing on the other side of the divider until it's too late to retreat. She forces herself to pretend she's indifferent. Slides her plate on the table and sits. It hurts her to see him, slender as a boy in his PJs, girded in the robe she gave him last year. Dark green to match the kimono he gave her the year before.

He clears his throat. "We need to talk."

We? She lifts her toast, which could be cardboard for all she tastes.

"I want to explain something."

She needs a sip of coffee to swallow her toast and doesn't take another bite. She doesn't want an explanation. The facts speak for themselves. He met someone else and now he's leaving.

"The other woman I —"

"I don't want to hear." She's proud that she cut him off.

"There's more you should know."

She turns away from him in her chair, ready to take her plate back to the kitchen. But what if he follows her? "So say it," she mutters.

"She's pregnant."

Joelle blinks. She understands the words and the concept. The sound, the logic, the meaning of the sentence. But not how any of that relates to Marc.

"I have to stand by her. She's very young. I have an obligation — because of the baby. I'm sure you understand that under these circumstances —"

Joelle shoves back her chair, carries her plate and mug to the kitchen. Dumps her coffee down the drain. Pushes through the door again, walks a straight line to the bedroom, closes the door behind her. Stares in her closet at her blouses, her dress pants, her skirts. If she had anywhere to go, she would pack her clothes and leave. She doesn't ever want to see Marc again. Anger pulses in her temples. Maybe she should take another Diazepam.

Pregnant. Baby. Those words in Marc's mouth simply make no sense. Toys underfoot, the domestic havoc, the demands. Getting his ankles smashed by a tractor. Over the years he let friends drop when they became parents. He said their brains regressed when they had babies. Maybe it was the diet — macaroni and cheese every night because that was all Bébé would eat. Or the brute, invasive force of a two-year-old's illogic. *Isn't he sweet?* No, Marc told Joelle on the way home, he's not. He always said, Any dog can do it, why are people are so proud? Yet look at him now, trying to make it sound as if he's been summoned for special duty.

When she finally hears the study door close, she grabs her purse, which she keeps in the bedroom now — her territory — and escapes down the hallway, pulls her coat off the stand in passing, yanks open the door.

∞

Nazim waits, legs crossed, on the sofa where Diane told him to stay put. She was in the kitchen making a special Boxing Day treat.

Since he's agreed to host Ghada's visit in their apartment, Diane has hardly mentioned her. She seems finally to have accepted the need for secrecy to protect his family. She was busy, too, with Christmas, working until nine every evening in the store. Diane's sister, Robin, had everyone to her place for tourtière on Christmas Eve, and again the next day for turkey. But even with Robin organizing the meals, Diane had to stand by to peel potatoes and carrots, chop celery and squash, mediate in the kitchen between Robin and their mom. Robin and André's little boy, Jérémie, careened from room to room yodeling to play. André and Nazim were supposed to keep him out of the kitchen. Diane had also asked Nazim to make sure Joelle wasn't lonely. Joelle sipped her wine and watched the family mayhem from the sofa. As far as Nazim could tell, she seemed all right.

He admits it will be easier to have Ghada stay here. He won't have to pretend that he lives at Abdullah's. Diane's apartment is obviously nicer than Abdullah's two rooms. But he still feels uneasy imagining Ghada sleeping in Diane's bed. Sitting at the table in Diane's spot next to the fridge.

Here comes Diane, scuffing her slippers down the hallway, moving slowly for once. She carries mugs of coffee piled high with whipped cream. He loves whipped cream. She sets the mugs on the table and kicks off her slippers. Under her robe she wears yellow long johns.

"Santé." She toasts in his direction.

He sips. And briefly, yes, he wishes Ghada could see him like this — on a lazy holiday morning at home with Diane.

"We don't even have to go out today. Robin gave me a care package of turkey and corn and tourtière that will last a week."

Both startle when the doorbell buzzes. Diane shakes her head at him not to move. No one they know would show up without calling first. Then the doorbell buzzes again, followed by a plaintive cry. "Diane…"

Diane swings her feet to the floor, but Nazim is already up and across the room. When he opens the door Joelle stumbles into his arms. He holds her up as Diane unwinds her scarf and unbuttons her coat. "Here now, here," Diane murmurs. She bends to tug Joelle's boots off. Nazim carries her coat down the hallway.

Diane leads Joelle to the sofa. Her eyes are swollen from crying. Yesterday at Robin's her hair shone and she wore earrings and a pretty eyelet sweater. No hint that today she would collapse like this.

"What is it, honey? Is it Marc?"

Joelle nods and begins crying again. "Marc."

Diane smoothes her hand down Joelle's back, offers tissue from the pocket of her robe, whispers comfort. Joelle must have seen Marc. Or maybe she saw Marc with the other woman. Poor Jo.

Joelle finally takes a big, heaving breath and mumbles, "A baby."

Diane leans close. "What do you mean, a baby?"

"He never wanted a baby."

"Are you talking about Marc?"

"Never." Reproach thickens Joelle's voice. "He never wanted a baby."

"Hold it. He didn't say he's leaving you because he wants to have a baby with this other woman? That's just cruel, Joelle! He's trying to make you feel that it's your fault he's leaving. He never wanted a child. That's what he always said. I heard him, too. Don't you take this shit!"

Softly Joelle wails, "She's already pregnant!"

Diane sits back. "That's preposterous."

Joelle sags against the sofa. "That's what he said."

"But that's..."

"It's what he told me."

Nazim appears with a third mug of coffee he's topped with the last of the whipped cream. He's changed from his robe and sweatpants into jeans and a sweater.

"Marc got this other woman pregnant," Diane tells him.

Nazim frowns, as if he couldn't possibly have understood. She nods. You heard me. He steps backward to leave the two women, but Diane motions with her chin at the stool by the bookcase.

"He told me this morning," Joelle says. Her blue-green eyes are more lucent than ever. Saltwater depths.

"Why didn't he tell you before?" Diane asks.

Joelle shrugs.

"Bastard," Diane says. "Can't even be upfront."

"…I don't ever want to see him again."

"Why is he even still there? I thought he was leaving. Why doesn't he move in with his preggie lady?"

"I don't know."

"Maybe she's married," Nazim says.

"Ha." Diane nudges Joelle. "Maybe he's not even the father. That would serve him right."

"I just don't want to see him," Joelle repeats.

"Do you want me to talk to him?" Diane asks.

Joelle scrapes her fingernail along the piping of a cushion. "What will you say?"

"Oh… there's lots I'd like to say to that man."

"I don't want you to yell at him."

"Why do you care if I yell at him? Don't you think he deserves it?"

"I don't want him to know…" Joelle sniffles. "…that I'm upset."

"Okay, here's what I'll say. I'll ask when he's leaving, so that we know when we can throw a big party."

Joelle manages a limp smile.

∞

Pa sent a Christmas card from Glacier Bay saying that he would call today at seven. The dishes are done, and Ma wears her good black skirt with a dark red blouse. She sits in the living room on the sofa next to the phone with Bastien valiantly trying to sit still beside her. Whenever he starts to wiggle again, she puts a hand on his knee. Gabrielle has plopped cross-legged on a cushion in the middle of the floor.

Ketia perches on the far corner of the sofa, her hands damp with anxiety. What if Pa asks… asks what? What could he possibly guess if Ma, who sees her every day, hasn't? Ketia's thoughts still ricochet crazily. She spreads her fingers, clenches them.

Suddenly she bolts from the sofa, runs down the hallway. She hears Ma calling but knows she won't follow with the phone about to ring. She swerves into the kitchen to the window. Stops with her cheek pressed against the grooved wood, her palm flat on the cold glass. Nothing out there but pock-marked brick. More windows like this one.

A hand on her arm squeezes hard and Gabrielle hisses, "Have you fucking flipped? You have to come back right now or Ma's going to ask. Don't be so stupid!"

Ketia wants to stay here, palm pressed to the window — as if it might dissolve and she could pass through to another world where everything was like it used to be. Then Gabrielle pinches the back of Ketia's hand, twists it.

"Ow!" Ketia jerks her hand away, cowering.

"You have to get a grip! Like right *now*. It's a phone call, okay? He's not going to see you. You just have to talk to him for a couple of minutes like you always do."

In the living room the phone rings. Gabrielle clutches Ketia's elbow and shoves her down the hallway to the sofa.

Ma has already passed the phone to Bastien, who's so excited that he stands on tiptoe, holding the phone with both hands, telling Pa about the yellow tractor he got for Christmas. "And you can turn it into a bulldozer, too!"

Gabrielle groans in disbelief. "Pa's calling from the other end of the world and *he* starts talking about a tractor?"

Ma shushes her. "This is his time. You leave him alone with his pa."

Each child gets three minutes. These calls from Pa's ship, via a special operator, are expensive.

Ma taps Bastien on the shoulder. He keeps chattering. More firmly she wags his elbow. He stops, mouth hanging, staring at Ma, who motions that he say bye-bye and give the phone to Ketia.

Ketia says hello so softly that Pa asks, "Who's that? My good girl or my naughty girl?"

Usually Ketia answers promptly. Now, her lips stiff, she says only, "Ketia."

"Ah, my good girl. You make us so proud. Are you still saving for university?"

"Yes," she whispers.

"I tell all of my buddies on the boat about you. My good girl — so smart and working so hard as a nurse, and soon you'll be getting your baccalauréat."

She grits her teeth against the gulping pain in her throat. Can't open her mouth when he asks if she's helping her mother. Thrusts the phone at Gabrielle and runs to her room.

Hunched on the edge of her bed. Pillow crushed to her face. She has no choice. She has to get rid of the baby. She can't do this to Ma and Pa. She can't.

∞

The doorbell buzzes. Marc, who is unpacking his socks, separating the black from the brown, ignores it. The landlady has already interrupted once to invite him to join her and her sister for a New Year's drink. Marc thanked her but declined.

He wonders if Ketia remembers that she promised to find a way to escape her family and spend New Year's Eve with him. Mind you, that was *before*. Everything has changed since. After Christmas she called in sick two days in a row. He assumes she's nauseated. That much he remembers about obstetrics from long-ago student days.

As he sees it, his role at the moment is to prepare their home. He's cleaned each nook and ledge, repapered the cupboards, scraped the tiles in the bathroom, sprayed bleach on the grout.

The doorbell buzzes again and this time the landlady calls through the door. "Monsieur? Monsieur?"

Marc descends the stairs slowly, dropping his weight on each foot. Let her know she disturbs him. He unlocks the deadbolt and opens the door.

She stands with a tiny glass of sherry held aloft. "You can't say no now! I've already poured it!" Her sister, equally short, her bulk sagging off the slope of her monstrous bust, stands next to her with a plate of store-bought cookies. "Bonne année!" they cry.

Marc sighs at such persistent goodwill and allows the two elderly women to cajole him into their living room on the main floor.

"Sit here!" The landlady pats the chintz cushions on the armchair.

"I can't stay. I have too much to do."

"Not on New Year's Eve!"

"Oui, Madame, even on New Year's Eve."

"Please call me Yvette — and this is my sister Evangeline."

He already doesn't remember which name belongs to which. He has no intention of telling them to call him Marc.

"You're expecting friends," Yvette/Evangeline asks.

"Not this evening, but soon enough. A special friend, yes." He doesn't sit, though again she prods and puffs the cushions.

"We heard you moving furniture."

Marc gestures at the TV where an orchestra plays, though the sound has been turned so low that the violinist seems a determined mime artist.

"The Millennium Concert!" Yvette/Evangeline beams.

Her sister asks, "Would you like to watch it with us?"

"No, no," Marc demurs. "My parents mentioned it."

"Do they live in Montreal?"

"In the Laurentians. In Val David."

"Lovely!"

Marc has drained his small measure of sherry. He steps backwards to the door.

"You're not worried about the..." She gestures at the TV. "What will happen at *midnight*?" she whispers.

He forgot about Y2K in the excitement of moving and getting the apartment ready for Ketia.

"We thought, well, we're so fortunate to have a man upstairs. You know, if the power goes off."

"Not much I'll be able to do in that case," Marc says. "I'm not Clark Kent."

"Of course, we're prepared. We've got water in the basement. *Twelve* jugs."

"Sh-sh," her sister cautions, as if she's giving away secrets.

"Thank you for the sherry." His lips a stiff grimace. "I really must go now."

"You're not celebrating New Year's Eve en famille then?" Their pouched faces, avid for gossip.

"Not this evening. I'm very busy... preparing the apartment — for my fiancée. I don't want her doing any heavy work."

"Your...?" Both gape at him.

"Fiancée," he repeats.

"But she can't live here!"

"What do you mean?" Marc draws himself up, not a tall man but he towers over these two biddies.

One flaps her hands, the other her mouth. "We've never rented to a couple! The flat isn't large enough for two."

"I would say that's my decision."

"And for us it will be too noisy. With just one person walking around upstairs, the ceiling cracks fearfully. You never said there were two of you."

"I wasn't aware that you imposed restrictions. And who knows? Perhaps we won't be happy here, either. Why don't we wait and see?"

One of the sisters drops awkwardly in the armchair. Her sister follows Marc to the door to lock it behind him.

Marc climbs the stairs, annoyed at how their meddling prompted him to say more than he'd meant. He should have let them meet Ketia first. Who could reject her?

He can hear the music from their TV through the floor now. Did they have it turned low before so they could track his movements from room to room? He's not used to hearing other people's noise. The condo was soundproofed.

In the kitchen he opens a bottle of Pinot Noir. He'd brought the last of the wine he kept stored in the laundry room with him. Truly the last. Joelle had drunk more than half. The idiot. All vintage wine and she probably only wanted to get drunk.

He can no longer recall the rationale of having left her the condo. Except for needing to escape her as quickly as he could — her and that busybody Diane. What was Diane after when she called, sounding so surprised that he answered the phone because she was *under the impression* that he had already left? He *was* leaving, he told her with asperity. That very afternoon.

He swirls the wine in the glass and inhales. Sour cherry, yes. And cloves. The taste almost smoky. Smooth on the tongue. Silky. An excellent wine that bodes well for the year to come. His new life with Ketia.

He raises a glass in a silent toast, sips again, and brings his wine to the bedroom. Back to sorting socks. Imagining Ketia's delight when he finally brings her up the stairs to show her their new home.

∞

Snow falls gently. Starry, 3-D flakes. Diane and Nazim tramp up the path that curves to the top of the mountain. It's dark — nine o'clock on New Year's Eve — but the snow reflects so much light they can see the trees on the slopes.

Diane noses her mitten through the crook of his arm. "Exciting, isn't it? Not just New Year's Eve, but a whole new millennium." She hears herself nattering, sounding too chirpy, but can't make herself stop. At least he's staying in the apartment when his sister comes. Even so, she feels nervous. She'd hoped for more assurance. For him to say he knows it's wrong that he never told his family about her. Or that he wishes he could — that he'll tell them someday. She'd say so, but she doesn't want to spend these last two days before his sister's visit arguing.

"I mean, think," she says. "People get excited when the century changes. But this is a thousand years. It's only happened once before."

"It's actually happened lots of times. People just weren't around to notice."

"Well, that's what I mean!"

He moves his arm against hers. "A couple of weeks ago you said you didn't know what the big deal was. Tomorrow morning you're going to get up and have your coffee regardless."

"We were talking about computers. I'm talking about *history* — what it feels like to be starting a whole new millennium."

"On my calendar it's only 1420."

Diane swallows a sigh. He won't even admit the evening is special. Maybe they should argue about his sister.

They trudge for some moments in silence.

Then he says, "The snow's perfect. Nicest I've ever seen. It's not even cold."

She leans against him. Understands it's a concession — a Moroccan who hates snow complimenting the winter landscape.

He hugs her arm closer. "And what did Joelle say she was doing?"

"Something about an elf. I didn't get it. I think someone she knows from work invited her over. But she was really clear on that — that she was doing something and she didn't want to spend New Year's with us."

"But you invited her."

"Of course. I don't want her to spend New Year's on her own." Though she's glad Joelle had plans. She wants to be alone with Nazim this evening.

They'd had hot chocolate in a café, then headed up to the mountain for a walk. At home a tajine was baking slowly in the oven.

Yesterday Nazim came home with a clay dish with a high conical lid: a tajine dish. He explained that back home it was set over a brazier of coals — the barest whisper of heat — for long, slow cooking. The toughest meat grew tender. The flavours of mutton, olives, pumpkin, and spices mingled. Ghada had a verse she muttered before she covered the mound of food in the dish with the lid. Nazim wanted her to make tajine when she came.

"Why don't we make one?" Diane asked. "I don't know about that verse, but I can follow a recipe."

"I don't have one."

"So who can we ask? Where did you buy this?"

Nazim pinched his earlobe. "At the butcher."

Today he came home with cubed lamb, carrots, prunes, honey, and spices.

"This is what the butcher told you to use?"

Nazim grimaced. "The butcher told me to get a wife. The woman at the cash told me how to make a tajine." He fished a piece of paper from the bag. Diane could read the numbers but the rest was in Arabic. Nazim sat at the table to copy the recipe into English.

She leaned over his shoulder and asked, "Spoons as in teaspoons or tablespoons?"

"She just wrote spoons."

It's almost eleven when they return from their walk on the mountain. Diane can smell lamb, cumin, and cinnamon as they climb the stairs. "Moroccan tajine," she says. "Made by your very own Montreal heathen."

Nazim doesn't answer, and she starts to worry. Maybe it doesn't smell the way it should. Stupid, she thinks now. Why did she try? He can do nostalgia with his sister. She should have made a big pot of ragout. Beef, mushrooms, and red wine. Remind him of what he loves about Montreal.

He follows her to the kitchen, standing back as she slides the heavy clay dish from the oven. She lifts the mountain-top lid and fragrant steam wafts into the room. Juices bubble softly around the chunks of carrot and lamb roasted a delicate brown.

Nazim leans close and smells. "Bingo."

His approval settles like an elegant mantle on her shoulders.

∞

Every second bar of light in the hallway was lit, but it still took Joelle a while to find the switches for the lights over the filing cabinets in the Colorectal Suite. They were on the wall between Dr. Collier's office and the housekeeping closet. Collier wasn't likely to see, much less touch them, so guess who was really in charge of the department? The true bright light?

Joelle snickers as she slots a chart in place, patting it down like a recalcitrant pup. "You stay now."

She lifts her mug for another sip. The bottle of wine stands on the floor by the leg of the table. She *is* at work. Though it's New Year's Eve. Even elves are allowed to get a bit drunk on New Year's Eve. Better than sulking at home like an abandoned wife.

Walking to the hospital she sidestepped people piling out of cars, en route to parties, pumping bottles over their heads, hallooing to each other. Hey ho, the new millennium. Blah blah blah.

When Diane asked if she wanted to come over on New Year's Eve, she said she had plans. She never had plans that Diane didn't know about, but Diane didn't press. Obviously Diane had plans. Joelle doesn't like feeling that Diane has to babysit her. And she did have this great idea about surprising everyone at work — and especially Pei Yi — by finishing the Colorectal cabinets.

She leans on her arms, head cocked at the stack of manila folders still to organize. She'd emptied a whole cabinet. Overestimated her energy. Underestimated the Rioja. Marc never drank Spanish wine, so that's what she bought.

He absconded with the last of the bottles in the laundry room. She arrived home two days ago to the study door open, the computer and Marc's clothes gone, gaps in the kitchen cupboards and dining room hutch. Though he didn't take everything. She supposed he'd tried to be *fair*.

Fair shmair. Pei Yi's brother is a divorce lawyer. Pei Yi told Joelle she could arrange a meeting — a coffee after work, something casual.

Joelle sips from her mug again. Makes a face. The wine's too dry for straight drinking. She wants something to eat. A bag of chips! There's a vending machine one floor down.

She has to return to her office to get her purse. Out of habit she locked it in her bottom drawer and hung her coat on the hanger behind the door. The floor in the hallway reflects the one-on, one-off overhead lights in stretched pools that almost touch end to end.

The dark offices don't frighten her. She feels safe in the hospital. No bogeymen here. Only words like malignant, necrotic, metastasis. If you could skirt those, the dark was easy.

Yet she hesitates before the elevator. Its sliding doors a steel maw. Decides to trip down the stairs that are brightly lit, even at night.

When has she last had chips? Not since the early days of the reign of Marc, who tolerated no form of junk food. Who lectured her on empty calories: if you consumed them, make them worth your while. Chocolate cognac mousse. Hazelnut praline.

Kachunk! The bag of chips tumbles into the tray. She snatches it up, rips the crinkly plastic. Elbows her way through the stairwell again, fingers already in the bag, greasy with salt and slivers of fried potato.

Coming down the hallway she wags her head to gauge how drunk she is. She steps only inside the spread pools of reflected light, trying to avoid their rims. Step on a crack, break your mother's back. It's not a crack, but why not? Stomp.

Up ahead a wall clock. 11:56. She trots to her office to turn on her computer. Wasn't this what Nazim and André were talking about at Christmas? A complete wipe-out at midnight. She knocks her chair around with her hip and drops on her bum. "Come on," she urges. The computer whirs and growls like it needs a laxative.

Where's her wine? Back in the Colorectal Suite. If she leaves her desk, she'll miss the crash. The numbers going from 99 to 00. The whole screen going blank. She hopes it happens. The government billing program zapped into cyberspace. Everything else, too. Let the whole world have to start from scratch again. Like she does.

"Move it!" She whacks the side of the monitor with the flat of her hand.

The minute hand on her watch has just nudged past midnight. The hospital logo blips into place. Same as always. Maybe her watch is fast. She clicks, double clicks, and the computer clock opens. 12:02. She clicks on the date. January 01—00.

Joelle slumps in her chair. So much for disaster. Her mouse is greasy from her fingers. What happened to her box of tissues? Stupid to be eating chips. She crumples the bag and drops it in the gabage, walks down the hallway to the washroom to clean her hands.

part *four*

Nazim scans the people streaming through the Arrivals gate. Many push trolleys heaped high with luggage, aiming for the gap in the roped-off exit. Here and there a family wanders less certainly, dragging their many bags and recycled suitcases bundled with string, too disoriented to focus on the relatives on this side of the cord who wave and call — until they're enveloped by cries and embraces, and in one case ululations. The men wear Western clothes, whether dress slacks or jeans. Some of the women are cloaked in heavy, brown burqas, though beneath, Nazim knows, they might wear a pantsuit — or an elegantly embroidered caftan. They're all strangers, yet he knows them. Knows where they come from, what they like to eat, what they think is proper. Knows how they will gaze at the dirty banks of snow piled along the highway, the insatiable spread of buildings, the streets lined with brick row houses. He never saw red brick before he came to Montreal.

Gathered in his arms he holds the parka Hatem's wife lent him. When he first arrived in Montreal — in March — he shivered inside the thin bomber jacket his father gave him to withstand the Canadian winters. Yesterday Diane asked if he wanted to borrow a couple of her sweaters for Ghada. He said they'd be too large. In fact, both women are the same size, but he doesn't want to trick Ghada like that. He already feels uneasy about her sleeping in Diane's bed. Wearing her sweaters would be an even more intimate deception.

A hand prods him. "You're looking at everyone walking by but me!"

How did he miss her? Her eyes and strong nose, her full cheeks — so like their mother's — her mouth wide in a laugh. They bump arms trying to hug. "Let me get at you," Ghada mutters, squeezing him through his bulky coat.

Ghada in Montreal! When they were children, they sometimes ran to the beach, where they clambered over the rocks to look for shells and tiny crabs in the mossy pools where the tide had receded. None of the other boys played with their sisters, but their sisters didn't bundle their djellabas to their knees and drop their slippers to scramble barefoot on the rocks.

"Look at you." He waves at her tailored trench coat.

She opens the coat to model her form-fitting jeans. "From Paris. A present from Asmae and Maha. They send their love, by the way." Asmae and Maha are friends, both married and with young children, accountable to their husbands for every dirham they spend. How had they tucked away enough money to buy imported jeans to armour Ghada in her flight across the world? *That* was true, lifelong, I-would-defy-a-war-for-you friendship. Nazim hears the subtext in all that Ghada does not even have to say.

"Mais tu sais," she leans close to whisper, "I had to put them on in the toilet before I got off the plane. They're too tight to wear sitting for all that time."

"Is that why the plane was late?"

She slaps his arm. "I have to look good for these Moroccan families we're going to meet — all your eligible brides."

Nazim's smile stretches foolishly.

"What's this?" She nods at the parka under his arm. "Don't you like my coat?"

"It won't be warm enough. Here, believe me."

Ghada rejects the coat with a lifted shoulder. She'll recant as soon as the first gust of frigid wind slaps her. Even with the shuttle bus, they've got to hike across an outdoor lot where he parked Badar's car. He begins to wheel the trolley upon which she's piled two large suitcases and a cloth market bag.

"Who lent you those?" He nods at the suitcases.

"Si Mohammed — who sends kind regards." She holds his arm as they walk.

"I borrowed my friend Badar's car to come to the airport. I don't have a car," he adds, being frank where he can.

"Who needs a car? *I* want to take the subway." She jiggles her arm against his. Excited.

"From where we — from where I live you have to take a bus to the subway. But we can do that, sure. We can take the subway." He talks quickly to cover his slip. She doesn't seem to have noticed.

"You know what I brought you? Smen."

"Mm-mm." He grins. "You know what I want you to make? Tajine."

"Tajine?" She scoffs. "I want peanut butter and cornflakes." She pronounces each syllable.

"If that's what you really want. But I've got a better treat: maple syrup." He's trying to remember if he has peanut butter. He doesn't eat it. Diane might have taken it with her to Joelle's. Yesterday they did a quick bachelor makeover of the kitchen, removing Diane's flowered apron and her new knit-sculpture calendar where she'd already noted a dentist appointment. Ghada will still question how strangely the kitchen is organized. Onions in the refrigerator? Onions belong in a wooden box in a cool, dark cupboard. So do potatoes. He had no wooden box, no cool, dark cupboard.

"I thought Montreal was so stylish," Ghada says.

"Why do you say that?"

She nods at the people before the sliding doors, about to step outside, tugging hats on their heads and knotting thick

239

scarves around their necks. Their mitts like large quilted paddles. "They look ridiculous — like Martians!"

"Keeping warm in the winter has its own kind of style." Nazim pulls his green toque from his pocket and fiddles his scarf free to wind around his neck. Again he tries to hand her the parka. "Put this on over your coat if you want, but put it on. Do it for me as a special favour. I'm your brother. Oblige me. There are mittens in the pockets."

Ghada rolls her eyes at him, but then opens her hands for the bulky shell with its flopping sleeves and hood. She still doesn't believe him — because doesn't she always know better than Nazim — but she sees how the other people zip up, looping scarves and shawls around their shoulders and necks, ducking their heads as if to butt the wind outside.

∞

Joelle carries two mugs of herbal tea to the living room, where Diane sits on the sofa with a crossword magazine.

"What do you think?" Diane says. "Five letters with a z in the middle."

Joelle curls into the other corner of the sofa. "What's the clue?"

"'To obtain by deceit.'"

Joelle smells mint and chamomile, feels the warmth of the mug against her palms, but in her mind images fold one into another... the metal armband of a watch, Marc's gym bag on the hardwood floor against the wall, Emile's bare ass between Francesca's thighs, a key thrown on a table, stir-fried shrimp on a plate, knife and fork set exactly. She doesn't know if she'll ever be able to eat shrimp again.

Diane looks up. "Are you okay?"

Joelle murmurs, "To obtain by deceit."

"Sorry," Diane says quickly. "I was too into this. I wasn't thinking."

"I have to get used to it. Every second or third patient who comes into the office asks about him."

"What do you tell them?"

"We're separated."

"Just don't make any excuses. It's not your fault."

Easy to say, Joelle thinks. But who knows? Did Marc meet someone else because he was unhappy with her, or did he become unhappy with her because he met someone else? The logic isn't as clear to her as it is to Diane.

Diane bends her head to her crosswords again. Joelle reaches for the new Marie Laberge novel Marguerite at work lent her.

Earlier this evening Joelle was in the kitchen slicing zucchini when Diane walked in and asked what needed to be done. Diane cut the chicken into strips and dredged them in flour. Joelle can't recall when she last cooked a meal with someone — certainly never in Marc's black granite domain. After they ate, Joelle stacked the dishwasher because Diane didn't know how it worked. When Diane wiped the table and Joelle set the salt and pepper mills on the hutch, Diane said, Why over there? We'll need them again tomorrow. Joelle put them on the table again. Like placing a cornerstone.

Nazim had dropped Diane off yesterday when Joelle was at work — because he had a car, Diane said. When Joelle got home, Diane was already installed in the study. Joelle only peeked in the room, though it no longer looked as if Marc had ever been there — two boxes in the middle, their flaps open on clothes, sweaters, books, tape cassettes, and crossword puzzles. A pair of jeans on the floor, a shawl tossed across the chair, which had been shoved from the desk. Diane ordered a pizza for supper. Joelle didn't tell Diane it was the first time pizza had ever been delivered to their condo. That night Diane slept with the study door open. In the morning when Joelle woke to go to work, earlier than Diane, she closed it. Diane slept soundly, one arm hanging over the side of the sofa bed.

Being at home feels entirely different with Diane here — more companionable. Comfortable. Even right now, though they're not doing anything together, they're both on the sofa with tea. Marc was always off in another room. Playing solitaire on the computer. Talking with his mother on the phone. Deboning quail.

Over the top of her book, Joelle watches Diane frowning at her crosswords. Her eyebrows arch as she prints a word. Must have been a hard one.

Joelle sips her tea. She's happy to have Diane stay with her. But she wonders about Nazim. She props her book face-down on the back of the sofa — another Marc no-no — and cups both hands around her mug. "Aren't you going to call Nazim?"

"I did — from work today and when I got here this evening."

"How is he?"

Diane shrugs. "Fine. You know Nazim."

"You don't..."

"I don't what?" Diane glances up.

"You don't have to sit with me all the time. You can call him if you want. He could come over, too. Why don't you invite him for supper tomorrow?"

Diane lowers her chin to her puzzle again. "He's busy. He's working on a project with a friend. It works out really well that I'm staying with you just now. Because he's really busy with this project."

"What kind of project?"

"Just some project. Something with computers."

Diane doesn't usually sound so vague. "Cozen," she says now, smiling to herself. "That's the word."

"Cozen." Joelle nods. The sound of the word fits the meaning. I cozen, you cozen, he cozens. Marc cozened her with pretense. He made it sound like he was leaving to forge a new life. He didn't mention that he already had a prop — a new girlfriend. And what he said about a baby. That still makes no sense.

Last night she had another nightmare. Marc was cuddling a bundle in his arms. He didn't look at all like himself, shoulders curved, hugging the blanket close, his hands delicate and lingering. Then his clothing morphed into Emile's worn jacket and jeans, and the blanket drooped. Not a baby, she saw now, but one of Frank's magnified, glistening tumors. She woke with her blankets kicked off the bed. The white pills only relax her during the day. At night her dreams are aggressive and ugly.

At work that morning she shoved the desk organizer with X-ray and lab requisitions farther along the cabinet and piled a stack of manila folders on top so she could no longer see Frank's photos from her desk.

∞

Ketia lies on the table, staring at the ceiling tiles. Row upon row. A curtain has been drawn around her table. She wears a blue gown. Her heels are secure in the stirrups but her toes, in the air, feel like they hang off a cliff edge.

Earlier, in the prep room, an attendant told Ketia to open her legs so she could shave her. The only sound was the scrape of the razor. Ketia felt disapproval in the jab of her gloved hand on Ketia's thighs. Her silence. Then she turned away from Ketia and clicked a switch on the razor so the head dropped in the garbage. "Close your legs," she said.

A social worker arrived with a clipboard to ask about her family. Mother, father, sisters, brothers. At the bottom of her page she drew a quick genogram of linked circles and squares, inking out Ketia's dead siblings in Haiti. Ketia wondered if she'd added an X'd triangle for her baby or if she would wait until it was done.

"Boyfriend? Husband?"

A husband, yes, Ketia thought, but not mine. Fit that on the genogram. "No," she said.

The social worker paused. "Should we discuss this?" Ketia

shook her head. "Have you notified anyone that you're here today?"

Ketia said her sister was in the waiting room. She couldn't tell from the social worker's face what she thought — probably that Ketia was the younger sister who got into trouble and that the older, more sober sister was waiting to take her home.

An OR nurse bustled in. "I see you're a nurse. I assume you understand the procedure?" She showed Ketia where to lie on the table, how far down to slide her bum. She propped Ketia's feet in stirrups, said the doctor would come soon, and swung through the curtain.

Lying there, Ketia can hear muffled voices, but no medical sounds — metal instruments dropped in a basin or electronic beeps. Under her thin blue gown she is naked, with only a small square sheet draped over her knees, her vagina exposed to the curtain, and if someone pulls that aside, the room. She angles her knees together so the sheet folds between them, but still feels air on the delicate, private skin.

Her thoughts shy away from imagining the steps of the procedure, though as a nurse she always chided patients who didn't want to know what the nurse or doctor was doing. But in the doctor's office, she hadn't listened either as his mouth opened and closed, explaining. When he slid the consent form across the desk, she signed.

She let Gabrielle drive them here, telling Gabrielle which street to take and where to turn. Gabrielle only had her learner's permit. On the way home Ketia would have to be conscious and alert.

In the waiting room Ketia had sat very still. Beside her Gabrielle crossed her legs and shifted, traced a brush heavy with pink glop on her lips, chewed bubble gum. She complained about the medicated smell. How can you stand working in a hospital? Ketia smelled nothing. What she felt was the brooding uneasiness of the people around her, the others — men and women — who were having different minor surgeries. Beside them, a middle-aged woman pinched the beads on her rosary. A nurse came out and said she could come see her daughter. Gabrielle whispered, What do you think her daughter had done? Ketia didn't want to know. She didn't want to talk, either. A young white woman and her Asian boyfriend sat across from them. He chewed the skin around his thumbnail, pushing the tip of his thumb between his lips like a soother, then examining it to see where there was still skin to bite. When the nurse called out a name, the young woman uncrossed her long legs and followed without even looking back at him. Ketia had become convinced that everyone in the room was having the same procedure as she was.

Hurried footsteps approach the curtain but pass. Why did the nurse bring her to the table if the doctor wasn't ready yet? To make her lie here in torture? Ketia remembers all the times she told patients — only half as a joke — that the reason they were called patients was because they had to be patient. She will never say it again.

In the car Gabrielle said that at least in a few hours it would all be over. "Doesn't that make you feel better?"

How could any of this make Ketia feel *better*? The closer time moves toward this moment, the more dread accumulates. Her hips and back soldered to the table, her vagina a tender wound about to be plundered.

The decided rhythm of high heels. "This bed?" someone asks and the curtain parts. Pascale steps in with her bright head nurse's smile. Her mouth straightens. She whirls back out the curtain again and returns with a larger sheet she flaps open to cover Ketia's stomach, legs, and feet. Ketia no longer feels the air on her open thighs and vagina.

"Thank you."

"I saw the doctor outside. He's coming soon. He had an emergency caesarean."

Ketia wonders how the same doctor can bring a baby into the world and kill one. One after the other.

Pascale lays her hand on Ketia's. "I'm sorry you have to go through this. Did someone come with you, a friend or family?"

Pascale had arranged for the gynecologist to see Ketia quickly, without fuss or questions. She gave Ketia two weeks' leave from work. And though she said she would be sorry to lose Ketia, she understood if Ketia would be more comfortable transferring off the floor. Pascale's kindness — the kindness and empathy of all the nurses when Ketia expected only judgment and blame — glimmers like a truth that has eluded her up until now. *She* was the one who judged them by thinking they wouldn't understand. She always acted like she was better than everyone, and look what she did. Yet they defend and protect her. Their unexpected goodness humbles her. Makes her realize that, even in her despair, she is fortunate.

"Do you want your sister?" Pascale asks. "I can tell them to let her in."

"No." Ketia closes her eyes but cannot stop the tears from seeping out. Gabrielle, too, helping her.

Pascale strokes her cheek until the doctor arrives.

∞

Joelle highlights and clicks, highlights and clicks. The billing codes are a thicket, one different from the next by only a single letter or number. For this program, a Y2K crash would have been a mercy killing.

She has yet to hear of a single computer or program that suffered even a burp from Y2K. Unfortunately, one of their patients, Mr. Hansblatt, was a victim of the paranoia. During the family New Year's Eve party his brother sneaked to the basement and switched off the breakers at midnight. Five-four-three-two-midnight! Mr. Hansblatt had a coronary. He's in the CCU now. If she can, she'll dash over later to see him.

She's alone in the office. No clinic today — January 4th — but every slot yesterday was double-booked. Every year the holidays usher in a wave of staggering intestinal malaise. Some of the patients had to sit in the hallway and kept returning to her desk, worried they'd been forgotten. Joelle had to assure and reassure. Couldn't they see that the doctor was rushing from one examining room to the next? Look, here was their chart. Right here.

Joelle hears tiny heels in the hallway. Only Pei Yi walks so quickly and lightly. She turns into Joelle's office — a burst of carnation ruffles down the front of her pink blouse, a flared black skirt. "So," Pei Yi says, "am I allowed to help with the rest of the colorectal files, or do you want to do them *all* by yourself?"

Joelle blushes, pleased and embarrassed. "That third cabinet isn't finished. I didn't have time. I just pushed them all back — the ones past... I can't remember. But I stuck a Post-It —"

"I noticed."

"I was trying..."

"It's great! I'll be there after lunch if you're free. And oh —" She swivels back on her heels. "It's fish and chips in the cafeteria today, if you want to come."

Joelle hesitates at the thought of all the calories and the grease — but she could have just a salad for supper tonight. She always loved fish and chips in her high school cafeteria. "Sure," she tells Pei Yi. "Thanks."

She's still smiling at the doorway when Emile appears, turning his head to watch Pei Yi swiftly tapping her tiny heels back to her office.

"Cute," he says, sauntering in, hands easy in the pockets of his sheepskin jacket. He could be in a bar about to order a beer. Or no, she remembers. His drink was scotch. *One* cube of ice and woe to the bartender who got it wrong. Single malt, the more guttural the brand the better.

Joelle could go back to her billing, but she doesn't. Emile is being admitted on the weekend for surgery on Monday.

Probably the next time she sees him he'll be in a johnny shirt, flat out in bed, maybe even unconscious.

He drops onto the chair by her desk, back slouched. "Had to come in for my P-A-T," he says. Pre-Admission Tests. He pronounces the letters as if they're a stupid joke.

"How were your holidays?" she asks, though she knows Emile never cared for them. It's the standard question of the week.

He squints, as if he can't remember. "Went to see the folks. Fa-la-la."

She's surprised — and then not so surprised. Maybe he finally understands how ill he is. "How are your parents?"

"She still talks non-stop and not a word of sense. He's turning into a 'tit vieux. All he wants is to sit in his shed in his ratty old chair and suck on a cigar." Emile sits up and smoothes his hands along his thighs. "I took him one. Hand-rolled and sealed in a tube. You know what he said? Dans la vie il n'y a rien mieux que ça. No wonder we're such a loving family. He never looked at a single one of us the way he looked at that cigar." Emile makes a wry expression. "What a sorry old bastard, eh? I never wanted to end up like him, but from the looks of it, I won't even get that far." He pauses. "What did you do for Christmas?"

"I went with Diane to her family. You remember Diane?"

His eyes close. "I remember Diane."

Briefly Joelle wonders why none of the men she's been with like Diane.

"And where was hubby? With his new lady love?"

"I have no idea."

"What's she like?"

Joelle's neck stiffens. "How would I know?"

"Aren't you curious? You know, to see if she looks like you. Or completely different."

Her head draws back. "I don't want to know."

"Me, I only ever went for pretty blondes. Like you. Nice shape, nice mouth…" He grins. "You were always my type, you know that."

She feels flattered in spite of herself — and though she knows Francesca was no blonde. And she saw how he up-and-downed Pei Yi.

"Come on, Jo, anyone would want to know what their rival looks like."

She wishes now she'd kept working on her billing. At least kept her hand on the mouse so she'd have an excuse to look at the screen.

"We're all animals when it comes to jealousy," he says.

"I'm not jealous. I got too used to it being with you."

"Maybe you should have told me. Maybe I'd have —"

"You wouldn't have anything!"

"Don't be so sure. A jealous woman puts out. Gives a little more action." He nods. "You and hubby aren't divorced yet, are you? Nothing's a done deal. Maybe he's just playing around. You always take things so seriously, Jo. Me, too, I was just chasing a bit of tail. I always came home again, didn't I?"

Under the desk Joelle's hands are clenched on her thighs. "You *packed* your stuff and left! Don't try to tell me now that you meant to come back."

"You're not listening," he drawls. "I'm trying to explain something here. Life isn't always so black and white, right and wrong, all that shit. You have to bend a little. What does it hurt, a bit of playing around? Don't harass hubby about his new girlfriend." He bats a hand in the air. "Act like you know you're better — and see if he doesn't get tired of his new game soon enough."

Joelle swings her head from side to side. "You're wrong. It's not like that."

"It could be, if you didn't get all worked up. Don't go cold on him. He's not in love, he's in lust. She's got her hands on his cock and he can't get enough. And you're probably playing the shy bride, right? What you should do is turn up the heat. Let him have a taste of what he's missing. And I mean taste." He juts his lips in the direction of her crotch behind her desk.

"Nothing turns a guy on like two women hot for him — and you're his wife. You've got your foot in the door. Play your cards, Jo. He'll think twice, believe me."

Joelle's lips are pressed tight. She's not going to tell him about the baby. She's not. Again she shakes her head. No.

He sighs and straightens from his slouch. "Okay, okay. Forget I said anything. I was trying to give you some pointers, but I see you're your old uptight self. Can't say I didn't try."

"It's not like that," she repeats, determined not to say a word more.

Emile gives a short, chopped laugh. "Believe me, it *is*. He's got himself a hot cunt and you won't get anywhere putting yours off-limits."

Joelle nearly tells him. But she still doesn't believe it. Or at least not the way Marc told her.

Emile wiggles a finger at her hand. "If hubby's history, why are you still wearing a ring?"

At home in the bathroom she twisted off her gold band and waved her hand in the mirror to see how her bare finger looked. She always slipped the ring on again. Even if it meant nothing now between her and Marc, she still wanted the world to believe she was married.

But if Emile thinks it means she still feels attached to Marc, well, watch this. She yanks off her ring and drops it on the appointment book. "There. I'm not wearing it. I'm going to sell it for scrap gold." Marguerite told her that's what she did with hers. The perfect end to seal a dumping.

Frank strides in, more a Broccoli Head than ever with his last haircut — short on the sides, high on top — and still in his blue OR scrubs. "Joelle," he begins, then notices Emile and the gold ring, a paralyzed O on the white page. And alarmed now, "Are you all right?"

Emile stands. "Keep your cool, doc. I'm leaving." He grins at Joelle. "See ya later."

"Are you...?" Frank asks again.

"I'm okay," Joelle says. She slips the ring on her finger again. She no longer wants to wear it, but she doesn't want to lose it.

"I need you to call Archives at Sacré Coeur and have them fax an OR report."

Joelle grabs a pencil to jot the details. She's glad Frank appeared when he did. She's not sure if he recognized Emile as a patient. Probably not. She's relieved that she managed not to tell Emile about the baby.

∞

A cloudless sky enamelled blue. Raw sunlight reflecting a mineral sheen off the knee-high slopes of snow that border the street.

Diane picks her way, tottering, sometimes skidding, along the single path between the slopes. Marie-Claude showed up at the boutique and asked if she wanted the afternoon off. Diane grabbed her coat. Business is slow after the holidays, and lately the solitary hours with her crosswords or a book make her restless — hemmed in by the glazed bowls, hand-carved spoons, and stitched slippers. All just *things*. Why doesn't Nazim call? At Joelle's and at the store she always sits with the phone in sight. A couple of times she's lifted the receiver to make sure there's a dial tone. He can't be with his sister every single instant of the day. Yet when she calls, his tone is evasive, his words curt.

The first time she asked, "Is she there? Just say yes or no. I'll talk on this end."

"I'm sorry, I'm busy. I'll have to reschedule at the end of January." The phone clicked and she heard the dial tone. She decided to laugh at how cleverly he dissimulated who was calling.

The next time she began, "Nazim, I miss you! Can't you —"

"You must have dialed the wrong number. There's no one by that name here."

She gripped the phone in anger. Between not talking to

her and tricking his sister, couldn't he sneak in a tiny message?

The second day, when she still hadn't heard from him, she called again. "You listen! Don't brush me off. Why don't you phone me at work or at Joelle's when your sister is in the bath or in bed? Or leave the apartment and go to a pay phone. Do I have to spell this out for you? You have to *call* me!"

"We already subscribe," he said. And more softly, "Goodbye."

Diane slammed down the dead receiver. Did he think he was being cute? Well, damn it, then she *wouldn't* call.

Another full day passed. Three days since he'd dropped her off at Joelle's. And she'd actually thought she'd feel more secure because he was still living at their place. Much good it did her! She only felt frustrated being able to picture him answering the phone, sunk low in their sofa, refusing even to pretend to do a marketing survey with her on the household consumption of beverages.

She should have let him take his sister to Abdullah's. Let her think that his life here in Canada was pathetic. Two barely furnished rooms reeking of hot oil and falafels.

She skids and slides along the frozen, slippery sidewalk and — "Shit!"— almost trips over a rubber edge protruding from a snow bank. A bicycle tire twisted by the kamikaze sidewalk ploughs.

Closer to her neighbourhood, she slows down. Pretends to stroll, chin high, looking up and down the street. Her story is that she's come to buy the brioches au chocolat that Joelle so particularly likes at the bakery around the corner. If she sees Nazim, she will say hello. If he doesn't introduce his sister, Diane will introduce herself. Nazim won't like it, but she has her excuse of buying pastries for her dear friend Joelle.

The other pedestrians are bulked out — disguised — in down coats, hats with earflaps, scarves, and boots. Why not, she thinks now, stop for a cup of tea in the café next to the bakery? Sit at a table by the window?

Then she sees Nazim about a block ahead. His coat, his green toque, his slightly splayed gait, walking with a woman she assumes is his sister, away from Diane.

Diane follows them. Though she's not really *following*. She's on her way to buy brioches. His sister can't keep her balance on the icy sidewalk. She clutches Nazim's arm, shouting and laughing at him, her tone loud and confident. Diane didn't expect her to be so animated. Nazim, too, leaning toward her. Not as hunched against the cold as he usually is. Forgetting how he hates winter in Montreal. Neither seems fettered by the bounds of tradition and religion. He grips her elbow, hoisting her upright. Both laugh as if the sidewalks were an insanely ridiculous joke. Who would possibly choose to live like this?

Diane slows before a window display of kiddie snowsuits. She's not so sure about hailing Nazim. And what if he turns around? He won't think it's funny. She can't even say that she's going to the bakery which is now two blocks back.

She steps inside the recessed entrance to the store, still watching Nazim. He shuffles and bundles his sister to the corner, where a bus heaves to the stop. They climb the steps and the door closes, but Diane still waits until the bus pulls away from the curb.

If she wanted proof of his sister's existence, she got it. Even from the back she didn't look the way Diane expected. Diane had somehow thought she would be smaller. More petite, like Badar's wife.

Only when she opens the door to the bakery does she remember Nazim refusing the sweaters she wanted to give him for his sister to wear. They'll be too big, he said.

Diane can't tell for sure with the parka his sister was wearing, but she guesses they'd have fit her very well.

∞

Since Diane has moved in, Joelle doesn't feel as bothered by the dark rooms. Still, she asked Diane to leave at least the hall light on when she left for work. Diane scoffed. All day long, when neither of us are here? What a waste of energy. Don't be silly. Joelle said, But I —

She can't explain to Diane, who has no patience for weakness. She still hasn't told her about the Diazepam, which she used to keep on her bedside table but now hides in her underwear drawer. Diane already borrowed a pair of socks without asking. There isn't a chance she'd fit into Joelle's bras.

Diane claims space with the sweaters she tosses over the backs of chairs, the crossword magazines she's told Joelle not to touch, her towel hanging off the shower curtain rod as if she doesn't see the rack on the wall. The smell of a robust beef soup she makes with carrots, barley, onions, and celery. Her old tape cassettes of seventies music — music Joelle hasn't listened to for years, as if she outgrew CSNY along with her hip-hugger jeans and apple seed necklaces.

It was Diane's idea, too, to push the sofa under the windows so that when you lie back, you see right up into the sky. Between the two of them, they carried the end table and the coffee table, but the sofa was too heavy. They shoved rather than slid it, and made a long, curved scratch in the floor. Not just the varnish, but scored right into the oak. The room looked off-balance now with the sofa, the end table, and the coffee table all in a row under the window, but they decided to keep it like that. Diane slapped her hands on her hips. "Up yours, Marc. We like things a bit cross-eyed, don't we?" Joelle was surprised by how aggressive she sounded. Marc dumped *her*, not Diane.

It's dark out now, but Joelle lies against the cushions on the sofa with the black sky above, comforted by the croon of Joni Mitchell's high, sweet voice. Men lost, men loved... When Joelle was younger, she danced to the inventive harmony of her singing. Now she listens, intent on the lyrics.

Diane stomps into the living room with a ball of fuchsia

wool and knitting needles. The first evening she announced that she was going to make herself a vest. She hated sleeves. You finished one only to have to start another. But a single front and back she could do. So far, though, she's only knit the ribbing for the hem.

Joelle tents her legs so there's enough room for Diane, who wields the needles like she's playing a sport with her elbows.

"What are you doing?" Diane asks.

"Listening to the music."

Joelle doesn't want to talk. She knows that if they do, she won't be able to hide how anxious she feels about Emile's surgery. How far the cancer has spread, whether Frank can even help him. And then Diane will lecture her again. Joelle appreciates the cozy, emotional cushion Diane plumps around her — her thick barley soups, her company on the sofa, the music — but at the same time Diane can never resist criticizing. Just like Marc.

The tape deck clicks. Joelle waits to see if Diane will get up to put on another cassette, but she keeps her head bent to her knitting, her posture hunched. Knitting seems to make her more tense, not less. She's not usually so quiet, either.

Joelle pushes herself up. "Do you want to watch a movie? I rented *La Reine Margot* — with Isabelle Adjani."

"Sure." More indifferent than interested.

Joelle stands to get the movie from her purse in the bedroom when the phone starts to ring. She turns to answer, but Diane has flung her knitting to the sofa and bounds across the room. What's wrong with her?

"Oui, allô?" At first Diane looks puzzled. "Just a moment. It's for you."

Who? Joelle mouths at Diane. Diane shakes her head. It can't be Marc.

"Joelle." A woman's voice.

"Yes?"

"It's Pei Yi."

"Oh!" Joelle relaxes. "How are you?" Pei Yi had offered to set up a casual meeting with her brother, the lawyer.

"I'm fine. My brother says he can see you for a coffee tomorrow after work. I'll come, too."

"Tomorrow? That's so soon." Joelle isn't aware that she rotates away from Diane, who watches her from the sofa.

"Just to talk. It's good to know where you stand."

Joelle fingers the smooth, oval pendant of her necklace. A turquoise eye at her neck.

"Tomorrow isn't good? I thought you said anytime."

"Tomorrow's okay, but isn't this... an inconvenience for your brother?"

"Not for my friend Joelle. Don't worry, we'll meet him near his office. He'll just have to come downstairs."

Joelle lets Pei Yi's decisiveness convince her. "Okay, thanks. I appreciate it."

She hangs up and turns around. Diane sits cross-legged with one hand on her hip. "Who was that?" she demands.

"That—" Joelle begins. Diane would yodel if Joelle said she was getting together with a divorce lawyer, but Joelle suddenly doesn't want to tell her. Not with Diane jutting her chin at her like that. "Just a friend. No one you know."

She walks to the kitchen, where she fills the kettle and plugs it in. At the cupboard she shuffles aside boxes of tea looking for the fennel she bought yesterday. It's so tightly packaged in cellophane that she has to wiggle a knife along the edge to slice it open.

Diane swings through the door. "I was in the same room, you know. I know you made arrangements to see whoever that was tomorrow."

"I was going to tell you. I'm just — I'm making tea for us."

"That's not very nice for me, you know. I moved in to keep you company and now you're taking off."

Joelle pours boiling water over the bags in their mugs. It would be easier just to tell her.

"Not very nice for me," Diane repeats. She takes an apple from the bowl on the counter and puts it back with exaggerated gentleness.

Why is Diane so angry? "I never asked you to spend every evening with me. And you don't have to stay here. Why don't you go see Nazim — wherever he's doing this project?"

Diane whirls around and bangs through the swinging door.

Just because Joelle won't say whom she's seeing tomorrow? Anyhow, what's wrong with Diane? Why doesn't she visit Nazim?

Joelle leans against the counter waiting for the tea to steep. When she carries their mugs to the living room, Diane sits huddled with her knitting again. No music plays. Joelle gets the movie from her purse, switches the TV display to video, and slides the VHS into the slot.

∞

Ghada stands before a life-sized poster of a woman sitting on a stool in tight jeans, knees elevated by heels, legs slightly spread, mouth a glossy vermillion O. The model's crotch is positioned just above Ghada's forehead. For a slightly shorter man the crotch would be at eye level.

The shopping concourse is busy with post-Boxing Day sales. People dawdle and stride past, swinging bags, sucking on soft drinks. As a rule, anything goes in Montreal. A young woman practicing opera notes on the subway. A boy with safety pins in his ears, and hair that looks streaked with egg yolk. An overweight pug being wheeled about in a baby stroller.

But people notice a simply dressed woman examining the crotch in a poster. Do they guess that she's only disguised as a Canadian? Under her parka she's a foreigner.

So far Ghada has stopped to scrutinize the lacy cups fit over a mannequin's poked-out breasts. A poster of an otherwise-naked man lying on a floor in form-fitting boxers. Of course, she's supposed to *see* the posters. That's why they're on the walls. But she's only supposed to look for that nanosecond that seeds the wish to buy this lipstick, these shoes, these boxers. Even the boxers, yes, since women shop for their men.

Ghada steps away from the poster of the woman in jeans with her legs spread. "What are they selling?"

Nazim points at the brand name of the jeans writ large across the bottom.

She flaps a hand. That wasn't what she meant.

Nazim has planned to take Ghada to Old Montreal, the Notre Dame Basilica, Château Dufresne, the Olympic Stadium. He will borrow Badar's car to drive to Mont Tremblant for a day.

But she wanted to visit Montreal's famous Underground City. He'd never heard of it. Diane had never mentioned it. He asked Hatem, Abdullah, Badar, and Yussuf. Hatem finally looked it up on the computer and discovered that the Underground City was the network of tunnels that connected the shops, commuter train stations, apartment buildings, banks, hotels, universities, and subway stations downtown — thirty-two kilometres of tunnels used by half a million people per day in the winter.

"You mean downtown?" Nazim said. He never paid attention to how the stores, subway stations, and banks were connected. He and Diane rarely even go downtown.

He doubts Ghada will like it, but he takes her. She can't believe he's found the right place. She was all set to experience *a city* under the pavement — not one store after another selling luggage, shoes, and scarves. "What is this place?" she says. "You can shop and buy muffins, shop and buy muffins."

Her hands stay in her pockets as they meander through the stores with their folded wares and price tags. Nazim says, "Pick something. Go ahead. I'll buy it."

She closes one eye. The gesture of diffidence that belonged to their mother. "I like the souk better."

Wobbly stalls. Tangled heaps of clothes. Shopkeepers gossiping over glasses of coffee. Prices an entente only reached after a corkscrew dialogue of innuendo, compliments, taunts.

"People here..." Ghada shakes her head and smirks. "They don't understand about shopping. They think it's just to buy. You have to talk, too. You want to know what you're getting. And the people who do the work, look at them. They shove what you buy in a bag and drag a machine across a plastic card. That young man —" she nods at a youth propped against a counter, eyes dull, in a shoe store. "He's going to stop breathing in that place. His face is already yellow."

Nazim remembers how back home, even going to the bank was a social encounter. You talked to the teller and the other people in line. People knew which day you were paid, which day you went to the bank, how much you withdrew. They knew when you made a transaction that was out of the ordinary and might even politely inquire. They felt they had a right to know, since there was only so much money at the bank, and they expected theirs, too.

Perhaps life is that intimate here, too, in small towns. Nazim doesn't know. He wishes he could bring Ghada to the boutique where Diane could tell her how the artisans glaze the bowls, weave the shawls, stitch the moccasins. Ghada would like that. But he won't dupe her so deliberately — only as much as he has to.

He and Ghada stop to sit at a joined table and chair unit in one of the many food courts. Without telling her what he's buying, he orders mango smoothies because he remembers how she loves mangoes.

"A frappé," she says once she's sipped from the straw. "Almost like on the beach back home. That's what I..." She stops.

"What?"

"I promised myself I wasn't going to ask why you live here. I thought I would understand when I came. But I don't. If anything, now that I see, I understand less than ever. The cold.

This —" She waves at the cavern of fast-food counters. "That you have to import all your fruits and vegetables."

"In the summer —"

"The summer!" she interrupts. "What about right now?"

He hoped she would be more impressed by the high-rises, the grey stone buildings, and cupolas against the skyline. How, on a short bus ride, you can hear French, English, Arabic, Greek, Spanish, Urdu, Tagalog, and more. There are churches, mosques, synagogues, and temples. They can eat Tonkinoise or tapas. It's all here: a mingle of people and cultures. But Ghada discerns little in the cold that turns everyone inwards, not just freezing Moroccans. And if she can't see the variety, she won't see the freedom that comes with it — if you want it. As he did.

She slides her jumbo smoothie cup away from her. "I'm trying to understand what holds you here."

What holds him now is Diane. What held him before was his decision to leave. Of course, he misses home — sharing bread and kefta with his family, the uncurling rope of surf along the beach, the horizon of grey-green water, the air so salty it rusts the blue shutters on the windows, the riding wail of the muezzin marking the times of the day, the stillness in the desert hills, gnawa music, the nutty flavour of argan oil in couscous. And yes, he hates winter. Every time he steps outdoors — and many days even inside Diane's cold apartment. But once you leave home and discover that the world can be different — in some ways better, in some ways worse — you can't return any more than you can be young again. He can't explain that conviction to Ghada. He didn't believe it himself until he experienced it.

Ghada drums her neatly trimmed nails on the table to remind him she's waiting.

At the next table unit, a teenage boy claps down a plate of oily noodles, swings onto the seat, and begins shovelling the noodles in his mouth in one smooth, practised movement: food-sit-eat.

Nazim shrugs. And weakly, knowing it sounds trite, he says, "Montreal is beautiful at any other time of year. You would fall in love with it, Ghada. Truly, you would."

"And it's worth eating hard strawberries all winter? Stale clementines? Having to mummify yourself every time you go outside?"

"It is."

She rears her head and closes an eye, not believing him. "Don't be surprised if one year, when spring comes and you crawl out from under all those layers of coats and sweaters, you've turned into a mushroom."

She's right. Every spring he's winter-pale, even clammy. His skin craves sun.

A redhead with an apron loosely knotted around her waist rattles past with a trolley of cleaning products, brushes, and pails.

"Fine, then," Ghada says. "That's established. You're staying here, so we'd better get started on finding you a wife." She sets her handbag on the plastic table and flips back the top.

Nazim's smile wilts. Eventually they were going to have this conversation, but he didn't expect it now.

"How about you look at these addresses and tell me where we should start — which are the easiest for us to get to. I didn't realize Montreal was so large." She fishes a folded page from an inside pocket of her purse and swipes her fingers across the table to check it's dry before she opens it. "Here." She turns the page toward him. "Sorry, I don't have pictures. Some offered, some didn't. In any case, character is what matters most in a wife, and you won't see that in a picture."

A photo of Ghada's bold, dark-fringed eyes and strong nose would speak very well for her take-charge character. Without actually reading it, Nazim sees a page with a dozen names and addresses. How did she find so many contacts in Montreal? She must have solicited people to ask people — farther afield than their small town. He wishes he didn't have to disappoint her.

Quietly he says, "I can't meet these families."

She sits back in her moulded plastic chair. "Why not?"

"Because I don't want to find a wife like that. I'm here now, in Canada. We do things differently here."

Ghada opens her hands. "I don't have any problem with that, dear brother. The problem lies with you. You haven't found yourself a wife yet. So..." She leans forward again and taps the page. "We fall back on the old-fashioned method."

He shakes his head. "No."

"They're expecting us to call."

"No," he repeats. "I never agreed to this."

"You knew that's why I came."

"I thought you came to see me."

He catches the glimmer of her eyes through her heavy lashes, although she folds the paper and tucks it back in the inside pocket of her handbag. She doesn't usually give up so easily. He knows she will show him her list of names again.

∞

For the last three days Ketia has stayed in bed. Often her cheeks are wet. Her breasts hurt and sometimes she thinks she's still pregnant. Gabrielle murmurs to stop worrying and pleads with her to get up. She brings Ketia bowls of ice cream and coaxes her to eat. Ketia can't taste it but she feels the cold on her teeth, in her throat. It's over now, Gabrielle whispers. You have to start to get better.

Yesterday Ma's slow steps trudged across the floor. The mattress sagged when she sat, her hip a rampart of flesh next to Ketia's leg. Ketia's breath came light and thin through her nose. Afraid of Ma. Could she have found out *now?*

Then Ma's deep voice. "Les peines d'amour." Her hand on Ketia's thigh, her palm pressed warm through the afghan. "You know... before your Pa there was a boy in Caprau." Each word came slowly, as if Ma would sooner not speak but felt that she must. "He said to me... en bon français... je prépare mon coeur à la nidation de ton amour."

Ketia's mouth softened, listening. *I prepare my heart to embed your love.* What happened to this boy that Ma didn't stay with him?

Ma's hand grew heavy. "...I wanted to die when they took him away. They had to tie my limbs. My grandmother burned herbs and killed our only chicken to pay the mambo to come. The priest said to untie me — but it was too soon. My sorrow was too big. It would have swallowed me." Ma squeezed Ketia's thigh.

"But it did not, you see. I married Pa and had my six beautiful babies." Ma squeezed again. When she lifted her hand away, Ketia missed its flat, warm ballast. The mattress bounced and resettled when Ma stood and scuffed from the room in her trodden slippers.

That evening at suppertime, when Gabrielle asked if she was getting up, Ketia said yes. She felt frail on her chair, almost as small as Bastien across from her. She ate little of her rice and beans. She kept sneaking looks at Ma. Gabrielle talked about going with her class to Sherbrooke to watch their school volleyball match. Bastien said he liked basketball better. "Good for you," Gabrielle said, but without heat.

When Ketia left her fork on her plate and sat with her hands limp in her lap, Ma told her to go back to bed and sleep. "Tomorrow you'll eat more."

This morning Ketia sits at the table while Gabrielle makes them toast. One of Gabrielle's sloppy toasts slathered with jam. Ketia cuts it in half and wants to scrape off some jam, but Gabrielle orders her. "You eat all of it. Ma's starting to worry you're anorexic. You got really skinny, you know."

Ketia forces herself to take another bite. She can feel from the way her bones fold that she's lost weight. Her legs and arms. Her hipbones are ugly now. She no longer touches them. And her breasts still hurt. She wishes she knew why — if it's normal.

Gabrielle says, "I want you to go driving with me today. I've got my test next week and I need to practice."

Ketia hasn't left the apartment since she came home from the hospital. It will be easier with Gabrielle. She shrugs and says okay.

She can hide in her pyjamas, but not when she pulls a pair of old jeans up her skinny shanks. A whole belt notch tighter. She picks a baggy sweater so Gabrielle doesn't notice.

They take the side stairwell, closest to the alley that leads to the back of the laundromat where Ketia parks her car. Gabrielle trips down the stairs on the balls of her feet, stopping on the landings and waiting for Ketia, who takes the steps slowly. Out the side door into the cold air. Ketia shivers. They don't talk. Ketia glances at the pale grey sky. The back of the apartment building next to theirs. The garbage spilled around a rusted blue dumpster. She tucks her chin into her scarf again.

She waits in the passenger seat, the heater blowing on high, as Gabrielle scrapes the windows. She remembers Gabrielle driving home from the hospital. Her womb empty. No baby. As a nurse she knows that doesn't mean she'll never have a baby, but deeper down her gut twists, worrying how God will exact punishment.

Gabrielle steers out of the alley onto the main street, drives past the pizza place, more apartment buildings like theirs, the pharmacy, the Vietnamese grocery store where they buy milk and sometimes eggs. Ketia watches but pays no attention. Gabrielle knows when to signal and how to advance to turn left. She doesn't need to twist so far whenever she looks over her shoulder, but that's how she is. She contorts herself as she tries to parallel park on the street in front of the church. She yanks the parking brake and turns the key off. "Here we are."

Ketia looks out the window at the church. A blocky, red-brick structure with a square steeple. A hairy carpet up the front steps to keep people from slipping.

"You have to go in," Gabrielle says. "Père Christophe is waiting."

"What?" Ketia struggles to sit up, her too-large clothes twisting around her.

"I made an appointment for you to talk with him."

"You *told* him what I did?"

Gabrielle fiddles with her gloves. "I told him what I did. That I helped you. I had to tell him because... I had to, Ketia." Her mouth trembles.

Ketia's shocked. She thought Gabrielle didn't care. "But I can't tell him that I —" Ketia can't say it out loud, even between the two them in the car.

"Père Christophe will help you."

"Help me *how*? It's too late."

A hand taps on the window. Père Christophe in a sweater and jeans. He opens the door. "Come, Ketia. I'm too old to be standing outside in this cold."

Ketia can't refuse with him waiting for her, though she drags her boots reluctantly, following him up the steps and into the church, down the side aisle to his office. He tells her to take off her coat and sit while he busies himself at the sink, filling the kettle and rinsing the teapot. His cluttered desk is shoved into the corner. The large wardrobe, its door ajar on his red and white vestments, dominates the room. His jacket lies tossed on a chair with his boots kicked underneath — as sloppy as Bastien. He lifts a small container of milk from the window ledge. Brings the teapot and two cups without saucers to his desk. He reaches inside his wardrobe for the purple stole he drapes around his neck, rotates the old wooden office chair with its quilted cushion toward her.

Ketia's mouth is so dry she can't swallow. She thinks she might start coughing.

He touches two fingers to his forehead, breastbone, left and right shoulders.

She does, too, but still can't speak.

He prompts her, "Bless me, Father, for I have sinned."

"Bless me, Father..." She grips the carved wooden armrests of the chair. Under her palms the wood feels hard, yet bald and smooth, the varnish worn away.

"I'm listening," he says gently, his head bent as if he can hear the thoughts that torment her.

"I..." He already knows if Gabrielle told him.

"Yes?"

She whispers, "I was pregnant."

He waits. She can feel her heart beating in her neck. She doesn't know what to say next.

"Do you have a boyfriend?"

"No."

"Who..." He seems to have to feel his way, too. "How did you get pregnant?" His hands lie still, fingers and thumbs loose brackets on his thighs.

Her lips dry as paper. "A married man."

He glances at her. "From this community?"

She shakes her head.

"And this married man... is he older?"

"Yes."

"Did he coerce you?"

She wants to scream *yes*, to blame Marc, and exonerate herself in whatever small way she can, but she wants to be forgiven, too. So she has to tell the truth.

The priest still waits. "You don't have to be embarrassed, Ketia. You can tell me. Did he coerce you?"

"No."

"And did you meet him only once, or several times?"

This is harder. She knows she did wrong, and did it again and again. "Several times." Her voice cracks.

Père Christophe leans forward to pour tea and milk. "Drink it," he tells her.

She doesn't want any, but she sips.

"Did you meet him because you loved him?"

"I…" Ketia has to sip tea again. "I thought I did."

"But you always knew he was married?"

She doesn't answer.

"Do you still see him?"

"No." The loudest she's spoken yet.

"What did he say when you told him you were pregnant?"

She looks at Père Christophe in confusion. Why would she have told a man who was married to someone else that she was pregnant? "I never told him."

Père Christophe tilts his head. "He was the father, wasn't he?"

Marc made her pregnant, but she never thought of him as the father. He was the man who did this to her. She didn't want him to know. "He's married," she said.

"So he didn't know and he didn't advise you."

A small shake of the head.

"Let me understand," he says slowly. "You discovered you were pregnant, but you didn't tell him. You didn't know what to do. And you felt desperate."

She nods. Tears dripping off her cheeks now. He's making her remember.

"And you didn't come to ask me."

Ketia's hands clench the armrests of the chair. "I tried."

"Yes." He touches his stole. "I saw you in the church, but I had no idea. I failed you, Ketia. I'm sorry. Truly I am."

Her breath catches. She's crying. She'll have to say it now. Even if he already knows. "I had…" she begins to sob. "…Abortion." She presses her yellow scarf to her face with both hands as she weeps.

He reaches for a box of tissue from his desk and waits as she cries. He makes the odd, consoling murmur, drinks his tea, and as her tears slow, urges her to drink hers.

When she's calm again — exhausted, cheeks hot, eyes puffy but dry — he says, "I'd like to understand how you came to this decision."

"For Ma," she says. She's thought this through again and again. "I didn't want to hurt her. She likes to stand so proud with all her friends. She would have been ashamed — she expects a lot of me. Especially with Gabrielle..." Ketia stops. She can't blame Gabrielle, who helped her. "Pa, too, calls me his good girl. And the kids at school would have teased Bastien. I had to protect my family." Even as she talks, she hears how flimsy the words sound.

Père Christophe purses his lips. "Your mother would never want you to do such a thing *for* her. Your mother is strong stuff, Ketia. She doesn't care about anyone's opinion. She follows her own counsel and her own good sense. She might not have been happy at first, but she would never reject your baby."

As he says it, she knows it's true.

"Who were you really protecting, Ketia?"

Ketia blinks. She thought she had no tears left, but she can feel them swelling again. "I didn't want Ma to be ashamed."

"Ashamed of who?" His voice soft. Coaxing her closer.

"...Me."

He nods — as if to say, you're almost there. Just another step, my dear.

∞

Marc drives to the condo. Jaw stern, mouth grim. He needs to act. Set events in motion. Do *something*.

His new apartment is ready with yellow Marguerites in a gray vase on the table, Egyptian cotton sheets, a duvet mattress cover, a set of Creuset he bought at a post-Christmas sale.

But Ketia still hasn't returned to work. He doesn't know why. There aren't any shifts marked next to her name on the schedule. Normally the nurses gossip so carelessly that the nursing station sounds like an instant soap opera, but no one mentions Ketia nor even seems to notice that she's gone. He's researched the risk factors for first trimester and can find nothing significant for a woman her age. Perhaps she's bleeding, which could be a miscarriage. She must have seen a doctor. Who's helping her through all this? Obviously not her strict mother. Ketia should be *with him*.

Every morning this week he's driven to her apartment building. She never comes out. But, of course, she won't if she's sick. Still, he expects her whenever the door swings wide. He's driven along all the surrounding side streets, but never found her car. There are two side doors and a back door to her building, but they're metal service doors. Probably fire exits. He always parks with the front door in view.

The front door isn't locked, but that doesn't help him if he doesn't know which apartment is hers. The stupid mailboxes aren't labelled. He knocked on a door on the ground floor and asked a man in a food-stained robe cinched around his drooping waist if he could please tell him where a young woman by the name of Ketia lived. The man backed up a step and closed the door.

Marc decided to try one floor up. As he waited before the door where he'd knocked, two big-shouldered boys sauntered down the hallway. "Hey, toi. What do you want?"

Marc pointed at the door as if he was visiting.

"Oh yeah? Well, guess who lives there? Me. And I don't know who you are." The larger of the boys flexed his wrist and clenched a fist.

"Mistake," Marc mumbled and sidled past them to the stairs to leave. Outside he walked past his car so they wouldn't know it was his. He bought a piece of pizza on the corner, bit into the tip, dropped the rest into the trash.

From his car he watches the girls who shuffle in treacherously high platform boots along the snowy sidewalk. Short, tall, gawky, overweight, underdressed, overdressed. None of the girls remind him even vaguely of Ketia.

Every so often he turns on his motor to keep warm. He imagines bursting through the door of Ketia's apartment, bundling her in a blanket, and carrying her to his car. The fantasy encourages him, even as he embroiders details — elbowing aside the overbearing, pigheaded mother who doesn't understand that his bond with Ketia supersedes hers.

Only after a while does he realize that the home where he imagines bringing Ketia isn't the apartment he prepared. The landlady was right. It's too small for a couple. With the computer in the bedroom, there's no room for the armchair where he thought Ketia would sit and watch the tree.

He wants Ketia in the condo — where he has as much right to live as Joelle does. In fact, even more now that he has to think of Ketia, too. She should be comfortable. He pictures her reclined against the pillows on the sofa, facing the dining room as he prepares a meal.

Joelle can move into the apartment he rented. It's all set up. He cleaned it. She only has to move her clothes. Of course, he'll buy out her share of the condo. He's not trying to cheat her. He only wants what's fair — for himself as well as her. He will speak with his parents about a loan. Joelle doesn't need all that space, living by herself.

He's only been gone a week, but when he sees the grey stone façade of his condo building, he feels that he's returning after a long, unaccountable absence. The broad, high windows. The stone archway engraved with the old college motto. HABE-BUNT LUMEN VITAE. He knows enough Latin from medical terms to recognize light and life — which is more than Joelle knows.

The lovely, high-gloss, stucco hallways. The marble floors. Though he hesitates when he sees strange boots in the tray. Heavy, flat-soled boots. Nothing Joelle would wear. And suddenly suspicious that the boots belong to a man — a man already! — he slides the key into the lock carefully.

Not quietly enough, though, because a figure bounds from the living room. Startled, he jumps back, then recognizes Diane's enormous bosom, her wispy fringe of hair that always looks like she needs a cut. And of course, already bellowing. "You can't just walk in! You don't *live* here anymore."

He brandishes his key. "This is my place, too! I own it — half of it."

"Half, you think? We'll see what a judge decides. You walked out on her, remember? To have a baby with someone else. So go. Have it." She swats a folded magazine between them as if he were a cloud of stink.

"What are you doing here? Where's Joelle?" He projects his voice down the hallway, convinced she can hear him.

"None of your business what I'm doing. And Joelle's not here." She sticks out her pointed witch's chin. As if her face weren't sharp enough already.

"I need to speak with her."

"Well, that's just too bad. Life doesn't happen exactly the way *you* want it to. I told you, get out!" She waves at the door with her magazine.

From where Marc stands he suddenly notices that the sofa is gone. "What happened —" He points.

"We moved it."

He stretches his neck and sees the edge of the arm. They've shoved the sofa under the windows. "That's a ridiculous place for the sofa."

"Matter of opinion. And at the moment yours doesn't count."

Diane stands too close, square on her feet, not moving. Marc can't see more unless he pushes her aside.

"Get lost!" she shouts. "I mean it, I'll call the police."

He feels a fleck of saliva strike his cheek and rears his head, revolted. Turns and yanks open the door to get away from her hysterics. He'll call Joelle at work. Or maybe he should call a lawyer.

Hand still on the door, he feels how she thumps it. The bitch.

∽

A tail of wind lashes Joelle and Pei Yi as they scurry from the hospital to the parking lot. Pei Yi's turquoise coat yells colour in the grey, brown, and white winter cityscape.

"You don't mind driving downtown?" Joelle asks.

"Why not?"

Joelle drives only rarely — and only when the road conditions are flawless.

Pei Yi revs the engine and reverses with a tight, neat turn. She pats Joelle's arm. "Don't be nervous. My brother is nice."

"I'm not nervous," Joelle protests too quickly. "Not about your brother," she adds.

Pei Yi accelerates to pass a bus. "You're just going to talk to my brother. Nobody says you have to get a divorce yet. Not until you feel ready."

Joelle has no idea how much Pei Yi knows about her and Marc. The other secretaries seem to know everything, but Pei Yi doesn't sit and whisper with the others over coffee and cheese Danish.

"He's already with someone new," Joelle tells her. "And she's pregnant."

Pei Yi purses her scarlet lips. "Easy," she says then. "Easy for you to get a divorce."

"It doesn't feel easy."

"No," Pei Yi admits. She flexes her gloved leather fingers on the steering wheel.

Joelle wonders what Pei Yi's marriage is like. Since she found out about Marc, she wonders about everyone's relationship. Being a couple must feel different when you both have to care for a child. She still can't imagine Marc in that role. Nor Emile. The men she's been with only ever took care of themselves.

"Where's your daughter now?" she asks.

"At home with her grandmother."

When Pei Yi turns into a parking lot, Joelle snaps opens her purse for her wallet. "I'll pay."

"We don't have to pay. Bingwen works here. I'm giving him a ride home."

"Does he live near you?"

"Two doors away."

They hurry across the scraped asphalt toward the café. As soon as they open the door Joelle smells dark roasted coffee. Only a few people sit at the small round tables and tufted leather booths. At one of the tables a man lifts his hand. His face is broad like Pei Yi's, but with a cleft chin. His suit jacket is dark grey, his shirt cream, his tie black and grey — his colours as conservative as Pei Yi's are flamboyant. He stands to shake Joelle's hand.

"Joelle, this is my brother, Bingwen. We tease him — call him Big Ben. Big Ben, this is my friend Joelle."

The women order hot chocolate. Bingwen already has an espresso before him.

He reaches for the slim briefcase on the floor and takes out a yellow legal pad. "Do you mind if I take notes?" He uncaps a pen and sets it at an angle on the page.

Joelle wipes her hands on her skirt and clears her throat. She's afraid to seem to be taking the first steps. Although maybe Marc is seeing a lawyer, too. He wouldn't tell her, would he? Pei Yi suggested she should be prepared.

She takes a deep breath. Pei Yi's slim fingers curve around her saucer. Bingwen's yellow pad with the pen on top. Both wait for her to start talking.

"What do I have to do?" she asks.

"To begin, have you considered dispute resolution — mediation with a counsellor?"

"Tell him," Pei Yi says.

Joelle tells her hot chocolate. "He's already met someone else and got her pregnant."

He balances his pen between thumb and middle finger. "Are you still living together?"

Joelle shakes her head.

"Who left the residence, you or him?"

He writes in short, scratchy strokes of black ink. He presses hard. The back of his hand is square. Larger than Marc's. Hairless. Joelle watches his pen move down the page as she speaks. When he gets to the end and flips it, the imprint of his writing is traced on the next page.

"What's the current market value of the condo?"

"...I don't know."

"And what other significant material possessions do you have? Real estate, automobile, boat?"

"The car was his."

"His because he bought it or his because he drove it? Did the money to pay for it come from your joint earnings?"

With each question, her shoulders feel smaller. She's ashamed of how little she knows.

"Do you have access to your financial goods? Bank accounts, RRSPs, bonds...?"

Joelle hasn't even opened the drawer yet, where Marc kept all the papers and the chequebook. No doubt, he took the papers. What if he hasn't even left her cheques to pay her bills? "I don't know. I don't think so."

The pen pauses. "It's all right. We can get access — unless he's transferred money to a separate account. Do you think he might have?"

Joelle softly clinks her spoon on the saucer. "He might."

"Does he want a divorce as well?"

"He should," Pei Yi says.

"Sh," her brother tells her.

"He hasn't told me. But he... doesn't tell me much. He didn't tell me about her. I found out from someone else. I know he wants to stay with her."

"So you don't expect conflict."

Joelle lays her hand flat on the table next to her cup. She's not wearing her ring. This morning she dropped it on her dresser. A thin rattling sound. She will use the money from selling it to buy herself something completely silly.

"You *do* expect conflict," Bingwen says now.

She curls her hand toward herself. "Not about the divorce. I don't know about the condo and the money. I didn't work for a couple of years and I make less money than he does now."

"Perhaps he'll have to pay you alimony."

She can't tell if he's joking. "I don't want his money."

"If you agree to retain me, how about you let me decide that?" He places his pen on the paper, textured and criss-crossed from the pressure of his writing.

"I..." Joelle hesitates. "How much do you cost?"

Pei Yi leans forward, finger poking her brother's arm. "Friend price!"

"Friend price," he nods. "But I'd sooner discuss that in my office." He closes his legal pad. "How about," he looks at Pei Yi, "we go for a bite. Since you drove downtown and already told Liang you were eating out with me."

"Oh, you!" Pei Yi scolds him in Cantonese. And to Joelle, "I can't tell my husband anything. He tells Big Ben."

Bingwen shrugs and says, "You, my dear, boss the both of us around." He tucks his yellow pad into his briefcase, slides his pen in his breast pocket, and signals for the bill. "Is she a bully at work too?" he asks Joelle. "I'm curious to hear if even half the stories she tells about the hospital are true."

Joelle looks at Pei Yi, surprised that at work she seems to pay so little attention to the goings-on only to spin them into stories at home.

Pei Yi doesn't deny it. She fits her turquoise beret on her black bob and nudges Joelle. "Aren't you coming?"

∞

Past eight o'clock and Joelle hasn't come home yet. Diane finally ate her spaghetti and ratatouille alone. She washed her dishes and left the rest of the food in the pots on the stove in the event that Madame would be hungry at whatever hour she finally deigns to arrive.

Diane huddles, knees up, on the same side of the sofa where she sits at home. She can't focus on her crosswords. She's flicked through the channels on TV and turned it off. Knitting her vest — still hardly past the ribbing yet — makes her feel like she's tying herself up in knots.

Earlier, when Marc walked in, her heart lunged with a burst that Nazim had finally managed to dodge his sister. But Nazim doesn't have a key. Of course it wasn't him.

Why is there no clock in the living room? She has to keep getting off the sofa and walking to the kitchen to check the clock on the stove.

She wonders what Nazim is doing. If his sister made tajine. Does he do the dishes when she cooks? His sister must ask questions about his life in Montreal. Can't she hear the holes in what he says? Instead of telling her about Diane, what does he tell her instead?

Diane groans. All right, then, *okay,* his sister is visiting and his family can't know about her. For some stupid reason she actually agreed to go along with that. But she cannot *bear* that he won't even talk to her on the phone!

She bounces her head back on the sofa, grits her teeth at the dark sky outside. She can't recall a time in her life when she felt like she was just... hanging in midair! Usually she can *make* things happen. She's not a puppet like Joelle.

What time is it now? Diane thuds her feet to the floor and stomps to the kitchen. Tomorrow she's going to a dollar store and buying a clock.

Eight-thirty already. Since when does Joelle have friends Diane doesn't know?

And what the fuck is wrong with Nazim that he can't pick up the phone and call? Simple manners, dammit! She's all set to accommodate whoever and however, but these past few days her tolerance has been zinged into orbit by the way

Nazim is behaving. He dumps her in silence and figures she'll just simper and wait on his pleasure like some sweet Moroccan wifey.

Oh yeah? She stomps across the room, snatches the phone, stabs the buttons.

"Allô?"

"Don't you dare hang up on me! I've had it, do you hear me? You say you're stuck between me and your family — between Montreal and Morocco. But you know what? You're not stuck *between* anyone. You chose them! I'm nowhere. That's what it —"

Diane hears the drone of the dial tone. She's not even sure when he hung up. She's so angry she could hurl the receiver against the wall.

She bangs her knee into the corner of the coffee table and curses. She sits with her feet flat on the floor in the middle of the sofa, ready to leap up again. What is he, some asshole she's been living with for two years and only now she's starting to smell how he reeks? And she actually thought they had a relationship! How can she ever live with him again?

She bounds from the sofa when she hears the key in the lock. "Where were you?" she demands.

Joelle hangs her coat on the stand. "I told you I was going out." She frowns at Diane. "What's the matter with you?"

"Marc was here. He didn't even knock, he walked right in."

"What did he want?" Joelle walks past Diane to the kitchen. She doesn't look or sound as upset as Diane expected.

"To talk to you."

Joelle pours herself a glass of water from the pitcher in the fridge.

"He wasn't happy to see me here."

"I'll bet."

Diane leans against the counter. "I made ratatouille."

"Not for me, I hope."

"You don't want any?"

"I told you I was going out." She sets her glass next to the sink. "I'm really tired now. I have to sleep. Work tomorrow."

Diane hears the bathroom door close. Joelle usually tells her everything. All through high school she recounted every play-by-play move with every guy she dated. The first time Emile invited her over for a beer, they had sex that very night. How Marc didn't creep his hand up her shirt until the third date. Why the big secret about this new friend?

Diane grabs one of the Italian glass bowls with plastic lids from the cupboard — no ordinary Tupperware for Joelle and Marc — and scrapes the ratatouille from the pot. She drops the metal ladle in the sink and bangs the pot, making as much racket as she can washing up. In the living room she turns the TV up loud. She squints against the wetness in her eyes. She is *not* crying. She is angry — and with good reason. With Nazim. With Joelle. With herself.

∞

Ghada stands at the counter skinning the green peppers she charred to make taktouka. When she moves to the sink to rinse her hands, she turns the cold water on first so she won't burn the djinn that lives in the drain. When Nazim first saw her do it here, he thought she was acting out of habit. Forgetting where she was. He finally teased her and she clicked her tongue. "Of course you have a djinn. Why wouldn't you? You think they don't live in Montreal? Watch out if you burn this one. She'll take revenge and burn your food." Another detail, he thought, that he would have to remember to tell Diane.

He loves sitting in the kitchen at the table while Ghada cooks. He closes his eyes and can almost believe he's home again. The tajine in the oven perfumes the air with citron confit, saffron, green olives, and shark. Earlier in the week she made couscous she flavoured with smen. He'd brought her to the Algerian butcher on Jean-Talon where she slid into a

Maghrebian patois — half Arabic, half Berber — questioning the butcher on how he'd spiced his merguez. Yesterday Nazim found her rooting through the plastic bags under the sink for one she could use as an ad hoc pastry bag to swirl dough into hot fat. Zlabia! As a boy he clamoured for the rose-shaped sweet.

Eyes still closed, he hears how Ghada moves quickly, like Diane, but... is it possible that a knife chopping on a board has such a personal rhythm?

Once indoors, Ghada peels off the form-fitting jeans that she believes make her the stylish equal of any woman in Montreal — nay, their better, because her jeans are from Paris. She slips into a blue floor-length djellaba. The robe sways around her hips and arms as she moves from the counter to the stove, reaches for salt and cumin. The bell of soft fabric adds a quiet shush and grace to her movements.

She brought a formal, embroidered djellaba for when they go visiting. Two days ago they celebrated Eid ul-Fitr with Hatem's family. Hatem told Nazim that his wife had promised on their eldest son's manhood not to divulge even a flick of the eye about Diane. Nazim thanked him, knowing how heavily Hatem would have to repay that debt.

Nazim has opened a bottle of Merlot to have with the tajine this evening. When he playfully made to set a wineglass before Ghada's plate, she slapped his arm. "Don't you dare!"

"You can drink water in a wineglass, don't worry. Allah knows the difference."

She shook her head. "Give me an ordinary glass."

The first day she scowled at all the wineglasses in the cabinet. How often did he drink wine? And how *much*, that he needed so many glasses? He explained they were decorative. People chose different styles for different wines and different occasions. Exactly like tea glasses. And in any case, the wineglasses belonged to the woman from whom he rented the apartment. Ghada didn't question this story about the woman who'd left to go work in Vancouver — too far away to meet.

She paced from room to room, marvelling at the space. But she wondered that he didn't mind living with such odd furniture. That sinkhole trap of a sofa. The bed so high from the floor.

Nazim pours himself a glass of Merlot and sips. His feet, crossed at the ankles, protrude past the edge of the table.

Ghada aims her knife at his feet. "Those are disgusting." He sits up straight and folds his legs under his chair. "Why didn't you tell me you needed a new pair of babouches? The only thing keeping those together are the memory of what they're supposed to be."

"I didn't think of it."

"I didn't think of it," she mimics. And in a more level tone, "Sins of omission are sins all the same."

"How about your sins of omission? You could have surprised me with a pair."

"Don't try to turn this into a joke. You know what I'm talking about. Those families I want you to —"

"No," he cuts her off. "I'm not meeting them. I told you."

"Listen to me." Ghada faces him now. "It took me over a year to contact all these families. But I'm not talking about me. Who cares about me?" She gives him a bitter smile. "I'm just Ghada. Trust me to patch up all the holes, see to this, see to that. But these families I contacted agreed to meet you — and they *expect* to meet you."

"Ghada, I'm not going to marry their daughters. It's absurd to waste their time, your time, and my time to sit and drink mint tea with them."

"It will be a courtesy. Have you become such a barbarian living here that you've forgotten courtesy?"

He knows what she means. These families have already ordered the pastries to serve with tea. M'hencha, sellou, chrik. The best filigree glasses polished and set on a shining silver tray. The parents may not like Nazim, approve of his job as service rep for an internet provider, care that he wears a sweater instead of a suit to visit. That's within their rights. For him not to visit, though, will be a grave offence, the shame of which will follow Ghada across the ocean to Morocco.

"Courtesy," she repeats more sharply, turning it into an order. Bangs the flat of her hand on the edge of the counter. "I made you tajine. I made you couscous. I baked cornes de gazelles. Now you behave like you should."

He rubs his fingers across his forehead, then up into his hair. What can he say? "I'm sorry, Ghada, I can't."

"It's because you already have a woman."

The flesh on his arms prickles. He expects her to glare, to sneer. But she looks at him with no expression.

"I'm not stupid, Nazim. If you don't want to meet perfectly nice women when you could, you obviously already have one."

His hand creeps toward his wineglass.

"You might as well tell me."

He takes a sip. "No."

"No, you don't have a woman or no, you won't tell me?"

"What you don't know, you won't have to lie about when you go home."

In the silence of the kitchen the oven elements hum awake. Nazim imagines he can hear the soft bubbling of the tajine baking slowly. Ever so slowly. The flavours mingling.

Ghada leans against the counter behind her. She might not like his logic, but she accepts it. "And that's definite?"

"It's very definite."

Finally she nods. Then sniffs. "How will I explain that at home — that I couldn't find you a wife?"

"Tell them I'm stubborn and stupid."

"We already know that."

She takes up the pestle she made him buy when she couldn't find one in the kitchen, and, hugging the bowl to her stomach, starts to mash the green pepper flesh and chilies. To the thump of the pestle on plastic she says, "Even if you're not going to marry these eligible brides, it would help if I could say that you had at least met them."

"Waste of time," he says again. "You're only here for three weeks —"

"No. This isn't about my time. Or even theirs. We've all agreed to do this. You're the one who has to wrap your brain around it."

"Ghada..."

"A glass of tea and some delicious pastries. *How do you do? How do you do?*" She peers into the bowl to see how smooth the mixture is. Keeps pounding.

"For form's sake," she adds. "Or how about you do it for me?"

∞

The door to the stairwell claps shut behind Marc. The floor seems calm — the linen trolleys against the wall stacked, the hampers that line the hallway empty. No one crowds around Lou's end of the nursing station. Marie-Ange stands with her enormous bum jutting into the hallway. The size of it strains the eyes, not to mention the seams of her uniform. The woman can't even walk normally. She should cut out the roti.

The housekeeper winks at Marc, nods at Marie-Ange, and grabs a fistful of air he mimes squeezing. Marc turns his head, pretending he hasn't seen.

In the change room he hangs his parka on a hook, grabs his stethoscope from his locker, loops it around his neck. Yadira bangs open the door. "Oops. Sorry."

Marc ignores her. These days he only comes to work to wait for Ketia. Every day he looks at the schedule to see when she'll be working again. The tension of not knowing and waiting adds to the unreality of his mornings sitting in his car outside her building.

In the nursing station, even though it's not busy and the nurses sit chatting, the counters are as messy as ever. X-ray films, patients' charts, lab requisitions, the bitten half of a donut tossed back into the empty box. The binder with the schedule pokes out from under a scatter of faxed lab results. He flips it open. Stands still. Very still. Ketia's name and shifts have been crossed through completely. As if... but no, even if she were on preventative maternity leave there's a code for that.

Marc spins around to where Raymonde listens to Aditi. "The order says to apply a dry dressing, but Wound Care told me N/S gauze —"

"What's this?" Marc interrupts, finger underlining Ketia's name on the schedule.

Raymonde bats a hand in the air. "I'm taking report. Can't you see?"

"You can still answer a question. What if it's an emergency? This is a hospital — you're a nurse! Can't you prioritize?"

Raymonde turns back to Aditi. "Did you tell Wound Care ID was here?"

Marc whirls around to see who else he can ask. They've all stopped what they were doing. A chorus of faces.

"What are you gawking at? I asked a simple question, and she won't answer. I remember when she was a student and she called a staff doctor stat because a lousy NG tube came out and she thought she'd killed the patient. So now she's a charge nurse. Big deal!"

Lou has snatched the phone to make a call, and now Pascale's heels can be heard approaching from her office.

"Marc," she says. "Come with me."

"Of course." He follows talking to her back. "I should have asked you, of course, but I didn't want to disturb you." He raises his voice so she can hear him over the repeated stab of her heels. "I asked Raymonde why Ketia's name was crossed off the schedule. Just because she's taking report doesn't mean she can't answer a question. I have no idea why she —"

"Close the door," Pascale says. Her office is tiny, her desk shoved against the wall with only enough space for her chair to rotate from side to side. The second chair obstructs the door from opening completely. Hooks on the back of the door hold a variety of cloth bags filled with irregular shapes. Shoes, Marc knows, because Joelle has the same kind of bags.

He waits for her to tidy away the contents of a folder she has open on her desk. "So," he begins again, "I wondered why Ketia's name was taken off the schedule."

She swivels her chair away from her desk, facing him, and crosses her legs. Her pointy black shoe with the fang-like heel hovers in the small space between them. "Ketia's name on the schedule doesn't concern you."

"You don't understand —"

"Let me speak." Her words and tone cut across his with all the severity of a reprimand — as if *he* were at fault. He is so shocked that his mouth opens.

"I've received several complaints about your behaviour toward Ketia. You've been observed pursuing her in the hallway, trying to surprise her in patient rooms, calling after her when she runs away, waiting for her after work — in short, harassing her."

"That's ridiculous! People don't understand. And they make things up. I can't believe you even take it seriously."

"Reliable sources, Marc — too many of them for me to ignore."

"But not Ketia," he says with absolute confidence. "Ketia never complained to you."

Her shoe nods once, up and down. "No," she admits. "Not Ketia."

He sniffs, convinced that he's trumped Pascale at whatever little trap she thinks she's concocted. "I don't care what other people say. It's not their business. Ketia and I understand each other. That's all that counts. You're no doubt aware that she's pregnant. Well…" He points a finger at his chest and smiles stiffly. "What I don't understand — what I was trying to ask Raymonde — is why Ketia's name is crossed off the schedule."

"Ketia no longer works here."

"No longer…?" He rucks forward in his chair but has to sit

back again or risk being impaled on the stabbing heel of Pascale's shoe. "You can't let Ketia go because she's pregnant!"

"Marc, you aren't listening. I called you into my office to discuss your conduct on the floor. I'm giving you a verbal warning now. If I get another complaint — from a nurse, an orderly, a family member — you'll get a written warning and a suspension. The hospital has zero tolerance for sexual harassment."

Marc lifts his chin. "Ketia didn't complain. You already said so."

Pascale uncrosses her legs and reaches for a piece of paper. "She might yet. I'm not sure why she's protecting you. Perhaps you threatened her."

"*Threatened her?*"

"You talk about her obsessively. She's terrified of you. I think it's very possible that you bully and threaten her."

Marc springs to his feet, legs rigid, glaring down at Pascale.

"Sit down! Or I'll call Security and have you escorted from the hospital."

He sits. Counts the memos pinned to the bulletin board behind her head. Blood thrums in his temples. He cannot believe how his own head nurse could misinterpret tales likes this. He'll take this to the union, he will!

"*Any* complaint," she stresses. "Just one. And you're suspended." She waits a beat. "Now you can go."

∞

Diane turns off the water she runs over the mushrooms. Joelle, who just came home, shuffles into the kitchen. "You're not supposed to wash them," she mumbles.

"What?"

"Supposed to brush them. Marc always said..." Joelle shrugs. "Forget it. He probably took his mushroom brush." She swings through the door again.

A mushroom brush? Diane shakes her head. As if life isn't

complicated enough already. Contorted. Ass-backward. A knot with no end — and her left holding it.

She tumbles the mushrooms onto the cutting board and begins slicing them. Each tock of the knife on the wood drives her frustration deeper.

Today she could have gotten a ticket for loitering, she hung around in the street so long before the red brick building where she lived with Nazim. Along the street, green recycling boxes stuffed with juice cartons, toilet paper rolls, wine bottles, and cans were wedged onto snow banks. Cars were parked at all angles in the bays dug with shovels and sweat. This narrow street was always one of the last in the entire city to be cleaned.

Diane could make out most of the apartment numbers scrawled on the recycling boxes. Theirs wasn't out. Nazim forgot. Three floors up, their tiny wrought-iron balcony — très Montréal — was heaped with snow. She dared herself to climb the stairs and knock on the door. Or — why knock? She had her key. She could walk in the way Marc did the other day. But she doesn't want to do anything like Marc.

The front door of the building suddenly swung wide and the neighbour from downstairs — Betty Boop and her wicked sex life — heaved her recycling box out the door, down the steps, onto the snow. Diane swung around and trudged off. She didn't care if Nazim saw her — in fact, she wished he did! But she didn't want to have to explain to the neighbour why she was out on the street with the garbage.

Mushrooms sliced, Diane wonders if she should start cooking. Joelle isn't in the living room but the bedroom, curled on the bed facing the wall. "Are you all right?"

Joelle says something Diane can't understand.

"Did something happen?"

Joelle twists around. "Emile had his surgery today."

Emile *again*. Why does Joelle never learn? That man will only hurt her — again and again and again.

"He did something so stupid. He wrote on his consent that

he refused a colostomy bag. Frank couldn't resect his bowel because the tumour was too big and then he couldn't do anything else, either."

Diane sighs loudly. "Can't you stay away from Emile?"

Joelle struggles up and swings her feet to the floor. "Don't you *listen?* Emile had his surgery today. And it *didn't* go well. In fact, it couldn't have been worse!" Joelle jumps up, arms like rods, fists tight. Diane backs into the hallway in surprise. "This isn't the time to give me a lecture on what I should and shouldn't do, as per my know-it-all friend Diane!" Joelle strides past, cheeks crimson, mouth trembling.

Diane swallows. She's only telling her for her own good. Doesn't Joelle realize? She shakes her hair off her forehead and walks to the living room.

Joelle sits huddled on the sofa, arms hugged around her legs.

Deliberately calm, Diane asks, "Why did you yell at me? You know I moved in here to help you —"

"To watch me!"

"That's not true."

"But you watch me all the time! Can't you just —" Joelle's breath catches. "Can't you stop telling me what to do?"

Diane moves to sit in her corner of the sofa. She hesitates, not sure if she should mention Emile again, but wanting to explain. "Emile makes me nervous."

"That's so crazy," Joelle moans. "You have no idea how pathetic he looks right now. And he's got this humongous tumour. Frank doesn't know if he's even a candidate for chemo."

Good, Diane thinks. One less sleaze on the planet.

"I'm going back to the hospital tonight to make sure he's comfortable. They're bringing him back to his room at seven." Joelle looks at her watch.

"I'll make supper, okay?" Slowly Diane stands, hands bracing her lower back.

"Thanks," Joelle says. "Diane…"

"Yes?"

"You don't always have to cook. There's a café not far from here where I used to have supper. We can go there, too. Or I can go and you can do something else."

"But I thought you liked when I cooked."

"I do, but you don't always have to." Joelle frowns, looks out the window at the sky, says nothing more.

In the kitchen Diane measures rice and water into a pot. Adds salt and a bay leaf. Joelle is going through a mixed-up time. She shouldn't take anything Joelle says right now too seriously. Shouldn't even listen. She pours olive oil into a heavy skillet, turns the flame on low, peels a clove of garlic. Her temples feel taut. The first sign of a headache.

∞

Nazim holds the door to the apartment building open for Ghada, who stomps her feet on the stone steps, then again on the rubber mat in the entrance. "Snow is worse than sand," she complains. "It sticks."

"But it melts," he says. Not like back home, where a dry wind blew in from the hills and you crunched granules of sand in your teeth.

Feet thunder down the stairs and Nazim moves aside for the neighbour, who seems about to barge between them. The downstairs neighbour Diane doesn't like. "Pardon," she says to Ghada, waggling her keys at the metal panel of mailboxes.

"Bonjour!" Ghada says, though she draws back a little, surprised by the woman's brusqueness.

"Salut," the neighbour mutters.

Nazim waves for Ghada to precede him up the stairs. Ghada looks at him, at the neighbour's shoulders, back at him. He has no intention of introducing her. For that matter, he doesn't even know the neighbour's name. Again he motions at the stairs.

The neighbour yanks a journal wrapped in plastic from her box, slams it shut.

Ghada pulls off her mitten and holds out her hand. "I'm Nazim's sister, Ghada, from Morocco. Pleased to meet you."

The woman frowns at Ghada's hand. Quickly Nazim says, "From upstairs. We're in the apartment —"

"Right," the woman cuts him off. Still not taking Ghada's hand. "Your girlfriend, who walks like the Jolly Green Giant. What did you do, kick her out? She was standing on the sidewalk today, gawking at your window. Probably stalking you. You should watch out."

Nazim desperately hopes Ghada can't follow the neighbour's quick words. He doesn't know who the Jolly Green Giant is, either.

The woman grimaces a fake smile at Ghada. "I hope you enjoy your stay chez nous à Montréal." And to Nazim, "Moroccan, eh? My boyfriend said you were Mexican. He's such a twit." The door swings shut behind her.

To fill the silence Nazim pulls out his mail key and opens his box. Remembers too late that there might be mail for Diane he'll have to hide from Ghada, but there are only flyers he tosses onto the stack of junk mail the tenants pile on the middle step. On recycling day someone adds it to a bin.

He and Ghada head up the stairs. He wishes he knew how much she understood of what the woman said. He can sense disapproval in the set of her shoulders, the trudge of her steps. On the landing, as he unlocks the door, she says, "Are all your neighbours that pleasant?"

He points at the door across the landing. "They're okay." A gay couple, always friendly the rare times their comings and goings coincide. He never remembers their names. But if they met Ghada, they'd introduce themselves. She wouldn't realize they were a couple.

He takes her coat and, as he walks down the hallway to the closet, calls, "Would you like tea?"

"I'll make it." She brushes past him — her hand on his arm more brisk than affectionate.

He hopes she doesn't ask what the neighbour meant. Hopes she remembers that what she doesn't know about, she won't have to lie about. He doesn't let himself feel how angry he is with Diane, because Ghada will sense that, too.

In the kitchen she rinses the bunch of fresh mint he bought at the Iranian store. At the rate they drink mint tea, he should have had a crate delivered. The silver teapot waits on the counter, lid open, the box of black tea beside it. The kettle heats on the stove.

She taps the stems against the edge of the sink and begins to pluck leaves she drops in a heap on the counter. He lifts two filigree tea glasses from the cabinet. Diane keeps them on the shelf next to the wineglasses instead of with the coffee mugs in the cupboard.

Ghada looks over her shoulder at the cabinet — Diane's cabinet, Diane's dishes — for a beat too long, her hands still busy with the leaves. Then at him. She knows.

"Three," she says.

"Three what?"

"Three families. You'll dress nicely. You'll be polite. You'll compliment the pastries, the tea, the house, the daughter. When I'm gone again, you can do as you wish."

∞

Dup. Dup. Dup. Dup. Marc's finger on the steering wheel. The dull pulse of waiting. A cheap brick apartment block with aluminum-frame windows. Beside it another. Beside that another. A laundromat. A dépanneur. Snow pocked with grit, plastic bags, Styrofoam cups, candy wrappers. The pizza shop on the corner where people buy a slice they cram into their mouths as they shamble along, drop the paper plate to the ground with a careless shrug, still chewing. They don't look for a garbage can. No one does.

How did Ketia, clothes so crisp, posture so regal, emerge

from this slum? Her family should thank him. Theirs is a fairy tale for the new millennium — he the prince, she Cinderella. He smacks his dry mouth. His eyes feel pouched, his spine, slouched against the car seat, fatigued. The tension of waiting and too little sleep exhausts him.

He dismisses Pascale's ludicrous insinuations, except for having marked the date in his agenda for when he'll make a grievance to the union. Sexual harassment? Ketia *loves* him.

Two girls in black coats walk slowly along the sidewalk, each carrying a bag of groceries. One is taller, with a languid elegance despite her bulky coat. The smaller one — her younger sister, he guesses — walks with her chin hidden in her collar. Marc is so tired that at first the yellow scarf doesn't register. Then they turn up the walk to Ketia's building.

He yanks open his door. "Wait! S'il vous plaît!"

At his cry both scramble up the steps, but Marc bolts after them. "I have to ask you something! Please, that scarf!"

The girl with the scarf cowers in the entrance. The taller one shoves her up a step and wheels on him, eyes focused with rage. "Get out! Or we'll call the police!" She jabs her arm at the door. "Fuck off, I mean it!"

"But that scarf — where did you get it? It's Ketia's," he pleads.

The girl with the scarf doesn't move, though her sister shoves her again and says something in Creole. At him she shouts, "Get lost, you fucking creep!"

"Please," he begs. "I need to find Ketia."

The girl heaves a sob and almost collapses on the steps. He would help, but her sister blocks him and yells, "Leave her alone! Fuck off!"

Apartment doors have opened. Two older black women scuttle out and pull the girl to the landing into the circle of their arms. Other tenants creep from their doors and crowd around them, holding babies on their hips, muttering, pushing out their lips.

"Don't any of you understand?" he cries. "I'm looking for Ketia!"

"Ketia doesn't want you!" the tall young woman spits. "Get the fuck lost!"

"But the baby —" he begins.

"There is no baby," she hisses.

Marc hesitates. She sounds so definite — as if she knows exactly what he means.

From behind the crowd on the landing a big-shouldered boy pushes through. "Hey, pansy boy! Thought we told you to crawl away. Do I have to step on your neck?"

"Ketia!" Marc shouts as loudly as he can. She's somewhere in this building.

The girl with the scarf turns her face. Ketia! But why does she stand so crookedly? Teeth bared, cheeks so thin, hair a frizzy cap on her skull. She sways against the two women, who bustle her into their apartment.

"Ketia!" he calls again, but with less force, not so sure anymore.

The boy with the thick arms shoves Marc, so he topples against the wall, then grabs him by his parka and throws him out the door. Marc falls down the two front steps, hitting the concrete with his hip and one arm. He lies sprawled. Doesn't move. Still too stunned by the sight of Ketia transformed into this wasted creature. That skeleton's grimace. What could have happened? Gone, her lovely, high-shouldered walk. Her modest charm. Why or how he doesn't know. Only that he's lost her.

Carefully he stretches his legs. He can move his wrist, but it feels like it's sprained. He staggers getting up, but manages to stand. His hip hurts when he puts weight on that leg. He rotates his neck. Thinks he bumped his head. He feels with his fingers to find the bruise.

He shuffles toward his car. Behind him hears, "Hey, cunt face! You're lucky you can still fucking walk. We see you around here again, you won't!"

Marc eases onto the seat, wincing. When he presses on the gas pedal his leg hurts. He pulls out without looking in the rearview mirror. A car horn blares.

Ketia must be very ill. She's so thin. Emaciated. Ugly. Disaster for her. Disaster for him. He doesn't understand what the young woman meant about the baby. Doesn't care. It's Ketia he mourns. Ketia, who roused him from the paralyzed routine of his life. All gone now. Gone.

He squeezes his eyes to clear his vision. Breathes hard against the grief that constricts his throat.

∞

Diane kneels on the floor unpacking a box of porcelain dishes, each swaddled in paper she has to peel free. Oval dishes with the lip slightly raised. Narrow leaf imprints swimming across the glaze like minnows. Diane sees but doesn't feel the pattern's delicacy.

She sits back on her haunches, hands on her thighs, fingers pressed into the ribbed corduroy of her trousers. Her anger with Nazim battles with her longing to hear from him. One moment she wants to storm their apartment, chuck his clothes and babouches over the balcony, tell him to go find another sucker who doesn't mind being a genie who has to evaporate in midair when *he* snaps his fingers. The next she yearns to sprawl with him on their foundering sofa while he reads the newspaper and she does her crosswords.

She can't even confide in anyone. Not Robin, with her ideal husband and baby. Nor Joelle, who spends her evenings at the hospital playing fetch-it for Emile — or getting together with new friends she won't tell Diane about. Diane doesn't ask anymore. Why should she? To have Joelle call her a know-it-all?

She reaches for another dish wrapped in far too many layers of paper. An overprotective potter. The dishes are ceramic

— not spun glass. Diane stops peeling and starts ripping. Hooks paper and tears. Nazim, you jerk!

And what about her? Pretty stupid, too. If another woman told her the same story, she'd scoff. You *what?* You let him stay in your apartment while you moved out and now he hangs up when you call? Send this douchebag to the moon. Send him fast.

But that's not what she wants, either. She wants for none of this to have happened. For her and Nazim to be as they were. She doesn't even care about his family anymore.

When the phone begins to ring she hoists herself up. "Boutique À Votre Goût."

"Diane."

"Oui?"

"It's Nazim."

"Nazim! Where are you calling from? It doesn't sound like you — it must be the phone. You're not at home, are you?"

"No."

"How are you? Where are you calling from?" She's babbling. She makes herself stop.

Silence on his end. "I thought we agreed..." His voice is low. "I thought we agreed that while my sister was here you would stay away."

She can't recall words that specific. It was understood, perhaps, but not the way he makes it sound — like a signed and stamped contract. "I *have* stayed away. In case you haven't noticed, we haven't seen each other once since she got here."

"The neighbour downstairs said she saw you in the street."

"Nazim, I haven't even heard from you! You haven't called once, and you won't talk to me when I call. I don't have a clue what you're doing — if you're even still alive!"

"You know exactly what I'm doing." Still that strange low voice. Strained. "My sister is here."

"Come on! Even with her there, you could call me — when she's in the shower or in bed. Or you could make an excuse to go out to buy milk."

"Says who?" A hard snip of words.

Her eyebrows lift. Why does he sound angry? She's the one who's being neglected. "I'm just saying, Nazim, that I think —"

"Could you for once"— he bites each word — "stop telling me what you think I should do? I'm doing what *I* think is right. Which is hard enough under the circumstances. All you're doing is putting me in an even more difficult position than I already am."

She's never heard him like this. He's furious. Her hand grips the receiver so hard against her cheekbone it hurts.

"Nazim, I..."

"The *only* time my sister will ever visit me." His breath strangled. Is he crying? "Three lousy weeks out of your great, big life. Can't you give us that? Can't you?"

"I didn't —" she begins, not knowing what she meant to say or how to defend herself. Then, whispering, "Yes."

"Please," he adds, his voice sounding more like himself.

"I'll stop," she says quickly, understanding that if she doesn't, she might lose him.

Neither speaks for a moment, and he says, "Goodbye."

Her hand aches when she replaces the receiver. She stares at the phone.

When the bells on the door of the boutique jingle, she darts to the small toilet and locks the door. Leans on the tiny sink. The words, what he said, his tone, as much threat as pleading. Three lousy weeks.

Through the thin door the clunk of an object dropped on the carpet. She straightens. Checks in the mirror that she hasn't smudged her lipstick. Makes herself open the door.

∞

Ketia felt how the urgency of Marc's voice could still pull her, but she knows he won't return. She heard how his voice changed when he finally recognized her.

Later, in their room, Gabrielle clutched her arm. "You got knocked up by a *white* guy? You are *so* damn lucky you're not having that baby. You would have put Ma in a coffin and hammered the nails down good."

Gabrielle described in detail how Gros Benji threw Marc out the door, booted him clear to the sidewalk.

There's no predicting what the neighbours made of the incident — or what they told Ma. Ketia waits for a reproach or a speech about shameful behaviour that gives the neighbours cause to gossip. But Ma says nothing. She cooks diri jon jon, Ketia's favourite dish of rice and dried mushrooms. In the living room she turns the ironing board so Ketia can see the TV, too. She tells Gabrielle to wash the dishes while Ma dries. Ketia says she can wash, but Ma waves her away. She treats Ketia like she's ill and still needs to convalesce — maybe remembering when she lost the boy who spoke beautiful French in a tiny Haitian village. She doesn't question that Ketia hasn't gone back to work.

Carlene and Marie-Ange call from the hospital to ask if Ketia wants to go for a drink and maybe dancing. Carlene insists and Ketia finally agrees, though they haven't set a date yet.

Today she took her résumé to the smaller hospital where she did a practicum as a student. The receptionist in Human Resources tapped her finger on the page. "You worked on Six East? They're hiring. You should scoot upstairs and see the head nurse."

Ketia hadn't left a note at home to say where she'd gone because she expected to be home again in an hour.

When, almost at suppertime, she opens the apartment door Gabrielle flits from the kitchen. "Tu étais où?" she cries, stepping aside so that Ma can see Ketia, too.

"I got a new job."

"Still as a nurse?" Gabrielle asks.

Ma tuts at her disrespect. What's wrong with a nurse?

"Yes, but at a new hospital."

Mama nods. "Good. That other place gave you craziness."

Craziness. Each considers the word for how they think it applies to what happened to Ketia. Ketia lowers her head, accepting the verdict. The three women — mother, daughter, sister — face each other, crowded in the hallway outside the kitchen. Bastien, who sits at the table, calls, "Can we eat now? Please?"

Ketia goes to the bathroom to wash her hands. When she returns to the kitchen she smells the cabri Ma stewed with yams cut into large chunks. Ma has begun to ladle food onto their plates. If Pa were home, he would get his first. Gabrielle always complains that in his absence Bastien gets served first — the *baby* of the family. What's fair about that?

Today Ma sets the first plate of food before Ketia. Neither Bastien nor Gabrielle object.

∞

The warm buffets of breeze promise daffodils, though spring is still months away. Joelle scuffs along, face lifted to the sun, the deep blue sky, the cutout horizon of Montreal cornices.

Frank told her to take the afternoon off. She decided to walk home, have a bubble bath, relax. She'll return to the hospital to visit with Emile before Diane gets home. She doesn't need Diane to remind her — again — of how Emile left her. She remembers the key left for her to find. That last phone call. You idiot. Stop harassing everyone.

So what? Look at Marc. For all his careful manners, he was mean, too. Devious mean. And never, even at the beginning, did he look at her the way Emile did. Emile's bold hands, his mouth. Marc never. Not even close. Marc spent longer in the shower after sex than having it.

Yesterday Emile asked about hubby. He come home yet? She shook her head. She wasn't expecting him, either. When she got back to her office she asked Pei Yi for Bingwen's number and made an appointment. She'd searched for the mortgage and RRSP papers, but Marc had taken everything. She no longer wanted to wait for Marc to decide what to do next. She wanted a lawyer involved, watching out for her interests.

She was able to get Emile admitted to the sixth floor, not the seventh, so she didn't have to worry about seeing Marc. But there were no semi-private rooms available, so Emile was in a ward room. An elderly woman with three daughters who argued non-stop about what would be best for Mum — to sit up or lie down, to drink prune juice or tea. A gaunt man who sat upright in bed, baggy pyjamas on his stick legs, knobby fingers holding *Le Journal de Montréal*. A young man with Rasta braids to his shoulders. His visitors sidled into the room as if it were a prison.

Emile lay in bed with an NG tube fed through his nose to his stomach, a bag to collect his urine hooked on the side rail, an intravenous looped from his arm, the needle embedded in his flesh. Naked under a johnny shirt, tied and stabbed in place.

Joelle asked if he'd told his parents that he was in the hospital. Why, he said. They didn't like to drive from Joliette to Montreal. They would know soon enough. She wondered if she dared call them herself. She and Emile's sister were never really friends, but they used to talk about clothes and hair.

There was little Joelle could do for Emile but sit with him. At least he had the bed by the window. She drew the curtain for whatever privacy that afforded. They could still hear the three daughters around their mother's bed. Look, Mum, I made you shepherd's pie. You love shepherd's pie. Don't force her if she doesn't want to. Let her rest. Easy to chew, Mum. I didn't put any corn in. For goodness's sake, how can you call it shepherd's pie if you didn't put any corn in? Will you be quiet? She has to eat. Eat, sure, but don't tell her you made something she loves when you didn't.

Emile never used to be interested in golf, but that was all he watched on TV now. As far as Joelle could tell, people mostly

stood around. The camera panned across the perfectly tailored grass. Now and then someone shifted from foot to foot,
squinted into the distance, and swung at the small white ball.

Emile murmured, "Watch how he releases the club."

Joelle asked, "Do you play golf?"

"I played there." He nodded at the screen. His thick neck
lost inside the shapeless johnny shirt. "Well, not at that green.
It's private. But in North Carolina. Oyster Bay."

Joelle faced the TV again. Tried to imagine Emile standing around on the grass. That graceful bend to his knee, the
disciplined swing.

When the orderly came to help Emile walk from the bed
to a chair, Emile's gown flapped open. Joelle looked away, but
not fast enough. His sad, little boy bum with a grown man's
fuzz of hair. His muscled thighs. She hadn't asked yet if he
would agree to chemo. Frank had told her that the oncolo-
gist wouldn't talk to Emile until the final pathology results
were in.

Joelle trips up the steps of her building, looking forward to
her bubble bath. A couple of welcome hours alone at home —
not thinking about Emile's prognosis, what Diane thinks, what
Bingwen will say, how Marc betrayed her, what will happen
next. Those darling little white pills help. She still keeps the
bottle hidden in the drawer under her bras. It's taken her all
these years, but she's finally realized that not telling Diane is
the best way to keep her from criticizing.

Joelle only slows, coming down the hallway, when she sees
boots in the tray outside her door. Why would Diane be home
in the middle of the day? Oh. No. Marc's black and tan suede
boots. The laces dropped inside, the toes aligned. As if he'd
never left.

She doesn't want to see Marc. Doesn't want him in the condo. Can she refuse him entry if he's half-owner? She should
have asked Bingwen.

A long, deep breath. Reminding herself that Marc left.

Made himself a new life with another woman. Maybe he only returned to pilfer some towels.

Cautiously she turns the key and opens the door, listening for a clue. His parka hangs on the coat stand. She eases the door shut and peeks in the living room. Pulls back her head. Shocked. The sofa has been pushed against the wall again. Even if it looks better there, he had no right to touch it.

She slips off her coat, still listening. There — the tap of metal on stone. His granite counters. She tiptoes to the kitchen doorway. He stands at the drawers, a sieve ladle in hand.

"What are you doing here?"

He starts. "I'm looking at…" He waves at the open drawer.

"You moved out. You can't just walk back in when you feel like it. You left."

Marc returns the ladle to the drawer, slides it shut. "We need to talk."

"I'm not usually home in the afternoon. You knew I wouldn't be here."

He gestures at the grocery bags she hadn't noticed on the counter. "I was going to cook."

His attitude — both certain and indifferent, assuming he can do as he wishes and that will be fine with her — makes her feel slightly nauseated. She steps back, bumping into the door frame behind her. Leans against it. Solid. More real than Marc.

He looks at his black granite counters. "Crown roast of pork with apple and kumquat stuffing."

"I don't want you to cook for me."

Stiffly he says, "May we at least sit?"

She pushes away from the door frame. Closest is the dining room. Pulls out a chair at the table. The salt and pepper mills are back on the hutch. What else has he moved?

He sits across from her, but one chair over. Jiggles his wrist, shakes down his watch. Still doesn't look at her. His face wan. His eyes pouched. He's lost weight. He never before had long hollows in his cheeks.

Why does he want to cook a meal? What does he want to say? She doesn't trust him anymore.

He frowns. "We need to discuss our marriage."

She opens her mouth, closes it again. Then slowly, "You left."

He nods, not agreeing so much as signalling that it's his turn now. "We've been married for twelve years."

"We were..." She speaks carefully, placing each word on a path she can't make out more than a step ahead. "We were married for twelve years when you said we should get to know other people."

"That was hasty."

"Hasty."

He nods. His turn again, but she speaks first. "What about her? The one you got to know?"

He straightens his shoulders.

Joelle slides her hands flat onto the table. "And the baby."

His mouth moves but nothing comes out.

"You might as well tell me. I'll hear at the hospital."

His jaw muscles clench. Finally, between thin lips, "She had an abortion."

Joelle almost laughs. She *knew* he never wanted a baby! Just as swiftly the impulse fades. Who laughs about an abortion? He probably made her have it. A man who can fuss in the kitchen, stuffing a pork roast with kumquats and apples, but won't learn the words to a nursery rhyme.

Joelle curls her hands on the table. Because Marc doesn't look at her, he hasn't noticed that she no longer wears her ring. He has one hand clasped inside the other so she can't see if he still wears his — though why would he?

He clears his throat. "We've been married for twelve years. I think we should try to work things out."

Again that nausea of disbelief. Is he crazy? "What about *her?*"

He doesn't seem to have heard.

"What about her?" Joelle repeats. "The woman you got pregnant."

Again his lips work before he can speak. "It's over."

"Because of the abortion."

His mouth stays closed, his eyes fixed on the wall across from him.

"You'll still see her at work."

"She no longer works there." Strain in his voice. Maybe pain, maybe hating to admit that he made a mistake.

And so... does he think it's that easy? She no longer trusts him. Not even sure she *likes* him, now that she knows what hides behind all his tidy routines and manners.

"We've been —" he begins again.

"Married for twelve years."

"Exactly. We should try to work things out."

"Because we've been married for twelve years."

His cheeks flush. "Well, we have."

Her breath comes faster. "Those twelve years didn't mean very much to you when you left. And for however long you were —" Involved with someone else. Got her pregnant.

He bows his head, acknowledging that she has the right to accuse him. But he doesn't actually admit it or apologize. He believes he's made his point. He's waiting for her to absorb it, and then he'll go to the kitchen and prepare a lovely meal. Maybe in a few months he'll meet another woman. Maybe this has happened a few times already.

She blinks against tears. "No."

"No what?" Marc frowns.

"You —" Anger blocks her throat. Jerks out tears. He hurt her so much. He's hurting her now, the way he sits there and assumes he can just come back. "You haven't once said that you love me or that you miss me. You won't even *look* at me!"

He rotates his neck, keeps his eyes level with hers.

But now she's crying, and doesn't want him to look at her. She flaps her hand in the air.

"We're married —"

"That was something else you said. You asked if I wanted to end up like my parents, married and miserable together. Well, I don't!"

"You weren't miserable with me. You were happy."

She shoves back her chair and blunders to the living room to get tissues to mop her face. From the other side of the wall divider she says, "*You* were miserable. You said you were. Like my mother. She used to come back, too, and everything was fine for a while. Then they started arguing again."

"We didn't argue," he points out coldly.

"Because you didn't even *talk* to me. You just fucked around — and then you moved out!" She slaps her bunched tissue against her hip. "You wanted to leave. So go. Get out."

"We're married."

Joelle shakes her head. "No, you left. You left, dammit! You *left*." She catches her breath. Tries to speak more calmly. "I've already talked to a lawyer. I want a divorce."

"Is *that* what you think?" He grips the edge of the table. "It won't be that easy. You're not half-owner. Remember who made the down payment. My parents."

"That was a gift to the both of us."

"We signed a prenuptial agreement. Obviously you didn't read it. Everything they gave us is mine if you divorce me."

His grim smile. The smug tilt of his chin. A man she used to think her saviour.

A key turns in the lock, and Joelle stretches out her hand for Diane to come quickly.

"What?" Diane stumbles over her boots she's still kicking off. "What — oh, it's you. Come to trespass again, have you?"

Marc pushes back his chair and stands.

"That's right," Diane says. "You're not welcome here."

"Don't tell me where I'm welcome —"

"Sounds like you need to hear it."

"— when I'm in my own home!"

"Oh, you've decided this is your home again, have you? Intending to move in with your preggie lady? Get her all comfy with her feet up on the cushions, set up a playpen?"

"Diane," Joelle tries to interject. But Marc has already wheeled around. He grabs his coat and slams out the door.

"Hope he runs into a concrete post," Diane says. "Head-on collision."

Joelle exhales a great breath she feels she's held since she walked in.

"What did he want?"

"To talk." Joelle grimaces. If she tells Diane now, she'll start crying again. Her hands hang at her sides. "I told him I want a divorce."

"Good for you!"

"But I won't be able to stay here." Joelle gazes around the living room. "All I ever really liked was the windows and the view."

"Hey!" Diane points at the sofa. "Did *he* push it back?"

Joelle suddenly remembers. "He left groceries in the kitchen."

"Anything worth cooking?"

"There's a roast. And if you know what to do with kumquats."

"I don't even know what a kumquat looks like."

Joelle glances at her watch. "I'm going to take a shower."

"And then back to the hospital?"

"Yeah." Joelle turns away.

"Can I ask you something?"

Joelle hesitates, expecting a snide comment about Emile.

"What did you mean the other night when you said I was a know-it-all?"

"You always think you know what's best."

"You'd sooner I keep my opinion to myself?"

"I'd sooner you remember that your opinion is your opinion — and that I'm allowed to have my own." Joelle shrugs.

"You've always been like that. Since we were ten years old."

"Why didn't you tell me before?"

"It didn't bother me before. But you're here now, and it's... too much."

"Okay." Diane nods. "Thanks." She thrusts both hands in her jeans' pockets and bumps through the kitchen door with her shoulder.

part *five*

Bastien crouches on the sofa, pressing a plastic bubble to make the dice inside pop. Ketia plays with him as they wait for their cousins from Laval to arrive.

She's had two visits with the therapist Père Christophe recommended. They meet in a small office near Concordia University. Shena carries her chair around the desk to sit close to Ketia as they talk. A gold crucifix on a chain rests on her collarbone. She tucks her wavy red hair behind her ear when she approves of something Ketia says, though her hair is short and soon springs free again. Shena suggests Ketia will come closer to forgiving herself if she can humanize her baby by, for example, naming him or her.

While Ketia was pregnant, she was convinced the baby was a boy. Lately, especially on the sofa next to Bastien with his elbows and knees excitement, his little-man shirts Ma starches for these Sunday visits, though soon he'll be galloping up and down the hallway, sliding on his socks, she wonders if her baby was a girl. As a nurse, she understands there's no way to know for sure. Yet when she tells Shena she thinks her baby was a girl, the therapist curls hair behind her ear.

The back of Ketia's throat prickles when she meets the neighbour with her baby girl in the stroller. Ketia stands back and explains that she's on her way home from work. No one wants hospital germs.

She won't be able to stand back when their cousins arrive, and Angélie clatters across the floor in her patent leather shoes. Ketia's hands sweat. She feels the tension in her neck and shoulders.

"You're not paying attention!" Bastien cries. "It's your turn!"

But then he leaps from the sofa at the knocking on the door. A distinctly adult knock with smaller fists pounding underneath. Monnonk Fritz steps in and around his legs scoot the boys. Ma clacks down the hallway from the kitchen, wearing her good slippers with heels.

All the commotion in the hallway. Greetings and whoops and laughter. Ketia stays curled on the sofa in the living room. Then tiny shoes tap across the wood floor and Angélie peeks in. But instead of running to Ketia as she normally would, she watches her with round eyes. Her hair knotted in little braids tied with pink satin ribbon. The frou-frou of her white crinoline under her pink dress. White leotards and shiny black shoes.

Ketia's hands tremble as she holds them out. "What is it, honey? You're not afraid of me, are you?"

Angélie toddles forward. "Tu pleu…" She points at the tears on Ketia's cheeks.

"Because I'm happy to see you." Ketia hefts her to her lap. "My own sweet baby."

∞

What would happen when Nazim's sister left? As the day approached, Diane decided she wouldn't even pack her clothes until she heard from him. Though there wasn't much to pack. She'd more or less been living out of boxes. All she really needed to grab at the last minute were her toiletries.

On the day itself she stripped the sheets off the sofa bed and stuffed them in the washing machine. They needed to be washed in any case. But she didn't fold the sofa bed yet. In the bathroom her bottles of shampoo and conditioner still sat on the rack in the shower.

Weeks ago, when Diane had scripted an entirely different scenario for Nazim's sister's visit — including sexy rendezvous in cheap hotels — she told Marie-Claude that she couldn't work today. She imagined a romantic supper followed by a sexy interlude. Or a sexy appetizer followed by take-out Chinese on the sofa. Now she wonders if Nazim will even call.

She paces around the living room, stands at the window, squints down at the cars driving along the street. Her toe traces the long, curved scratch she and Joelle made in the wood floor with the sofa. She drums her fingers on the window sill. Then on the glass. She breathes on the glass to fog it and lifts a finger to trace a D, hesitates, then wipes it away with her sleeve. The minutes stretch, falter, lag. She doesn't know when his sister's plane is leaving and can't call to find out, since it isn't a direct flight.

In the sixteen days since that terrible conversation, she's understood that Nazim won't necessarily do what she thinks best. That, in fact, he might have another idea altogether. She hopes he gives her points for not having tried to see or talk to him again.

She reads the titles of the books in the cabinet against the wall. The anatomy text must belong to Marc. He's called twice and left a message on the answering machine to ask Joelle when she's leaving, so he can move back. Joelle's lawyer told her to stay put for the moment. Diane's glad Joelle has a kick-ass lawyer.

She plops on the sofa, drums her fingers on the armrest. A ragged edge of nail scrapes the fabric. She bites the nail, spits, then picks the almost invisible scrap off the floor, takes it to the kitchen. When the phone rings, she bounds across the room to snatch it. "Allô?"

"It's Nazim." In the background she hears flight announcements.

"You're at the airport."

"Ghada just went through the gate."

Her breath shivers. He called her as soon as he could. He didn't call her for three weeks, but now that his sister is gone, he called her immediately. She clutches that certainty.

"I called you at work, but Marie-Claude said you had an appointment. I wasn't sure where you were."

"Here." She doesn't trust herself to say more, because she doesn't want him to hear that she's crying.

"Should I come get you?"

"Yes."

"I'll be there soon."

In the bathroom she splashes water on her face, but her cheeks look splotchy. Joelle has foundation and powder. The powder smells like it would make her sneeze. She dabs some pink foundation on her finger and smoothes it under her eyes, but it streaks and won't even out. She washes her face. Now she looks scrubbed. The tips of hair around her face wet.

She should call Joelle. Let her know she's leaving.

Joelle has patients in the office. "Are you sure?" she whispers into the phone. "Everything's all right between you and Nazim? Because I was starting to wonder..."

Diane forces a laugh. "Of course, everything's all right! He's coming to get me."

"Oh. Good."

Diane bobs her head to whatever smarts kept her from telling Joelle. Joelle doesn't need to know. And what would she think now, if she knew what really happened and why, and then heard that all Diane wants is to see Nazim again? Diane can't explain.

And suddenly — yes — Diane understands why Nazim didn't tell his family about her. They don't need to know. It's too complicated. Diane doesn't even care about his family anymore.

She checks that she hasn't left any books in the study next

to the sofa bed, which she closes now. Carries her two boxes to the door. Folds the sheets from the dryer and puts them in the linen closet. She clutches her arms around herself, hangs her head, paces.

When the buzzer sounds, she makes herself walk slowly to the door, opens it.

Both hesitate. For an instant they're strangers. Then Nazim says, "Diane," and steps forward to enfold her. His hug is firm, one hand on the back of her neck, fingers in her hair.

She nuzzles his scarf, breathing in the smell of his skin, the wool, his leather jacket.

"Let's go home," he says.

In the car she asks, "Your sister had a good visit?"

He nods and takes his hand from the steering wheel to clasp her knee. "Don't worry, Diane. No one else from my family will come."

Never? she wants to ask. But of course doesn't. She wants to believe it, too.

∞

Joelle grabs her yogurt from the refrigerator in the lunch room and sits next to Pei Yi on the chairs against the wall. Two secretaries from Neurology have spread their microwaved meals on the table.

"Want some?" Pei Yi offers Joelle salad from a plastic container. The green leaves match her dress.

"Thanks. This is enough for me."

"You're going to visit your friend?"

Joelle nods, spooning up yogurt. "I don't want to eat in front of him."

Last week Emile was allowed fluids, and for one meal even regular food — although he objected that tofu spaghetti wasn't regular food. The next day he had cramps and his abdomen was distended. The residents took him off all food, including liquids. Now, after a few days of not eating, he's on fluids again. But he scowls at the plastic tray of apple juice and Jell-O, says he has no appetite.

"You're a good friend," Pei Yi says. "Very loyal."

"Very loyal? That's funny. I'm filing for divorce."

"That's different."

Joelle lobs her yogurt container in the garbage. "I've got to scoot. We've got patients this afternoon. I can't be late."

"Nice skirt. It suits you."

"Thanks." Joelle smoothes her hands down the hips of the new tweed skirt.

"Big Ben says…"

Joelle, who's already taken a step, turns to hear.

Pei Yi winks. "Too bad you're a client."

Joelle shakes her head, not sure if Pei Yi is teasing.

Often now, when Joelle walks into Emile's room, he's sitting in a vinyl armchair with a blanket across his lap. His NG tube and the urine bag have been removed, but he still has an intravenous. She's offered to have him moved to a semi-private, but he said he prefers to stay in his corner by the window. Maybe he likes hearing the other patients and their families.

Of the original group, only the elderly woman with the three daughters remains. A few times Joelle has found one of the daughters with the curtain pulled aside, talking with Emile. She'd thought the daughters were middle-aged, but saw now that this one was probably her age. Joelle likes her blunt way of telling Emile to stop saying he doesn't care whether he lives or dies. "Of course, you care," she says. "Or you would be dead already. What matters now is whether you have a comfortable or a miserable death." Emile calls her Madame No-Guff.

Two days ago Madame No-Guff stopped Joelle in the hallway. "Are you his girlfriend?"

"A friend."

"He doesn't have any family?"

"He didn't tell them he was in the hospital."

She snorted. "Was he always stupid like this? Or just now when he's sick?"

Today Emile's curtain in the corner is drawn around the bed. Madame No-Guff and her sister hover and stoop by their mother. The sister scrapes a fork through a piece of fish, breaking it into bite-sized pieces.

"You have to eat, Mum."

"Aren't you hungry?"

"Give her some juice to drink. Then she'll eat."

Across from them a man with an amputated leg discusses last night's hockey game with the orderly.

Joelle nods hello all around and approaches Emile's curtain. "Knock, knock," she calls, pretending to knock on the cloth.

No answer. She gropes along the curtain for the edge.

Emile lies on his side with the sheet pulled up, legs tucked in a fetal curl, arm with the IV resting on his hip. He faces the window. The grey duvet of clouds outside.

She steps close to the bed. Looks at the sky, too.

Acknowledgements

Thank you to friends who read pages, listened, encouraged, and gave me feedback: Kelley Aitken, Danielle Devereaux, Kim Edelstein, Lina Gordaneer, Saleema Nawaz. Especial thanks to my special writing buddy, Mark Kline.

I gratefully acknowledge the staff on 4NW — nurses, house staff, and residents — who kindly answered my many questions. For specific help with linguistic, cultural, nursing, medical, and hair care details, thank you to Jean-Claude Napoléon, Mehnaz Tariq, Caryl Tabanay, Rytchelle St. Pierre, Clara Lauture, Nancy Brennan, Miss Ross, Beth Collins, Sadeesh Srinathan, Lara Maalouf. Any errors in interpretation are mine alone.

My sincere appreciation to Mona Abou Sader for facilitating the final block of time I needed to edit this book. Thank you to Deidre Skelton and Shari Alleyne.

I have only the best memories of the 2007 Banff Writing Studio, the faculty and writers I met there. A deep nod to Suzette Mayr and Michael Helm for reading the long and messy first draft of this novel.

Thank you to the Canada Council for the Arts for their generous support during the writing of this book.

I cheer for the amazing team that was and is at NeWest Press. Thank you to Lou Morin, Paul Matwychuk, and Andrew Wilmot for their savvy and dedication; Michael Hingston for his quick eye and bag full of commas; Natalie Olsen for her wizardry at distilling an image from words.

I am profoundly grateful to my editor, Suzette Mayr, for her expertise, commitment, good humour, and ongoing belief in this book.

My whole-hearted appreciation and love belong, as always, to Robert Aubé.

Originally from Ontario, Alice Zorn lives in Montreal. She has published short fiction in magazines, and placed first in *Prairie Fire*'s 2006 Fiction Contest. Her collection of short stories, *Ruins & Relics,* was a finalist for the 2009 McAuslan Quebec Writers' Federation First Book Prize. *Arrhythmia* is her first novel.

❡ The text for this book is set in Requiem, designed by Jonathan Hoefler and completed in 1999.